THE SUNKEN

Book one of the *Engine Ward*

S.C. GREEN

GRYMM & EPIC PUBLISHING

Grymm & Epic Publishing

Auckland, New Zealand

http://www.grymmandepic.com

Cover design: Vail Joy

Author photo: Jess Manning

To "the Bogans." for your friendship and unfaltering support.

About the Author

S. C. Green lives in an off-grid home in rural New Zealand with her husband, two mischievous cats, and a medieval sword collection. She's the author of *the Engine Ward* series, as well as the humorous fantasy novel, *At War With Satan*, under the name Steff Metal. Find out more about her work on her website: www.steffmetal.com.

CONTENTS

PROLOGUE

1820

"This beam engine pumps water from the Thames directly into those reservoirs and the water tower. The mains run seven miles to Campden Hill and it supplies water to most of West London — Nicholas Thorne, are you listening?"

Master Brunel fixed him with a withering stare. Nicholas, who had just turned fifteen and normally loved watching steam engines at work and hated to disappoint his teacher, shoved his crumpled Navy papers back into his pocket and tried to look interested as the Master led his four pupils into the pump house. But he couldn't think about steam engines today.

Inside the shed, Nicholas followed his teacher and the other three pupils onto the observation floor. He pressed his back against the wall of the thin wooden platform and tried to focus his attention. The beam engine was just approaching full speed, and he clutched his papers even more tightly as the floor and walls vibrated with each rotation. The fifteen-ton beam soared over their heads, crashing down with a sweeping stroke to slam the pistons into the condenser and release great clouds of steam.

"Father says this is the first engine to use a separate condenser," said Isambard, Brunel's son, his face lit up with excitement. "The engineers are really starting to get to grips with reciprocating engines—"

"I'm leaving London, Isambard." Nicholas said.

"I know. Tomorrow."

"I might never see you again. Don't you *care?*" He frowned at his friend.

Isambard looked hurt. "Of course. You and James are going to earn your fortunes at sea. And I must stay in the Engine Ward with the Stokers and repair furnaces for the rest of my life. But that's not 'till tomorrow. Today …" He gestured to the beam engine, "I can pretend that maybe, one day, I would be able to create something like this."

"Isambard—"

"No. Just thank Great Conductor you weren't born a Stoker."

James Holman elbowed Nicholas in the ribs. "Isambard's right — we have plenty to be grateful for. We're going to see the world. We'll sail great ships across the ocean and have all sorts of adventures. Don't you *want* to go?"

"What I *want* has had no bearing on my life since my father disowned me. If I stay in London, I'll be a pauper. My money will run out sooner or later, and none of the engineering sects will take on an apprentice without family money. I'm not like you, James. I've had quite enough danger and adventure in my life already, thank you very much—"

"Out of my way, Your Lordship." Henry Williams shoved Nicholas into the wall as he pushed past, pulling his dragon Mordred behind him on a thick chain. Nicholas smarted at the nickname — given to him by Henry because Henry couldn't understand why anyone who was the son of a Lord would come to live in the Engine Ward of his own volition.

Henry Williams was also a Stoker — one of the "Dirty Folk," as the Londoners called them — but he was the favourite son of an important Stoker family — a long line of dragon-hunters. Nicholas hadn't met Henry's brothers — the priests Oswald and Peter and Henry's twin, Aaron — but he'd heard enough about the Williams family from Isambard to know he didn't want to.

When the Stokers first moved to London from the swamps, Henry's father had given him the juvenile swamp-dragon as a pet. Henry, who liked the fear the three-foot-high dragon invoked in his fellow Stokers, took Mordred everywhere, including places dragons shouldn't go, like on this field trip.

Mordred looked up at Nicholas with wide eyes, and Nicholas felt the familiar sensation of the creature's thoughts sliding into his own head. The dragon loved Henry, despite the rough treatment he received, and his mind hardened with determination to protect his master from the beam engine, which he perceived as a large, shiny predator. The noise and the steam inside the pump house clouded Mordred's senses, and terrified the dragon. Every muscle in Mordred's body was poised for danger, and that unease was now mirrored in Nicholas' mind.

Nicholas reached out a hand to pat Mordred's snout, sending a calming thought back to the dragon. He hadn't told anyone in London about his *sense*, — his ability to hear the thoughts of animals as if they were his own — not even Isambard or James, his closest friends. It had cost him too much already. He'd chosen to come to the city — to cloister himself in the world of machines — to escape the voices and the pain they caused.

"Don't touch my dragon," Henry snapped, yanking Mordred's chain back so hard the creature yelped in protest.

"He's not technically a dragon," said James, clutching his books close to his chest. "Dragons have wings in all the books. And breathe fire."

"Those are make-believe dragons. English swamp-dragons stand on two legs, have cold skin, and could bite you in half with one—"

"*Boys.*" Master Brunel rapped his stick against the metal platform. "The engine is up to full-speed now — six and a half rotations per minute. Would you like to go down and have a closer look at the condenser?"

James shook his head. He didn't share the others' fascination with machinery, especially if it involved descending into the bowels of an unflinching engine.

"Well, if you're too scared to come closer," said Henry, "hold Mordred for me. He won't fit on the platform."

James looked stricken, but he held out his hand, and Henry pressed the lead into it. Mordred stared at his master, confused.

"I want to look at the engine," said Isambard. "Nicholas, you should come down with me."

Reluctantly, Nicholas followed Isambard and Henry down a narrow ladder onto an even narrower platform, suspended just above the main cylinder. Above his head, the beam made another rotation, driving down the piston and sending up a cloud of steam that soaked his clothes in sweat.

He peered over the railing into the bowels of the machine, struck by the elegance of its simple function, and the simple line and symmetry of the frame. Beside him, Isambard leaned even further out, his face alight as he took in every rod, every cylinder, every bolt.

Master Brunel came up behind them. "Now, boys, who can tell me how the condenser works?"

Behind him, James shouted. Something heavy jerked the platform sideways and crashed against Nicholas' ankles, slamming him against the railing. His vision spun, his scream caught in his throat as he swung out, dangerously close to the piston. The platform jerked again, and he fell back against the metal grating beside Isambard. Blood gushed from a cut in his friend's cheek.

"Where's Henry?"

Nicholas spun around, just in time to see Mordred, dragging his chain behind him, leap across the lurching platform, desperate to reach his master. *How had he got free?* The platform lurched forward as the dragon bowled into Henry, who sailed into the railing and toppled over the edge.

Nicholas grabbed the railing to steady himself as the platform lurched again. He pulled himself along the railing and peered over the edge. Henry, his face white with fear, clung to the outside of the railing.

His arms straining under his weight, Henry managed to pull himself up and hook his feet over the edge of the platform. Nicholas inched along the railing and extended his hand to Henry, just as a stray thought entered his head.

No, Mordred, No!

Nicholas tried to grasp the creature's mind, to stifle Mordred's thoughts with his own, but he was too frightened, too weak. Mordred's mind slipped through his and the dragon bounded across the platform again and leapt at his master, knocking Henry off the platform and sending him sailing onto the piston rod just as the beam came down.

Blood splattered Nicholas' face, clouding his vision. He couldn't hear Henry cry out over the slam and hiss of the engine as it tore the boy to pieces. More blood flowed over the platform, but the machine did not stop, heedless to the cracking of bones and the sizzle of blood and flesh dripping into the condenser.

His mind filled with pain. He let go of the railing and clutched his head, crying out as Mordred's anguish pressed against his skull. It was as though Nicholas himself had knocked Henry off the platform, as though he himself had seen the person he loved most in the world crushed under the great steel beam.

He howled, pressing his head into the grating, trying to force out the horrible thoughts. Hands grabbed him, dragging him back, wiping the gore from his eyes. He was dimly aware of Master Brunel shaking him, calling his name. Over his shoulder, Isambard watched, his face drawn.

"You're all right, boy. You're all right."

Through the haze of steam, Nicholas saw Mordred slumped on the platform beside him. The tendrils of Mordred's thoughts — of the loss and pain and guilt — reached deep within Nicholas, summoning up every memory of his past. He reached across and laid a bloody hand on Mordred's chest, above the creature's heart, and tried to give Mordred some sort of release, tried to pull back the pain, to hold it in himself.

A fog swirled inside his head, and everything went black.

***

Nicholas woke up on the cobbles outside the pump house. Master Brunel pulled him to his feet, and they trudged past the pump house and back to the omnibus station. Nicholas had no idea how long he'd been unconscious, but the place already swarmed with constables and journalists and a gaggle of onlookers. He turned away, not wanting to see them removing what remained of Henry.

They caught an omnibus back to the Engine Ward — the industrial heart of London, where the Stokers lived and worked, tending the engines that kept the city running. Each boy sat silent, lost in thought. Nicholas sat on the edge of the bench, his face outside the window where the wind might dry his tears. He cradled Mordred in his arms, pressing his cheek against the creature's cold skin, and tried to push away the pain that threatened to overwhelm them both. Beside him, James, unusually silent, stared at his hands.

"That was *amazing*," said Isambard, breaking the silence.

"Not the word I would use to describe it," said James, his voice hoarse. "It was all my fault. I didn't hold Mordred tightly enough." Tears rolled down his cheeks, and he turned away.

Isambard carried on talking, oblivious to James'

distress. "Henry was foolish, hanging over the edge like that. You have to respect a machine, especially one as incredible as that beam engine. I never much liked him, anyway. Did you see how the steam inlet valve closed when the piston reached the top of the cylinder?"

Nicholas pushed aside the pain, and stared up at his friend. Isambard's eyes glowed as though a fire had been lit behind them, and he could hear him muttering calculations under his breath. *While James and I saw our schoolmate torn to pieces, Isambard sees only the power of the machine.*

The thought turned his blood cold. Mordred gazed up at him with warm, frightened eyes, and Nicholas looked from the dragon to his friend, and knew nothing would ever be the same.

PART I:
THE VAMPIRE KING

1830

Dear James

You may have some idea what has become of me since we parted in Portsmouth. If you had followed the papers you'd know the Cleopatra *stayed for a year on patrol in English waters before setting out on duties in the Mediterranean. After being in an engagement, she put in at Gibraltar for repairs and her crew was decommissioned. You may have even read of a young lieutenant who killed his superior officer in a brawl and evaded the authorities by escaping into Spain.*

I had intended to buy passage home to England and begin life anew as a student of architecture, but I had not counted on Napoleon making a particularly spectacular decision. Blockading England basically drew a line in the sand — with Industrian England on one side, and Christian Europe on the other. There was not one ship that could take me where I so dearly wanted to go, and French hostility toward Industrians forced me into hiding.

I've been in the mountains for nearly three years, studying architecture with some of the foremost European masters, but circumstances permitted that I return to England with haste, and I hope to find work there under a new name. I will not burden you with the details of my illicit journey, lest this letter fall into the wrong hands. Suffice to say that at the time of writing, I am in the North, and it does my heart well to once more walk on English soil.

I arrive in London on Tuesday, and would greatly desire to meet you for dinner, at 6pm at the Butchers Hall Beef House. You must come alone, and tell no one who you are seeing.

You cannot write to me in return, but I shall wait for you on the appointed day.

Yours
Nicholas Rose

JAMES HOLMAN'S MEMOIRS — UNPUBLISHED

The history books — the thick sort written by *real* historians — will tell you England's troubles began when Isambard Kingdom Brunel knocked Robert Stephenson from the post of Messiah of the Sect of the Great Conductor, and became overnight the most powerful engineer in England. But they do not have the full story.

The *true* origin began many years before that, with George III — the Vampire King — and the damage wrought by his naval defeats, and his madness. His depravity might have been held in check were it not for a mild spring afternoon in 1830, when a dragon wandered into Kensington Gardens and ate two women and a Grenadier Guard.

I happened to witness this occurrence, although witness, my critics would say, is a word I am not permitted to use, on account of my complete blindness.

I had been granted a day's leave from my duties at Windsor Castle to come into the city. In my left hand, I clutched two envelopes. One contained a thick, pleading letter to my publisher, written on my Noctograph in large, loopy letters to arouse their sympathies, humbly requesting a payment for royalties due on my book. The second contained a request for a period of extended leave to travel to Europe, addressed to the Duke and signed by my doctor. In my other hand, I held the brass ball atop my walking stick, rapping the pavement and listening for the echoes whenever I felt myself veer from my path.

I arrived at the offices of F., C., and J. Rivington, my publishers, a little after four, and was surprised to find their offices empty, the door locked, and no one about. I ran my fingers over the door, but could find no notice. Perhaps they had taken an extended luncheon? I sniffed the air, remembering the delicious pie shop on the corner beneath the barbershop. Yes, perhaps I should look for them there.

I had no sooner taken a step across the street, my mouth watering with the anticipation of pie, when coach bells jangled, whistles blew, hooves thundered, and a great commotion rumbled down the street — a carriage speeding over the cobbles, the inhabitants crying out as they were flung back in their seats. I yanked my boot back just as the carriage screamed past and several Bobbies blew their whistles at me. Boots pounded along the street as the usual gaggle of reporters, thrill-seekers, and layabouts chased after the carriage, anxious to see the cause of the commotion.

Of course, being somewhat of a thrill-seeker myself, I shoved the letters into my jacket pocket and followed. I didn't need my stick to follow the sound of the carriage, and I fell in step amongst the crowd and allowed the jostles of the nosy to pull me along. I collected details in my mental map — a right turn here, a left there, the rough cobbles giving way to silken lawn and neat, paved paths. We'd entered Kensington Gardens, tearing through the squared hedges of close-cropped yew and prim holly, cut and shaped to mimic the bastions and fortifications of war. Hydrangea and rose perfumes drifted on the breeze, until the coo of songbirds was interrupted by piercing screams as women scuttled between the hedges, looking for a place to hide.

Then, I heard the roar.

The sound was so low it shook my insides about, so my organs felt as though they had sunk into my socks. The crowd around me, only moments ago hell-bent on moving forward in search of the commotion, scattered in fear, diving into the trees flanking the Round Pond and leaving me in the centre of the path to confront the scene before me.

Though I could only hear and not see what unfolded, the vivid accounts read aloud to me by friends from the papers allow me to picture it now as clearly as anything. A female swamp-dragon (*Megalosaurus bucklandii,* in the new taxonomy) appeared from nowhere beside the Round Pond, obviously in need of a drink. She bent down, fifteen feet of her, to lap at the water with her thick tongue, her leathery green skin catching the midday sun. The gentlemen who had been preparing to launch their boats on the water scattered, but their women were busy setting up the picnic tables and laying out the tea settings, and did not notice the commotion until the beast was upon them.

A woman cowered under her table, clutching a crying baby and trying to muffle its sobs beneath her skirt. But the dragon — like me — saw the world with her ears. She drove her wide snout under the table and tore at the unfortunate woman, tearing out her pretty arms and staining her dress with blood.

Crème scones and Wedgewood china flew through the air as the beast charged the picnic tables, snapping up morsels of womanly flesh. The screams brought more bystanders — lovers strolling along the Serpentine, the Royal Horticultural Society, who'd been admiring the hydrangea beds, and, finally, a nearby guard on duty with his shiny blunderbuss.

The shots rang in my ears for several moments, and I leaned on my stick, suddenly blinded to the world around me. The ground trembled as feet thundered past, and I turned to move after them, but a voice broke through my panic.

"You sir, don't move!"

I froze. Now I heard the hiss of air escaping the dragon's nostril, and the click of its claws as it stalked across the garden path toward me. The air grew hot, carrying with it the smell of butchery — blood and flesh mingled with the beast's fetid breath. At any moment it would be upon me. The panic rose in my throat, and I fought the urge to run.

"Easy does it, girl." The man murmured, and I heard the footsteps slow. The creature stopped and sniffed the air. It grunted, turned, and thundered off into the trees.

I dared not move, sucking a silent breath and

listening for her return. Something grabbed my arm, and I lost my composure, sobbing to be spared.

"Woah, easy, chap!" It was the man's voice, the man who had driven the dragon away. "I don't mean any harm!"

The voice was husky from sucking in coal dust and engine fumes, and his hands were rough. He was a worker, probably a servant of one of the engineering sects. I allowed him to take my hand and lead me to a nearby bench, where I sank to my knees, confounded.

"How did you defeat the monster?" I asked, wiping my sweating face with my kerchief.

"That is a secret of mine," the man said. "But she shant be coming back again, of that I am certain."

I knew he had used no weapon, for I would have heard the shot fired or the slice of steel pulled from a scabbard, and the creature had given no sign of a struggle. It had simply changed its mind. This man had turned the creature away with naught but his own mind.

Interesting.

"Tell me, good fellow," I leaned forward. "Did you *think* the dragon away?"

"Such a thing is preposterous." There was the hint of a smile in his voice.

"Not so preposterous, especially as you have saved my life. I have a friend, whom I think you should meet. We served as lieutenants together in His Majesty's Royal Navy, and he has just returned to London after spending some years abroad. He too can influence the minds of animals from his own thoughts."

The man leaned forward also, intrigued by my bold

statement. But when he spoke, there was hesitation in his voice.

"I should not think any man of your acquaintance would speak to the likes of me. I'm a Stoker, sir, born amongst the rail trenches and boiler boxes of the Engine Ward, a servant of the Great Conductor."

I should have known him a Stoker by the scent of coal on his clothes. Although the Stokers performed one of the most important and dangerous jobs — they were the mechanics of Engine Ward, maintaining the machines and furnaces of London's engineering churches — their dirty, underground work and insular, fanatical society meant Londoners both hated and feared them. "The Dirty Folk" were shunned by polite society and thought to be incapable of innovation until recently. Isambard Kingdom Brunel — the boy I'd left behind in Engine Ward and had not seen for ten years — invented a new type of steam locomotive and took for himself the title of "Engineer", a title protected by law and never before given to a Stoker. Brunel's innovation had ignited the religious and scientific elite, and this man was right to assume most men would prefer not to associate with a Stoker.

"I think you'll find Nicholas and I most accommodating. My mother was a Stoker, although she was fortunate to marry a rich Aetherian so I did not grow up inside the Ward, though it holds a place in my heart. Nicholas sheltered there for a year as a boy, hiding from a cruel father. Both he and I were childhood friends of your engineer, Isambard Kingdom Brunel." I used the word *engineer* — a word many say Brunel should not be allowed to use — to show I harboured no ill will. I extended my hand. "James

Holman, at your service. I am eternally grateful."

He took my hand and gave it a firm tug. "I am Aaron Williams, and it is an honour to meet you. Forgive me, but am I speaking to *the* James Holman, the celebrated Blind Physician?"

His statement surprised me. Not many Stokers could read, and my book — a treatise on the effectiveness of various "cures" for blindness — was hardly a popular volume. "I wouldn't say celebrated, sir. My book was rubbished by the critics. The *Times* concluded a blind man had no right to pen a medical treatise."

"Nonsense. Isambard speaks fondly of you, and he cherishes his copy of your book. I know all about you … and Nicholas. Isambard and I became friends after you left, and he always speaks of his schoolmates with reverence. I was never permitted to attend school myself, but I know all your stories as if they were my own."

I beamed at the praise, and clasped his hand. "I cannot allow such an avid fan of my work to escape into the London gloom without buying him a drink. I am meeting Nicholas for dinner, and I'd be honoured if you would join us."

He seemed reluctant, but I insisted, and tugged on his arm 'till his protests fell silent. I was due to meet Nicholas at the Butchers Hall Beef House at six o'clock. With Aaron leading the way through the busy streets, we made it there shortly after five, so I led Aaron to the end of a long table and paid for three pints of beer. I allowed Aaron to regale me with renditions of his favourite parts of my book 'till I heard a familiar voice behind me.

"James Holman, it's good to see your face again."

"And to hear your voice, old friend." I rose and shook Nicholas' hand. I could not see him, of course, so I did not know how his physical features had changed, but his handshake was firm, his fingers rough with the calluses of a seaman. His voice had lost none of its kindness. "It has been a long five years since I left you in Portsmouth."

"You shouldn't have come home so soon, James. The war only got interesting once you left. I have much to tell you — but who's this ragamuffin sitting in my chair?"

His voice betrayed something: *Reproach? Fear?* I remembered the letter he'd sent me, asking to meet. He'd chosen his words carefully, the tone perfectly congenial — as though he had seen me only yesterday — and explaining nothing. It was as if he were afraid of being followed. Suddenly, I wished I hadn't brought Aaron along. I should have guessed Nicholas wanted to talk privately.

Aaron must have sensed Nicholas' apprehension, for he spoke kindly. "I am Aaron Williams, sir. Mr. Holman—"

"Call me James," I interjected.

"Mr. Holman invited me here to speak to you, on a … private matter."

"I see he's already plied you with ale, so it must be a very private matter indeed." Nicholas sat down, resting his hat on the back of the chair and grabbing the remaining glass. "Unlike most men, James Holman's tongue clamps shut under the influence of any brew, so one cannot wrestle a secret from his lips even with the liberal application of lubricants."

His words were jovial, but his voice trembled as he spoke. Yes, he was definitely afraid.

I grinned at his words, trying to put him at ease. "I met Aaron in Kensington gardens today—"

"Ah, yes, nasty business, that. I heard the screams all the way from the Society of Architects." Nicholas had spent the years since the war ended training in France as an industrial architect. At least, that's what he'd told me in his mysterious letter. "Trust the Blind Physician to be first on the scene. I see you're not nursing a dragon-tooth-shaped wound?"

"I am fine, thanks to Mr. Williams. Nicholas," I lowered my voice, "he *thought* the dragon away."

Nicholas drummed his fingers against his glass. I waited for him to digest this. Aaron finished his glass and clattered it on the table.

Finally Nicholas said. "So you hear them, also?" The fear had left his voice, replaced by barely concealed excitement.

"I do, sir. It is a power I inherited from my grandfather. Apart from him, I have never met another who possessed the power."

"Nor I, Mr. Williams," Nicholas smiled. "The sense is a mystery. No one in my own family ever possessed it, or if they did, they kept quiet. You have, it seems, greater control of your power, as you call it, than I, for I would never be able to hold — let alone control — the mind of a fully grown dragon. You must tell me how it felt to enter her thoughts. To loosen your tongue, I'll even buy you another drink."

"It was quite something, sir," said Aaron as Nicholas placed another glass in front of him. "A feat I'd experienced only once before, when I was a boy and my mother took me to see a swamp-dragon in a travelling menagerie. The sadness of the animals, trapped in tiny cages with little food, dying slowly in a land far from their home, drew me in. When my mind grasped the thoughts of the dragon, their ferocity knocked me down. I saw as it saw, smelt as it smelt, and I looked up at my mother's stern face and imagined devouring her flesh. The thought so excited and frightened me that I *pushed,* heaving with my mind to escape the terrible thoughts, and then my head felt clear, but I had pushed too hard. The dragon and all the animals broke through their cages and tore their cruel master to pieces before the guards finally shot them down.

Aaron's voice grew cold and angry as he spoke. I sensed a deep, smouldering temper behind his placid exterior.

"To be inside the mind of a man-eater … it is both fascinating and wholly repellent. Their thoughts narrow, every thread of their mind coiling, poised for the kill. Today, inside her head, I could *smell* Mr. Holman as she smelt him; wild and peppery and absolutely delicious. Against the desire to bite his head off, I *pushed.* I pushed with my whole mind, and she forgot her hunger, and retreated toward the swamps, where a line of constables and Royal Guard waited with blade and blunderbuss."

Silence descended. I did not feel it proper to speak, as I did not share this unique experience. Finally, Nicholas rapped the table and declared another round of ale. He asked Aaron what his grandfather had done with the power.

"My grandfather hunted the dragons in the fens. It

was he who first led the Stokers to success as dragon-hunters, before we were brought to London to work in the *Engine Ward*." He practically spat out the last part of his sentence.

"Hold on," I leaned forward, my heart racing. "Are you in any way related to Henry Williams?"

"He was my twin brother," Aaron said. "He died many years ago, in a—"

"—beam engine accident," whispered Nicholas. "We know. We were there."

We lapsed into silence as the barmaid slammed three pints of beer on the table, followed by three plates of stewed beef. I dug into my food, glad of the distraction. Aaron did not realise he was dining with the man who'd caused his brother's death. I was holding Mordred, but I was so excited about leaving for the Navy that I was barely concentrating. I'd put the chain down — so stupid — wrapped it once around the railing — not tightly enough — so I could check my pocket for my papers again, so I could glance again at the bright drawings of the port of Halifax that would soon become my home. And Mordred had seen Henry out on the platform and leapt across, taking the unsecured chain with him.

The accident had been all my fault. But I hadn't liked Henry anyway, and I certainly didn't want his death to postpone my embarkation, so I left for the Americas without explaining to anyone what I had done.

And Marc Brunel, who'd already been in trouble for innovating without the sanction of the Council, had been blamed for Henry's death, and sentenced to thirty years' penal servitude in Van Diemen's Land.

Thinking of Henry's death and Marc Brunel's deportation turned my stomach, and the coagulated gravy on the beef stuck to the roof of my mouth.

"Isambard never speaks of that day," said Aaron. "I thought only he had witnessed it."

A fresh wave of guilt coursed through me. Not only had I caused the death of Aaron's brother and Isambard's father's deportation, but I'd left Isambard to bear the pain of it alone. "We left for sea the next day," I said, struggling to keep my voice even. "We were not here when Isambard's father was sentenced."

"No wonder Isambard does not wish to speak to us," said Nicholas.

"What do you mean?"

"I have been away from London for ten years, and for five of those years, I wrote to him every month. He has not answered any of my letters," said Nicholas. "Have you managed to contact him, James?"

A new guilt flared in my stomach, and I clutched my glass to keep my hands from trembling. Even though I'd been living at Windsor Castle for three years and Brunel's profile had been growing in the city, I had never tried to contact him. I could not face him, knowing my carelessness had cost him his father. "I have twice requested an audience with him on my visits to London," I lied, "and he has twice refused."

"Of all us schoolboys, he was the one destined for greatness. And despite everything, look at what he has achieved — an engineer with his own church — the only engineer ever to rise from the Stokers' ranks." Nicholas smiled. "He was my dearest friend at a time when friends were few. More than anything, I would like to see him again."

"I am still close to Isambard," said Aaron. "Perhaps I could talk to him on your behalf. I am sure there is a reason for his coldness."

***

Aaron left around 9pm to begin his shift in the Engine Ward. Reluctant to retire to his desolate lodgings, Nicholas walked with James along the Strand, the Thames to his right and the magnificent city sprawled out in all directions. Watchmen darted in front of them, lighting the streetlamps that twinkled between the buildings like fireflies. Businessmen hurried home to wives and children, or darted through the alleys to the taverns and bawdy houses of Fleet Street and Covent Garden, ducking to avoid the Metic preachers on the street corners, who yelled at the top of their lungs about the evils of Imperial measurement.

Downriver, the London docks lay shrouded in shadow — the once-vibrant port over-run with weeds and vandals. Only one ship waited for cargo, and she was likely moving up-country, rather than across the water. Hardly any ships had crossed from London to Europe in three years — not since Napoleon had blockaded the waters around England and forbade any god-fearing Christian country to trade with Industrians. King George's navy, vastly depleted from his previous losses, had so far failed to dislodge the blockade.

For Nicholas, this was a bittersweet homecoming. After ten years away, he was back in this city, penniless and lost. He'd left England to escape his father's wrath, to make a name for himself, and lose the voices of the animals in the emerging world of warships and industry. Now this Aaron Williams had shown up and in a single night rewritten everything he thought he'd known about himself.

James — his face averted, his eyes sewn shut with golden threads — walked in silence beside Nicholas, his stiff gait betraying the pain in his limbs. Both men wallowed in their uncomfortable thoughts, 'till Nicholas broke through the silence.

"Thank you for meeting me," he said. "I was afraid I didn't have a friend left in England."

"I'm stuck in that tiny boarding house at the castle with only the six decrepit Naval Knights of Windsor for company. I would've rescued you from France myself if only for a little adventure."

"James Holman, I read your book. You spent four years sneaking into lecture halls and dissecting corpses at midnight using only your fingers as a guide. That's adventure enough for any man, let alone a man in your condition."

"Pfft. Any young gentlemen with a taste for wine and a strong stomach can become a doctor. I have a more lofty ambition." Holman raised his head to the sky, almost as if he could see it in his imagination. "One day, Nicholas, I will circle the globe."

"In a ship?" Nicholas knew from their days in the Navy what time at sea did to James' health.

"Even if an Englishman could still buy passage on one, I cannot afford a ship. I will go on foot, crossing Russia and Siberia and passing over the great land bridge."

"That's suicide!"

"That is the life I seek."

"You haven't changed a bit. Didn't all those years

on the *Cleopatra* teach you that the world's the same no matter where you go? Miles of ocean and endless voices."

"I believe differently," Holman said simply. "I *must* believe differently."

They wound their way into increasingly poor districts, slipping between crowds of drunks spilling from the public houses and ducking under the outstretched arms of haggard beggars. Nicholas shrugged away a bangtail who'd grabbed hold of his coat.

"There's adventure enough right here, James, if only you thought to look for it." They came out on the edge of the Thames again, and Nicholas stared across the water, watching as the black cloud over the Engine Ward swirled and stretched. Fires crackled and belched within it, creating a maelstrom that churned and circled above the city. Although he was no engineer, but an architect, he felt an inexorable pull toward the place — the only place that had ever been a home to him — the angles and pylons like some intricate tapestry draped across the city. *The Gods of Engine Ward working their elemental magic.*

"I can no longer *look* for anything," Holman said cheerfully. "This city has lost her magic since the border closure. If I stay in England, I am doomed to live the remainder of my days in Travers College at Windsor Castle with only twice-daily prayers to Gods I don't believe in to occupy my mind. I have my Royal Society membership, but I've no stomach for politics, and what engineer would hire a blind man? I might have been some use to Isambard, but he does not want me. But if anyone can carve a future for himself in these *interesting* times, it is you, Nicholas Rose."

Nicholas smiled at the ease with which his old friend had adopted his new name. "You think too much of me, James. I have returned to England with *nothing*. I am … in danger. I cannot tell you more than that. If I do not find some means of keeping myself, I will be no better than these people." He swept his arm about the street, indicating the unsavoury characters occupying the cobbles, forgetting James couldn't see the gesture.

Holman shook his head. "You have a new name, a clean slate. And you have your mind, and that's more than many can say. You managed to sneak back across the border from France, the country most hostile to England's Gods. That is remarkable, and remarkable men don't go long without work. Isambard always looked to you for guidance, Nicholas, and who knows? Maybe he could now look to you for building design. He's just a minor name now, stirring shit in the Society, but his ideas could transform England forever. He could change what it means to be an engineer, but with you at his side, maybe he will change what it means to be human."

Nicholas stared at the black cloud blotting out the moon. He shivered, wondering if James was right.

***

ENGINEERS TO RID LONDON OF DRAGON MENACE

The Times, London, Friday, 20 July 1830.

HMK George III called an emergency session of the Council of the Royal Society last night, following yesterday's dragon attack in Kensington Gardens, during which two women and a Grenadier Guard were killed and the dragon in question caused hundreds of pounds worth of damage to the hydrangea beds.

Dragons have been sighted in the city with increasing regularity over the last few years, but attacks on the public have begun only recently. So far, twelve Londoners have been killed or seriously injured after meeting with dragons in our public parks and squares.

"The hunting and drainage activities in the swamps have caused irreversible damage to the dragon environment. Now that they're no longer being hunted, the species has been allowed to repopulate, and they are moving south and east in search of new sources of food," said Sir Joseph Banks, biologist, Royal Physician, Prime Minister, Messiah of the Aether Sect, and President of the Royal Society. "The dragons are attracted to London because of the warmth from our fires and factories. There is a high concentration of food here, and no competing predators. They will continue to attack with increasing ferocity unless we do something to stop them."

In the wake of the Kensington Massacre, the Council today declared its intention to solve the problem once and for all. "Clearly," said Banks, "Something must be done. The dragons are a menace to public safety."

The Council of the Royal Society — the nation's foremost religious and civic body — are sponsoring an engineering design competition. Engineers from all over the British Empire are invited to submit proposals for an ingenious solution to London's dragon problem. The prize includes the engineering contract to build the proposed design, the sum of £1200 from the Royal purse, and the rank of Presbyter within their chosen engineering sect, if not already occupying this post.

HMK George, addressing the Royal Society for the first time since his recovery from a bout of illness that has seen him unable to attend his duties for several months, encouraged engineers from all the sects to enter the competition. Engineers can submit their proposals to the Royal Society at their residence in Somerset House. His Majesty and the Council will decide the winner, who will be announced at the next Society meeting.

Meanwhile, the Royal Society has commissioned the printing of a pamphlet to be circulated throughout the populace. This pamphlet explains how to keep your home and family safe from dragon attacks, and includes "There be None of Beauty's Dragons", a poem by Lord Byron and a woodcut of several dragon booby-traps designed by Robert Stephenson. The public is reminded to report any dragon sightings to their nearest Police Office.

***

In the deeper recess of the Engine Ward, Aaron Williams pushed a shovel of coal into the furnace, shut the door, and moved onto the next. He had thirty furnaces to monitor on his shift, mostly the Cornish boiler units, which supplied the steam to the traction pulley systems of the churches above.

Only the Stokers — the mechanics of Engine Ward — were permitted into these underground chambers. A year ago, a Morphean engineer had snuck in and sabotaged the furnaces, causing a great fire to engulf the west wing of the Engine Ward and boiling three congregations of Metics in their prayers. That was only days after an Aristotelian boiler "malfunction" roasted an altar to Lord Byron, Messiah of the Church of Isis.

Aaron was perfect for the job, being a little shaky on the subject of religion. He had been on dubious terms with his own god — Great Conductor — ever since his childhood friend became the only living Stoker to invent something. And these days, inventing something didn't just mean you were clever — it meant you were favoured by the Gods. The closer Isambard got to religion, the less it appealed to Aaron, any sense of faith he once carried inside him long since replaced by a cold resentment for the Stoker's position in the city.

One could not have found a less likely religious leader than Isambard Kingdom Brunel. Their friendship had risen from their mutual grief: Aaron had lost a brother who, despite his flaws, he had loved the most of all his rotten family. And Henry's death had been the last straw for the Royal Society in the case of Isambard's father, Marc Brunel. Incensed at his continued breaches of conduct, the religious court had Marc Brunel banished to Van Diemen's Land.

Born a tenth-generation Stoker, Isambard Kingdom Brunel should never have invented anything. After they hunted the swamp-dragons to extinction and had no means of sustaining themselves, King George had allowed the Stokers into the city to work in his newly formed Engine Ward, but the Stokers would never be accepted as part of the engineering elite. They did not mix with folk who weren't their own, nor were they invited to join the Royal Society or speak in the great churches. They had one purpose, and one purpose only — to keep the Engine Ward operational; to oil the great industrial machine of London.

So for Brunel to design and build a new locomotive and create his own church was doubly impressive. Aaron had seen it coming, of course: only a few years before he'd been helping Isambard spy on the lessons of the other engineering schools. He'd stolen books for his friend from the nearby churches of Grandfather Clock and Meticus, he'd pored over Isambard's technical drawings, and marvelled at the intricate designs. Aaron had always known Isambard wouldn't be content to shovel coal in the engine rooms, and nor did he long to return to the swamps — he had none of Aaron's affinity for animals.

After selling his first steam engine to a wealthy industrialist (who used it as a garden ornament), Brunel purchased a scrapped furnace chimney from the Metics and converted it into a functional, albeit modest, church. Soon, he would complete his second and third locomotives.

London society buzzed with news of this "upstart mechanic" who dared to take the name of "engineer" and create locomotives. Brunel had supporters, too: engineers who sought a change from the strict religious confines of the Royal Society, and they glorified Brunel and his locomotive design as the future of British engineering.

And though Aaron stood by Isambard's side and rejoiced in his success, he could sense the attention was affecting Isambard. His ambitions — once grounded by his poverty and standing — reached ever wider as his influence grew within the Engine Ward.

Even as they drank together after the workday had finished, Aaron could sense Isambard's mind ticking away like a Dirigire clock, whirring and churning over future possibilities.

Above Aaron's head, steam hissed through a pipe, blowing a shrill whistle. He shut the last furnace, checked the oil in the pistons, and hung up his shovel for the night.

With his concentration broken, the voices flooded in. It should have been quiet on the lower levels, but of course *they* got into the pipes and travelled as they pleased. *They* were compies — the small, lizard-like dragons that had beaten down the rat population to become London's most prolific vermin. Their minds sang like a choir in harmony, for they moved and thought as one. Aaron had become so accustomed to their chorus he could sometimes send out a thought and have them pick up on it, forcing them to change direction or stop in their tracks.

I wonder if Nicholas can do that, Aaron wondered.

Isambard was working on installing steam-driven elevators on every level of the Ward, but he'd been distracted with his locomotives, and the elevator down on the sixth level remained unfinished. Aaron clambered up the stairs, listening to the clang of his boots against the steel grating as it echoed through the machinery.

Bootsteps clanged towards him. He tipped his hat at Quartz, who came to replace him. His grandfather's closest friend since before Aaron was born, Quartz had cared for Aaron after both his parents died. A swamp man from way back, even his years in the city hadn't tamed Quartz's feral spirit. His weathered, greying features suggested an age and wisdom far beyond his years, but from behind his yellowed teeth often burst the most blasphemous profanities. If Aaron was unsure of the gods, Quartz was downright malevolent.

"His Eminence wishes to see you." Quartz's wild eyes glimmered as he clapped his hand on Aaron's back. Aaron staggered forward, but managed to keep his balance.

"Did he say why?"

Quartz shrugged. "He wouldn't presume to tell me, a mere mortal, now would he? He should be finished at the pulpit within the hour if you felt like skinning your knees in his presence."

Like all the engineers of the Ward, Brunel delivered nightly sermons from his church, mostly on matters of locomotion, mathematics and the science of machinery. Tonight, he was speaking on his favourite topic: the advantages of his broad gauge railway design. With Brunel's name gaining notoriety, there would be a crowd for sure. Aaron slapped Quartz on the shoulder as he passed, and clambered up to level two.

Aaron took a shortcut through the tunnels and emerged on a staircase, which he ascended into the shadows at the rear of the Chimney. Brunel had extended the shell of the old chimney into a high circular nave, and had incorporated some of the Stoker workshops into wings that stuck from the structure like the legs of an insect. The rest of the workshops — and the shacks and tenements the Stokers inhabited — were hidden behind the complex. From the street the building was dwarfed by the majestic churches surrounding it, but Brunel had already extended many of the Stoker tunnels deep underground. If the Royal Society ever found out …

Lit by strings of flickering Argand lamps cascading from the vaulted ceiling, and enclosed by the comforting sounds of shuffling feet and subdued coughing, the space seemed homely, a place of solace and learning. As Aaron had suspected, every pew was full. He recognised the faces of many prominent engineers — influential men who wanted to see this upstart Stoker for themselves — and in the far corner, nearly concealed by the shadows, Aaron recognized the gaunt face of Joseph Banks, President of the Royal Society.

What's he doing here? He has done nothing but denounce Isambard to the other sects. If Banks was listening to Isambard's sermon, it meant he must consider the Stoker "engineer" a real threat.

As Isambard spoke — his tone rising and falling with vehemence as he explained why broad gauge railway would be the future of England — Aaron felt the tension in the room rising; a palpable film of outrage and antagonism clung to the air. While Isambard was popular among the workers of Engine Ward, here among the elite, among his true peers, he had few real supporters.

At just twenty-five years of age, Isambard was an imposing presence, even to his childhood friend. Despite his short stature, he carried himself with an air of quiet confidence, his work in the Engine Ward keeping him thin and muscular. His eyes — wide and sparkling — betrayed his boyish enthusiasm. He didn't rest his arms or elbows on the pulpit, as other preachers did, but kept them at his sides, occasionally raising or lowering them to emphasise a point. His voice, clear and animated and tinged with a rasping edge from his time by the furnaces, soared through the vaulted metal nave, so every soul present heard every word, though they would not understand them all. Aaron barely understood anything Isambard said these days.

When the sermon finished, Aaron watched as Banks got up to leave, slipping quietly into the retreating crowd so no one would notice him. A Messiah could not be seen in the church of another sect without arousing suspicion, as the fear of plagiarism was rife. Wealth, status, and prestige followed the men who invented the most useful and brilliant machines, and everyone wanted a part of that. It was not unknown for men to become mercenaries of scientific information, trading ideas and designs between competing engineers, but it was a dangerous profession — one wrongly recounted fact and an experiment could literally destroy an engineer. If Banks was here himself, it meant understanding Brunel's innovation must be worth the risk.

Aaron waited 'till the church had emptied before approaching the pulpit. Above the altar, a dusty skylight cast a shaft of light down on Isambard's crouched form. He leaned over his notes, furrowing his brow and rubbing his temples, as he always did when he was stressed.

"I took these numbers from a book of algorithms, but I think they're incorrect," he mumbled, scribbling notes in the margin of his page. "It will take me days to correctly compute these sums."

"Charles Babbage is creating a machine that will

calculate the equations itself, eliminating the problem of human error," said Aaron, who'd heard gossip about it from Quartz.

"I know, and I wish he'd damn well hurry up about it. I heard he's been charged with blasphemy — not much hope for a counting machine now. Come down to the workshop."

Isambard's workshop mimicked the secret basement room they had used in their youth. He'd built it several storeys below the church, accessible only by a steam-powered lift or a winding staircase guarded by several booby traps. He pushed Aaron inside the tiny lift shaft, and cranked the handle to send them on their way.

"I want to show you something," he said. "You're the first to see it, and I want your honest opinion."

"Is this your entry to the King's competition?"

"Ah, so you saw the article in the *Times*." He mimicked Joseph Banks' refined voice. "'If the Stokers hadn't killed all the tricorns, the dragons would never come to London and eat all our bonny bangtails.' And how many times can the man say the word 'engineer' in one sentence? He would do anything to sour public opinion against me."

"He hardly needs to worry. I don't know why you're bothering, Isambard. They will never vote for a Stoker design, even if it is brilliant."

"And yet, I have made all this," Brunel swept his hand through the air, indicating the clanging elevator, and the Chimney, high above. "The King believes in broad gauge, Aaron. That's why he allowed me to build all this. That's why he sent Banks here tonight to spy on me."

"So you saw him, then?"

Brunel ignored Aaron's question. "King George created the gods and the churches and the Royal Society, so he can bend them as he wishes. And if I *could* win—"

"You hope for too much."

But Brunel wasn't listening. "Presbyter!" his eyes danced. "Imagine one of the Dirty Folk being able to jump to the rank of Presbyter! The winner will sit on the Council of the Royal Society — imagine that! The result of this competition could alter the course of Stoker history."

The elevator creaked to a halt, and Brunel pulled the grating open. Aaron followed him across the tiny landing to the heavy iron door, which stood open most of the time (being rather difficult to move) but was now shut and bolted.

"I didn't want any prying eyes to steal my idea," he said. He unlocked the door, slipped off the bolts, and he and Aaron each leaned a shoulder against the door and pushed.

The door creaked open to reveal the high, airy chamber, at odds with its underground location. Ventilation shafts carried fresh air from the city (if any air in London could be defined as *fresh*), and a system of pipes discharged waste and fumes into rubbish pits behind Engine Ward. Long workbenches lined every wall and stretched across the centre of the room, covered in every manner of contraption imaginable. In the far corner, a furnace flared, sending flickering shadows across the room.

Aaron had visited many times before, but still he found himself in awe of the expansive space. Isambard seemed utterly at home here, as though he had become part of the machinery himself.

Brunel strode across the workshop and pointed to a model spread across the central workspace. "Look!" he cried, his eyes dancing with excitement.

Aaron bent over the model, seeing immediately it represented an exquisite miniature cityscape of London, perfectly rendered in clay and metal. Around the entire boundary of the city proper, a great wall towered, the smooth sides high and imposing even on such a small scale.

"It's a *wall*," he breathed, at once grasping the simplicity of Brunel's plan. "A wall to keep out the dragons."

"Not just any wall. One-hundred foot high, made of iron, and powered by steam. With controlled entry and exit points, not only will she protect London from further dragon attacks, but she'll help with crowd control and the checking of goods coming in and out of the city. And when the French finally get up the balls to invade, she'll help our army to protect and defend the city. And the best news of all, she'll be wide enough to run a rail line around the city. A broad gauge line."

He showed Aaron the working model of a locomotive and two carriages, which he placed on the rails on top of the wall. Aaron watched in awe as the train wound its way around the model, passing tiny stations in each district.

A wall — so simple, yet so ingenious. A solution employed by cities for thousands of years. Aaron smiled at his friend and said, "You're sure to impress the King with this design, Isambard."

"I pray you speak the truth, friend."

"Do you have any idea what Stephenson plans?"

Isambard spat. The very mention of Stephenson's name induced a deep fury within him. While Brunel toiled in the Engine Ward, building his first locomotive engine from stolen plans and snippets of overheard lectures by the eminent locomotive engineer and Messiah, Richard Trevethick, Stephenson, son of a wealthy civil engineer, had built his locomotives using his "standard gauge" of four feet, eight and a half inches, and had laid down track for a line between Stockton and Darlington in the north of England. With money at his disposal and a ten-year head start, Stephenson was poised to be the man to accomplish Isambard's greatest dream — to build a cohesive, functioning train line between every city in England.

After Trevethick died, Stephenson's work had earned him — or, as Isambard claimed, *bought* him — the honour of being declared the Messiah of the Church of Great Conductor, the God of steam machinery whom the Stokers — along with Stephenson's Navvies and some other, smaller churches — worshipped. As Great Conductor's representative on earth, Stephenson had complete power over England's expanding rail network, and he constantly blocked the proposals of smaller engineers and bought up the choice plots of land. Besides this, Stephenson was responsible — in Isambard's mind, at least — for his father's deportation. It was no wonder Isambard grew ever more hateful of the man he deemed his greatest rival.

If the winner of the King's competition were granted the position of Presbyter, then that man would have a vote in the dealings of the entire sect. Stephenson would no longer be able to ignore him, and Isambard wanted that honour more than anything.

If only Isambard could win, which he wouldn't.

"I shall complete the plans shortly," declared Isambard. "And take them to Somerset House within the week. What do you think, my friend? Do you believe I have a chance?"

"More than a chance," Aaron lied, lifting the tiny locomotive in his fingers and watching the pistons moving the wheels around the shaft. "We'll be building this Wall together by next month, of that I am certain."

"The only problem is the exterior." Brunel threw a set of drawings on the table. "The King favours designs with a strong aesthetic, and I have no eye for such trivialities. My Wall is ugly, and this will count against me. But I won't have someone from the Church of Isis turn it into a Romanesque bauble. I need an industrial architect, someone who cares more for steel pylons than Corinthian columns and acanthus leaves!"

"As fortune would have it, there is an architect just arrived in London," Aaron said. "I met him on Tuesday, after I rescued his friend from the dragon in Kensington Garden. He has trained in France."

"He sounds perfect. What is his name?"

"Nicholas Rose, although you might know him as Nicholas Thorne."

Brunel's face paled. "And his friend you rescued?"

"James Holman, the Blind Physician."

Brunel slumped into his chair. "Both James and Nicholas? In London — *together*?"

"Nicholas has only just returned from France under strange circumstances. How he got across the blockade he didn't say, but they both asked after you most profusely. They are anxious to meet you, and wonder why you have not answered their letters."

With trembling hands, Brunel reached behind him and withdrew from the desk beside the furnace a small drawer. He tipped a stack of letters into his lap. "All unopened, all unread. I thought they blamed me for Henry's death, for I was the one who dragged them on to the platform. I blamed myself ... and then my father was sent away. I just wanted to forget, to throw myself into the world of machines. And so, I could not bring myself to answer either of them. But now it is too late. It has been so long—"

"If they did blame you, that blame has long faded. They express only concern, and pleasure at your success."

Brunel's eyes did not leave the stack of letters in his lap. "They truly do not hate me?"

"They worry that you harbour hatred for them."

He looked up then, and Aaron saw the beginnings of tears glistening in the corners of his eyes. "Tell Nicholas I would be honoured to receive him, and that I have urgent work for him if he requires it."

***

Nicholas had seen the paper, too. He'd paid a matron of the guesthouse a small fortune to get him a copy of the *Times* with his breakfast, and he'd roused himself from his melancholy long enough to flip open the pages. He hadn't seen a British newspaper in several years — they were in short supply on the ships, and they'd been banned in France since George III denounced Christianity. Not that he could've got his hands on one anyway from his mountaintop prison—

He scanned the headlines. The announcement of the engineering competition sounded vaguely interesting — perhaps he could find work with whoever won. Suddenly, a sentence popped out at him.

"Excuse me?" he called to the landlady. She bustled over with her tray of tea things, but he held his hand up to stop her filling his cup. He pointed to the article. "The paper talks about the King recovering from an illness. When did this happen?"

"Gor, you been living under a bridge, sonny?"

"Something like that," he said gravely. "I had no news where I've been. Last thing I'd heard, he'd made a complete recovery from his malady and sent his eldest son to the block."

She snorted. "That nasty business was some years ago, now, though the next two sons is dead too. The King was distraught — he's only got daughters left now, and he keeps them locked in the castle for their own protection."

"What did the princes die of?"

"Well, that Joseph Banks — he was only the Royal Physician then — said it was venereal disease on account of all the ladies they were having relations with — but both of them within days of each other? Most say 'twas poison, the poor dears. George hasn't married again, and with none of his immediate family still livin', no one knows who'll be crowned when he dies — I get men in here all fired up over the Council debates, an' they think we're headin' for another Cromwell. But dammit if George ain't ninety years old and no sign of him bein' infirm 'till he took ill a few months ago—"

"And that's why Banks—"

"—is now the Prime Minister. You're a clever lad."
She patted his shoulders. "More tea?"

He obliged, hoping she didn't charge extra for the
tea. His financial situation was already dire. He'd left
France with all he had, but that wasn't much. He could
only afford a few more nights at this guesthouse —
one of the cheapest, seediest ones overlooking
Convent Garden — before he'd be on the streets.

*Everything must go well with Isambard today, or I
am doomed. How fitting that my future now lies in the
hands of the schoolboy whose own future had seemed
the bleakest of all.*

Wringing his fingers in the napkin until the ends
turned white, Nicholas stared at the crusts of his toast,
his mind unfocused — travelling in endless circles.
Another guest entered the dining room, dragging a
mangy dog on a chain. The mutt yapped at the table
legs, its eyes wide as it took in the room. The dog's
thoughts floated into Nicholas' head — the curious
smells emanating from every surface, rising like clouds
and swirling together into a haze of colour. Nicholas
rubbed his neck, feeling the bite of the chain against
his skin.

*If I return to the Ward, to the machines, perhaps
the voices will finally be silenced.*

Nicholas retired to his room to prepare for his
meeting with Isambard. He spread his things out on his
desk. He didn't have much — he had brought only a
small satchel from France — some papers, his faded
lieutenant's jacket, the cuffs stained with blood, a
Lammarchean bible, a tiny switchblade, and a small

flask of his favourite whisky. He stuffed the switchblade into his pocket. Clasping the bottle, he unscrewed the lid and swallowed the entire draught.

"You know, most Englishmen drink tea at this time of the morning."

Nicholas jumped, startled. He turned around and saw Aaron leaning against the door to his room, his face and clothing even blacker with coal dust than the previous day. A trail of dirty footprints followed him up the hall.

"Isambard sent me to collect you." Aaron pushed past Nicholas and surveyed the room. "By Great Conductor's lead-soaked testicles, this room is barely better than my Stoker hovel."

"I *am* capable of walking to the Engine Ward myself."

"Suit yourself, but the place is a madhouse — engineers rushing everywhere, trying to finish their designs for the competition. Everyone is terrified their idea will be stolen. They're not letting anyone in or out without an insignia. Here." Aaron pushed a Stoker pin — the insignia of St. George's cross made of gauge nails adopted by Brunel's church — into Nicholas' hand. "Put this on."

Nicholas pinned the tiny crossed railway nails to his lapel. Taking his ratty satchel in one hand, he tipped his hat to Aaron. "Ready to go."

***

In the muddy London daylight, Nicholas could finally see the Engine Ward in all her glory. For the briefest time he'd once called that neighbourhood of handsome churches and soot-cloaked workhouses home, but now he could only regard her with the awe of an architect confronted with the greatest masterpiece of his time. The Engine Ward had tripled in size since Nicholas had last seen her, her smoky expanse engulfing the surrounding tenement blocks, pushing the bulge of black smoke further out across the city. The surrounding wall — built slapdash of riveted iron plates — did little to hem in the continual hiss and slam of beam engines, the roar of the furnaces or the hammering of metal, but seemed instead to amplify it, so the very streets trembled with a furious energy.

As they walked toward the Ward, the city changed. The streets were empty of people — those who did go out darted between buildings, their faces and clothing stained with soot. They passed block after block of tenements, the windows smudged with a black slime so thick the tenants must live in constant darkness. The usual city noises — hooves clopping against the cobbles, street vendors yelling the daily specials, clerks scribbling away in stifling offices — fell away under the hum and belch of the Engine Ward.

The thoughts drifting in and out of Nicholas' head had been the usual cacophony of city animals — horses thinking about warm hay, pigs wondering what the nice man with the knife would be getting them for lunch, pigeons scouting out the perfect gentleman's hat to use as a convenient latrine. But one by one they too fell away, and he was left with a humming chorus of voices — rodents, all thinking together. Not rats, like in Paris, but something even more intelligent.

As they neared the wall, they passed blocks of

abandoned tenements, their crumbling walls streaked with filth and gutted by fires. So thick and poisonous was the air not even the poorest people in London would live in the streets surrounding the Engine Ward. His eyes stinging, Nicholas pulled his kerchief from his pocket and held it to his face.

"Do you hear it?" Aaron asked. "The choir?" Nicholas nodded, instantly understanding. The rodents' voices rose in volume as they neared the gates, the thoughts coming to him in waves, rising and falling in pitch like the chorus of an opera. Their thoughts — harmonious, like a song — sent complex messages, and Nicholas saw maps of the rodents' tunnels impressed in his thoughts.

"It's the compies — they took over from the rats about five years ago. They're the only creatures who feel at home in the Ward. Besides us Dirty Folk, of course."

As Aaron had said, the towering iron gates were locked tight, and a crowd of engineers and acolytes blocked the street, their brightly coloured robes flapping about their bodies as they banged on the doors and yelled insults at the guards on the wall above. Aaron grabbed Nicholas' hand and began pushing through the crowd.

As people realised it was a Stoker trying to push through, they stepped back, tripping over each other to avoid having to touch him. "Oi, Stoker!" called an Aether engineer. Aaron looked up, and the engineer spat in his face. "You ought to wash your face," the Aetherian smirked. A man wearing the purple robes of the Isis Sect swept his hand along Aaron's arm, then folded it into his sleeve and pretended it had fallen off.

His companions sniggered.

Aaron kept his chin high, and did not acknowledge their taunts. Nicholas stared at the Stoker's blackened overalls, his ears burning as the crowd whispered to one another about the shabby gentleman being led by a Stoker.

Once through the crowd Aaron pulled Nicholas into an alleyway, and pushed open the door to an empty tenement block. He motioned for Nicholas to enter.

"Aaron, those engineers back there. They—"

Aaron shook his head. "C'mon Nicholas, you can't have thought things here would be any better? You're lucky — you're a stranger to them. You have freedom men like me can only dream of. You could be *anything*. Are you sure you want to get in with Isambard and the Stokers?"

Nicholas looked into Aaron's eyes — gleaming against the blackened skin on his face like two orbs of hard, cold marble. *He hears the voices. All my life I thought I was the only one.* "I am no more free than you are," he said, and ducked inside the tenement. Aaron closed the door behind him.

Aaron led Nicholas down a pitch-black staircase into the cellar. He pulled a rotting doorway off the wall, picked up an Argand lamp that lay abandoned beside the wall, and shone the dim light behind the door, revealing a low stone tunnel. "I presume you remember the existence of these tunnels below the Ward," he said. "The Stokers use them to move between areas of the Ward. Now we have some, like this one, that stretch beyond the Ward – we use it when we need to move outside the Wall without being harassed. If the Council were to discover these tunnels, we'd be in a lot of trouble. So don't be surprised if folk down here aren't friendly to a stranger, do you understand?"

Nicholas nodded. As he peered into the darkness, the chorus of compies turned into a roar, thundering against the sides of his skull with such force he cried out and jammed his fists into his ears.

"It comes in waves," Aaron said. "You get used to it. Follow me. You got that Stoker pin still?"

Nicholas nodded, and followed Aaron into the tunnel, ducking his head to avoid scraping it on the low stone ceiling. The tunnel sloped sharply downward, and Aaron's Argand hardly penetrated the gloom. Nicholas held onto the bare brick walls, trying to keep his footing on the damp slope.

Down they went, 'till the tunnel widened out into a round antechamber, lit by flickering Argand lamps and a faint shaft of light from a ventilation shaft above. Aaron met a guard, and both he and Nicholas displayed their Stoker pins before being ushered into the hall beyond.

Here the stone walls were barely visible behind bank after bank of machinery. At one end of the long room, four men took turns shovelling coal into two Cornish furnaces, while another stood ready to rake the coal flat over the fire. Hundreds of pipes crisscrossed the expanse of the cavern — nearly more than a hundred feet long in all and sixty wide, with at least twenty men swarming about on two levels, pulling levers, checking gauges, and yelling at each other in an incomprehensible language.

"One-twenty for boiler seventy-two, C Quarter. Better pump her up!"

"Wheel's shot out in D quarter — get Oliver on it!"

'Williams!" a croaking voice called. Nicholas turned to see a hunched man, his face pinched and crumpled with age, leaning over the gangway leading to the upper level of the galley. He gestured for Aaron. "Don't stand there like a useless Navvy. We're losing pressure in seventy-two—"

"Not now, Quartz," Aaron called, his stern face breaking into a smile as he tipped his head at the old man. "I'm on church business."

"Of course you bloody are." The man smiled, revealing a row of rotting teeth, and made a rude gesture at Aaron before returning to his work.

Aaron led Nicholas down another tunnel, pushing past several Stokers jogging in the opposite direction. "Don't mind Quartz," he said. "He's the closest thing to a father I have. We're a little uncivilised down here."

Nicholas noticed how the Stokers in the tunnel moved to the side so everyone could get past without pushing, the men calling friendly insults to each other as they passed. "If you want to see uncivilised," he laughed, "you should visit France."

They ascended a set of metal steps, and Aaron pushed open a heavy iron door. Nicholas, his eyes accustomed to the dimness, squinted as light flooded the stairwell.

He stepped out into an open square, surrounded on each side by the towering cathedrals of the four richest sects: Aether, Isis, Morpheus, and Great Conductor. From the lofty spires of these great edifices the Messiahs worked — Shelley penned his verses, Turner painted his landscapes, and the great plume of smoke and debris spewing from the top of the Aether Church suggested Banks was conducting some kind of chemical experiment. Worshippers crowded the marble steps — the Isis acolytes in floaty dress, setting up their easels and positioning the courtesans they'd hired from Convent Garden, banging elbows with the Aetherians and their chemistry sets, while the Morpheans called insults across the square and scribbled their favourites down in their notebooks. Only one church remained silent, the front doors firmly locked. Stephenson's worshippers had gone north to build his railway, leaving Brunel the most prominent Great Conductor Church in London.

Engineers from every sect crammed the square, their arms laden with plans and supplies as they pushed against the tide of people, dodging the elaborate shrines built by prominent politicians. Along Industry Street — the main thoroughfare for the Ward — drivers yelled obscenities as they attempted to navigate a traffic jam that stretched right back up to the gates. The horses spluttered and neighed in protest as they were forced to stand in the soot-blackened air.

Nicholas gripped Aaron's arm as he was pulled through the surging crowd, ducking into the alley between the Isis and Aether cathedrals and emerging on one of the side streets. Smaller churches crammed the roadside, built leaning up against each other and jutting out at odd angles. These churches didn't have the patronage of wealthy Royal Society members, so they built their houses of worship with what they had available — usually wood, brick and metal salvaged from the now-defunct shipyards. Some of these religions were affiliated with official Gods of Industry, while others, like the Metics and Dirigires, were cults devoted to strange foreign deities. (The Metics — who believed imperial measurement was an affront to the Gods — and the Dirigires — men who flew great balloons and worshipped a goddess of the sky — were both French religions, which meant they'd never found much favour in England.)

Down another side street, only a block from where Nicholas had attended Marc Brunel's school as a boy, Aaron stopped on the corner and pointed up. "Here you are: the Chimney."

He gazed up, unable to believe Isambard had really created this. The Chimney was a modest building, the spire a disused smoke stack that had formed one of the earlier Ward workshops. The Stokers had reshaped the workshop, widening the space and creating a vaulted nave. Short wings protruded from either side, slotting into the gaps between the giant Lord Byron shrine and Joseph Banks' Aether Church that flanked the structure. The giant iron doors were closed. Engineers wearing the robes of the Great Conductor sat on the steps, and Stokers rushed in and out, attending to various chores.

Aaron rapped his knuckles against the door. A slot opened and two beady eyes peered out suspiciously.

"We've no services today," the mouth belonging to the eyes said.

"Don't pretend you can't see me, Peter. I've brought Nicholas Thorne to see Isambard."

Nicholas paled. "Please don't use that name," he said. "It's Rose now."

"Nicholas *Thorne*?" The man spat. "The scoundrel who done killed our brother?"

Nicholas stepped away, shocked by the

resemblance between Aaron and the priest. Although at least ten years his senior, the priest shared Aaron's piercing eyes, curled black hair, and gaunt features. Nicholas remembered the fearsome reputation of Henry's elder brothers among the Stokers — priests who delighted in finding religious transgressions within the Ward to bring before the Council. They'd been particularly diligent in weeding out troublesome Stokers, and had played a crucial role in convicting Marc Brunel. Nicholas decided it was prudent to keep his mouth shut.

Aaron had no such qualms. "Henry got himself killed with his own stupidity, and you will too if you don't open this door."

Aaron's brother slammed the cover over the slot, and with a hiss of steam, the door swung inward. Peter — who towered over them both in his silk robes — scowled at them. "What's *he* doing here?"

"Priests don't ask questions," Aaron said. "That's the price you pay for not ever having to get your hands dirty."

"You'd better watch your tongue, or I'll report you to Oswald." But Peter sloped off into the shadows, leaving them alone in the Nave.

"Oswald?"

"My other brother. He's Head Priest, and not as angry as Peter, but even more dangerous. You'll meet him in time."

"I thought your brothers were priests in Stephenson's church."

"They were — and a fine penny they were making from it, too. But Stephenson refused to take them with him when he left for the north. Being Stokers, he didn't consider them trustworthy." He snorted. "They'll do anything to avoid manual labour, and Oswald was smart enough to realise the priesthood of Isambard's church would incur no wrath from the Stokers. It's less power, less money, but it's an easy life. We take the elevator here."

He pulled aside a panel decorated with a pattern of rivets forming a Stoker cross, and stepped into a metal cage. Nervous at once again entering the darkness, Nicholas stepped in beside him. Aaron closed the panel and leaned his weight against one of the levers sticking out from the floor of the cage. With a jerk, they lurched downward.

Aaron had brought no light with him, and Nicholas had plenty of time, lost with his thoughts in the darkness, to wonder what awaited him at the bottom of that elevator shaft. It occurred to him briefly that maybe he was being set up. Maybe Isambard had used Aaron to lure him here, to exact revenge for Nicholas' part in Marc Brunel's sentence. The knife in his pocket felt heavy, and Nicholas wondered if he would have to use it.

The din of the compies still came upon him in waves, but it was abating. *Not even the compies would come this far into the earth.*

Finally, the elevator jerked to a stop. Nicholas heard Aaron pull open the grate, and a hand grabbed his sleeve. "Through here," Aaron said, directing him through a low door.

The workshop was dim, lit by a roaring furnace in the far corner and a row of Argand lamps scattered across the benches. Nicholas could barely make out the shapes of the long tables, laden with strange machines and rolls of technical drawings smudged with oily fingerprints. Sheets of metal, half-formed cogs and stacks of miscellaneous parts leaned against one wall.

"Nicholas."

The voice startled him. He whirled around as Brunel stepped out of the darkness and rushed forward to greet him.

His emotions on edge, Nicholas' first instinct was to step back, his hand flying to his pocket. Isambard, seeing his distress, held up his hands in surrender. He extended one, and after a few awkward seconds of staring at it, Nicholas stepped forward and shook.

"It's been too long, my friend," Isambard said, his cold, bony fingers entwining with Nicholas' own. "Please, sit with me."

Isambard pulled a stool in front of the furnace, and Nicholas sat on it gingerly, still nervous in the presence of his old friend. Isambard sank into a wing-backed chair opposite him. Once opulent, its fabric was now blackened with soot and the stitching was unravelling around the arms. Aaron sat on the floor behind Brunel, his thin legs stretching across the floor.

"I'm sorry, I do not have any tea to offer—"

"You did not answer my letters," Nicholas blurted out.

"No, I did not." Isambard stared at his hands. "I treasure them, every one, but I could not bring myself to read them, let alone reply. You have to understand … I felt like a failure. You and James went off on your adventure, but I was trapped in Engine Ward. You would both return as gentlemen, your Stoker heritage forgotten, and our friendship could not continue, for gentlemen do not associate with Dirty Folk. I knew your letters would be filled with new sights, strange smells, great adventures ... but I had no stories to tell in return. I woke up, I shoveled coal into the furnaces 'till my fingers bled, I fell asleep, and I did it all again the next day. I wanted to wait 'till I had *this*," he gestured around the room, "to show you, but by then you had stopped writing. But you're here now, and can see it with your own eyes."

"And it is truly amazing, but Isambard, you should have known James and I would not judge you. We knew against what you've fought. You must be the bravest man I know to have built this church right under the nose of Stephenson and the Royal Society."

Isambard's face brightened. "Wait 'till you see my locomotives. But please ... I want to hear about your adventures. Aaron tells me you came to England from France. A border crossing is no easy feat—"

"No, it is not. And you must appreciate that I can't discuss it," Nicholas said, his voice sharper than intended. He didn't mean to offend Isambard, but he had to keep the details of his flight as secret as possible. His survival depended on his presence in London remaining undetected.

"But you have been studying at one of the French schools?" Isambard pressed him.

"I have not sat for a degree," Nicholas answered, not willing to explain any further. "But I have studied under many of the great European architects. My knowledge of architectural principles is sound. Aaron tells me you have a job for me?"

Isambard led him to a table, covered in a grimy cloth. He whipped away the cloth, and Nicholas leaned over to get a better look at the intricate model that spread out across the bench. The model of London city sprang to life, clockwork gears crunching under the table as the figures crossed the narrow streets. Around the perimeter of the city, bisecting many of London's richer suburbs, was a high wall. Atop this structure, a locomotive and two carriages made a lazy circumnavigation of the city.

"This is my design for the engineering competition," said Brunel. "But I am a man of machines, Nicholas. I know how to make something work, but I don't know how to make it appealing to the discerning eye. The poets and artists of the Isis and Morphean sects are going to have something visually stunning, and for my Wall to impress the King, it needs the touch of an architect."

"You want me to—"

"Make my Wall beautiful." He handed Nicholas a sheet of paper. "The fee is modest, I'm afraid, but there will be a permanent job for you with me when we win."

"*If* we win," Aaron corrected.

Isambard laughed. "Mr. Williams doesn't share my optimism." He circled the table, pointing out details of the design. "Each gate operates with steam-powered doors. These pistons drive the locks. If the French ever think to invade, they'll have to break through these first. And here." he pointed to the districts of Belgravia and Kensington. "We will build the Wall double height."

"Why?"

"The richest people in London — including the men on the Council — have residences in these suburbs, and they will want to maintain an atmosphere of exclusivity. When I build the railway, it will go through a tunnel in Belgravia, and so their garden parties and croquet games are unspoiled by the soot and steam. We'll install separate gatehouses and private train platforms, also."

While Brunel explained the various features of the Wall, Nicholas scribbled notes and watched Aaron out of the corner of his eye.

Aaron leaned back against the workbench, closed his eyes, and rested his head against his chest. Within moments, he'd fallen asleep, his head bobbing against his chest as he let out a loud snort.

Brunel noticed him watching Aaron. "He often falls asleep down here. His wife must keep him busy at night," he said, smiling.

Suddenly, Nicholas realised the reason for his friend's slumber. He'd been so awed by entering the workshop and seeing Isambard again, so thrilled with the prospect of working on the Wall, he hadn't noticed the most remarkable thing of all.

Down there, in the depths of the earth below London's churning engines, nothing stirred. Not a rat or a compie or even a lowly earthworm. They were down so far, behind so many walls of solid metal, that no animal's thoughts penetrated his skull. Nicholas' mind, for once, was silent.

***

Soaking his cloth in the bowl of warm water beside him, Joseph Banks unscrewed the medicine bottle on his lap and tipped a few drops onto the sodden rag. He turned toward His Majesty King George III and motioned for him to remove his clothes.

The King lifted his tunic over his head, and Banks once again marvelled at the results of his treatments. He'd been physician to the King for nearly forty years — for as long as England had been without a Parliament — and his medicine had not only cured the King's madness, but had remarkable effects on his person. At ninety-two years old, George's muscles still retained their firmness. His skin pulled taut around his body, showing none of the telltale brittleness of a man his age. His physique was that of someone forty years his junior, aside from the burns and blotches that marred his once flawless skin — a side effect of Banks' unusual treatment.

George had barely aged since Banks had begun administering to him. As a wide-eyed youth just out of medical school, Banks had been appalled at the King's rapidly deteriorating condition. The court doctors were stumped, and Queen Charlotte — May Aether protect her soul — had called on him after reading his revolutionary essay about the healing effects of certain lead-based tinctures.

His Majesty had been so incoherent, so close to death, they dragged his son before Parliament and declared him Regent before Banks had even uncorked a medicine bottle. No one expected him to recover, but he did. With remarkable control of his faculties, King George III marched down to Parliament and disbanded it, declaring the Council of the Royal Society the new governing body, and had the Prince Regent — his own son — executed for treason. The other princes died a few months later of an "unknown" illness (brought about by a certain substance Banks added to their brandy), and several of the more outspoken politicians met with a similar fate.

England's new government handled both religious and secular affairs, and proved remarkably effective. The country ran so smoothly that, despite some of his more radical decisions — such as closing the borders of England to foreigners — no one had questioned George's sanity since. At least, not openly.

While Banks tended to his wounds, the King discussed the competition entries. Rolls of drawings, scale models, and intricate moving machetes decorated his private chambers. Whatever entry King George chose, it would be Banks' job to force this decision on the rest of the Council at their meeting tomorrow. *It will take all of my persuasion to convince each Council member not to vote for his own church's designs.*

Banks' hand slipped, knocking a blister off one of the sores. Bright, metallic blood oozed down the King's torso. Banks went to wipe it away, but the King swatted his hand. "Enough of that, Joseph. I have something to show you."

The physician set down the medicine, and the King handed him a roll of drawings. "This is the winning design."

Banks unrolled the first drawing, revealing a detailed map of London, completely encircled in a wide iron wall. His eyes widened as he recognised the hand who had designed it.

"Are you *certain,* sire?"

"Of course I'm certain." George pulled his tunic on, fastening the buttons with deft fingers. "He couldn't have designed anything better if he were privy to my plans. Since Stephenson refuses to budge, I don't see why Brunel shouldn't be the one to build me what I need."

Panic rose in Banks' throat. "But sire, it's *Brunel.* He shouldn't have even been allowed to enter the competition. The Council will never agree—"

"That is why I have you, Joseph. With your powers of persuasion, I'm sure they'll soon see things our way. I knew it was the right decision letting him into the Society."

Banks sighed. "Choosing Brunel will anger the poets, the Aetheriuns, Turner's folk, not to mention Stephenson and his Navvies. This could drive a wedge between the sects that we cannot repair." *It will shift even more power into the Great Conductor Sect,* was what he didn't say.

"Then it will be time again to purge the Council of my enemies. I want this Wall, Joseph, and any engineer who opposes Brunel also opposes me, is that understood?"

Banks choked back his fear, and opened the plans again. This time, he tried to imagine this monstrosity surrounding the city, the high iron wall crisscrossing the districts, more of a fortress than a city. There had been an attempt, at least, to make it appear less intrusive — the architect had decorated the outer faces with rows of straight Ionic columns supporting a row of decorative arches and pedimental sculpture — homage in iron to the classical motifs so in vogue right now.

George watched Banks scrutinise the plans as he smoothed his clothes. "The design is certainly commendable," Banks managed at last.

"Who is the architect?"

Banks squinted at the name scrawled in the corner. "Nicholas Rose. I've never heard of him. He's certainly not a member of the Royal Society."

"I wouldn't expect Brunel to work with one of the established architects, not with most of them joining Turner's church. You're to bring Brunel to me, Joseph, tomorrow. And I'll see this Nicholas Rose, as well, if you please."

Joseph was about to protest, when a loud crash sounded from across the palace, followed by a long scream, cut haltingly short.

Banks turned to the King, horror in his eyes. "Sir, not again—"

"Attend to that for me, won't you, Joseph?" the King smiled. "It seems another of my children has broken free of the nursery."

***

Lieutenant James Holman, Esq.

His Majesty King George, Prime Minister Joseph Banks and the Learned Council of the Royal Society cordially invite you to attend a special meeting of the Royal Society on Thursday the 15th of July. On this illustrious occasion HMK George III will announce the winner of the engineering competition, and following this, Charles Babbage, engineer of the Metic Sect and inventor of the Difference Engine, will answer the charges of treason brought against him by the Council.

Formal dress required. Brandy and light supper provided.

***

In the days since they'd handed in the drawings, Nicholas had spent every spare moment in the Chimney with Isambard, returning to the guesthouse only to sleep. Isambard cut him a key, so he could come and go as he pleased, and even offered to let him sleep in the workshop. Nicholas had to admit the idea of spending the night without the voices was tempting, but he did not want to take advantage of his friend. Also, he was afraid Peter might sneak downstairs and kill him in his sleep.

Both Nicholas and Isambard had guarded their thoughts for years, but the more they talked, the more conversation came easily. Nicholas wondered if he could ever trust Isambard enough to tell him the truth about why he'd fled France. Isambard, who had now read all of Nicholas' letters, knew his friend's story up until the time he left the Navy, and so filled Nicholas in on his own life in a haphazard fashion. He would talk fleetingly of people, of deaths and births and important events, dwelling for hours on revelations in the design of his locomotive — the construction of the chassis, the drive-wheel, the pistons.

Aaron joined them whenever he could, but his work on the furnaces and his wife kept him busy, so mostly they were left alone in Brunel's workshop. The time there passed quickly, and in the gloom it was impossible to tell when one hour ended and the next began.

One day Nicholas inserted the key Brunel had given him into the heavy padlock, hefted off the chain, and swung open the door to the Chimney, to find Brunel sitting at one of the pews, waiting for him. "I want to show you something," he said, standing to greet Nicholas. "Not here — out in the workshops."

Curious, Nicholas followed Brunel behind the pulpit, and down a flight of steps leading out behind the church. Isambard led him past row after row of pitched roofed structures, through which Nicholas could hear all manner of hammerings, whirrings, and men swearing. Finally, Isambard stopped in front of one, nodded to the guard who leaned against the wall, pushed aside a long wooden door, and darted inside.

Nicholas followed him, and stopped short, in awe of the sight that greeted him. Occupying every inch of that shed were the towering forms of two black locomotive engines. He'd seen drawings of these peculiarly English inventions in some of the contraband French journals, but he could not have imagined the sheer scale or raw beauty of them.

Built for Brunel's broader gauge rails, each wide chassis sat on her own bed of track, holding court with the dignity of Egyptian sphinxes. The formidable wheel arches rose at each side, and the open cab gaped from the expanse of iron like the mouth of a dragon, from where a tongue of flame might shoot out at any moment. Stokers crawled over every inch of the engines, fitting parts, taking measurements, welding and shaping raw metal into the zenith of engineering beauty.

"There they are," Brunel whispered, his eyes dancing with delight. "My two darlings. They won't be finished for many months yet, but if I win the engineering competition, they'll be the first locomotives to run in London. In order to meet the demands of broad gauge track, I've had to place the boiler on a separate six-wheeled frame behind the engine itself. The 2-2-2 engine is the *Hurricane* and that 0-4-0 beauty over there is the *Thunderer*."

"You *built* these," Nicholas breathed, awed by their size, their complexity. They seemed to rise up from the earth, beautiful flowers in a garden of machines, as if Isambard had somehow imbued them with his own spirit.

Brunel nodded. "My first engine — the one I sold to pay for this Chimney — was a cruder version of these. Aaron and I built it together, in secret. It took us nearly nine years. Already I'm making improvements."

"And Stephenson's … are they anything like this?"

"Hardly." Isambard snorted. "I've seen his *Rocket*. A piddling thing, it can barely pull two carriages up a slight incline. Throw a pebble on the track and it derails. Broad gauge is stronger, faster, and more robust. The sooner the Royal Society understands that, the better."

Brunel pointed to the guards stationed at either end of the workshop. "They ensure only Stokers can enter here. Stephenson has Navvy spies all over London, not to mention those in the pay of the Council, who want me prosecuted for engineering. I can't afford to have my ideas compromised."

They walked around the engines, Brunel stopping men in their work to discuss their progress and the problems they'd encountered. He listened as they explained parts that wouldn't fit, questioned flaws in the design, and discussed mechanical processes Nicholas couldn't even begin to understand. Brunel did not dismiss any opinion, but each time offered an answer that seemed to please the men.

"Your men respect you," said Nicholas. "I wager not many engineers can say that."

"The Stokers are clever men," replied Brunel. "They understand a machine intuitively — as if it were an extension of their own bodies. They have only to glance at the plans to tell you what works and what will not. There is no reason — apart from the arrogance of certain powerful men — why Stokers cannot be engineers in their own right, or whatever they wish to be … if given the chance."

"And this is your dream? To have Stokers in the Royal Society? To give them seats on the Council?"

"Freedom is the dream of every man, don't you agree?"

Nicholas said nothing. Brunel stopped walking, and turned to face him, his dark eyes fixed on Nicholas' own, searching relentlessly for an answer.

"We dance around this question," he said. "But we are old friends, and I tire of the dance. I have not heard from you since they closed the borders, and yet, here you are again, returning at great risk to London, changing your name, wanting to work in secret, and with barely a shilling in your purse. Now the best I can figure, the only reason a learned man would want to return to London is if he were running from a woman, from the law, or from someone who was trying to kill him."

Nicholas' mouth went dry. He raked his tongue across his teeth, desperately trying to think of something to say. "You may be right on all three counts," he managed.

"You should tell me what has happened. I could help."

"If I tell you, Isambard, I throw everything you've built here into jeopardy. Someone may come for me at any time, and I will not drag you into my problems, any more than I already have."

"Nicholas—" Brunel stepped toward him.

"Isambard," Aaron's voice interrupted. Nicholas jumped. He hadn't even heard Aaron come down the stairs. *How much has he heard?* "I don't mean to disturb you, only there's a messenger from the King waiting in the Nave. He wants you and Mr. Rose to accompany him to Windsor Castle promptly."

Isambard's face changed instantly. His conversation with Nicholas forgotten, he dropped the plans onto the table and raced to the elevator. Nicholas jogged behind him, his heart leaping in his chest. *The King? He wouldn't concern himself with the affairs of a minor engineer. The only reason he could want to see us would be if he'd got to him, if he'd found me—*

Nicholas gulped.

***

"—you are not under *any* circumstances to speak to him on any matter other than that which he requests. You must *only* answer his questions, and be quick about it. Do not otherwise initiate conversation in any way. There will be some small sandwiches and cakes on the table, but the King will not touch them, and so neither should you. You must raise only the teacup to your mouth, and return it to the saucer after each sip. You must not slurp. If he speaks to you, address him

only as 'Your Majesty'. Do not touch him in any way
—"

The steward kept up a constant stream of instructions as he frantically brushed lint off Nicholas' jacket. The complex protocol and fussing attendants were only serving to make Nicholas more and more nervous. Beside him, Brunel was having his hair plastered into place by two grunting attendants, while a third was trying in vain to steam out the stains on his overalls. He looked utterly unfazed to be standing in Windsor Castle, about to meet the King.

Nicholas and Brunel had arrived at the castle in the messenger's carriage, only to be whisked around the back to a servants' entrance and locked in a small waiting room, where they had remained for the past two hours, subjected to various barbaric beauty treatments in preparation for their audience with King George.

"Is this all really necessary?" Brunel asked, as one of the attendants tied a pair of starched white cuffs around his wrists.

The steward glared at him. "His Majesty has never had an audience with *Stokers* before. We hadn't anticipated how long it would take to make you presentable. And since you won't co-operate—"

"These overalls are a symbol of my heritage," said Brunel. "I will not remove them, not even for the King."

"—then we've had to do the best we can with what *little* we have available to us. At this rate, I don't think you'll be able to meet with him at all today—"

There was a knock at the door. "The King will receive them now," a voice called through the panel.

"They are not ready!"

"He won't wait any longer."

"We're perfectly presentable," snapped Brunel, disentangling himself from the attendants. He grabbed Nicholas' hand and pulled him toward to door. Nicholas met his eyes, and Brunel smiled, as if trying to reassure him.

Frowning one last time at the state of them, the steward sighed loudly, and pushed open the door. Brunel stepped out, his face calm, and Nicholas followed him, his legs shaking with nerves. Brunel reached a hand up and ran it through his hair, deliberately messing it up. Nicholas smiled weakly, but the effort just made him feel ill.

They were met by a guard, who looked them up and down with a disapproving scowl. "Are you certain you should wear *that*—"

Brunel glared at him. The guard shook his head, and beckoned for them to follow him down the hall. They paused outside two ornate wooden doors, which the guard pushed open, revealing an expansive drawing room, the walls and ceiling decorated with exquisite friezes and gilded mouldings. Nicholas gulped, forcing himself to resist the urge to turn on his heel and run.

"Mr. Brunel. Mr. Rose." The King waved them from the doorway. "Please, you may enter and take a seat. I will have the staff fetch you some tea."

Nicholas, his palms shaking and coated with sweat, stared at the chair the king wished him to use, its heavy oak legs carved in the French style, inlaid with delicate details leafed in gold. It probably cost ten years of an engineer's salary. He perched gingerly on one edge and looked up at the King, who stared down his nose at them both with a stern expression. King George's eyes sparkled with intelligence, and neither his posture nor his features betrayed his age. Nicholas tried to read his expression, to see if what he feared were true.

He's *found me,* he thought, his chest clenched. *He's making the King send me back so he can torture me—*

Joseph Banks stood behind the throne, his hands floating awkwardly at his sides and a leather satchel stowed between his feet. He pursed his lips, glaring at Brunel with vehemence.

"It is an honour, Your Majesty." Unlike Nicholas, Isambard seemed calm, collected. He sat upright in his chair, mimicking the King's strict posture. "If it pleases His Majesty, I wondered why you have called two lowly engineers into your presence today?"

Nicholas cringed at his easy use of that loaded descriptor. He did not wish to claim any such title for himself, especially not when he knew exactly what the King wanted. Banks' eyes flashed with anger, but King George did not seem to notice.

I'm sorry, Isambard. I didn't want to drag you into this.

The King smiled, sending a chill down Nicholas' spine.

"Many of my *current* ministers," the King shot Banks a filthy look, "have dismissed your broad gauge railway as quackery, but I've been reading your papers with interest. It has not escaped my attention that you've entered my engineering competition, and although I cannot reveal the winner of that contest before Thursday's Royal Society meeting, I would urge you not to miss that meeting."

What? Did he just say ... Brunel is ...

Not even the presence of royalty could keep the boyish glee from Isambard's face. "Your Majesty, it is an honour."

"It is still *not* decided," Banks snapped, freezing the smile on Isambard's face. "The Council are not yet in agreement."

The King dismissed Banks with a wave of his hand. "Don't mind Joseph. Eventually, he comes around to seeing things my way. However, the matter I'd like to discuss today is of a different nature. The plans, please Joseph?" The Prime Minister handed the King a set of drawings, who spread them out on the table, positioning weights over the corners to keep them flat. Nicholas squinted at the delicate lines, trying to comprehend.

"I want you to build me a railway," said the King. "Build it as fast and as well as you're able, and if I like it, I shall give you the authority to build railways all over England."

Brunel sucked in his breath, and he grabbed Nicholas' arm as though he might fall over at any moment. Nicholas stared, dumbfounded, from his perch, wondering how such a remarkable fortune could have fallen into Brunel's lap.

"But Your Majesty," Brunel's voice came out high-pitched. "*Why?*"

"I intend to move my household and affairs of state into Buckingham House, in the heart of the city. I want Windsor Castle to remain a religious centre, a place where I can find respite with my gods, and where pilgrims might travel to give offerings at St. George's Chapel. But my main residence shall be moved to

Buckingham, and I need a railway to transport the court and my furnishings between these residences. I intend to run it through these old sewer tunnels," the King rapped his finger against the map. "So they will need widening and reinforcing. And I need the entire length of track to be secure — I don't want any threat of assassination. But most of all, I want it to be *fast*. So fast I can make the trip to Windsor before a messenger could arrive at Somerset House on horseback."

"No, I mean, why *me?* Surely choosing me over Stephenson will cause friction on the Council?"

"The nature of this project requires absolute secrecy, Mr. Brunel. Not a single citizen must know of this railway's existence until I declare it so, do you understand me? Stephenson would not comply with this. Also, his standard gauge just won't reach the speeds I require, and I feel he has designs for England that don't comply with my own. I would not worry yourself about Stephenson — despite the animosity on the Council, you have a lot of support in the Royal Society."

Isambard leaned over the table, his eyes taking on that glazed look Nicholas recognised from the pump house all those years ago. Nicholas felt sure the task was impossible, but Brunel, unblinking, took in every inch of the proposed line, all twenty-six miles of track, the tunnels to be constructed and reinforced, the complexities of secrecy on such an ambitious project. Finally, he settled back into his chair, and smiled.

"I will need to make improvements, of course," he said. "Will I be given a workforce?"

"You will pull men from the Stoker workforce — men who can be trusted. I will pay you whatever you need from the Royal Purse. It will fall upon your shoulders to ensure this railway remains hidden."

"What is the completion date?"

"Four months from today."

Nicholas sucked in his breath — that deadline was *impossible.* But Brunel said nothing, merely bending his head towards the King, and continued the conversation in hushed tones.

Nicholas, who had not even seen a railway before, let alone had any experience of building one, sat back in his chair, trying to calm his thundering heart. *You're safe, Nicholas old chum. For now, at least. But you must be more careful. If you're going to work for Isambard, you're going to have to be invisible—*

Something interrupted his thoughts. A noise, like a muffled screaming, came from some far-off wing of the castle. He raised his head to the door, straining to hear. There it was again — a short, sharp scream, cut off abruptly by another sound, almost like the snarl of an animal. Banks met his eyes and shook his head, but Nicholas stood up and walked toward the open door, listening intently.

Another sound; closer this time. It came from one of the rooms on the corner of the hall. A snarl, low and menacing, definitely some kind of animal. *A dragon, perhaps? But how did one get in here? And why can I not hear its thoughts?* He turned to tell the King something was in the hall, when out of the corner of his eye he saw a shadow move across the tapestries. He jumped.

"Nicholas, what's wrong?" Isambard looked up from the table, his eyes concerned.

"I heard a noise." Nicholas turned back to the hall.

"A scream … a snarl … like an animal … and when I looked into the hall, I saw—"

Banks frowned. "You're seeing things, Mr. Rose. There's nothing in the hall."

"No, there's *definitely* something moving—"

A figure dashed across the hall.

His heart pounding, Nicholas stared down the dim hall. "It's a man!"

With lightning speed Banks crossed the room, shoved Nicholas aside, and slammed the doors to the audience chamber shut. "Of course it was a man," he said, his eyes flashing. "You probably saw one of the servants trying to snoop on the King's private audience. They do like their games."

"He was naked," Nicholas insisted. "And that doesn't explain the *snarling*—"

He was interrupted by the King, who let out a gasping breath and collapsed across the table. Blood splattered across the plans, causing Brunel to leap back in alarm. Banks dived for His Majesty's body, pulling it back onto the couch and bringing his face into the light. As Banks pulled at the King's high collar, Nicholas could see George's eyes — bleak and bloodshot and tinged with green. In fact, his very skin seemed to give off a pallid green tinge. Banks ripped the collar open, and more blood pooled from a large scab that burst in his neck.

"Get out!" Banks screamed, shoving the King across the couch and reaching for his medicine bag. "Both of you!"

Their eyes locked on each other, Brunel and Nicholas did what they were told: they bolted for the door and ran.

***

"What *was* that?" Nicholas asked, his shaking fingers clutched around a chipped teacup.

Brunel had taken the carriage back to London to begin preparations for the King's railway, but Nicholas, still shaken by the events at the castle, now sat with James Holman in the dining room of Travers College, a modest building outside the walls of Windsor Castle that housed Holman and the other Naval Knights of Windsor.

"He has been ill these past months, but I was told he'd made a full recovery. There have been some very peculiar happenings around the castle recently," said Holman, carefully setting down his own teacup and pouring the boiling water. He used a finger hooked over the rim of the cup to check the liquid level.

"You never said anything before."

When Holman had been forced from the Navy after his illness had ravaged his joints and left him blind, he'd returned to England and, not wanting to live the life of a beggar, had applied for a post in the Naval Knights. The order consisted of seven superannuated or disabled Lieutenants, single men without children, "inclined to live a virtuous, studious and devout life." The Naval Knights were expected to live out their days in the modest rooms at Travers College; their only duty was to attend mass at St George's Chapel twice per day.

At twenty-five years of age — the same age as Nicholas and Isambard — Holman was the youngest of the Naval Knights by a good forty years. Although they were only allowed to absent their duties on medical grounds, he had managed — although how he had done so still remained a mystery — to secure an extended period of leave to attend medical school in Edinburgh, about which he had written his first book.

"There didn't seem much to say. The King stopped conducting the services at St. George's, preferring instead to sit in his wheeled chair beneath the pulpit. I've heard the servants talking about sounds in the castle, screams, skitterings in the halls, and some maids and stable boys have disappeared, although I can't imagine that's out of the ordinary with such a large staff."

"Have you noticed anything else? Wild animal noises, maybe?"

Holman shook his head.

"What do you suppose this all means?"

Holman shrugged. "Whatever secrets the King and this castle are hiding can't remain secret for much longer. He has to give the presentation at the Royal Society meeting. Let us see how he fares then."

***

Jacques du Blanc shifted, pulling one cramped leg out from under him and stretching it across the pile of bibles on top of which he crouched. Not allowing himself to show discomfort in his face, he stretched out the other leg, kicking a stack of books over so they scattered across the humming deck of the dirigible gondola.

He watched with interest as the leather-bound volumes slid toward the furnace, following the dip and sway of the flying machine. He didn't bother to pick them up. Let the coal-boy deal with that.

The pilot gestured to him, yelling something Jacques couldn't hear over the roar of the furnace and the howl of the wind. Above his head, the envelope — a huge fabric bag inflated with hydrogen, providing the craft with the means to float high in the air — shaded the deck from the sun, the wind whipping over the edges of the gondola, and tugging at his clothes and hat. The pilot turned the rudder suspended below the envelope, his eyes fixed on a point somewhere on the horizon.

Jacques followed the pilot's gaze over the edge, and saw that they were no longer flying over water. They'd crossed the Channel and now floated over a patchwork of green fields, their bright hue visible through the smoke belching from the exhaust. England; he'd made it to England.

Fields soon gave way to forests, dense with oaks. The dirigible rose over the canopy, heading north along the edge of the valley, 'till Jacques could see plumes of smoke rising between the clouds. As they dropped through the clouds, the spires of Meliora appeared. The city jutted precariously from the trunks of the ancient oaks, each trunk spliced and threaded with platforms and winches and punctured with mechanical devices.

The Dirigires (The Steerers) — a radical sect who worshipped the goddess Mama Helios and their ballooning Messiah Jean Pierre Blanchard — had fled to England after Catholic France began persecuting worshippers of the Industrian gods. King George had welcomed them, for they brought their skill with clockwork and flying machines. He'd given them land on his private hunting estates so they could build their city, and Meliora had risen up into the clouds.

Now, with England blockaded, the Dirigires were richer than ever. They had fused gondolas and steam engines to their balloons, creating for the first time lighter-than-air craft that could be manoeuvred. With the British navy otherwise engaged with attempting to dislodge the French ships, the Dirigires could now dominate an illicit trade route between England and the rest of Europe. If you wanted it, the Dirigires could get it — bibles and illegal Christian artefacts, French wine, German books, illegal passage between England and Europe — for any man who could afford the fee.

Jacques du Blanc was a man who could afford the fee, and the Dirigires didn't bat an eyelid at his fine clothes and the curved rapier strapped to his belt. They got all types on this crossing.

Even above the splutter of the dirigible's engines, Jacques could hear the seamless tick of the city. Before the purging, he'd fought alongside Dirigire priests at the Battle of the Pyrenees, and they had told him tales of their fantastical city, a shrine to their goddess of the skies. Now, it seemed, he would see her for himself.

The pilot let out the regulator, and the dirigible jerked downward, sending more bibles sailing across the deck. Jacques watched the scene on the landing pads. Workers swarmed around the dirigible, tying down the lead ropes and pulling down the deflating envelope so it didn't catch on anything. If a single spark caught the flammable hydrogen gas inside, the explosion would probably be felt in Paris.

As soon as the envelope was down and the gas

pumped away, a crew of men stormed on board to unload the cargo. Bibles, casks of wine, and boxes of holy relics all left the ship to be sent out across the countryside to buyers.

Jacques hugged his portmanteau to his chest and tried to squeeze his way through the workers. A high priest waited on the platform. As Jacques swung his legs over the edge of the gondola and descended the ramp, the priest reached up and steadied him. Jacques tipped his hat in reply, his legs wobbling as he accustomed himself to solid ground once again.

"Don't walk near the edge for a few hours," the priest said. "Your mind and body need time to adjust to the height."

The effort of lifting his portmanteau left him breathless, and his temples throbbed. Jacques gasped, desperately trying to remain upright in the pounding wind, his lungs hungry for air. He'd been some months away from his home in the Pyrenees, and his body had already forgotten the rigors of high-altitude breathing.

"Are there … rooms available … in the city?" he huffed.

"We've prepared one already," the priest replied, reaching for Jacques' portmanteau. "Your name is known in the city. Many remember you from the *Acadamie,* before the purgings. We're not often visited by such noteworthy men."

They were joined by the pilot, who thanked Jacques in grating English for flying with him and offered a cigar. The priest drew one from the box, and Jacques followed suit. "We should get out of the wind," he said in French, his legs shaking more than ever.

To Jacques' relief the pilot led them to a tavern two levels below the landing pads. They descended on a staircase that moved of its own accord, a belt that circled around on a series of giant cogs, powered by steam from an engine room far below. Jacques closed his eyes and gripped the balustrade with white knuckles. He knew better than to look out over the expanse of Meliora.

Inside the bar the pilot dropped a crate of champagne on the counter, pulled one bottle out, uncorked it, and poured them all a drink. He lit up the cigars, and leaned back in his chair, scuffed boots on the table, his gaze making Jacques nervous.

"So *you're* du Blanc," he sneered in that horrid English accent, draining his wine and running his tongue around the rim of his glass. "I never bagged you for a toff, hiding out in the mountains for years while the rest of us risked our necks for liberty. They say you went wild and ate a girl—"

"Show some respect," the priest snapped. "This man's crusade has preserved our rights to worship whom we choose."

The pilot looked unconcerned. "Did you get a lot of crusading done on the top of that mountain?" he asked.

"Tell me," Jacques said, not bothering to answer the pilot's question. "A friend of mine made this journey, not two months ago now, and I'm desperate to find him. An Englishman, though his French would be impeccable. He wouldn't have been carrying much — a portmanteau, maybe? He had sandy hair, probably hidden under a hat or cloak, and grey eyes—"

The pilot shrugged. "Everyone looks the same to

me. Ask around in the city — if he stayed a few days or bought passage with one of the traders, someone will remember him. But don't expect to get answers for nothing, even in your fancy clothes. We do a fine trade in secrets here, Mr. du Blanc."

The pilot picked his boots off the table and sauntered toward the door. The priest wiped the table with the edge of his sleeve.

"I apologise," he said, reverting to his native French now the pilot had gone. "Some of the wealthy families insist on sending their boys off to English schools. They all return sounding just like him. I am François, the High Priest of Meliora, and I may be able to help you in your quest."

Jacques set two coins down on the counter. The priest eyed them with interest. "The man," he said. "Did he come here?"

"When a man passes through Meliora, he prefers our folk not knowing the reasons. We'd be a poorer people, sir, if we gave out every slip of information on our passengers. We'd soon find ourselves with none."

Jacques set another coin down on the counter. All three pieces disappeared into the priest's sleeve in an instant, his eyes never leaving the Frenchman's face.

"He stayed here two nights," the priest offered. "He had nothing with him save a tattered portmanteau. He travelled under the name 'Nicholas Rose', and I never saw him change clothes. He bought passage with one of the traders, heading for London, though whether he intended to travel the whole distance or not, I cannot say. This was a month ago, now."

"You've been most kind. Where might I find transport to London?"

"No wagons are due for another three days, but if you take the railway, it'll get you as far as Bristol, and that's a traveller town."

The sweet smoke curled around Jacques' head. He lifted his cigar to his lips and took another deep drag, a smile creeping across his thin lips.

I'm coming for you, Nicholas. I'm coming for what's mine.

***

JAMES HOLMAN'S MEMOIRS — UNPUBLISHED

At precisely eleven minutes past nine on the fifteenth of July I strode across the lobby of Somerset House, Nicholas trailing at my heels. I bowed my observance to the Industrian gods — represented by ten alabaster statues set into two rows of niches flanking the long hall — and entered the vaulted chambers of the Royal Society. As I suspected, our late carriage had conveniently missed the opening prayers (which, with ten Gods, do go on for some time), and the pre-lecture drinks had started in earnest.

When I had been invited to join the Royal Society after the publication of my first book, I had thought it nothing more than a weekly meeting of learned gentlemen interested in pursuing the "natural philosophies". With numerous influential members and centuries of Royal patronage, the Society enjoyed much influence and stocked an impeccable cellar of the world's finest brandy, which I admit somewhat swayed my decision to accept membership.

But it seemed my opinion of the Society had been very much mistaken. Since His Majesty abolished the Church of England and disbanded Parliament, the Royal Society had become the foremost power in England, answerable only to King George himself. The eminent minds of our bright new age chose their gods, started their own congregations, and became as power-hungry and dogmatic as the priests of the church they had outlawed. Inventions became no longer the work of intelligent men, but the manifestations of the Gods of Industry on earth.

The world had given up polytheism centuries ago, and we suddenly had a Parthenon of gods thrust upon us. Fifty years after the change, England still struggled to comprehend it. Learned men clung to the same values that has seen civilisation through thousands of years of history — ignorance, and fear, and intolerance.

The Society continued its weekly meetings, but they had become nothing more than a church service — the forced attendance of hundreds of clever men, going through the motions of religiosity before they could get their hands on the brandy. Placing several gods in a room in the hope that they would jointly think up new and innovative ideas seemed sound in theory, but in practice it led only to competition, suspicion, and, ultimately, outright hostility. Faraday wouldn't talk to Herschel, and Turner secretly had popular artists killed in their sleep. Charles Babbage raised a quantitative error in one of Sir Humphry Davy's calculations and, combined with his scathing rebuke of the Society's excesses, managed to displease every member of the Council at once. The man who had once been a shoo-in for Presbyter of the Metic Sect was tonight going to be sentenced for treason.

I pushed the door ajar, tapped my stick on the oak-panelled floor, and listened. Voices rose into the vaulted ceiling, and I caught snippets of hundreds of conversations — half understood mathematical principles, fragments of engineering genius, the first inklings of original thought.

"Marvellous," Nicholas breathed, pushing past me to step into the room.

"Terrifying," I corrected him, thinking of the power wielded by the men present.

To my right I heard the unmistakably fake cough of William Buckland: Oxford biology professor, fossil collector, and longtime friend. Renowned for his work with swamp-dragons, Buckland first discovered the connections between modern creatures and the skeletons of giant ancient reptiles he called "dinosaurs". I moved along the wall toward him, hoping my late entry hadn't caught the attention of any of the Council members.

"You're conveniently late," Buckland whispered in my ear, placing a glass of brandy in my hand.

"Pesky omnibuses. They're so damn unreliable." I sipped my drink. "Has my absence been noted?"

"I informed Prime Minister Banks you were outside getting some air, but I think he's becoming suspicious," Buckland observed. "Perhaps we both ought to show up on time next week."

"Or come up with a different excuse."

Buckland and I had been amusing ourselves by turning up later and later to the regular Royal Society meetings. We'd even established a rotating roster.

Every second meeting one of us would be late, and the other would cover for him. We devised a giddy, schoolboyish joy from cheating the Messiahs of our attention.

"I see you've brought another unfortunate along to witness this farce."

"Buckland, this is Nicholas Rose. He and I were in the Navy together. Nicholas is an industrial engineer just arrived in London from his studies in France."

I felt Nicholas' body tense up with my casual mention of his illegal crossing, but Buckland just laughed. "France, eh? How'd you get back across the border?"

"I had help," Nicholas replied evasively. The men shook hands, and I noted that Nicholas quickly shifted the subject to Buckland's work. Buckland, who loved to talk about himself, acquiesced with pleasure, but I wondered — not for the first time — how Nicholas had indeed managed to return to England at all. Our borders have been tightly patrolled ever since Christian Europe united in opposition to our new pantheon of industrial gods, and one cannot simply row across the Channel. If Nicholas had come to England from France, he had come illegally — probably by way of an illicit air crossing. I listened to my friend talk, wondering what had happened to him since I'd left him at Portsmouth.

Nicholas had come to the Society meeting as my guest. He'd been nervous about coming under the public eye, if it was indeed true the prize was being awarded to Isambard (giving further credence to my worries that he'd been involved in ill dealings back in France). Isambard, too, thought it better that Nicholas didn't declare their friendship in public, but for a different reason. "We don't know how the engineers will react to the chosen winner," he'd said. "As much as you think you're a danger to me, Nicholas, it is your association with me, and not what transpired in France, that might lead to your death. Better to have engineering circles know you as an associate of Holman's than as an accomplice to my blasphemous works."

Buckland, flattered by Nicholas' attentions, began asking him for his opinion on the outcome of the engineering competition.

"I heard Shelley's had a team of poets working non-stop on his creation," said Nicholas, who'd been keeping up with the design proposals in the papers. "And Sir Humphry Davy has apparently concocted a most efficient poison. Then, of course, I've heard rumours about the brilliance of Isambard Kingdom Brunel, that young Stoker engineer—"

Nicholas sucked in his breath as he realised what he'd said. I leaned forward, listening to the conversations around us, hoping nobody had heard.

Buckland lowered his voice. "You shouldn't speak that name so freely, Mr. Rose, especially not in present company. But I'm glad to hear you're a Brunel man, also." Buckland patted Nicholas on the shoulder. "Isambard's a good chap. He won't win, of course — the Council won't accept that — but he's got a head full of clever ideas and the tenacity to forget what he ought not to say. I don't take with all this anti-Stoker nonsense. An engineer's an engineer's an engineer, I say. But my dear fellow, I've been talking you ear off and your hands are still empty. Allow me to remedy my oversight!"

Buckland went to fetch Nicholas a drink, and Nicholas and I bent our heads together so he could describe the room to me.

The Society hall — which had always resembled a church with its podium and rows of carved wooden and velvet pews — had been divided into two by the addition of a long wooden stage, covered with exquisite carpets and festooned with bright garlands of flowers and idols of the Gods of Industry. Our pantheon of gods-on-earth — the Messiahs, Presbyters, and other men of rank — strutted around the room, flanked by their high priests wearing various church regalia.

The room was more crowded than usual, and the pews had been pushed aside to make room for all of us. On a raised dais at the edge of the stage sat His Majesty. Banks and the other officers of the Council were seated beside him. A gaggle of contest entrants — would-be engineers, scientists, and architects — clamoured for the King's attention.

"You can tell those men apart from the rest of us," noted Buckland, returning with a glass of brandy for each of us, "by the outright desperation on their faces. Each one dreams he will be the recipient of this most enviable prize, and fame, fortune, and immortality will be his."

Nicholas and Buckland described for me some of the familiar faces. George Combe, the eminent phrenologist of the Church of Morpheus, paced up and down along the wall. Turner, the artist and arrogant Presbyter of the Isis Sect, held court in a private circle in the corner, his trilling, whining voice rising above the clamour. Not wanting his position to be compromised by one of the newer artists or poets, Turner had submitted plans for a mural to be painted across the west-facing walls of each of the city's buildings — scenes of terror and desolation, of hundreds of Redcoats armed with muskets and bayonets, ready to strike at any dragon that dared impose upon the city.

Percy Bysshe Shelley, the dark, brooding "engineer of words" who'd became Messiah of the Isis Sect in Lord Byron's absence, slouched across one of the velvet pews. Shelley had submitted a spectacular design for a high-walled pleasure garden containing plants like garlic and fenugreek, which the dragons found abhorrent. He planned to suspend these gardens or "mobile Eden" across the city, so citizens afflicted by dragons could wait in safety while the beasts were apprehended. I knew his design would find favour with many of the noble men on the Council, and he certainly acted as if he knew the prize was already his. He mocked protocol by bringing his wife, Mary, as his guest, and she sat beside him, dressed in her finery, the subject of many lascivious whispers amongst the learned men.

Brunel stood in the corner of the stage, and Aaron stood behind him, frantically trying to pull the hems of Brunel's too-long formal robe from under the feet of the marauding deities. "Isambard's face betrays nothing," Nicholas said. "His is the only steady gaze in this room of posturing. Do you wish to see him?" he asked me. "Isambard has been so kind to me, James. I'm certain he will welcome you as a long lost brother."

The blood froze in my veins. I shook my head, unable to bear the thought of facing him, of talking to him or Aaron, knowing my actions cost the lives of a brother and a father. "Perhaps another day," I said "Brunel will not want to think of the past when his future may well change forever." Nicholas waited for me to explain further, but I didn't.

"How does the King look?" I asked, changing the subject.

"Strangely fine," Nicholas replied. "He's still sitting in the wheeled chair, but he lifts his head and talks to people — mostly to Banks, who has just slipped him a small bottle of something. The skin on his face shows no signs of the wounds he received. I do not know what to make of it."

"And no sign of Babbage?"

The Council judged cases of state and religious crimes. Babbage was charged with blasphemy, and he'd opted to defend himself rather than accept a Council-appointed lawyer. As far as I knew, he'd found no man willing to speak in his defence.

"He has declined to attend his own trial," Buckland said. "No point, really, is there? They have him under guard in the Engine Ward — his last free night to work on his calculating machine."

Even I could sense the tension in the room. Shuffling my Noctograph from one arm to the other, I flipped back the glass lid on my pocketwatch and felt with my fingers for the engraved watch face. We had been waiting over an hour, but now all the Messiahs — save Robert Stephenson, who often absented himself from Society business, preferring to remain in the north with his railway — were present, we could finally begin.

Sir Joseph Banks called us to order. There was a mad scramble as men rushed toward the front of the room, but we remained in our circle in the corner, our reactions hidden from the scrutiny of the stage. Buckland, who would be reciting the evening's sermon, nervously folded and unfolded his lecture notes. He was a man who secretly (or not so secretly, thanks to Babbage) still worshipped the Christian god, and the presence of so many religious men unnerved him.

There was still no sign of Charles Babbage.

Banks rolled the King's chair across the stage, and released an injector valve, which raised it above the podium with a puff of steam.

"For thousands of years, man has long sought to hold back the natural world." The King's voice held no sign of age or illness. Strong and deep, it soared over the cavernous room. "From the moment of our birth in the great Forge of Creation, we've fought to control fire, pull up the flora, and tame wildlife. And now, as we proceed through the nineteenth century, we are closer than ever before to achieving dominion over all the earth's forces. In this room stand the men who've made this possible — the engineers, physicians, adventurers, scholars, artists, and poets who've shaped this age of iron and industry.

"Our final task lies before us. We must keep this city — the capital of iron and dreams — free from the menace of the dragons, the last great remnant of our barbaric past. We must assert, once and for all, our dominion over the beasts. After a week of deliberation with the committee," he said, "I have decided who among you shall lead this city into the new age of industry. I would like to ask Isambard Kingdom Brunel to join me."

A collective gasp rose from the room, followed by frantic whisperings as tongues wagged. Even though Nicholas had told me what the King had said, I still couldn't believe the Council had chosen Brunel.

"Mr. Brunel's design is composed chiefly of a great Wall, which will encircle all of London like a fortress of old, making her impenetrable to the dragons as well as any other enemy that may present itself. The Wall shall also benefit our local trade and security, as it will monitor the coming and going of people and goods throughout the city, and will one day run passenger trains throughout London. In light of his industry and forward thinking, I present Brunel with this certificate of patronage, and his new Godhead as Presbyter of the Sect of the Great Conductor, replacing William Adams, who will be stepping down immediately."

The applause came in spatters, overwhelmed by cries of protest. "He's not even an engineer!" cried Shelley, leaping from his chair and upsetting his brandy all over his velvet breeches.

"Silence!" boomed the King. "The Council's decision is final. Brunel has won the competition. Need I remind you that questioning my divine authority and insulting church leaders are answerable to charges of blasphemy and treason."

That shut everyone up. In stony silence Brunel walked across the stage, his heavy worker's boots clanging on the oak. He accepted his award and kissed the King's ring.

"He looks rather chuffed," whispered Nicholas.

"Wouldn't you?" Buckland said. "This is an incredible honour. Perhaps the Council is finally allowing men without money or status to pursue the sciences."

"Not likely," Nicholas replied. "Look at Shelley's face. He looks as though he's ready to commit murder."

Banks tapped on the lectern, his fingers rapping against the wood and Brunel's footsteps on the wooden stage as he returned to his seat the only sounds in the room. The King gestured for the ceremony to continue.

"To our second matter," Banks said. "We must address the opinions published by Charles Babbage in the *Society Gazette.* I know many of you have read this document, but for those of you who have not, Babbage insinuates Sir Humphry Davy, Messiah of the Aristotelean Sect, had not added his calculations correctly, and suggested an alternative equation based on his own calculations. Clearly, you must all be as appalled as I am by Babbage's actions — to accuse a Messiah of erroneous calculations — such a thing is blasphemy! Mr. Babbage's writings have sullied the good name of Mr. Davy, the *Gazette* editors, the Society, and the deities we serve. When asked to speak in his own defence, Babbage declined: his absence only confirming his guilt."

"Declined, or was kept away?" Nicholas whispered. I nodded. He was beginning to understand the kind of men we were dealing with.

"As you know, the punishment for blasphemy is excommunication. But, as this is an organisation of equals, I would not be so arrogant as to make this decision myself. Is there anyone in this room who would speak for Mr. Babbage? Anyone who would offer an argument for him to remain?"

No one spoke. I knew the thoughts of my friends mirrored my own. If free thought and debate were still welcome within these walls, than why was Charles Babbage being vilified for expressing his?

Banks, however, didn't appear to notice this discrepancy, as he announced the decision had been made. Charles Babbage was no longer a member of the Royal Society and would be stripped of all his royal and church patronage. Any further infractions against the church would be dealt with more harshly.

After that announcement, we heard two sermons — one from Sir Humphry Davy himself, who informed the congregation in a smug tone that his calculations were, in fact, correct; and the second, much longer, from Buckland on some recent fossil discoveries of Great Dragons: the larger, prehistoric ancestors of the very swamp-dragons that continually attacked our city. I took a seat on the edge of a pew and rested my Noctograph in my lap, using the metal and string frame to guide my notes in straight lines across the page.

Normally a compelling, engaging lecturer, Buckland stammered throughout his speech, dropping his papers from the podium and losing his place. I understood his nervousness — his discoveries pointed toward a catastrophic flood wiping out the great dragon population, which, coming from the mouth of a known Christian, sounded even more blasphemous than Babbage. Luckily for Buckland, the Council members had found the brandy stash, and no one paid much attention to his sermon.

The meeting closed and we were free to drink our fill of brandy and talk amongst ourselves. Men — mostly lesser engineers and those from the poorer classes — swarmed around Brunel, offering their congratulations and requesting meetings.

Aaron managed to slip away from the chaos and joined our circle. "He won! Could you ever have imagined such a thing?"

I wondered why Brunel had not told Aaron about the hint that had been given during the meeting at the castle. For friends, we all of us seemed to harbour secrets.

"It's a great day for the Stokers," he said, clinking glasses with us. "With Brunel's appointment, we may finally become an important part of learned society."

"As long as your new Presbyter doesn't let all this religious nonsense go to his head." I gestured to the gaggle of engineers gathering in the centre of the hall, singing the Hymn to Great Conductor and shouting jeers at the leaders of other sects.

"If anyone can keep his head screwed on right, it's Isambard." Aaron replied.

"Pity about Babbage, poor old chap," said Buckland. "He was a bright spark, head of his own little Metic congregation. A brilliant mathematician — Charles had this idea to create a machine that could calculate mathematical tables."

"I bet the computers like that idea," Nicholas smirked, referring to the men who were paid to calculate and write mathematical tables.

"Not one single bit, but that's not why he got expelled." Buckland dropped his voice. "He was a good man, but blinded by his own intelligence. He never thought of the consequences of anything he did. Babbage just wanted the Society back the way it was, back the way it is *supposed* to be — a stimulating discussion of various scholars."

"I wish they would choose one god and stick to it," Aaron said. "I've grown up with Great Conductor, but I don't mind Morpheus or even that Mama Helios the Dirigires are so fond of. I wouldn't even mind having that Jesus fellow back — after all this nonsense, his claims of transmutation and necromancy seem rather inoffensive."

"You know," Nicholas leaned forward, lowering his voice even lower. "Since this society no longer cares for natural philosophy, we should take our discussions elsewhere."

"You mean … start our own society?"

"Why not? Men are still allowed to meet each other at pubs or in the privacy of our own homes. I don't see why we can't extend a dinner invitation to a select few free-thinkers."

"Leave the invites to me," I said. "Buckland, you're invited, of course, if you're interested."

"Wouldn't such free-thinking inquiry be … blasphemy?" Buckland could barely keep the smile from his voice.

"There's no blasphemy in a few gentlemen getting together over a game of whist to drink brandy and smoke cigars." Nicholas again lowered his voice. "We could each take turns preparing a lecture and a topic for discussion."

"A brilliant idea," Buckland said. "I would love to give a true and accurate account of my discoveries —

instead of the bogus lecture I gave this evening, if this new Society would have me."

"We could meet in my rooms at Travers College," I said. "It might be a little crowded, but between the madness and deafness of my roommates, there's little chance we'll be overheard."

"It's settled. The first meeting of the Free-Thinking Men's Blasphemous Brandy and Supper Society will take place in Holman's rooms tomorrow evening." Nicholas' eyes twinkled, and he rubbed his hands together in delight. "Now, I trust Buckland will provide the teacake, but who will bring the brandy?"

***

After the meeting had finished, Holman, Aaron, and Nicholas pushed against the tide of engineers and scholars stampeding for the doors, and found Brunel slumped against the edge of the stage. Nicholas handed him a glass of brandy, but he set his glass down on the stage and embraced Nicholas.

"Thank you, my friend." he said. "Without the designs of Nicholas Rose, I would not have won this honour."

As Nicholas stepped aside, Brunel's gaze fell upon Holman, and his expression turned to one of surprise.

"Congratulations, Isambard," Holman said quietly, his face angled toward his feet.

"James Holman, is that you?" Isambard reached across and embraced the blind man. Holman, surprised, dropped his walking stick, and patted Isambard awkwardly on the back.

"Look at you — you haven't changed a bit! Apart

from the eyes, of course. You shall have to tell me of your adventures. You are a Member of the Royal Society? How did I not know this?"

"I-I-wrote you letters," Holman stammered.

"I never received them, but let us not worry about that. The old gang, back together at last! Please, will you all walk with me to Engine Ward? I'm afraid I'm rather giddy with excitement."

Isambard led them out of Somerset House and down the Strand toward Waterloo Bridge, pushing his way through crowds of brightly dressed characters from the seedier quarters of the city that spilled over to the riverside at this time of night. Isambard, a spring in his usually measured steps, led the way over the bridge, chattering nonstop, firing question after question at Holman, who answered in halting stammers.

"I cannot believe it," Aaron said, smiling from ear to ear. "Isambard, you've done it! You're a Presbyter! A Stoker Presbyter!"

"Your name will be known throughout the kingdom," said Holman, who walked behind Nicholas, his head turned toward the ground.

"Our fortunes are changing," said Isambard, dodging around two streetwalkers and turning down a narrow alley. "The Stokers will finally have a place—"

"Wait!" Aaron held out his hands, his voice tight and urgent. "Don't move!"

Nicholas' head snapped up, wondering what was wrong. He looked around them, but could see nothing out of the ordinary. A bawd, her face drawn and haggard, chased two of her girls through the alley, while drunks cheered them on, and near the street an

Isis priest preached from one of Shelley's books of poems.

Then he felt it — the sinking feeling as a creature's thoughts pushed their way into his head, crushing the other voices and his own thoughts under their intensity. A predator, feeding on flesh — focused on the deliciousness of the meat, its senses on full alert for possible challengers to its meal.

A dragon. And it was close by.

The others couldn't see it, and Brunel opened his mouth to protest. Aaron held up his finger, urging them to remain quiet. The men inched forward, deeper into the alley, Nicholas and Aaron taking the lead, exchanging between them a knowing, frightened glance. Nicholas fumbled in his pocket for his knife.

Aaron has turned a dragon away twice before, he thought. *He could do it again.*

He could have turned back, sent Isambard and James down another street, but the meat pulled him — the smell of the fresh kill tickling his nostrils. His stomach rumbled, and saliva rolled from the sides of his mouth. *So hungry ...*

The alley ended at the wall of the close-packed tenement blocks. An even narrower path — barely as wide as a man — ran between the tenements and a workhouse. One by one they wriggled inside, their feet splashing in the mud and filth that formed at the bottom of the gutters. The smell of sweet, tender flesh grew stronger, pulling him onward.

"What's going on? What's happening?" James asked, but neither Nicholas nor Aaron had the mind to reply.

The passage widened out, leading them into another

alley. They rounded the next corner, the smell of blood filled the air, and Nicholas' mouth watered as the dragon's desires overcame his last human defences, and he seemed to become the beast he was now confronted with.

This dragon, another female, stood as high as a man, her tough brown skin dappled with green spots, and the scar of a burn along her muscular shoulders revealing a previous fight with a hot iron. She bent over the body of a man — a local butcher — her twin rows of serrated teeth making short work of his leather apron. She had dragged the body some way from the street, for the intestines stretched in a tangle down the alley.

In the distance, someone was screaming. The images floated in front of Nicholas' eyes. In one instant he was inside his own head, looking on at the dragon, and in another he was staring down at the corpse from *inside* her head, the taste of that fresh meat sliding down his throat.

Isambard sucked in his breath. Holman, even though he couldn't see the beast, sensed something was wrong, for he grabbed Nicholas' arm, his fingers digging deep.

The head came up, and the dragon sniffed. Nicholas' breath caught in his throat. He could smell himself and his companions as the dragon smelt them — four men, cornered and frightened. He smelt dessert.

Suddenly, another hand squeezed his. It was Aaron. Nicholas couldn't hear his thoughts, but he could *feel* the dragon slipping, confused. It wanted to ignore the intruders, but it didn't know why. The dragon's thoughts receded, and his own mind slipped back into his head. Nicholas gathered his senses and concentrated on pushing out one thought, giving it to the dragon. *Ignore the people. They're no threat.*

Holman, not able to see what was happening, but smelling the blood and the stench of the kill, whimpered.

Ignore them. They're nothing.

The dragon's head whipped around, and her yellow eyes bore into Nicholas. He pushed harder, knowing the dragon could leap at any moment, knowing this was the only way he could save his friends.

Ignore the people. Ignore the people.

The dragon snorted, dipped its head, and returned to feeding.

Aaron glanced at Nicholas, and they pushed Isambard and a terrified Holman around the corner of the building and circled on to the main street. They huddled under a streetlamp and caught their breath.

"That was … that was …" Holman could only stutter. His fingers around his cane were white as bone.

"Two dragons in as many weeks," Aaron teased. "You must smell mighty tempting, James."

Shaken, they pressed on toward Engine Ward, the towering funnel of black smoke growing larger with their every step. As Nicholas walked alongside Aaron, the air between them seemed to sizzle with energy, like lightning bolts flicking between their fingers. Nicholas knew it had been mostly Aaron who had stopped the dragon, but he wondered what they might be able to do, the two of them together, if they could again direct their minds to the same purpose.

The Ward gates stood open, and the usual gaggle of

priests and intellectuals passed to and fro, some going to the midnight masses held in the vaulted cathedrals, others leaving to take their pleasures in the bawdy houses and bagnios. Here, progress was slow, for men kept stopping Brunel to congratulate him on his appointment. He chatted with each of them, not scolding them for interrupting, paying as much attention to the ill-mannered rakes as to the sycophantic priests. Nicholas caught the sounds of music and revelry on the breeze, and as they neared the Chimney and the Stoker quarter, he could see Stokers dancing around great bonfires, already celebrating Brunel's appointment.

Brunel didn't go to them straight away, but stood on the steps of the Chimney, his gaze sweeping over the scene. Nicholas and Aaron watched him, and James faced the fire, each man lost in his own thoughts.

Finally, Isambard said. "I cannot get the image of that dragon out of my head. All we have built here — this great city of brick and stone and iron — cannot *control*, cannot protect those who dwell within her."

Nicholas thought back to that horrific day, ten years ago, when Henry had been crushed in the beam engine and Isambard had regarded the incident with this same rapt curiosity. He shuddered.

"When you finish your Wall," said Holman, "they will no longer be a problem."

"They will always be a problem, as long as we fear them and don't try to understand them," said Isambard. "The Stokers understood them, back before I was born, when they lived in the swamps. Unfortunately, we understood them so much we used their own tactics against them — we hunted them practically to extinction. It seems only fair they should come to this city to kill us."

"Is that why they're in London, do you think?" Aaron asked. The idea seemed to intrigue him.

"I couldn't say. Something is drawing them into the city. Why could it not be revenge? Do we so readily assume vengeance is the sole dominion of man?"

"I wonder why the Royal Society has never sent someone to investigate the dragons," said James. "Surely someone like Buckland could study them in the swamps to ascertain the reason for their exodus."

"Yes," said Isambard. "I don't understand this myself. But now that I'm a Presbyter, perhaps I can begin to unravel this mystery."

"Let's get this wall of yours built first," said Nicholas.

Across the street from the Chimney, a man emerged from one of the warehouses. He bent down, a briefcase bursting with papers clutched tightly to his chest, and fumbled with the lock. Nicholas didn't recognise him, but the moonlight caught the man's face, and he thought his expression almost impossibly sad.

"Would you excuse me for a moment," said Isambard. "There's a matter I need to attend to." Before Nicholas and Aaron could say another word, he broke away and slipped into the street below.

***

With a strangled sigh, Charles Babbage dipped his quill into the inkwell and scrawled his signature on the last of Clement's many cheques. He folded the stack inside a crisp envelope, added his seal to the front, and dropped it into his satchel.

He would deliver the cheques tonight, after he closed up the office, and then he would go home and drink all the brandy in the cupboard. And then maybe he'd start on that bottle of port Francesca had bought him on their wedding anniversary. He would drink until he forgot all the trouble he was in, and if he drank so much he didn't wake up in the morning ... well, so much the better. He would drink 'till he forgot Clement, and the Royal Society, and the ridiculous blasphemy charges, and that could take a very, very long time.

Clement, the self-made precision engineer whose detailed drawings had brought Babbage's dream of a Difference Engine to life. Clement, who could fashion a tool for any purpose and create minute parts so similar one could not tell them apart even under a microscope. Clement, the bastard son of a whore and a cheat, who'd been deliberately delaying completion of parts of the Difference Engine to extort more money from their open-ended contract. Clement, the rotten blagger, who'd robbed Babbage of every penny he had, cost him his Royal patronage and turned his congregation and the whole of the Royal Society against him.

Babbage locked the door to his office and stalked down the hall of the old shipping warehouse, now home to several small-scale engineers and their tiny, floundering churches. Some would go on to become great names in the sects of Great Conductor or Morpheus or Aristotle; others had been great once, but their fortunes had waned as new and greater inventions took hold of the people's fickle interests. And some, like Babbage, had never really invented anything at all.

He closed his eyes as he passed by his workshops; dark now, and deserted. He couldn't bear to see his beautiful engine, the racks of numbered wheels lined up against the shelves, ready to be assembled onto the great steel frame. And now they would never turn, would never execute the complex calculations for which he had designed them.

He jammed his hands into his jacket pockets. It wasn't bloody *fair*. He had devised one of the most singularly useful machines in existence — a calculating engine. No longer would engineers, mathematicians, and astronomers be forced to rely on the erroneous ledgers of equations calculated by the computing men. They could instead crank a handle and receive an accurate answer calculated by the machine.

When he'd first approached the Royal Society with his idea, they had immediately seen the benefit, and offered him a stipend of £1,500 to complete the first prototype. Then Joseph Banks had suggested he hire Clement — the most accomplished precision engineer in the Sect of the Grandfather Clock, and a Society favourite. And that was where everything had gone bloody wrong.

Outside the window, an organ grinder passed by, the high, tinny notes of "Down in the Sally Gardens" sealing his doom. Babbage ground his teeth together. The only thing he hated more than Clement was organ grinders. They knew it, of course, and worked together in teams to follow him all about the city, taunting him with their repeating, off-key tunes.

He turned away, hunching as he pulled the door shut behind him, locked it for the last time, and shoved the key back into his pocket. He turned, and his stomach dropped to his knees as a dark shadow emerged from the buttress of the Metic Church and floated towards him. He fumbled for his pocket knife, but barely had time to draw breath before the figure was upon him.

"Isambard, you startled me!"

"I'm sure many have said the same thing to you in past weeks," Brunel smiled. "You were missed at tonight's meeting, Charles."

"I'm in no mood for mockery, Isambard."

"It's the truth. You're not the only one who thinks the Society should focus more on constructive reasoning and less on robe-kissing. Davy's calculations were wrong — it seemed a simple matter to me."

"Hardly. This simple matter has had me excommunicated. Banks informed me yesterday I shouldn't bother to defend myself." Babbage started walking, briskly, across the courtyard in front of the church, hoping Brunel would take the hint and leave him be. But the Stoker met his stride with ease, his casual demeanour only increasing Babbage's unease.

"A move I'm certain you anticipated with great joy. After all, now you are unbound from their rules and scrutiny. Now you're free to push the limits of your science."

"The limits of my bank balance, more like," Charles sniffed, cutting across the pavilion at the rear of the Church of Grandfather Clock. "This blasted engine is not even a quarter complete, and Clement has taken all his drawings, all my money, and all the precision tools he created to fashion the mechanisms. And without the Royal Society's stipend, I cannot hope to afford the price of another engineer. No, sir, the Difference Engine is doomed for the scrap heap."

"If that's the case, then what I've come to offer will brighten your day."

"What do you *want?*"

"I want you to renounce your god, assemble what sections and plans remain, and join me in the Chimney."

Charles snorted. "Join the upstart Stoker who plays at engineering? That would do wonders for my reputation."

"That's upstart Presbyter to you."

Babbage stopped. "You didn't—"

"Can't you hear them praising my name?" He gestured behind him at the revellers. "I've been awarded the prize in the engineering competition, and I want you to work for me. It's not as abhorrent as you make out, my friend. Think about it — you have a Difference Engine lying in pieces all over your workshop, an engineer who's run off with your only means to fashion the precision parts, dwindling finances, and a church that's about to desert you for someone less risky. I have a need of your analytical mind and work to occupy you, and what's more I now have the funds and tools to help you complete your masterpiece."

For a second, just a *second,* Babbage was tempted to accept. But then he looked up, into Brunel's eyes — the eyes of London's newest religious fool — and what he saw stopped him short. Flickering behind the clear surface was that same fanatical gaze he saw in

Clement, in Banks, in everyone at the Society. *No,* Babbage decided. *This Industrian nonsense will go to Brunel's head, just like it does to every other learned man, and I'll have no more of it.*

He shook his head. "I'm doing just fine on my own, thank you, Isambard."

"As you wish," Brunel tipped his hat. "I must say, I am disappointed. I greatly admire you, Charles, as a man of brilliant intellect who's caught the short end of the Council's stick. You would find plenty of worthwhile endeavours to occupy yourself in my employ."

"I have enough endeavours of my own to employ my intellect for the rest of eternity."

"Very well." Brunel took a thin metal plate from his pocket and threw it at Babbage, who fumbled and dropped it in a puddle. Scrambling to pick it up, he heard the Presbyter say as he departed: "If you change your mind, bring that plate to the Chimney. The offer will still be open to you."

***

The walls of the state chambers of Windsor Castle echoed with the sounds of shattering crockery, as King George III of England proceeded to break every bowl in the china cabinet over the head of Alison Cooper, the newest maid.

Brigitte Black hid behind the door and listened, her heart beating hard against her chest. With every shout and scream and smash, silent sobs escaped her, the salty tears blurring her vision. After a while, Alison ceased to scream, but still the tirade raged on.

Finally, the King ran out of plates. But he did not leave Alison. Brigitte pressed herself against the door, struggling to hear what was going on. She could just make out a light sound, like a sucking or … *lapping* of liquid, before the King let out one final bellow and stormed off to his chambers. Brigitte waved to Cassandra, who tiptoed down the hall to check the way was clear. When Cassandra waved back that the King had gone, Brigitte nudged open the heavy door, and bit back a scream.

Alison lay facedown in a pool of her own blood, her pressed white uniform now stained bright pink. Her arms were spread at either side, the bare skin crisscrossed with weeping gashes, as though she had reached out to embrace the King while he thrust the crockery into her. Ceramic shards stuck out at odd angles from her skin and her matted, tangled hair. Beside her head, a teacup — the only piece of china in the room still intact — sat upright on its saucer, holding a few drops of her blood.

Cassandra let out a great sob, clamping her hands over her mouth as though she might be sick. Brigitte reached out with trembling fingers to touch the girl's shoulder.

"Don't—" Cassandra sobbed. Brigitte didn't blame her. She didn't want to see, either.

As Brigitte's fingers brushed the raw skin beneath the torn dress, Alison groaned. *Perhaps she's still alive. Perhaps we're not too late, after all.*

"Alison?" she said, trying to keep her voice even.

Alison groaned again, fainter this time. Brigitte clasped her hand around Alison's shoulder and pulled her back, trying to get her to turn onto her side.

Alison's head lolled back, causing some of the shards to fall out and fresh blood to pool from the wounds. Blood dribbled over Brigitte's apron.

But Brigitte barely registered the stain, transfixed as she was by the girl's face. Alison's eyes were half-closed, glassy, and unseeing. The skin on her cheeks hung in torn strips, slivers of Staffordshire sticking out like porcupine quills. Long gashes crisscrossed her neck, as though he'd tried to behead her with the dinnerware. Blood dribbled from cracks in her lips.

Brigitte recoiled in horror. She dropped Alison's shoulder, and fled to Cassandra's arms. The two girls met each other's eyes. "Miss Julie," they said in unison.

Brigitte gestured for Cassandra to grab Alison's legs, and she dug her hands under the girl's shoulders. Shards tinkled on the marble floor. Together, they heaved her off the ground and hobbled into the hall. Between Brigitte's legs, Alison's head flailed back and forth, spraying blood all over the French carpets. Luckily, the maids' staircase was only down the adjacent hall.

Brigitte held the door open with her back while they manoeuvred Alison's limp body inside. Cassandra bent down to wipe the blood dribbling down her stockings. "This is horrible!" she sobbed.

"*He* is horrible." Brigitte grunted as she lifted Alison again and started backing down the staircase. "The sickness is making him positively cruel."

"I hoped this time Banks had cured him for good." Cassandra lifted Alison's legs over the corner balustrade. "Do you remember this time last year, when they had to chain him to his chair? Or when he babbled incoherently in the drawing room for fifty-two hours straight? I'd give anything to go back to the babbling. Just last week I overheard two ministers in the drawing room discussing his deplorable behaviour at the Royal Society. Apparently, he sent three Whigs to the Tower for pronouncing the God Morpheus' name wrong. They fear he won't recover his sanity again."

"As right they should," Brigitte winced as Alison's head knocked against the wall. "At least now maybe they'll talk about a regency, even if the princesses aren't yet old enough. May we all survive long enough to see the end of him."

"May we all." Cassandra looked down at Alison. "Quickly now. Miss Julie will know what to do."

Brigitte kicked open the door at the foot of the stairs, and they dragged Alison's body into the kitchen. A plump, sour-faced woman looked up from the kneading to scold them, but then she saw the blood.

"Out of my way!" She flung the rolling pin over her shoulder, scooped up the unfortunate Alison in one beefy arm, grabbed a wool blanket in the other, and dashed into the sleeping quarters. Brigitte and Cassandra sprinted after her.

Miss Julie flung the blanket over Alison's bed, laid the bleeding girl out upon it, and began picking out the ceramic shards. "Bring me water, a cloth, and the vinegar!" she barked. Cassandra raced off. Brigitte stayed in the doorway, unable to move, her teeth biting down on her fingernails while she watched Miss Julie work.

Cassandra returned with a tub of water, a stack of rags and the bottle of vinegar. Miss Julie soaked one of the rags in the water, rubbed a little vinegar on it, and started mopping up the blood. Alison's eyes fluttered open, and she moaned a little before disappearing again. "It's all right, child," Miss Julie said. "We'll have that pretty face of yours back in no time."

To Brigitte she said, "most of the cuts are quite shallow, but on her face and neck — these are serious. Tear those rags into bandages."

Her hands numb and shaking, Brigitte picked up one of the rags in the pile and tore jagged, clumsy strips, which Miss Julie soaked in the water and vinegar and wrapped around Alison's head. Alison moaned, lolling her head from side to side. Brigitte knelt beside her, stroked her hand, and whispered her name, but Alison didn't seem to be aware of her presence.

When Miss Julie had finished, she stood up and wiped her hands on her apron. "I've done all I can, the rest is up to the Gods. Now, what happened?"

"It wasn't her fault, Miss!" Brigitte burst out. "She was dusting the china cabinet, and she slipped from her ladder and dropped a plate. She even managed to rescue it before it smashed on the ground. His Majesty was sleeping in his chair in the corner and she must have startled him awake. He tore from the wheeled chair, tipped the cabinet upside down, and threw all the plates at poor Alison's head, howling all the while. He — he — he —"

"He assailed her even when she was no longer screaming," said Cassandra. "We heard the whole thing from the hall. Oh, Miss Julie, it was horrible!"

Brigitte thought of the strange noises she'd heard, and the blood sloshing at the bottom of that one pristine teacup, and she wondered if she and Cassandra had even grasped the true horror. She hugged her knees to her chest.

"You girls have had a terrible fright." Miss Julie stroked Brigitte's hair. "And you know what cures the willies — a good run at the wringing machine. There's a load of bedclothes a mile high that needs wringing and hanging, and we'll be covering Alison's chores 'till she recovers, so we'll need to look lively."

Cassandra sobbed, but Miss Julie would hear none of it. With one last, lingering look at Alison, her head covered in bandages and her tiny body punctured with wounds, Brigitte left the room and returned to her chores.

***

When she collapsed into her bed that evening, Brigitte leaned over to watch Alison. Miss Julie had obviously been in to change her bandages, for now only a thin layer covered most of her face. One of her eyes had swollen shut, puffed up like the casing on a mince pie, and the other stared, wide and unblinking, at some spot beyond Brigitte's shoulder.

"Alison?" she whispered.

The eye met hers, wide and frightened. Alison tried to say something, but all that came out was a strangled, hoarse sob. She was the third new maid in as many months, the other two disappearing from the castle in the night, their beds found empty in the morning, and their meagre belongings still stuffed into the pillowcase.

"Hush, it's all right now. You don't have to be afraid. He can't hurt you here—"

Alison screamed, the sound hollow and hoarse, as though she had not the energy to make a sound. But her one eye screwed shut and she opened her mouth again in a gaping, silent screech. Horrified, Brigitte turned away, buried her head under her pillow, and tried to forget.

***

For days Alison remained in a state of flux: catatonic one minute, screaming the next. It was as if she lived inside a permanent nightmare, flailing herself against the sheets in a desperate attempt to wake herself up.

Miss Julie had cleaned up the blood and crockery on the third floor. The King hadn't left his chambers since that horrible morning, though Banks had been attending him night and day. Brigitte hoped he stayed there forever.

After a week, Alison's condition had not changed. Miss Julie took some money from the jar under her bed, and went into the village. She returned with a man in a dark suit, carrying a leather case. They shut the bedroom door while they examined her, so Brigitte could not watch, but she listened through the door and could hear Alison sobbing. Ten minutes later Miss Julie and the man emerged. The housekeeper's usually ruddy complexion had become drawn and white.

"Alison will be going away," she said. Brigitte demanded to know why, but Miss Julie rapped her across the knuckles for insolence. She was sick, Miss Julie said. The man would take her somewhere she could get better.

But Brigitte's mother had gone away with a pale-faced man with a leather case too, and she'd never got better and she'd never come back. Brigitte sobbed and screamed and cursed at Miss Julie, who didn't scold her this time, but took her in her arms and said it really was for the best. The man returned to the bedroom, bundled the sobbing girl in her sodden sheets, and carried her outside to his waiting carriage. As Brigitte watched through the barred windows, the carriage sped out of the gates and along the castle wall, 'till it finally disappeared from sight.

Brigitte knew she would never feel safe in the palace again. She and Cassandra cleaned as a pair, one manning the mop or broom or polishing cloth, while the other walked behind, eyes nervously darting into every hall and alcove, checking for signs of the King. Whenever they heard the creaking of the wheeled chair on the bright marble floor they would hide in the nearest room, holding each other and praying to their Gods that he would not find them. Neither wanted to end up as the next victim of the King's rages. Neither wanted her cheeks flayed off like poor Alison.

***

"He doesn't want to see no one."

"He'll want to see me." Nicholas stooped down to look through the slot in the door. Peter's face scowled back at him.

"I know it's you, Nicholas. He doesn't want to see you, neither. You could go down if you want, but he's chained an' padlocked the door. Working on something top secret, he is."

"Fine. I'll wait in the church."

Nicholas didn't understand. *We have only four months to get the Wall and railway completed. Isambard said we needed to begin immediately, and here I am, ready to work, and Isambard has locked himself away on some whim?*

He didn't really know what to do with himself. He had no desire to return to the guesthouse — the compies in the walls were louder than ever — so he lay down on one of the pews at the back of the church, and fell into a dreamless sleep.

He awoke later, to the uneasy feeling of someone standing over his body. The dark shape stood in the shadows just out of view, tall and thin, like a rake leaned against the wall by some careful gardener.

"There you are. I've been waiting for you for hours. What are you messing around with down there? We have a Wall to build—"

"Hello, Nicholas."

It wasn't Brunel. The man stepped out of the shadows and loomed over him, his priestly robes sweeping along the floor and his bulk blocking the light from the gas lamps above. Nicholas sat up and met the man's gaze. The man didn't speak, but simply stared back — his expression hard, his eyes blazing.

Finally, Nicholas said. "And you are—"

"I am Oswald, the eldest son of Henry Williams, Senior. I believe you went to school with my brother."

"However much you blame me for Henry's death," Nicholas said, uneasiness creeping into his head, "I cannot bring him back."

"I'm here to talk about Aaron," Oswald said. "I want you to stay away from him."

"Why?"

"You're not a Stoker, Nicholas, so I don't expect you to understand. Aaron is young, and you—" he gave a sinister smile, "you have not exactly sailed under cover of darkness. Once I heard you returned I had to know everything there was to know about Nicholas Thorne. You had a brother once, didn't you? But he died in very mysterious circumstances. *Very* mysterious indeed. And then you came to London, and my brother died, and you conveniently shipped out the very next day. So I looked up the Navy records, and what did I find? You killed a superior officer, and fled into Spain to escape your punishment. But you're in London now, so you've crossed the border illegally, and that can only mean you've left an even bigger mess behind in France than a murdered lieutenant."

He leaned in so close Nicholas could see every lump and furrow of his pock-marked skin. "We're simple folk, us Stokers, but we have our own rules, and we care about our families, Nicholas Thorne. I've already lost one brother because of your presence—"

"Henry's death was an *accident—*"

"And *accidents* seem to follow you everywhere, don't they? I won't have Aaron caught up in whatever clandestine dealings you and Brunel have dreamed up." He swept his arm around, indicating the Nave, the Chimney, the flickering lamps, and Brunel's whole operation. "He believes that because I work for him I'm blind to his ambition, but I've *seen* things, Nicholas Thorne. I've *seen.* You're planning something, the two of you, and it's un-Stoker-like, and Aaron will have *no* part in it."

"But we're not—"

"Also," he added, holding out a thick palm, "I see the bulge of a purse in your pocket. I'll have that, if you please."

"But—"

"If you please, Mr. Rose. I'd hate for the authorities to find out about your presence in this city, and your real name."

Nicholas pulled the purse from his jacket and threw it at the priest. Oswald caught it in midair, pulling it open with eager fingers, and feeling for the coins inside.

"That will do … for now."

"This is absurd. Isambard has done nothing but look out for Aaron. And I hardly intend to—"

But the priest had already turned away. "I trust," Oswald called over his shoulder as he descended the steps towards the priests' cloister, "you won't forget this little meeting."

"Your words, your *Holiness*, are forever etched into my memory."

"Good." And he was gone, his robes swishing against the stairs.

Nicholas' stomach growled. He thought of the two shillings he'd had in his purse — the last of his money 'till Brunel could pay him. *It will be another night with an empty stomach, another night kept awake with the threats of this new enemy hanging over me. I should have never returned to London.*

***

JAMES HOLMAN'S MEMOIRS — UNPUBLISHED

As declared, the first meeting of the Free-Thinking Men's Blasphemous Brandy and Supper Society took place in my cramped dormitory at Travers College, requiring the members to travel twenty-six miles from London to the grounds of Windsor Castle. I spent some of my meagre savings on a spread of fresh-cut meats and cheese and several varieties of tea, not to mention a fine bottle of brandy.

I raced back and forth between the common room and my quarters, arranging chairs, setting up bowls and spoons and polishing the tea settings. Every time I passed the oak writing desk opposite the door, my fingers brushed the letter that I had leaned against the inlaid drawers. Occasionally I picked it up and fingered it, brushing against the Duke's seal, imagining what it might say.

The letter had arrived that morning, and it could only be a response to my request for extended leave to undertake an adventure. At twenty-two, I was the youngest of the Naval Knights by a good forty years. Although we are only allowed to absent our duties on medical grounds, I had managed, with a recommendation from a doctor friend, to secure a previous extended period of leave to attend medical school in Edinburgh. My new application sought permission to travel extensively across England, though in reality I meant to escape our closed borders and pursue my dream to conduct a circuit of the world.

Of course, I couldn't read the letter, and I didn't want to ask one of the cantankerous Knights to read it for me. So I had been fidgeting in anticipation all afternoon, pacing across the floor and cracking my knuckles in a most un-gentlemanly manner.

Nicholas and Aaron arrived promptly at four, sharing a carriage. Both men handed me their coats — Nicholas' a fine woolen cape in the latest Parisian fashion, worn and thin around the edges; Aaron's the tough canvas of a workmen, reeking of soot — and settled into the mismatched chairs I had placed around the cramped room.

"No Isambard?" I asked, secretly relieved.

Aaron shook his head. "He's been most peculiar these past two days. He's locked himself in his chambers and has not emerged, not even to give orders to begin construction of the Wall. I've no idea what he plans, but he certainly does not wish to leave his workshop for any reason."

"Too bad, he's missing out on this." I presented the brandy to the gentlemen, and poured a glass each for Nicholas, Aaron, and Buckland, who had just arrived by carriage from Oxford.

"It's nothing like the Royal Society lays claim to," I observed, feeling each man's fingers brush mine as they took their glasses. "But I feel our club should enjoy the fineries of intellectual countenance."

"I'll drink to that," said Buckland, raising his glass to his lips. As requested, Buckland's wife had indeed baked a cheesecake, and Nicholas had stolen a box of hot chocolate from the kitchen at his guesthouse. He stirred his brandy into his hot drink and sipped, giving a sigh of contentment.

We exchanged pleasantries while we waited for the final two guests to arrive. When I could no longer contain myself, I slid the envelope across the desk toward Nicholas. "Please?" I said.

Images swam inside my head — images of things I could no longer see but might one day hear, and smell, and feel. *Paths unwandered, specimens undiscovered, ingenious peoples whose fascinating customs yearned to be documented ...*

He slit open the envelope with his bread knife, and read the contents aloud. "... on behalf of His Royal Highness the Duke of Edinburgh, we regret to inform you that—"

I froze, my heart galloping in my chest. I didn't hear the rest of the message. I must have looked horrified, as Nicholas reached across and took my hand.

"I am sorry, James. The current political climate is rather prohibitive to adventuring. Perhaps you will have better luck if you apply again in a few years."

My application had been declined. I would be stuck in Windsor for eternity, my dreams of travel and adventure remaining simply that — dreams.

The food I had so lovingly prepared tasted sour after that loathsome news. Aaron and Nicholas did what they could to keep the conversation light, but my mind returned again and again to my fate, to live out the rest of my days trapped in these infernal chambers with six crotchety old men, the only travel the gruelling hundred steps I must endure twice per day to reach the chapel.

The maid knocked on my door and announced the arrived of my final two guests: Mr. George Lyell, a biologist, and Dr. John Dalton, a chemist currently researching color-blindness, and the friend whose medical evidence had once succeeded in earning my freedom. Nicholas stood up to introduce himself to the men, and they greeted him warmly, offering their own platters of food for the feast.

When each man had been seated and their glasses filled, Nicholas rapped his knuckles against the chair arm and cried. "I hereby call the first meeting of the Free-Thinking Men's Blasphemous Brandy and Supper Society to order."

"Hear, hear!" Buckland was already halfway through his second glass of brandy.

First, we discussed the problem of keeping minutes of the meetings.

"It's imperative we record our intellectual discussion," said Dalton. "We might well make important observations that need to be recalled. Often, it's when returning to the notes from such discussions that the true nature of a phenomenon becomes apparent."

"But if a written record of our meetings ever fell into the wrong hands ..." Buckland's voice trailed off. We all knew what had happened to Babbage.

"The obvious solution," said Aaron, "is some kind of code."

"Aaron is right," said Nicholas. "However, we face the less-common problem that not all of us can read." He paused, and I could feel all eyes in the room fall on my Noctograph — the wooden and string frame I used to guide my hand while I printed — lying unused in my lap.

"Worry not about me, friends," I replied, my cheeks burning despite myself. "I'm used to storing intellectual notes in the recesses of my cranium."

"Nonsense," cried Buckland. "We should not leave

any one of our members without access to written notes of our proceedings."

"What about a code printed in raised shapes on a sheet of metal?" said Aaron. "Like rivets on plated steel? That way, Holman could read with his fingers."

"Brilliant!" I beamed.

Nicholas set his glass down on the table. "Aaron, of all of us, you have the most ready access to a workshop of tools. And I have some skill with ciphers from my time in the Navy. Should we two work together to write our code?"

With that decided, Nicholas — who seemed to fall into the role of master of ceremonies — moved on to the main event of the evening. The first member responsible for presenting research was Buckland, who had spent the summer on a caving expedition in Wales where he'd discovered a human female skeleton, stained with red pigment, amongst the bones of the ancient Great Dragons.

Geologists have already established that many large animals from the *Dinosauria* family — similar to the neckers, iguanodon, compies, swamp—dragons, and other creatures abundant in the British Isles today — had died out before the appearance of man. But never before had a human skeleton been found alongside them, and never one who, like Buckland's, carried unusual rings and amulets made of the bones of the beasts. Buckland was trying to come to terms with the find before he published his paper.

"There is a Roman settlement nearby," said Buckland. "Perhaps she discovered the bones in a nearby cave and carved the jewelry from them."

Lyell shook his head. "The bones would have to be

carved when they were still hard. You said the decomposition was the same? It seems your red lady was contemporary with the beast."

"The bestial skeleton is old, probably pre-flood — I mean, pre-*catastrophe*. I can't suggest that humans lived then. That's counter to the whole Industrian dogma. You saw what happened to Babbage!"

"Relax, William," said Dalton. "Unlike the Royal Society, it matters not to us what you write in your papers to please the Church. We've all written similar plaintive."

Nicholas reached over and topped up Buckland's brandy glass. "We're interested in what *you,* as a scholar of biology and geology, think was going on in that cave."

Buckland sighed. I felt a surge of pity for the man. I too knew what it was like to struggle against the bonds of society.

"The artefacts indicate she lived either before or during the Roman occupation," he finally said. "And when this woman lived, Great Dragons still inhabited England. Not a word of this must leave this room, for it is blasphemy—"

"Great Dragons and humans … together?" Nicholas' voice shuddered. "It is a terrifying thought."

Sensing the panic in Buckland's voice, I changed the subject. "Tell us, Buckland, as the expert on animal behaviour, why do the dragons now come into the city in such force?"

"It's funny that you should ask, James." Buckland shuffled forward in his chair, his voice steadying as he regained control of his emotions. "I've spent the last two days discussing the exact same subject with the new Presbyter."

"Brunel?" Now it was Aaron's turn to lean forward. "What interest does he have in biology?" his voice took on a new urgency.

"I don't rightly know. He spoke little of his own thoughts, only wanting to listen to my theories. Not that I can give a conclusive answer, but I think I may offer the beginnings of an explanation."

"And that is?"

"After the *catastrophe* that killed off the big dinosaurs — the Great Dragons and the twelve-foot tricorns — the swamp-dragons became the largest and most fierce predators in England. Their skeletons appear uniquely adapted for the fens, explaining why we don't usually see them outside the great swamps. For perhaps fifty years they were hunted near to extinction by the Stokers, their skins and teeth used for expensive clothing and jewelry. My first inference is that since the Stokers moved to the city in 1765, the dragons have been able to rebuild their numbers."

"Makes sense," said Aaron.

"So if the swamps are free to them once more, what would turn them toward the city with such increasing frequency? There could be only two possible explanations. One is that the food in the swamps has become so scarce that they can no longer sustain themselves and so seek to pick off meals in our overpopulated city."

"This doesn't seem likely," said Aaron. "My grandfather used to tell me stories about the swamps. Even when the Stokers left there were plenty of animals and fish the dragons could eat."

"Both Brunel and I thought so, too. The second

explanation — and the one that seemed to particularly interest him — is that some other factor — a change in environment, most likely the introduction of another, larger predator — has pushed the dragons from their usual habitat. It was the same in pre-*catastrophe* times, when tricorn numbers were at their height."

"Because the tricorns ate the trees and reeds, where so many of the dragons' prey lived?" Dalton asked. Buckland nodded.

"The Great Dragons moved on to other areas. Many of the Great Dragon species found a new niche in the forests of the north, before they too died out."

"But what could be causing the dragons to flee the swamps now?"

Buckland shrugged. "No man of science has cared enough to investigate the swamps. These days, if you want real glory from science, you impress the King by manufacturing a steam-powered shoe-polishing machine, not by venturing knee-deep through England's bogs."

Aaron spoke up. "My grandfather was the greatest dragon-hunter this country had ever seen, so great, in fact, that it was believed he shot the last dragon in the swamps, and forced the Stokers to come to London to work on the engines. If anybody could figure out what makes the dragons flee the swamps, a Stoker could."

"Are you volunteering, Mr. Williams?" Buckland laughed.

"Maybe I am."

***

The discussion of catastrophe-theory, dinosaurs,

and Buckland's mysterious red girl continued around him, but Nicholas listened with only half an ear. He watched Aaron, whose intent expression belied the enthusiasm with which he took part in the conversation.

Thinking back to his encounter with Oswald the previous evening made the blood boil in Nicholas' veins. *Who is that man to dig up my past? How dare he try to keep me from the one man who understands what I am?* After tossing and turning for several hours during the night, replaying the conversation over in his mind, Nicholas had decided to ignore Oswald. After all, the man had no real power. He would tell Isambard of Oswald's threats as soon as he emerged from his workshops, and Isambard would deal with Oswald as any religious leader might deal with a wayward priest.

Inside Nicholas' head, the stray thoughts of animals flicked in and out, as they did every minute of every day. The compies in the basement, the birds sitting on the eaves outside, the sheep grazing on the slope behind the college — these mundane manifestations blurred together in a constant layer of noise that filled his head, pushing aside all other thoughts save the one he chose to concentrate on. He stared across the room at Aaron, knowing he must hear the noises also, knowing he must, at that moment, be exerting great energy to push them down.

Why then could he possibly want to go to the swamps?

Aaron had insisted they share a carriage on the way to Windsor Castle. Nicholas, not seeing Oswald anywhere in the vicinity, did not refuse. He had so many questions, about Aaron, about his grandfather, about his life growing up with Brunel. Oswald's words echoed in his head as he bombarded Aaron with questions, not knowing if he'd ever get another chance.

"My father resented my grandfather," said Aaron. "He was a hunter too, but he didn't have the *sense*. He felt it was my grandfather's fault we had to leave the swamps. Not one of his children has even seen the swamps — not even Oswald. To a proud Stoker like my father, that's abhorrent. But Grandfather knew he was only doing what was best for the Stokers, for our survival."

"What happened to your grandfather?"

"He died when I was five. The pox got to him. Many Stokers died of it then — it seemed to rise from the swamp mists. Now we die in machinery accidents, of dust in the lungs, but nothing much else has changed. He was the only one who knew—"

"What happened then?"

"My father followed soon after, and my brothers attempted to look after me while Mother drank herself to death. No one much cared for me — Henry was always the favourite. Even though we're twins, we were nothing alike. He was strong, built for hard labour in the furnace rooms, and I was smaller and had a way with animals — a useless skill in Engine Ward. After Henry died, Oswald and Peter turned nasty, especially when they discovered I'd become friends with Isambard. After Mother died, I went to live with Quartz, and good riddance to them."

"They care about you, though, in their own way." *If blackmail could ever be construed as caring.*

Aaron shook his head. "They care about keeping their priesthood, even if it means working for a man they abhor. They care about our family name, for what it's worth in Stoker society. They don't want me to mess everything up. It would be much better for all concerned if I just went away. But I can't leave Isambard."

He'd changed the subject then, and said no more of it. And now, to hear him talk about the swamps with such reverence, Nicholas began to see the cause of the silent fury that bubbled beneath Aaron's skin. He could discern it, but he didn't *understand* it.

Nicholas was in London because he was running away … he'd never really stopped running since he'd left his father's estate twelve years ago. But Aaron had lived in London his whole life. He'd known the peace that came from surrounding himself in high walls, but still he yearned for the swamps — a spiritual homeland he'd never even seen. Nicholas could not fathom why Aaron would want to abandon all he had here for the wild, a place which must be torturous to minds like theirs.

We have everything we could ever want, right here in London. Here we can dull the unceasing onslaught of voices. And more than that, you have family. You have work. You have Brunel. What would make you wish to leave all this?

***

The carriage dropped Aaron back outside Engine Ward just as the evening's celebrations inside began in earnest. As he picked his way through the darkness of the tunnels, he could hear the talking and laughing filtering down from the streets. The Stokers — joined by some of the other sympathetic factions within Engine Ward — had been celebrating Brunel's victory for three days straight. They dragged wood and rubbish — anything that would burn — into the cooking pits and lit a towering bonfire.

As Aaron emerged from the subterranean world behind the Chimney, a wave of heat washed over his body. He shielded his eyes from the bright inferno that leapt unencumbered from the central courtyard of Engine Ward. The press of people immediately consumed him, bearing him against his will into the joyous crowd.

"Aaron!"

Someone grabbed his arm. It was Quartz, his face flushed with booze. Laughing, Aaron slapped the old man's back and clung to him, allowing Quartz to lead him closer to the blaze, where the women crowded around, balancing cooking pots filled with meats and stews, which they placed in the embers 'till the smells rose over the whole camp. Aaron waved to his wife, Chloe, who waved back as she leaned her pregnant belly against the pot, lifting the lid on her creation and dishing stew into several outstretched bowls. Generations of working in the swamps or with the machines had rendered most Stokers without smell or taste, yet even the most ancient, hardened worker smelt this particular meal.

Men dragged out musical instruments that had gathered dust for years, and the children skipped and sang the old folk tunes, including at least three renditions of "The Stoker and the Navvy's Wife". Even Quartz had got into the spirit of things, although Quartz could be guaranteed to get into the spirit of any occasion provided there was a free flow of alcohol.

"It's amazing," said Aaron, helping himself to a mug full of stew and clambering behind Quartz up onto the leaning roof of a nearby shack. "When we first showed the engine, most of the Council wanted to see him hanged for daring to call himself an engineer, and now, he's the most celebrated engineer of all."

"Mmmmph," Quartz didn't look so impressed. He slugged back the dregs of his drink and wiped his mouth with the back of his hand. "Never you mind all this, boy. After the party dies down, then we'll see what Isambard will make of all this attention. And where is old Iron-Bags tonight, eh? I thought he would have shown up for his own party."

"I don't rightly know. He's been locked up in the workshop ever since the announcement. Have you any clue what he's doing?"

"I wouldn't know. Us mere mortals aren't allowed within those hallowed walls." Quartz scowled at the Chimney.

"Isambard's work is *good* for the Stokers, Quartz."

"Bollocks. Isambard's work is good for Isambard. The sooner you understand that, the better off you'll be. This city embraces him not because he is a Stoker, but because he has overcome *us* to become one of *them*. We're not even allowed to work on this new Wall of his, since it stretches outside Engine Ward."

"If you knew him—"

"You've always been in his shadow, Aaron. I never liked that boy — too much thinking. Too many secrets locked up in his scheming head. Three days a Presbyter and he's already as slippery as the rest of the priests," Quartz growled. "No good will come of this, mark my words, lad. He's sending me away, you know."

"What?" Aaron hadn't heard anything about that.

"Back to the swamps. He's building some fandangled railway from London to Plymouth, through the worst of the dragon country. It runs on air-pressure or some such nonsense. Bloody stupid idea, if you ask me—"

"The Atmospheric Railway?" It had been one of Isambard's more ambitious schemes, an idea that he'd submitted to the Council for funding on three separate occasions without success. Instead of steam, the trains were propelled by vacuum pressure through tubes running along the centre of the track. The train was controlled by opening and closing flaps within the vacuum tube.

"It's a farce, Aaron. He needs an engineering project to appease the Council, to hide what he's really doing. He wants to find out what's scaring the dragons out of the swamp. He sent for me yesterday evening. Right into his lordly manor I had to go so he could inform me I am to be one of the foremen in charge of overseeing this little venture."

Aaron remembered what Buckland had said earlier that evening about Brunel's sudden interest in his biological theories. He wondered why Isambard hadn't told him about the Atmospheric Railway.

Quartz read his expression. "See, he's not one of us anymore. Stokers belong in swamps, Aaron. Engineers belong in the city. He's getting rid of us to become one of *them*."

"I'm certain he doesn't mean that. Besides, I thought you wanted to return to the swamps?"

"Not for what he's paying me," Quartz spat. "There are no lodgings for us, nothing left of our old camps. We're expected to build our own from the measly stipend he's granted us. There's no roads to carry in equipment, nor boatmaster that will dare venture that far into dragon-infested waters. And don't you forget, if Buckland is right about the reason the dragons are leaving the swamps, there's something in those swamps so fearsome not even the dragons want to face it. I don't know what I'm going to find out there. At least in the city, I know *exactly* the nature of the boy who dares to lord it over me like he's the Duke of bloody Gloucester. Out there, your brothers will be in charge."

"Oswald and Peter?"

"Aye, and a horde of their priestly vermin in the bargain. I'd rather take my chances with the dragons here than fall under the command of that lot."

"Be careful around them, Quartz. They may be priests, but they're clever, especially Oswald. Don't get on their bad side."

Quartz spat in reply. They sipped their soup in silence. Finally Aaron said "When do you leave?"

"Apparently we're waiting for a factory at Swindon to deliver the sleepers so we can start laying the track for this bloody railway through the middle of a dragon-infested swamp. No Navvies are building out that way, His Lordship said. Of course they aren't; they're far too sensible."

"I'll miss you, Quartz."

"Yes, you will." Quartz poured himself another drink.

***

His head swimming with too much drink, Aaron clambered down from the roof and pushed his way up the crowded steps to the Chimney. The stern face of his brother Oswald glared at him through the door.

"Stokers are forbidden to enter."

"Open the door, Oswald. I'm in no mood for this."

"I'm under specific orders not to disturb him."

"Then don't disturb him. I'll be the one rapping on his door, not you. If you don't let me pass I'll just go down through the tunnels, and I can't be responsible for who, or what, follows me."

The door swung open, and Aaron brushed past his brother, swinging the grating open on the elevator.

"Aaron," Oswald began. "You can't continue to behave in this manner—"

"In *what* manner?" Aaron whirled around to face his brother. "In what *exact* manner are you referring?"

"This *exact* manner, brother. I'm not your enemy, you know. I'm the head of this family, and it's my duty to keep an eye on you."

"What are you talking about?"

"I've seen you with that Nicholas Thorne, or Rose, as he's calling himself these days. He's dangerous, Aaron."

"Henry's death was an accident. He didn't have that cursed dragon of his under control. You can't blame Nicholas—"

"If he's so innocent, why is he using a fake name on his drawings? Who is this Nicholas Rose? Did he tell you about *his* brother — the one that died on his father's estate in a most curious manner mere weeks before Nicholas showed up in London without a penny to his name? Did he tell you about his dishonourable discharge from the Navy? Did he tell you about his dealings with French fanatics or his illegal crossing into England—"

"I don't have time for this." Aaron jumped in the elevator, slammed the grating closed and stomped on the lever without another word.

As he wound his way down into the earth, he felt the voices slipping away — the compies and insects and rodents that hid in the corners of the church. His mind calming, becoming clear, made Oswald's protests and Isambard's behaviour seem all the more unusual.

The elevator came to a shuddering stop. Squinting in the darkness, Aaron fumbled for the entrance, and found that — as it had been for three days — the heavy iron door had been pulled shut, locked with three heavy padlocks, and swathed in lengths of chain bolted by yet more padlocks. Aaron picked up one of the chains and slammed it against the metal door, the sound echoing up the elevator shaft.

"Isambard, open up. I need to talk to you!"

Silence. Aaron slammed down the chain again, giving the door a kick for good measure. He was just about to call out again, when a muffled voice called to him from the other side of the door.

"I'm pushing the key under the door," Isambard said. A second later, Aaron heard a small metal object scrape across the floor. He bent down and retrieved a ring of keys. Responding to Isambard's shouted instructions, Aaron fumbled with each lock in turn, finally dropping all three loops of chain to the floor.

Leaning all his weight on his shoulder, and with

Brunel pulling from the other side, he finally inched the door open wide enough for him to squeeze through. He found himself in total darkness, save a short flickering of light from the far end of the workbench.

"Nicholas is arriving shortly. There's a lantern on the shelf to your left. You'll need it." Brunel pushed the door almost shut, plunging the workshop even deeper into darkness. A thin sliver of light from the lamps in the shaft outside lit up the shelves near the door.

Aaron fumbled for the argand lamp, lit it, and directed it across the floor of the workshop. He saw nothing out of the ordinary — the long benches covered in various metal shapes and protrusions lined each wall. At the far end, Brunel's furnace — usually lit, giving a glowing light and warmth to the room — stood cold, the wingback chair Brunel had pulled in front of it empty of the usual piles of books and drawings.

Aaron squinted into the darkness, a sudden fear seizing his chest. "Isambard, what's going on?"

"Why did you come down here, Aaron?"

The question hung in the damp air, carrying with it a twinge of malice. Aaron shivered, but pressed ahead with his inquiry. "Quartz told me you're sending a crew of Stokers into the swamps to begin building the Atmospheric Railway?"

"That's correct. With the money from the Society and the Royal contract, I can finally afford to realise some of my projects. Once complete, the line will provide a speedy goods route between London and Plymouth. I'm hoping the men will be able to leave within the week."

"Lying doesn't become you, *Presbyter*." Anger rose in Aaron's throat. "You've been talking to Buckland."

Isambard smiled. "Buckland talks too much. It's true, Aaron. I want to find out why the dragons are coming to London. It could aid the construction of the Wall, and the Wall absolutely *must* work. Anything that aids it ..." he shrugged. "It's a secret because I don't want to reveal my intentions to the rest of the sects. It will make me appear weak, unsure, especially in front of Stephenson. I don't see what has you so upset—"

"Isambard, you *know* how much I want to go to the swamps. Why didn't you ask me? Quartz is old. I fear for his health—"

"Quartz's *health?*" Brunel laughed. "The man has more grog in his system than blood. It's the swamp that best look out for him!"

"You *know* I'm more comfortable around animals than I've ever been around machines, and I've always wanted to see where my grandfather hunted—"

"Of course. Aaron Williams Senior — the Great Dragon Hunter. Clearly, he wasn't as great as everyone thought, or we wouldn't be building this Wall to keep out the dragons he supposedly hunted to extinction."

Aaron gritted his teeth. "All the same, I'd like to go."

Brunel shook his head. "That's out of the question. I need you here, Aaron. You're the only one I trust. I have another job for you, one that's even more important."

"I don't *want* your job. You're not *listening* to me. You only care about what's right for Isambard. I want to be with Quartz, I want to go to the swamps."

Brunel reached out in the darkness and clasped Aaron's hand.

"As always, my friend, you are right. I thought this was what we had been working for. We're on the cusp of creating a better life for the Stokers, and I need you by my side."

Memories flooded Aaron's mind. Peering in the windows of the engineering schools, watching Isambard scrawl complex formulas onto scraps of paper and old bits of tin. The two of them, working away in silence in their secret workshop, building the locomotive that would make Isambard great. The way Isambard had embraced him when they finally got it to work. "This is only the beginning," he'd said. "The beginning of a new life for the Stokers. And you'll be here to live it with me, Aaron. Whatever changes, you'll be here."

Aaron said nothing.

"Aaron?"

He sighed. "Of course, Isambard. I won't leave you, not if you need me. What is this job?"

***

His hands shoved deep in his pockets, his face down to avoid eye contact, Nicholas pushed his way through the crowded, rowdy streets behind the Chimney. Here in the Stoker camps, the buildings leaned inward, the tips of the tin roofs pressed up against each other — a precarious maze of well-balanced scrap. Stokers filled every available space, dancing and drinking together as they celebrated the dawn of a new life. Steam rose from raised vents in the pavement, obscuring the narrow alleys with thick, haunting mist. Occasionally, a tongue of flame shot from the sewer gratings, and the revellers jumped back to avoid being singed, laughing all the while.

It was a mistake to come here. He would never find Aaron in this crowd. Someone crashed into him, slamming him against the wall of a shack. The drunk picked himself up, calling an apology with a cackle. His fetid breath wavered past Nicholas' face.

He'd no sooner righted himself when he leapt out of the way, landing on his hands and knees in the mud, having narrowly avoided crashing into a speeding carriage pulled by two cackling youths. Its cargo of two fattened pigs screeched in terror and kicked at their wooden cage. Nicholas was picking himself up when one well-timed kick to his jaw sent him reeling into the mud again.

"Here, let me 'elp you up."

It was a woman. She was young — not a year past eighteen — her eyes sparkling from her soot-caked face. Her clothes, like all Stokers', were made of rough canvas and leather, patched and repaired in several places. She smiled at him, and her face seemed impossibly kind. He held out a hand and she pulled him to his feet and wiped the mud from his coat and ushered him into a nearby courtyard, less crowded, probably because it was filled with barrels of foul-smelling alcohol. He gripped the wall, his head spinning from the stench, hoping he wouldn't pass out.

His rescuer, who seemed not to mind the smell at all, squinted at him as she wrung out a rag in the well and dabbed at his clothes. "You're dressed awful fine for Engine Ward. You ain't from around here, are you?"

He shook his head. A loud mob of men entered the courtyard, grabbing one of the barrels and rolling it out toward the street, splashing the foul liquid over Nicholas and the woman. "I'm looking for Aaron Williams!" he yelled over the din.

"What?"

"Aaron Williams! He's a Stoker—"

"—and a right bloody pain in the arse." She smiled. "You must be Nicholas. He's talked of little else since he met you. I'm Chloe, his wife. He was talking to Quartz last I saw him, out by the bonfire — apparently he's gone up to the Chimney to have words with Isambard."

"What about?"

She shrugged. "Quartz said he was hopping mad. If you see him, tell him he's not to come home if he's had even a drop o' this." She gestured to the barrels behind her. "I only just cleaned up the mess from his last revels."

"Thank you. I shall look for him there. It's a pleasure, ma'am." He tipped his hat to her. She gave his hand a push.

"Don't you ma'am me. We're Stokers out here, scum the lot of us."

Mounting the Chimney steps three at a time, Nicholas rapped on the door, reeling when he saw the hard eyes of Oswald staring back at him through the door.

"Aaron is down in the workshop," the priest said.

"Isambard is expecting me," Nicholas said, passing a paper through the hole in the door. "He sent this message to my lodgings this morning. If you don't let me in, he will suspect something, and you will be questioned. I can hardly do wrong to Aaron in his presence."

Oswald snatched away the message. Scowling even deeper, he slammed the hatch shut — nearly taking Nicholas' fingers with it — and swung open the door.

"Don't forget our little talk," Oswald growled.

"I couldn't possibly," said Nicholas as he stepped into the elevator.

Once the elevator had creaked into the shaft and he was out of sight of Oswald, Nicholas withdrew his notebook from his coat pocket. Bound in leather and tied up with heavy twine, this book was on his person at all times. In the back, he'd written out a simple code for the Free-Thinking Men's Blasphemous Brandy and Supper Society, and he knew Aaron would want to see it. Tonight might be his only opportunity, while they were together in Brunel's presence.

When he reached the bottom he was surprised to find Isambard's door, which had been locked for the last three days, was ajar. Inside he could hear voices — Aaron's and Isambard's. They sounded as if they were fighting.

"You're not *listening* to me," Aaron hissed. "You only care about what's right for Isambard. I want to be with Quartz, I want to go to the swamps—"

Nicholas recoiled. *Aaron wants to leave the city?* He remembered how Aaron talked about the swamps with such reverence. *What could possibly be there for you, my friend, besides mud and the unending clamors of the voices? Why would you leave the city now, when we have just met each other?*

The voices lowered, and seemed friendly again. He coughed loudly.

"Ah, Nicholas." Brunel called from inside the darkened workshop. "Come in."

The furnace was unlit; the only light a faint glow from an Argand lamp in Aaron's hand. He squinted at his friend in the darkness, saw his face set into a stony expression.

"Isambard was just informing me of his secret project," Aaron said, his tone even.

"You're building the London railway?" asked Nicholas.

"The King wants you to build a railway in London? Isambard, this is—"

"Amazing. Miraculous, Incomprehensible, I know!" Isambard's excitement filled the room. "It's only a small section of track, but it's a start. He wants me to build a railway from Windsor Castle into Buckingham House. It will be the first railway inside the city. Apart from the first mile of track across the castle grounds, the entire railway will be underground. And it must be built in four months."

"That's preposterous!" Aaron said. "You've only built one railway before, and that hardly stretched a mile, and it took a lot longer than four months."

"Especially not when work on the Wall begins next week," added Nicholas. "That too shares that same impossible deadline, and since it stretches outside the Ward and will be in full view of the public, the Stokers are not permitted to work on it. Where are we going to find men?"

"I *am* aware of both these issues. That's why I've

been holed up in here for the last three days, trying to come up with a solution. Now that you're both here, I can show you what I've created."

Brunel reached over and, with fingers that seemed unusually cold as they brushed Nicholas' arm, pushed the light toward the far corner of the room. There stood two machines that made Nicholas recoil in fright.

"Isambard—"

"What is *that?"* Aaron demanded.

"You can approach them." Brunel grabbed Nicholas by the shoulders and dragged him across the room.

"They look so—so—"

"I know. Aren't they beautiful?" Brunel reached out and stroked the belly of one of the machines, angling the light to give Nicholas and Aaron a better view. "I call them my Boilers. They will revolutionise the manufacturing process."

Each Boiler stood a little higher than Brunel — round furnace bellies balanced on metal skids, with a complex labyrinth of wheels, tubes and gauges protruding from the top. Their shape appeared too natural, too human, to be made of iron, but iron they were, and ingeniously designed. Clawlike limbs extended from the furnace body, and where one would expect a head, Brunel had given each a double chimney. More dials and gauges protruded from the rear of the furnace, and Nicholas recognised some of the controls from Brunel's steam locomotive designs — a regulator, a water glass. Obviously prototypes, the metal was rough, unfinished, but Nicholas immediately grasped the basic idea.

"They're … workers?"

Brunel nodded. "There aren't men enough in England to finish the railway and Wall as soon as the King wants them, but with machines to work day and night, and men like Aaron to run them, we can do it. These are just prototypes, of course, but fifty units are being finished in the workshops as we speak. I plan to have the first Boiler workgang operational by the end of the week. Watch."

He opened the furnace of the nearest one and stoked it up. It spluttered to life, churning steam from its double chimney. Brunel worked the controls from behind the Boiler, stepping aside when it lurched forward. Aaron stumbled back, tripping over Nicholas as the Boiler barrelled toward them, claws outstretched, steam billowing from its mechanical neck.

Panicked, Nicholas rolled out of the Boiler's path, dragging Aaron back with him. But the Boiler wasn't after them. It tore straight past Nicholas and picked up a length of pipe from the bench behind him. Holding the pipe in its clawed hands, it bent the length into a perfect U, fitted a pressure gauge on the end, then fitted it to another pipe protruding from the wall, tightened the whole apparatus, and stood back, awaiting its next instruction.

"See?" Brunel clapped his hands together. "The Boiler will repeat that task, again and again, until he is given new instructions. Aren't they the most amazing invention that ever your eyes did see?"

Aaron grabbed the lamp off the bench and directed the light toward his friend. Nicholas watched Isambard's eyes gleaming with excitement. He knew that look well — the expression of pure glee Isambard always wore when he'd found the solution to a particularly perplexing problem.

"Isambard ..." Nicholas' head spun. He hadn't expected *this*.

Aaron spoke first, his voice dripping with anger. "If these machines can build the railway and the Wall, they could also run the furnaces of Engine Ward, and then what will the Stokers do? Isambard, your own people will no longer have any place in London."

"Nonsense. These are *machines,* Aaron. They need men to run and manage them. These Boilers merely enable the Stokers to take their rightful place — as overseers, foreman, and innovators in their own right."

"I don't know, Isambard. The men won't be happy to share their work with these ... these *machines*", replied Aaron.

A note of irritation crept into Isambard's voice. "I thought you'd be happy. You're the first to see them, of course, apart from the King, who approved the design. *He* thought them marvellous."

"The King is, it has been firmly established, stark raving mad."

"Well, what do *you* think, Nicholas?" Isambard snapped.

"I ..." Nicholas fought for words. "They *are* marvellous. I'm simply trying to understand how their use will affect society. Machines that take orders from a master? Nothing like this has ever been conceived before."

"Think of your own people, Isambard," said Aaron. "Their livelihoods depend on the work you and the other engineers give them. With machines to do that work for them, our men cannot feed themselves. How do you expect them to embrace these terrifying metal beasts?"

"That's where you come in."

"I don't understand."

"The men listen to you, Aaron. I need you to get them to see the brilliance of the Boilers. You will oversee the construction of the King's new railway. It must be kept secret from everyone — our men, Quartz, the priests, the Royal Society. *Everyone.* Do you understand?"

"I understand."

"You need to handpick ten Stokers to work on the project and learn the mechanics of the Boilers. Choose the most intelligent and trustworthy men you know. They don't have to be strong — the Boilers will do most of the work."

"But the Stokers can't work outside the Ward. How will we—"

"The King has granted special permission in this instance." Brunel grinned. "Our fortunes are already changing, Aaron."

"I lead men, Isambard, not machines—"

Something tore Nicholas' attention away from the conversation. In the darkness of Nicholas' mind, a voice prickled at the edge of his consciousness, weak and in pain. It was a compie — the tiny mind barely a whisper within Nicholas' jumbled thoughts. He wouldn't have noticed it at all, except that the voices never came to him down here. The workshop was too deep, too well fortified. *What's happened to you, little fella?* Somehow, it must have found its way into Brunel's workshop and got itself trapped beneath some equipment.

He tried to push aside the little voice and concentrate on his two friends. Isambard was explaining the particulars of the railway to a stony-faced Aaron.

"We're creating a secret branch of the railway line, stretching through the old sewer tunnels below Buckingham Palace. You'll be laying the track in those tunnels, widening them when necessary, and constructing a platform in the specially prepared room under the palace."

"All within four months? I must learn the secrets of these machines and instruct them to build an underground railway all within *four months*? I don't have a choice, do I?"

"There's always a choice, Aaron." Brunel held out his hand. Nicholas watched Aaron take it, feeling odd, as though he were witnessing something private. "You choose our friendship, or you choose to shun me, a Presbyter, which is heresy. You decide."

He said it with lightness, but Aaron's face contorted in anger. Nicholas was stunned by the thinly veiled threat. A feeling of dread settled in his stomach. Brunel continued to talk, his voice rising with excitement as he discussed the Boilers, the new railway, his plans for the Wall. He stroked the barrel of the Boiler again, his eyes betraying a tenderness Nicholas had never seen before.

He seems as I've always remembered him: driven, intelligent, excitable. But these Boilers ... I don't trust them—

Help me, the tiny mind called, forcing out his own thoughts. Nicholas felt it trying to voice the thought, to scream out to its brothers, but it couldn't. Nicholas' chest clenched as he felt what the compie felt — the terror of dying alone.

Nicholas tried to send a comforting thought back, but it was as if his sense met a wall of iron — he could not push the thought out. Inside his head, the compie screamed.

He watched Isambard tinker with the mechanisms on the back of the Boiler's neck, leaning his whole body over as if embracing the metal worker. Nicholas felt like screaming, too.

***

After their meeting with Brunel ended, Nicholas and Aaron took the elevator together. Nicholas patted the faded notebook under his arm. "I was hoping to find you tonight. I've made a draft of our code for you to look at, but Oswald does not want me to see you—"

"So he's been at you, too? I wouldn't worry about him. He won't risk his comfortable life enacting any threats — not that he can do much from the swamps, anyway," said Aaron, his tone dark. "Chloe won't expect me home for many hours yet. Not with all this grog and merrymaking in the streets. I'll take you to a workshop, and we'll look at it together."

"I met her tonight. I went to look for you in the Stoker quarter, which turned out to be a mistake. She saved me from being decapitated by a pig."

Aaron sighed. "She's a good woman. She tolerates my drinking and my temper, and that's no easy task sometimes. She does not know about the voices, but she suspects … something. This is why she worries so. Isambard asks so much of me, and I wish—" He shook his head. "Never mind."

Oswald was waiting in the Nave when they stepped out of the elevator. Neither man said a word to him, but as they crossed the Nave together, Nicholas could feel Oswald's eyes boring into his back. Aaron pretended not to see him, joking with Nicholas as he pulled open the door and stepped out into the night.

Nicholas followed Aaron through the dark, labyrinthine streets, littered with scrap and moaning bodies — wallowing in the night's libations, or rutting together in full sight of their neighbours. Through the tightly packed warren of Stoker shacks, they emerged in front of a row of low warehouses, their windows cracked and lewd graffiti scrawled across every surface. Pushing open the door to the first, Aaron said, "These have been empty since the Navvies moved up north. We won't be seen in here."

Aaron lit the Argand lamps along the walls, while Nicholas spread his papers out on the long, low bench occupying the centre of the warehouse. "I went to the British Museum today and saw some Sumerian tablets containing a curious, indecipherable script — each glyph made of straight sections and triangles — easy for the ancients to write with a triangular chisel or reed pen. I thought adopting this idea for our code might provide James enough distinction for each letter."

Aaron measured each symbol with his finger. "I think this could work," he said. "Is it a simple substitution cipher or something more complex?"

Nicholas showed him the code sheet. "I've based the key to the code on the name of our club, and have included several shorthand symbols for common words and letter combinations."

Aaron frowned at the page. "Some of these won't work when I emboss the plate. Hand me a pen."

They worked for hours by lamplight, engrossed with the intricacies of the code language. Aaron embossed a series of plates using the code, ready to show to James at the next meeting. As the early rays of sunlight danced on the glass shards in the windows, Aaron said: "Did you know he was creating those … *Boilers*?" He spat the word, as though it would poison him.

"I knew he was attempting to devise a solution to the King's impossible timeline. But I had no idea of the extent … already his priesthood has changed him."

Aaron shook his head. "He's the same Isambard, all right. He's been waiting, Nicholas, storing up all his cunning for the day he was given that first shred of power. He is relentless, and poverty can no longer curb his ambition."

"Aaron, do you truly wish to leave the city?"

"So you heard my conversation with Isambard." Aaron's voice was hard. "It has been my dream since I was a child to be with the animals in the swamps, like my grandfather. I see no reason to stay in a city that will soon replace me with a machine."

"But why? I grew up in the countryside near Salisbury. The voices beat relentlessly against my skull, and I longed for peace. Every moment I spend in the Engine Ward surrounded by steel is a celebration of clarity."

"It is funny how men always yearn for that which they do not have. I spent my entire life within these walls, yet desire nothing more than to escape to the countryside, to embrace the voices and hold them to me. I stay only because of Isambard." He gave a bitter laugh. "He needs me as much as I need him. At least, he used to."

Something had been bothering Nicholas. "Why have you never told Isambard about the sense?"

"My grandfather told me never to tell a soul, and I honoured his plea. Besides, Isambard would see me differently — I would become a curiosity to him, some natural principle he had to understand. I need his friendship, not his scrutiny. Isambard can see my great affinity for animals, and that is enough. But you did not tell Isambard, either?"

"I was afraid. When I came to London," Nicholas said, "I was a fugitive. I killed … there was an accident on our estate, and my brother died. If my father found me, he would've seen me hanged. I hated myself, hated the power that had caused me so much pain and had cost me my family and my future. I did not want to be anything but a normal boy, and so when Marc Brunel found me and offered to teach me at his school, I saw a chance to forge a new life, one where no one knew what I had done or what I was capable of doing."

"But Mr. Holman—"

"James found out later, when we were stationed together on the *Cleopatra*. He caught me one night on the prow of the boat, calling up a sea-necker. But that was back when things were different, when things seemed hopeful." He gulped. "But we can trust James — he knows a thing or two about secrets himself."

"And so does Isambard," said Aaron. "But I'm not sure I would trust him with this."

"Isambard has been nothing but a friend to us."

"We've been friends for ten years now, long

enough for me to realise he doesn't see friendship the same way you or I do. Isambard sees people — friends, enemies, associates — as parts of a great machine, one he can re-forge and bend to his will. When his face lights up, like it did over the Boilers tonight, that's when he's at his most remarkable, and his most dangerous. We're part of his plan, Nicholas, and our own hopes and dreams matter not. He's sending Quartz away to the swamps — along with Oswald and Peter and some of the other Stokers. Quartz is the old man you met in the tunnels." Aaron paused. "He's looked after me ever since my parents died. Isambard knows how important he is to me, how old and frail he's getting, but he's still sending him away. And Quartz says the Atmospheric Railway is a cover — Isambard wants him to figure out what's made the dragons leave the swamp."

Nicholas leaned forward. "That explains his sudden interest in Buckland's theories."

Aaron nodded. "And these Boilers … they're only the beginning. He's planning something big, and I can't fathom what."

Nicholas shuddered, remembering something. "I heard a *voice* down there."

"In Isambard's workshop? No animal could find its way down there. Not without us seeing it. Besides, I didn't hear anything."

"I know what I heard," Nicholas said, remembering the suffering that had washed over him. "It was a compie, and it was in great pain. But it was faint, as though I were hearing it through water. I could not return thoughts to it. I could not calm it—" His voice cracked. "It was dying, Aaron. And I know we both hear animals die all the time, but it was in so much pain, terrible pain, and just hearing the one voice, isolated like that—"

"It doesn't make any sense," said Aaron, pulling the door shut behind them.

"No," said Nicholas. "It doesn't. Since Isambard was made Presbyter, nothing makes any sense at all."

***

The train chugged through green hills, rolling across the countryside and through green woods. Here, apart from the heathen priests in their bright robes pushing engineering tracts into grubby hands, and the shrines to Great Conductor overlooking every station, the north of England seemed barely affected by the country's Industrian fanaticism. At times, the locomotive pulled them into forests so dense and wild Jacques could swear they were back in the foothills of Mount Canigou, where he'd been hiding for the past four years.

For most of the day, he was the only person in the first-class cabin. This pleased him, for he didn't much care to converse with the uncouth English and give his origin away. A Frenchman outside of Meliora would find few friends in England. He passed his time by staring out the window and imagining how he might like to kill Nicholas when he finally found him.

At the tenth stop, a large man, his jacket buttons stretched tightly across his belly, clambered on board, lifted his nose at the four empty benches and settled himself in the bench opposite Jacques, placing his satchel down on the cushion beside him. He tugged a tin from his pocket and popped several mints into his mouth, smacking them against his cheeks in an undignified fashion.

He leaned over and offered the sticky tin to Jacques, who declined with the shake of his head, hoping the rotund man would get the hint.

But the man seemed anxious to talk. "Do you come by train often?" he asked, his accent betraying his northern roots.

Jacques shook his head. "This is my first time," he said in English, hoping the man wouldn't question him about his obvious French accent.

But the man seemed more interested in talking about the train. "She's a beauty, yes? She is my *Rocket* — every piston and rivet is of my design. She'll have you in Liverpool before suppertime, for she's the fastest way to travel in all the Empire. Not that we have much of an empire, anymore."

"You made this train? We had no such transportation in France."

"Nothing like this in all the world, my friend." The man extended a hand. "But soon there will be. I see no reason why France, or Spain or even Norway can't have their own locomotives, just as soon as our blasted King gets over his rudding religious bollocks and allows us to trade with Europe again. But forgive me — I've not introduced myself. Robert Stephenson, at your service. I run the only railway company in England, servicing the mills at Manchester, the northern mines, right down to the Liverpool port, and we're hoping to get a line in all the way to London by the end of next year."

"Pity. I'm travelling to London. I would have liked

to go all the way by train."

"I'm going to London also. I could share a coach with you, if you wish, after we disembark. Not that either of us look like men who need to share, but I could do with the company." He paused. "Do you pay much attention to church politics?"

"Not I," replied Jacques, who had long since given up hope of a silent journey, but wasn't about to reveal his identity to this portly stranger. "Too many churches, too many gods and Messiahs and priests — I can't wrap my head around it. I'd rather admire the machines without worshipping the men, if you don't mind my saying."

"Not at all. It all seems a load of Oxford poppycock to me, and I'm the Messiah of one of the bloody things. The churches run a false economy right out of the heart of London. Out here where the *real* industry is, it's business that matters, not any of this religious nonsense. It's when you start mixing the two you get into trouble. But try telling that to my men."

"Your men?"

"A Messiah has got to have men, sir. Mine are the Navvies — they're good workers, but too damned superstitious." He sighed. "A young upstart has just been made Presbyter of my church. A Stoker, even — they're nothing but London's furnace fodder — and it's set my men off something awful. I thought Stokers couldn't innovate their way out of a grog barrel, but here's this Brunel character, trying to make a locomotive of his own, shouting in Royal Society meetings that I've no right to turn a profit from my own investments. So I'm going back down to that cursed city to put a stop to it."

"But surely this Brunel would need patronage to fund his locomotive? I would think a man of your ample—" he cringed as Stephenson sucked back another candy, "—*means* would have nothing to fear from an imitator."

"That's just the problem — he's won some renown in the city, and the potty King's given him a lucrative contract. He's hired this architect, Nicholas Rose, who no one's ever heard of—"

Jacques jumped. He couldn't believe his luck. "Did you say Nicholas Rose?"

"Aye, that was his name. Have you heard of him?"

Jacques laughed bitterly. "A man — a guest in my household — murdered my wife. He's fled, and I've reason to suspect he's gone to London. He is using the name Nicholas Rose."

"If he's a murderer, you should simply hire a thief-taker to find him for you."

"I haven't the coin for that."

Stephenson clicked his tongue sympathetically. "I hear they've established a Metropolitan Police Force in London now — very French, tsk tsk. They can circulate his likeness in the papers. He won't hide for long."

"This is …" Jacques searched for the right words, "a delicate matter. I'd rather authorities weren't involved."

"Dear me," Stephenson dabbed at his face with a kerchief. "Come to my offices when we arrive in London. I can put you in touch with some men who may be able to help you."

***

Six days after he was granted the contract to build a Wall and a railway in just four months, Isambard Kingdom Brunel commenced the construction of his Wall on the edge of the Belgravia district by driving in the first rivet. A crowd had gathered to watch, and they cheered and hooted as Isambard held up the hammer in triumph. Nicholas clapped too, smiling up at his friend, but his stomach fluttered with anxiety.

Aaron was not in the crowd, nor were any other Stokers save the priests. They were all occupied in Engine Ward preparing the Boiler workshops for production. Oswald scowled down at Nicholas from his position of honour behind Isambard. He'd been watching Nicholas with hawklike eyes ever since Isambard had emerged from his workshop. Nicholas stayed close to Isambard, only leaving the Ward well after midnight and carrying his knife in his pocket.

But the crowd was mostly made up of engineers, priests, and officials of other sects and churches, wishing to show their support for the new Presbyter. Among them were many from the smaller Great Conductor churches — congregations led by engineers whose ideas hadn't yet gained notoriety. But there was the artist Turner with a number of his men, as well as priests from Banks' Aether Church — Isambard's most vocal enemies on the Council.

Nicholas stood near the back of the crowd, his ears pricked to hear the words of these men.

"I'll not bow to a Stoker, no matter his rank. I'll not!"

"This Wall is preposterous! I don't understand what the King was thinking when he commissioned it."

"He wasn't thinking — that's the problem. If ever

we needed more solid evidence that he's not of sound mind, we now have it."

"I wouldn't worry about Brunel," said Turner, twirling the corner of his moustache around his fingers. "The King has given him an impossible deadline. Four months — he'll never finish, and then the Council can dismiss him from his post. I heard Stephenson's coming down from the north. He'll soon put a stop to Brunel's nonsense."

The crowd dissipated, leaving the workers to the serious task of building a Wall and a railway. Nicholas, who had no experience of actual construction projects, planned to simply observe from a distance, but Isambard climbed off the scaffold and gestured for him to follow.

"I've made you foreman of Team D," he said.

"Isambard, I *can't*. I'm no engineer. And I can't be seen in such public view like this. What if I am recognised? What if one of the men were to give me up?"

"Seen by whom? All who knew you in a past life have already welcomed you home again. Whoever you're running from is all the way across the Channel in France, and if a constable were to walk through this site right now, none of these men would be sober enough to say their own names, let alone yours. "

He couldn't talk Brunel out of it, so he scrambled into some overalls and had a lesson from Isambard on handling steel, then spent the remainder of the day up in the scaffolding in the pouring rain, helping the men to raise the struts and clip or rivet them in place.

He was just coming down the ladder for a cup of tea when he felt the familiar, dreaded creep of a creature's mind forcing its way into his own.

He turned, and saw the dragon's tail flicker behind the stacks of iron supports. It crouched low, silent, watching. Two men leapt off their ladders and moved toward the stacks, chatting idly as they bent to pick up a heavy beam. He called out a warning, but they couldn't hear him over the din of the construction crew. With the beam supported on their shoulders they set off back toward the Wall.

As Nicholas watched, horrified, the dragon pounced, knocking down the first man and snapping his neck in one swift movement, slamming the iron strut down with such force it flung the other man into one of the smelting fires. The worker lay there a moment, stunned into silence, before he noticed his skin clinging to the hot iron plate. He screamed, high and terrified, and it was that that alerted the other workers on the Wall to the presence of the dragon.

Someone threw their chisel at her, and this bounced off her head, leaving a shallow gash across her cheek, which she didn't seem to notice. She held down the man's body with her thin forearms and tore off a chunk of flesh in her teeth. Blood pooled into deep puddles. Crying out in anger, the men at the top of the ladders threw their tools down upon her. Nicholas yelled at them to stop, but their anger had caught hold of them.

Now enraged, the dragon tore through the site, crashing through the skeleton of the Wall and sending ladders tumbling down and men flying for cover. One man swung down off his ladder with one hand, and pressed his torch against her leathery skin, singeing a bright welt across her back. Nicholas' vision flared into red dots, and he saw the man's face through the dragon's eyes as she swung around and snapped off his arm.

Bang! Bang!

Gunshots rang out, ricocheting through the iron skeleton. One caught the dragon's belly as it reared up, and Nicholas felt a new pain, white-hot as it stabbed at his stomach, arch through his entire body. He looked down and saw he wasn't hit — it was the dragon's pain, and it slipped away as the constable put another bullet into her head.

The men refused to return to work, and Nicholas had to close the construction site early. The first day, and two men had died, several had been injured, and only a few skeletal yards of the expansive Wall had been erected.

If Isambard doesn't get those Boilers running soon, there won't be a man left in London willing to work on the Wall.

***

From the ledge above the water tower at the back of the Stoker workcamp, Aaron and Quartz had a clear view of the Wall construction site. They shared a bottle of whisky as they watched the men clamber up the scaffold to secure the steel struts. Unlike the Stokers, who had an intricate knowledge of industrial buildings and machines, these men were labourers who worked on farms during summer and spring and came to the city when the cold weather set in. They were thick as engine oil and lazy besides.

"We should be out there," said Aaron, anger

bubbling inside him.

Quartz dismissed the notion with a wave of his hand. "Let Brunel solve his own problems. There's work enough in here for all the Stokers, for now."

It was true — they'd never been so busy. Isambard had ordered every Stoker that could be spared to work in the Boiler workshops — he wanted them operational within the week. He'd secured some rusting factory machines from the old Navvy sheds, and they needed pulling apart and refitting to engineer and fit the precise parts of the Boilers, and new, precision parts custom-built for each specific task. With overtime pay on offer, Stokers rushed from one shift in the furnace rooms to another in the workshops, and there had never been such a great bustle of activity in the Engine Ward. But soon it would be quiet again, for when the workshops were operational, Quartz and two hundred Stokers would leave for the swamps.

"I don't understand Isambard's thinking," said Aaron. "There's a Wall over there that needs to be built quick as lightning, and here's Isambard occupying his own workforce in making cursed *Boilers* and frolicking in the swamps."

Quartz drained the final drops of whisky, threw the bottle into the scrap heap below, and pulled a fresh one from the pocket of his greatcoat.

From outside the Ward, in the direction of the new Wall construction, Aaron heard screaming. From this distance he could not hear the creature, but he could guess.

"Dragons," said Aaron. He saw the workers scrambling off the scaffold. *I hope Nicholas is all right,* he thought.

"All this over a couple of dragons," said Quartz.

"People just want to feel safe, I guess. I wish I felt safe here. But everything is changing so fast; Isambard becoming Presbyter, you going away ..." *meeting another who shares the sense.*

He took another swig from the bottle, and the roar of the compies in his ears became fainter, as though he were listening through a layer of mud. He thought about what Nicholas had said last time he'd seen him — about the voice he'd heard down in Isambard's workshop. *"It was a compie, and it was in great pain."*

But if Nicholas heard something and I didn't, what does that mean? Is my sense somehow broken? Is his?

***

Nicholas paced the length of the opulent receiving room, waiting to be admitted to the King's private audience hall. His fingers drummed nervously against his leather document case.

Brunel, far from showing any sign of nerves, seated himself on an overstuffed French chair, folded his hands in his lap, and whistled "The Stoker and the Navvy's Wife". Nicholas shot him a murderous stare.

"I don't see what you're all worked up about," Brunel remarked. "Your plans are brilliant, and with my new Boilers, I have the means to bring them to fruition."

"The King wants a Wall and a railroad built in four months! And your plan ... your *only* plan ... involves a machine that exists as two heaps of scrap-metal in your workshop. We should be spending this time pressing as many men as possible into service, not sending the Stokers away to the swamps and trying to fund yet another engineering experiment."

"I have every confidence in the ability of my Boilers." Brunel smiled. "Just you wait."

The outer door creaked open, and a maid entered, wheeling a tea-trolley and dressed in austere black skirts and a white apron. She can't have been much older than eighteen, and was possessed of a rare natural beauty — porcelain skin, bright, intelligent eyes, and pert, delicate lips.

"Sorry to disturb you, sirs," she said, giving a short curtsey, "but His Majesty thought perhaps you would like refreshments while you wait for him to prepare for your meeting." She smiled at Nicholas, a warm, dazzling smile that made his head feel fuzzy.

Nicholas gratefully accepted a cup of steaming tea and a tiny scone, which she pushed into his hands with such delicate grace his nerves rather got the better of him, and they jerked uncontrollably, splashing scalding tea on the seat of his trousers and all over the French chair.

A flush crept across the maid's cheeks. "I'm so sorry. Allow me to clean this for you, sir."

"No, no, it was my fault. You don't have to—" But she was already dabbing at the stain with a white handkerchief, her eyes downcast, concentrating on her work.

A few strands of her hair escaped from her bonnet in a tangle of brown curls, cascading down her face as she dabbed at his trousers. He fought the sudden, unbecoming urge to grab her by her beautiful hair and press her face to his.

No, Nicholas. Concentrate. You're here to visit

with the King.

His own cheeks flushed, and, as he leaned forward to help her up, his fingers brushed against her arm. That simple touch of soft, warm skin sent a shiver through his entire body. She leapt away, averting her gaze once more, fussing with the items on the tea-trolley.

She set a teacup and saucer down on the ornate oak end table beside him, and dabbed a spoonful of clotted cream onto a scone. He watched her intently, not caring how rude he must seem. He saw her sneak a glance at him through her pretty curls, and quickly look away again. Behind him, Brunel gave an ungentlemanly snort.

A guard entered from the inner door, his rifle resting against his shoulder. "The King will see you now." He addressed the girl. "Bring his tea." The girl followed with the laden tray.

Nicholas had expected exactly what he saw — an opulent chamber, dimly lit, and festooned with exotic silks and damasks. What he hadn't expected was to see the King lying facedown upon an oak couch of German design, while a waifish girl wearing a thin chiton kneaded his back. The last time they'd visited Windsor Castle, George had been immaculately presented, receiving his guests in the stately drawing rooms, his clothing perfectly pressed, his wig and makeup flawless. Even at the Royal Society when he was confined to his chair, the King still maintained a dignified air.

Compared to this earlier image, his current state was deplorable. The King's wig was askew, hanging over one eye and revealing the thin, matted hair beneath. His bloodshot eyes blinked rapidly in the dim light, the skin around them drawn up so they bugged out of his skull like an insect.

"The Presbyter Isambard Brunel and his architect Nicholas Rose to see you, Your Majesty." The guard darted away, as though he couldn't bear to remain inside that chamber a moment longer.

"Your Majesty?"

King George raised his head, ever so slightly, and regarded them with his bulging, wild eyes; the pupils dark and slanted like an animal. Pushing himself onto his hands, he rolled over and faced the two visitors. Nicholas struggled to tear his gaze away from the blisters covering the King's cheeks, from the skin that pulled around his mouth, revealing his long, blackened teeth and gums. As he stared, the King's robe fell open, revealing a cluster of fresh, bulging pustules, and dark scars crisscrossing his chest. Nicholas averted his eyes, ashamed to see the monarch in such a state.

"Sit, sit." His voice, calm and strong, seemed at odds with his deplorable condition. The King waved them to a formal couch. "You bring me the finalised plans, I see."

Brunel unrolled the drawings and set them out on the table. "Mr Rose and I have been puzzling over how to meet your Majesty's request to have the Windsor/Buckingham railway completed within your timeframe, to coincide with the completion of the shell of the Wall. We believe we've finally come up with a solution that will satisfy all parties."

The King leaned over the table, his eyes poring over the drawings. The girl shuffled forward, trying to continue her work. He growled and pushed her away.

Pouting, she flounced into the darker recesses of the chamber. As she turned, Nicholas caught the same crisscrossed scars and puncture wounds on her shoulders and back as he'd seen on the King only moments before.

Behind the King's couch, the beautiful maid hunched over her tea-trolley. The King sat up and she handed him a cup of tea — a strange brew that appeared reddish in the dim light. As she straightened herself, King George's eyes swept over her body, and he licked his lips. She backed away and returned to her tea-trolley. Nicholas' eyes met hers, and he was surprised to see terror there.

"Four months," the King murmured. "It is not enough. I need it sooner. Two months."

Nicholas blanched, but Brunel simply nodded. "As you wish, Your Majesty."

"You are certain these … *machines* … will complete my railway on time?"

"Oh yes, sir," Brunel said. "I am certain."

"Very well." The King pushed the drawings aside. "You shall have as much money as needed to complete the job. Show me the latest designs for the Wall."

Brunel unrolled the next drawing. "There she is, higher and wider than has ever been attempted before. As you can see, sir, we'll be building new stations in Belgravia—"

"There are too many gates." The King frowned.

"People still need to move freely about the city. Otherwise, the Wall would disrupt commerce. The gates are controlled using my unique steam-driven turbines. Once closed, only a command to the control room in Engine Ward will open them again."

"And this will seal off the city?" The King's voice rose in pitch.

Brunel nodded. "No men or dragons will be able to penetrate those walls."

"Good," the King nodded, rubbing his thin, hooked nose. "That's good."

The King's eyes shifted erratically, and his head lolled to the side. As he moved, the wounds across his chest wept blood. He didn't dismiss the maid, and so she stayed, crouching quietly in the corner so as not to be noticed. Nicholas met her eye, and smiled. She gave a little wave, and smiled back, though her eyes darted back and forth between the King and the bangtail at the back of the chamber. She was terrified. He didn't blame her. The King was acting in a most peculiar manner.

Nicholas shifted in his chair, and accepted another scone from the tray in an effort to calm his shaking hands.

Brunel and King George bent their heads together and continued their discussion in low whispers. Pretending to be fascinated with some detail in the plans, Nicholas leaned over the table, tore a new page from his journal, and scribbled a note. Discreetly, while Brunel was demonstrating the positions of the new railway stations, he folded it and slipped it up the sleeve of his jacket.

The King nodded his satisfaction. Brunel held up his page of notes. "I shall see His Majesty's requests worked into the final plans," he said. The King waved them away, and called for his nymph to return. The girl in the chiton skulked from the shadows and draped herself over his couch. Nicholas looked away, not wishing to see.

As they rose and moved toward the reception room, he passed the tea-trolley and slipped the note into the pocket of the girl's apron. She looked up at him, her eyes wide. He gave a tight smile, and left.

I should not have done that. But his steps felt lighter as he walked with Brunel back to the Engine Ward, his mind awash with the memory of her sweet smile.

***

After Brigitte put the tea things away, Miss Julie rattled off a long list of chores for her to finish. She rushed through the washing and the dusting, the note burning a hole in her pocket. Even so, it was well past dinner before Brigitte could extract herself from Miss Julie's clutches and hurry to her chamber. She unfolded the note with shaking fingers, and laid it flat on her pillow, smoothing out the corners and admiring the gently sloping, elegantly curled handwriting of the handsome gentleman.

She couldn't read it, of course, for she had never learned to read. Her mind raced with myriad imaginings of what it could say. She thought of the man who'd passed it to her: his soft features, the curl of his hair over his ears, his kind grey eyes tinged with sorrow. Her stomach fluttered.

A crash started her. Crying out, she dropped the note and turned to see Cassandra hobbling across the floor clutching her foot. "Hurt me toe," she gasped, collapsing onto her bunk.

"You might be more quiet about it."

"Why? You're not sleepin' or nothin'. Hey, what's that?" Cassandra's eyes fell upon Brigitte's pillow.

"It's nothing." Brigitte shoved the note under her pillow. Her answer seemed to satisfy Cassandra, who rolled over, kicked off her stockings, blew out the candle, and fell promptly asleep.

Brigitte rolled onto her side and listened to Cassandra's snores, her mind reeling with the events of two weeks: the King's attack on Alison, his strange temperament and the peculiar marks all over his skin, the screams and snarls echoing through the castle halls, and now a gentleman was giving her notes. Finally, her eyelids fluttered closed, her hand feeling under the pillow for the note, and her dreams filled with visions of a certain grey-eyed gentleman.

***

"—and don't go chasing after dragons. And listen to what the priests say, even though they're idiots, they're in charge, and they have the power to make your life miserable, and—"

Aaron and Quartz stood together under the giant iron arches that formed the gates of Engine Ward. A row of carts lined the street, some to carry the large crew of men, others stacked high with supplies — sleepers, building materials, tools, and chests of food and drink. Peter and Oswald and the other priests stood under the gates, their faces stony as they directed the workers. They didn't look happy to be leaving the city.

Aaron clasped Quartz's shoulders, rattling off long lists of instructions and platitudes, babbling so he would not have to face the silence of his own thoughts.

"—come back to London if you're in any trouble —"

"Aaron," Quartz grinned. "I aim to *make* trouble."

"That's what worries me."

Quartz nodded his head in Aaron's direction, and climbed aboard the cart. At least twenty men crowded in after him, so Aaron could no longer see his jolly, wrinkled face. He turned away, slinking back through the Ward before the carriages even pulled away.

His shack felt enormous, empty, without Quartz. He lay down on the bed and pulled Chloe close, hoping to lose himself in sleep, but he would not get his wish. After an hour of tossing and turning, he got up again, and opened the cabinet to find a bottle of whisky, only to discover Quartz had left it bare. Sighing, he looked under the bed, found a bottle with a few drops left in it, and took this outside with him. He went up to the top of the boiler tower, where he had sat with Isambard only a few years previously, and gazed out across the Ward and the city of London stretching on into eternity beyond her walls.

For the first time in his life, he was suddenly, inescapably alone.

***

They disembarked at Liverpool, and Stephenson went off to procure a carriage while Jacques relieved himself in the public latrine. The Frenchman sat by the platform and watched the men loading and unloading the wagons, marvelling at the weight of cargo the locomotive could transport. At the edge of the platform was a small stone shrine containing a votive statue of

Stephenson that seemed to lurch under the weight of the floral wreaths that covered it.

These locomotives could make England rich, he realised. *The richest country in the world, if only they had a king who wasn't mad.*

Someone called his name. He saw Stephenson waving at him from beside a comfortable carriage, while the footman helped two women settle into the carriage and tied their portmanteaus to the roof.

The woman introduced herself as Annabelle Milbanke, and, upon hearing his accent, insisted on addressing him in flawless French. Her daughter Ada, who must have been fifteen or so, tugged at her dresses and flipped through a notebook open on her lap.

He knew who she was, of course. One couldn't go a day in Paris without mention of the famed poet-turned-Messiah Lord Byron and his tumultuous marriage to and divorce from Miss Milbanke, followed shortly thereafter by his daring escape across the closed English border into Greece.

He settled into the sliver of space left on the bench beside Stephenson, and as the carriage pulled away from the station, he addressed Miss Milbanke.

"What sends you fine ladies to London?"

"Why, the first sermon of Robert's new Presbyter, of course," said Miss Milbanke. "Ada writes often to eminent members of the Society, and we've been sent transcriptions of his lectures, which we've studied with great interest. He's got some remarkable ideas about locomotion, Robert. He thinks you're going about it all wrong."

Stephenson's face darkened. "He's got this fandangled idea that a wider rail gauge will make the trains run faster. But my trains run plenty fast enough, don't they, Mr. du Blanc?"

Jacques nodded.

"I've even heard he's got the notion of a railway that doesn't run on steam at all! And his Wall design is preposterous — ridiculously expensive and an inefficient use of men and resources. I don't know what the Council was thinking. If you've come to London all the way from Kirkby Mallory for Brunel's lecture," Stephenson continued, "I'm afraid you're going to be horribly disappointed."

"Don't forget, Mother. We're also visiting Mister Babbage!" Ada piped up in a singsong tone, never looking up from her study.

"Now there's a thing," Stephenson said. "There's not many who would admit such an acquaintance in public, young Ada."

Miss Milbanke sniffed. "Ada and Charles have kept up quite a correspondence. She helps him with his calculations, you know. I myself am not sure he's an appropriate companion for her, not since that business with the corrections and his disgraceful excommunication. But try telling that to a headstrong girl."

"Mother!" Ada huffed.

"See, now, Babbage I approve of," said Stephenson. "Smart man, and probably right about the calculations, but he got caught up in the politics. That's all the city is good for, is politics. That's why I left as soon as they gave me the jewels." He gestured at the emerald-encrusted medallion — the mark of a Messiah — hanging around his neck. "In the north there ain't no politics getting in the way of good engineering.

Babbage would have done fine if he'd been in a university, but he wanted to start a church—"

They chatted on about church politics and famous engineers, and though he found their talk fascinating, Jacques' thoughts wandered back to his own mission. If he had the protection of a Presbyter, finding Nicholas in London wouldn't be easy. He patted the hilt of his sword, resting reassuringly against his thigh. *Somewhere in this world of engineering priests and mechanical gods, you're hiding, Nicholas, but I will find you.*

***

By the third morning Brigitte was desperate. She could no longer keep the note secret if she hoped to discover what it said. It was barely light outside their grubby window when she dug the note — now much crumpled and torn in the corner — from under the pillow.

The roosters in the kitchen garden outside began their morning call, and Cassandra rolled over and groaned. "My feet are killing me. And I've another day polishing the armory to look forward to. I don't never want to see another ceremonial sword again — Brigitte, what you starin' at?"

"Cassandra, can you read?" Brigitte held up the note.

Cassandra snatched the paper from under her nose. "Cor, you got an admirer?"

"No," Brigitte blushed. "At least, I don't believe so. The gentleman who visited the King with Mr. Brunel, he gave it to me."

"Oooooh, a gentleman! Was he rakishly handsome?"

"I'll give you rakishly handsome in a minute if you don't tell me what it says."

"I dunno," Cassandra threw the note back into Brigitte's hands. "I can't read it. Ask Miss Julie."

"And have her find out a gentleman friend of the King has been slipping me notes? No, I don't think I'll be doing that. I'll have to find someone else to read it to me."

"What was your gentleman meeting His Majesty about?"

"He's not *my* gentleman." Brigitte felt her cheeks grow hot. "The King was approving Mr. Brunel's plans for the Dragon Wall. At least, when he wasn't doing something unsavoury to that bangtail he brought in last week." Brigitte wrinkled her nose.

"Better her than us."

Brigitte nodded, remembering the scars crisscrossing the woman's skin, and Alison's face, the flesh barely hanging from the bones.

"So who's gonna read yer note for you?"

"I think I know just the person." Brigitte swung herself down from her bed and tucked the note into her pocket. "If Miss Julie asks after me, tell her I'm helping with the gardening."

***

Maxwell — a stooped, wind-beaten man with a face marred with liverspots but possessed of a jolly laugh — squinted at the scrap of paper, turning it every which way and rubbing his grubby beard in concentration.

Brigitte leaned forward, her hands wringing her skirt. "What does it say?"

Maxwell turned it upside down, squinted again, and burst out laughing.

"Maxwell, this is *not* funny!"

Wiping his dirty hand across his brow, the castle gardener held out the note, his grey eyes twinkling, that laugh booming from somewhere deep in his chest. She grabbed it from his thick fingers, scowling at him as she folded it reverently, and replaced it in the secret pocket of her apron.

"He wants to meet you, Miss Brigitte, in Kensington Gardens this afternoon."

"This afternoon?" Her eyes grew wide. "But that's … today!"

"It surely is. You'd best make it down to London quick smart."

Brigitte ran her hands through her hair, strewn with straw from helping Maxwell in the barn. Her hands, rough from the week's polishing, caught in the tangles. She knew her face must be smudged with dirt.

"I'm hopeless," she moaned.

"Nonsense." Maxwell patted her shoulder, leaving a smear of dirt across the ribbon. Brigitte sighed.

"You best show this to Miss Julie," he said. "She'll know what to do."

"But she'll forbid me from going. She'll—"

He put his finger to his lips. "Best you not go underestimating Miss Julie. Now, go. Land yourself a gentleman."

***

When Miss Julie saw the note, her eyes grew wide and she pressed her hand to her chest, as though she might pass out at any moment.

"He handed it to me as he left the King's chamber, Miss. I swear I didn't—"

Miss Julie yanked her arms above her head.

"Off with that dress," she commanded.

"Wha—"

"Stop arguing, Brigitte. We have precious little time and lots of work to do. Cassandra!" she bellowed. "We need a tub of warm water and my wire brush!"

***

"With the salary Isambard's giving you, you could afford something much more ostentatious than this." Aaron puffed as he manoeuvred an old oak desk — Nicholas' only new purchase for the austere rooms he'd rented — across the landing of the boardinghouse stairs and into the office.

"I like this place just fine," said Nicholas, sharper than intended.

Aaron shrugged, and kept on pushing.

The truth was, Nicholas had chosen the apartment because the landlady didn't require papers to sign the lease. He wanted to stay Nicholas Rose as long as possible, in case someone from France showed up in the city. Brunel had offered him a private room in the new wing he was planning to add to the Chimney, and Nicholas was sorely tempted by the prospect, but if Jacques ever came for him, the Engine Ward would be the first place he'd look.

After Aaron had wrestled the desk into place, Nicholas invited him to stay for tea. The cupboards in his larder were bare, save a half-eaten loaf and a small square of cheese left over from his breakfast, but he — being a proper Englishman — had already purchased a lovely tea set.

"What do you hear now?" he asked Aaron as he set the cup in front of him.

Aaron knew instantly what he meant. "I hear compies under the floor, scrabbling in the gap between the floorboards. They have a hole into number sixteen that they're patrolling, waiting for the family to leave so they can sneak in and steal the ham. I hear worms in the dirt, their thoughts singular, based on instinct."

"What about birds?"

"Their thoughts flicker; predatory, maternal, hunger, joy. I see London as they see it, from the air, a hodgepodge of warrens and labyrinths. They have traps — dead ends into which they funnel their prey. Thankfully, I don't hear any dragons nearby." Aaron set down his cup. "It is so strange to talk freely about the *sense*. I haven't been able to do this since my grandfather was alive."

"I was there when the dragon attacked. I couldn't stop it." He stared at the table, the image of the man's skin burning against the iron floating through his mind.

"We could've stopped it together, if I were allowed to work outside the Ward. This whole situation is ridiculous, Nicholas, and you've got to tell him so. We've got a high-profile project upon which Isambard's entire career hangs that must be built within four months—"

"Two months."

"What?"

"I was at Windsor yesterday, and the King has decided it must be built in two months."

Aaron threw up his hands. "Then what are we to do? The finest industrial workers in the country are not able to work on the Wall. Instead of figuring out a way to get the Stokers on the Wall, he's building mechanical workers and shipping us off across the country on a wild dragon chase."

"Aaron, if you told Isambard about the sense, he would let you go into the swamps, too."

"I've already explained — it's out of the question. And don't you tell him, either. You'll live to regret it."

They lapsed into silence after that, each lost in their own thoughts. Nicholas knew he should be worried about Isambard's decisions, about the new deadline for the Wall, but every thought was occupied by the image of a timid maid and her head of shimmering curls.

You fool! What were you thinking?

He would go to the gardens this afternoon, and he would wait, but she would not show up. It would be imprudent of her, especially given whatever mysterious circumstances prevailed at the castle. So he would wait, and she would not show, and he could return to his life devoid of brightness.

***

An hour later, Brigitte held up a bronze mirror to her face and gasped aloud. Miss Julie had worked a miracle. Brigitte's hair stood in a firm bun, demure but attractive, with two ringlets peeking mischievously from under her bonnet and secured with a pretty brass pin, also taken from a box of the princess' things. She'd pulled a dress from the box hidden at the back of the scullery.

"This used to belong to Princess Amelia," said Miss Julie, measuring it against Brigitte's trim frame. "When King George took the princesses away for safe-keeping, he left all their pretty things behind, gathering dust. He ordered Maxwell to burn most of it, but I saved a few things. Such fine tailoring — I couldn't just throw this away."

The dress fit Brigitte perfectly, draping across her shoulders, the blue bodice giving her a beautiful waistline, the crisp skirts swaying about her feet. She hoped no one would notice her grubby boots peeking out from under the fine silk.

"Hurry, child. You're already running late!"

Maxwell bustled her into a carriage, and Cassandra and Miss Julie waved from the servants' entrance as she clattered toward the gate at high speed. Her heart raced even faster than the horses. She hadn't set foot outside the castle for two years now, and to be leaving for Kensington Gardens to meet a rakishly handsome gentleman, dressed in a frock last worn by a princess, seemed like a dream.

With Maxwell driving the countryside passed by in a blur. Brigitte could hear the coach's axles wobbling in their stays, and she had to grip the edge of the door tightly to keep from slipping off her seat. As the carriage passed through the towns, people stopped on the street and waved to her, perhaps thinking her an eccentric courtesan out for a ride in the country. Not knowing what else to do, she waved back, her cheeks flashing red.

They hit traffic coming into London along the Strand, but Maxwell ducked and swerved with a tenacity Brigitte had never seen in the old gardener. By the time they pulled up outside Kensington Gardens, she was only a few minutes late.

She leapt from the coach, Maxwell circling her, wiping dust from her sleeves and smoothing the hem of her dress. Then she scanned the park for a sign of him. *Maybe this is some kind of joke. Maybe—*

Her heart leapt into her chest as she recognised him.

He was waiting on a bench by the pond, and as she walked toward him — her legs shaking so much that each step was a challenge — he turned and saw her, and his whole face lit up.

She froze, her eyes locked with his, searching out every detail of him, as though she expected him to turn to dust at any moment. He stood a head taller than her, his back straight and posture proud. His clothes — the same as he had worn at the castle, she recalled — were of fine quality, but worn and threadbare. His hands — the skin smooth, the fingers long — fell at his sides. She knew she was being frightfully rude, but seeing him again in such extraordinary circumstances had robbed her of the power of speech.

Finally, he smiled. "Hello, again," he said. She nodded. That was all she could manage.

He shook hands with Maxwell, who would act as her escort, and bent to kiss her hand. As his fingers touched hers, a shock ran through her hand and all the way up her arm. His eyes met hers and danced with delight, and her stomach churned.

"Would you like to stroll among the garden?" he asked, offering his hand.

She could hardly speak, he was so handsome. Maxwell nudged her forward with his boot, and she stumbled over the hem of her dress and grabbed his arm to steady herself. Nicholas caught her, placing his other hand on her hip to keep her steady, the warmth making her stomach squirm even more.

She gave a nervous laugh, and he laughed also. She took his arm and he led her along the path at the edge of the pond. Maxwell followed at a short distance, just within earshot of their conversation.

"I hope you will forgive me for the forthright nature of my note," he said. "I do not know what came over me. I do not even know your name."

"Brigitte," she choked. "My name is Brigitte."

He smiled, melting her heart a little more. "Then that is at least something. I am Nicholas Rose, and I am pleased you could meet me today, Brigitte. You've been foremost in my thoughts since I first saw you."

Her stomach flipped. "I— I—"

"Please don't be nervous. I want nothing from you other than your company. Did you read my note yourself?"

"Maxwell—" she pointed to the figure behind them. "He read it for me. I cannot read."

"That is no matter. Many who can are not as beautiful as you. If I may be so forthright, tell me about yourself; how did you come to be a maid in the palace?"

"It's not a very interesting story."

"It's interesting to me."

She took a deep breath, found her voice, and steadied herself against his warm, strong arm. "I was born in Whitechapel. My father worked at the docks, and my mother ran the kitchen at a public house. We didn't have much money, but we could afford rooms and food most days. That is, until my parents died. First my father caught a plague from the foreign sailors coming off the ships. At first, he complained of throbbing aches throughout his body. After a few days, he couldn't stand. He lay in the blankets we used as a bed and coughed up blood ... so much blood. It splattered over all our clothes, our cooking pots, my mother's books. Then, one morning he didn't cough anymore. I helped my mother carry him downstairs for the man to collect. A few weeks later, my mother went mad, shivering and babbling. She broke all the windows in the doss house in one of her rages, and a man came and took her away to a sanatorium. I was eight years old.

"When it became clear I could no longer pay the rent, the landlord dumped me at an orphanage. The puritan nuns resented my presence — another mouth to feed. They beat us most nights, locked me in a dark cupboard for days at a time, and once forced me to eat leather as a punishment. I hated them, and I realised that if I were to ever escape from their cruelty, I would have to find myself a profession. So I started cleaning. First, I cleaned the pub next door in exchange for fresh bread. Then, I cleaned the homes of the publicans. I listened to the gossip at the tables and realised many well-to-do Londoners came to Whitechapel to taste the ladies of ill-repute, so I made sure to bring them their drinks and make myself known to them."

"My first wealthy client, Joseph Banks, was so pleased with my efforts that he recommended me to his entire social circle, and I came to the attention of the King's staff. At £6 a year the job offered more money than I'd ever earned before, with food and board included. Without telling the nuns where I was going, I packed what little things I owned, and came to the castle."

"Do you enjoy your work?"

She paused, wondering if he was asking about the King. He nodded for her to continue. "Sometimes. I enjoy touching the fine things, making them shine. But I hate the futility of it all; rooms and rooms of exquisite artwork, precious metals, and dazzling jewels, all of it dusty and unseen. You can spend hours polishing, but really, you're just moving the emptiness around. If I ever own beautiful things, I shall enjoy them every day."

He turned off onto a divergent path, leading her through the rose bushes toward a covered gazebo. He said, "It's a curse of the rich to covet such beautiful things and yet to never truly enjoy them."

"Are you a lord?"

He laughed. "I could have been, Miss Brigitte, but instead I am an architect. I designed the exterior of Brunel's Dragon Wall. If you look toward the river you can see the shape of the first section being erected now."

They sat on a bench beside the gazebo, watching the pigeons pecking at scraps along the edges of the path and the gardeners repairing the flower beds damaged in the dragon attack. He asked more questions: her favourite flower (water lily), her favourite foods (mutton and minted peas). Had she ever travelled outside London? (Once, to the country, when she was younger.) Which God did she worship?

(She always liked Isis — she was the prettiest, and all the artists whose work hung in the castle worshipped her, too.) She wanted to ask him something of himself, but he avoided all questions, simply turning each inquiry back upon her.

The world around her disappeared, and she was lost in him, in the sound of his voice, the movement of his lips, the gentle creases at the corners of his eyes as he laughed at one of her tales.

Someone tapped her on the shoulder, startling her out of her trance. "It's time to return to the castle, Miss Brigitte." Maxwell held up his pocket watch for her to see.

Nicholas stood and offered her his hand. "Will I see you again?"

He wants to see me again! This can't be right. It must be some kind of cruel joke. Perhaps he is dangerous—

"I must go." She gathered her skirts, eyes downcast, suddenly afraid. The spell had been shattered, and now she wanted to get away.

"But will I see you?"

"I — I don't know."

"You will come to the palace again?" Maxwell asked.

Nicholas nodded. "Brunel will meet with the King and the Council members next Friday to give an update on the Wall's progress."

"After your meeting with the King, you will go to the courtyard outside the Curfew Tower. Brigitte will be waiting there."

Nicholas pressed a handful of coins into the gardener's hand. Maxwell tried to push them back, but the architect held up his hands. "For your kindness," he said, "and your silence."

He held her hand out and kissed it, his warm lips lingering for an eternity, his vivid grey eyes boring into hers. She trembled, though she was not cold. Finally, he tore himself away. "Good day, my Lady."

"G— g— good day," she choked. He turned and strolled away. She waited 'till he was out of sight before sinking back into the park bench. Maxwell had to grab her and lead her to the carriage.

Only when the carriage pulled out onto West Carriage Drive did she let out the breath she was holding. Maxwell smirked.

"Why, Miss Brigitte, I've never seen your face so flushed."

"It's the heat. This dress is awfully stuffy."

"Of course," he laughed. "The dress."

***

While Nicholas met Brigitte in the park, Aaron took his two deputies out to Windsor to lay down the survey pegs for the site of the Windsor platform of the King's secret railway.

He'd wanted to take more men, but there was not a Stoker to spare. A skeleton crew ran the furnaces — men working sixteen-hour shifts just to keep the Ward functioning — and even the women were assembling Boiler mechanisms. Work on Brunel's two new locomotives had ground to a halt, and he'd had to go into the sheds at 6am and drag out two of the best men — William Stone and his son Benjamin — for this cursed job. Aaron hated leaving the Ward with so much work that needed doing, but since Brunel still believed they could make the King's impossible deadline, they had to press on with haste.

He'd never even been outside London, let alone to the imposing Windsor Castle, looming over the Berkshire countryside. He hung his head out the window and drank it all in — the tiny cottages, the towering barns, and the cacophony of thoughts from a myriad of animals. Sheep and cows grazed in the paddocks, birds and raptors circled the trees, horses pulled carriages and coaches that passed them on the narrow road, and neckers, those long-necked beasts bred in Scotland, pulled huge wagons of goods toward London for market.

He enjoyed the slow thoughts of the neckers the most: they'd walked the same stretch of road many times before, and they knew each turn by heart. He relished seeing this world — so new to him — through their knowing gaze.

The trip was over all too soon, and they introduced themselves to the guard at the castle gates, using the story Brunel had coached them on: the King had commissioned them to build a new shrine in the garden. The guards had evidently been given the same story, for they opened the gates and directed them to the edge of the terraced garden without further questions.

Aaron unfolded the plans and, being the only one of the three men who could read, directed the placement of the stakes and recorded the measurements. Hidden behind the high garden wall and located at the bottom of a steep terrace, the station would be invisible to anyone outside the castle or walking through the garden from the main path. It was to be a simple structure — a wooden platform, a shed to keep the locomotive and two carriages dry (which would probably be scrapped from the plans due to time constraints), and the trackbed itself, disappearing down into the natural valley of a dry stream bed that ran along the outskirts of the township toward London.

Aaron wanted to get the basic structure of the platform built today, so he and William unloaded the shovels and thick lengths of wood and steel, while Benjamin, a young lad with a strong back, began ripping up the lawn to dig the post holes. They worked for three solid hours in the biting cold wind, with only the sounds of the birds and their voices for company. William and Benjamin had many questions about the railway and its purpose, none of which Aaron could answer.

After lunch, William went up to the castle workshops to borrow a set square, and came back screaming, "The King is coming!"

"Don't be ridiculous. The King wouldn't—"

William dragged Aaron up over the edge of the terrace and pointed toward the castle. Aaron raised his head, squinting. He saw a line of tiny figures emerging from the inner gate and descending down the hill toward them. The procession was flanked on both sides by men carrying the Union Jack flag.

"By Great Conductor's steam-driven testicles, it *is* the King! Quick, William, clean up those tools! Benjamin, stack up the beams—"

They scrambled around, frantically trying to make their work area look less like a work area. When Aaron looked up again, the procession had reached the crest of the hill.

The King slumped forward in his wheeled chair, as though the leather straps around his arms and legs were the only things holding him up. Joseph Banks stood behind the King, his thin hands clasped so tightly around the handles of the wheelchair his knuckles were white. Flanked by his guards with their towering helmets dwarfing the figures of his retinue, the King seemed impossibly frail.

As they stopped on the slope of the hill, Aaron, William, and Benjamin bowed. Banks snapped his fingers and ordered them to rise. The King didn't acknowledge them, flapping his head against his shoulder and mumbling something unintelligible. Aaron saw his cheeks and the skin of his forearms were covered with dark, blistering marks. And his eyes, they were the most frightening of all — they were not the listless, unfocused eyes of a sickly man, but contained the fierce, rapacious gaze of an animal, a predator zeroing in on his prey.

"You are Isambard Brunel's men?" Banks barked.

"We are, sir." Aaron stepped forward. "I'm Aaron Williams. This is William—"

"I don't care who you are. The King wishes to inspect your progress on his railway."

"As you can see," Aaron gestured behind him, "there is not much progress for His Majesty to inspect. Today we're marking out the position of the trackbed and erecting the posts to support the platform."

"And how long will it take you to finish the entire railway line?"

"I'm not yet privy to all the plans, sir, but we're working with haste to have it ready within His

Majesty's two-month deadline."

"That's not nearly soon enough. The King needs the railway completed within the month."

"That's impossible, sir. Laying the rails alone will take six weeks—"

"Then lay them faster," Banks snapped. "Your king has commanded his railway be built within the month, and so you shall build it. Brunel's a clever engineer — he will work it out."

"With all due respect, sir—"

In a matter of moments Banks thrust the handles of the wheelchair into the hands of a waiting steward, crossed the lawn, and grabbed Aaron by the collar.

"Tell him," Banks whispered, his eyes bulging. "If this railway isn't completed by the end of the month, all the titles and renown in London won't save him from the King's wrath. Tell him, that he has thirty days to finish this railway, or I'll hang him with my own hands, to save him the agony of what the King will do to him."

***

The journey back to London passed in silence, each man staring out the window, lost in his own thoughts. Aaron's mind was dark — the sounds that had so delighted him that morning were nothing but a muddy blur.

A month to finish the railway was *preposterous*. He would laugh at the notion, had it not been for the menace in Banks' voice. It was as if they were treating Isambard and the Stokers to some great practical joke. He wondered if Banks and the King were laughing over their teacups as they watched Aaron, William, and Ben work at record speed to drive in all the piles.

As the carriage passed over London Bridge, Aaron caught a glimpse of the first section of the Wall, a few yards of scaffolding and steel pylons mounted in the ground. It seemed woefully small — just looking out across the great expanse of London's skyline brought home the fruitlessness of the whole task. This angered Aaron beyond all measure, and he balled his hands into fists.

As their carriage pulled up alongside the Boiler factory, Isambard was already outside, waving at them.

"Successful trip?" Brunel asked, after he'd shooed the Stone Brothers inside and practically dragged Aaron from the carriage.

Aaron snorted, and told Isambard what had happened at the castle. "It's over, Isambard. You won the prize, you built the Wall, but it's all a joke at the Stokers' expense. We were never going to change anything."

"There must be another explanation."

"What other possible explanation could there be? I'm afraid we've been set up to fail by Joseph Banks. The King is clearly too far gone to have any say in the construction. Think about it — you said yourself he's become increasingly unintelligible in your meetings with him, and Nicholas said his entire body is covered in burns and cuts. But Banks is always with him, speaking for him. And he never wanted you to win in the first place, did he?"

Isambard was silent for a moment. Slowly he nodded his head. "You're right. But it's not over, Aaron. We're going to build the Wall, *and* that railway."

"In a month? Don't be ridiculous."

Brunel threw open the door of the shed. Inside, Aaron saw at least fifty Stokers working along an assembly line, some shifting raw materials and slag into huge furnaces, others manoeuvring parts into place or watching the progress of the new high-pressure engine as it shaped and hollowed lumps of metal. Along the front of the workshop, their unseeing eyes surveying the work, ten shiny Boiler units stood to attention.

"Another ten will be finished tomorrow," said Brunel. "And ten each day thereafter 'till the job is done. By the end of the week we shall have fifty units, and that should be more than enough to lay the sleepers and rails on twenty-six miles within a few days. A Wall and a railway in a month, Aaron! If we can do it, can you imagine?"

Aaron stared into the cold, flat faces of the Boilers, and the anger in his belly turned to fear. "Yes," he said. "It's my imagination that worries me."

***

When Isambard told Nicholas over breakfast that the schedule had been moved from two months to one, he spat tea across the table in a most ungentlemanly manner.

"That's impossible!"

Isambard frowned, gesturing for the priest who hovered at the door of the chamber to clean up the stain. "Aaron thinks it's a plot by Banks and the Council to discredit me, to prove I'm no engineer. I'm rather afraid he's correct."

"What are you going to do?"

"The only thing I know how to do. I'm going to *work*, Nicholas. I'm going to pull out every trick I can think of, and a few I haven't yet dreamed up, and I'm going to get the Wall and railway finished if it kills me. But I need your help."

"How? Isambard, I am no engineer."

"I have a month," Isambard said, his voice grave. "I don't know why the King is in such a hurry, but I do know to disappoint him would mean my death, and the death of hope for the Stokers along with it. It is in *both* our interests," he said pointedly, his eyes fixed on Nicholas, "to complete this Wall on time. If I were you, I'd finish that cup of tea as quickly as I were able, and report to the workshops—"

He was interrupted by a young acolyte, who raced into the chamber and leaned against the table. "Presbyter," he gasped, "a package has arrived for you from the swamps."

Nicholas' ears pricked up. *The Stokers have sent something to Isambard?*

The Presbyter didn't seem surprised by the news. He shovelled another forkful of egg into his mouth. "Well, bring it here, then!"

"It's arrived on a wagon, sir. A *large* wagon."

Brunel leapt to his feet and dashed from the room. Nicholas and the acolyte followed close behind. What could be so large it needed an entire wagon?

The wagon had been parked outside the Boiler workshops, practically blocking the door. It was as wide as the roads would allow, and needed four horses to pull it. The six axles sagged under the weight of the crate — as long as the wagon and higher than a man — roped to the back of the wagon.

"Special delivery," said the grizzled man who sat on the footplate, the reins of the tired horses clutched in his shaking hand. He lifted the corner of his hood up and met Nicholas' eye — it was Quartz.

He's back. This will please Aaron—

The thoughts hit him like a wave smashing against a rocky shore, fracturing his own thoughts and sending him reeling against the wall of the Chimney. He rubbed his temple, not understanding at first. Through the haze, his mind clutched on to the truth.

There was something alive inside that crate. It was large — larger than the biggest creature he'd ever seen — and it was dangerous.

What does Isambard want with an animal?

It can't be. But it was. The way the thoughts narrowed, the hunger in his belly, the insatiable malice that crawled over his skin. His sense told him that inside that crate was a dragon, bigger and more frightening than any of the dragons he'd encountered in London. *But why?*

He watched Isambard lean in and exchange a few words with Quartz, then waved him onward, in the direction of the Boiler workshops and the entrance to the underground service tunnels. Pushing the horses to their last, painful trot, the old man leaned in toward Nicholas as he passed.

"Don't tell Aaron I was here," he said, pulling his hood low over his face. Nicholas could see a fresh cut running across Quartz's face. "And don't let him go to the swamps, neither. I won't have him become a part of this."

Nicholas nodded, watching the wagon wind its way through the Stoker camp toward the service entrance to the tunnels, the hunger of the dragon settling in his stomach, and the frightening thoughts of the creature slipping from his mind.

Now what is going on?

***

Aaron watched, transfixed with awe, as the Boilers whirred away, flinging down the sleepers, bending and cutting the rails to fit, driving down the nails and compacting the ballast, then rolling forward to begin on the next section. They used no tools, their mechanical arms completing each assigned task with frightening speed. Under Aaron's feet, a length of perfectly straight, perfectly laid broad gauge railway track stretched back into the darkness.

"They've laid ten miles of track in two days," he breathed, unable to believe it.

"And it's straighter and more accurate than we could've ever done." William stared at the pristine sleepers below his boots, his mouth agape in bewilderment.

Aaron had spent all day Monday with Nicholas and other workers, getting to grips with the Boiler controls. After several false starts and a couple of disastrous hours where the Boilers laid half a mile of sleepers on *top* of the rail, they were running through their tasks faultlessly. Aaron had programmed ten of the machines to machines to widen the old sewer tunnel ready for the locomotive, and another five carried away the debris. He set a twenty-four-hour guard on the machines, but after two days and nights of endless work, his men reported no difficulties.

It's easy, he thought, coughing as the Boilers discharged a cloud of soot from their chimneys. *It's too easy.*

"Well," William dusted his hands on his overalls. "If that's all the work that needs doing, I'm going home."

"But, you can't—"

"I *can*, Aaron. My shift is over. I've done my job. There's nothing I can do here that the Boilers can't do faster and better." He yawned. "All this standing around watching machines work has made me awfully sleepy. You can tell Brunel for me that these Boilers are the greatest invention ever. He's gonna make a fortune."

"I will. Goodnight, William."

The greatest invention ever. Aaron wondered whether William was right. *They* are *remarkable. We'll be able to finish projects at lightening speed. Every engineer in England will want their own Boiler workforce.*

He watched the machines bang, slap, bend, drill, and hammer with their eerie, remarkable precision. They did not talk and joke with each other, as men did. They did not drop tools or curse or misread the measurements.

They're the perfect workers.
So where does that leave me?

***

Nicholas had taken over foreman duties on the

Chelsea section of the Wall, which now stretched five miles across the district, thanks to the speed and efficiency of the Boilers. He was thankful to escape the Engine Ward, knowing that Isambard had brought in a dragon.

He hadn't seen Aaron, and was grateful, for he didn't know how he could keep the whole affair from him. Had Aaron heard the dragon, or had Isambard taken it too far away? What was it even *doing* here? Why did Quartz not want Aaron to know about it?

As foreman, his main task was to oversee operation of the Boilers. The Boilers operated using what Brunel called a "program", an experimental term coined by Charles Babbage to mean a series of commands that the machine repeated over and over. Using a panel of switches and gears, Nicholas could make the Boilers twist, bend, secure, rivet, hold, and stack objects. He'd practised for half the night in the Boiler sheds, 'till he could program precise movements without mistakes. The units needed men watching them constantly, for they sometimes malfunctioned. But as Nicholas watched in amazement, in less than two hours, ten Boilers erected the skeleton of the next half-mile of Wall.

As construction raced forward, onlookers lined the streets to gawp at the Boilers. "What be those?" asked the greengrocer as he huffed under the weight of a cart heaped with vegetables.

Nicholas explained how the Boilers worked, and his face lit up. "Gor, that Brunel is a clever chap. I'd buy one for meownself, so I didn't have to push this cart no more."

By lunchtime they'd run out of iron, and with the

next shipment not due 'till the following day, the men packed up their tools and wheeled the Boilers — their fires still stoked — onto the wooden wagons, strapped them down, and drove them across the city for demolition work. Hundreds of buildings had to be torn down and streets pulled up to made way for the Wall, but the Boilers made light work of such an impossible chore.

"These here contraptions are all right," said one worker, giving the nearest Boiler an affectionate pat. "I wouldn't mind one in me own home, make light work of the woodpile, wouldn't ye?"

The Boiler, of course, made no reply, staring forward with an unseeing gaze. For the first time, Nicholas felt the knot of fear in his stomach untie itself. Maybe Isambard really had found a way to build the Wall on time. Maybe the Boilers would save all their lives.

***

The breakneck pace of construction had not escaped notice. What should have taken months was completed in days, and already the skeleton of the Wall stretched from the Engine Ward right across the Thames to Paddington. In Chelsea, whole blocks of residences were demolished to make way for an ornate gatehouse. Tongues wagged — *just who did this Brunel think he was?*

Each day, the Wall's growth increased exponentially as more and more Boilers poured from the factory sheds. Soon more than a hundred Boilers worked the Wall, each one doing the work of fifty men without food or drink or pay.

As the shell took shape and the men grew confident with the machines, Nicholas gave up his job as overseer and got to work on the exterior design. He commissioned a team of craftsmen from the Isis Sect to construct the pediments and steel arches that made up the classically inspired exterior.

The Free-Thinking Men's Blasphemous Brandy and Supper Society met at their regular time. Aaron and Nicholas presented their code to James, who thanked them gratefully and set about committing it to memory.

Discussion quickly turned to the speed and efficiency of the Boilers, and other applications for the machines. Buckland saw them as great earthmovers, able to shift tons of dirt or rock to reveal the hidden stories of the biological past. Holman pointed to their application as mechanical servants, eliminating the need for men and women to perform chores about the house. Even Dalton could see uses for the machines in his medical practice. Aaron remained silent, but his surly expression gave his opinion away.

"Brunel must be careful," Buckland warned. "Powerful men are watching this Wall, and they're not as easily impressed as the London mob."

Nicholas barely contributed to the discussion. He watched Aaron carefully, worried about his state of mind, wondering if he too had heard the voice of Brunel's dragon. Twice, he almost blurted out what he knew about Quartz, but he didn't want to anger Aaron further.

The Royal Society met on its usual night, but when Isambard and Nicholas entered the room all conversation died away. The faces that met Isambard's gaze did not show awe or admiration, but rather suspicion and fear. If he noticed the mood in the room, he cared not, and he carried on his sermons as if nothing were amiss. Nicholas knew the Council — who did not know of the King's secret railway — would not continue to allow Isambard such free rein.

***

Nicholas' suspicions proved correct. Ten days into the assigned month, Brunel received a summons from the Council. He was to report to Windsor Castle the very next day to answer questions by Council members on the alarming progress of the Wall.

"This is perfect," he said, folding the letter precisely and tucking it into his pocket.

"As always, friend, I am confused by your enthusiasm," replied Nicholas. "Surely the Council means to curtail your progress on the Wall, maybe even prosecute you?"

"Prosecute me for what? I've done nothing wrong. The Council members have not seen my Boilers in action, so they are right to hold my methods under suspicion. But tomorrow I can win their support." A Boiler unit stood silent and un-stoked in the corner of Brunel's workshop. Isambard walked over, took a rag soaked in oil, and began to lovingly rub away the dust that had accumulated on its surface. "Once they see my beauties operating, they'll all want one for themselves. Servants that don't have to be paid or whipped, workers that never tire — politicians are, above all else, greedy, lazy men. They would keep as much of their money in their own pockets as possible, and they will see the use in my Boilers, of that I am certain."

Nicholas had other things to think about. Tomorrow he would have his chance to see Brigitte again. With nerves wound tight as engine coils, he tried to formulate a plan to slip out of the meeting; perhaps when Brunel began his speech? He obtained his map of the castle and went over Maxwell's instructions 'till he had them memorized.

That night he tossed and turned, unable to sleep for his fears. *What if I am caught sneaking around the castle? What if Brigitte is caught and punished? What if she has changed her mind about me?*

Early the following morning, Nicholas arrived, bleary eyed, outside the Boiler factory, where Isambard waited for him beside a private carriage. A small crowd of Stokers peeked from inside the factory, curious about the commotion.

He had never seen the Presbyter so excited; Isambard jiggled back and forth on his feet, practically dancing while the men manoeuvred a Boiler inside a tall wooden crate, nailed it shut, and heaved it onto the back of the carriage. The two men climbed aboard and the driver sped toward Windsor.

Isambard kept up a stream of conversation about his Boilers and the Council and the progress on the Wall. Nicholas tried to listen, but his mind was on Brigitte. He shoved his hands into his pockets and balled them into fists, hoping Isambard hadn't noticed the sweat pouring down his forehead.

Once at Windsor, Nicholas walked beside Brunel across the quadrangle toward the official entrance of the state apartments, one arm clutching his rolls of drawings, the other fingering a delicate porcelain figurine of a duck — a present for Brigitte.

The castle loomed before them. Some of the most influential men in England loitered in the courtyard, the robes of the Councilmen flapping in the wind as they huddled in tight circles. Politicians in their smart tailored suits passed around cigars. Eyes landed on Isambard and Nicholas and quickly looked away. Nicholas shuddered. *Isambard will have a difficult time impressing this lot.*

Brunel wrung his hands together, his brow creased in concern. He stopped to address two men, politicians and lesser priests of the Isis sect who proudly wore Stoker pins in support of Brunel. They fell into quiet discussion and Nicholas tuned out, his mind on Brigitte.

A maid. He'd fallen for a maid. All hope of avoiding the pain of love, of re-integrating himself in his father's favour had died the moment he'd laid eyes on that beautiful face.

I do not care. My father gave up on me a long time ago. But lovely Brigitte, she is my future.

The minutes passed and the men congregated on the lawn began to move toward the castle entrance, walking a wide circle around Isambard as if he might poison them with his presence. Nicholas felt their eyes boring into him and wondered if he'd even be able to sneak away.

They passed through the entrance and into the Crimson Drawing Room. Many members of the Council had already gathered, huddled in groups of threes and fours and talking in hushed voices, scuttling around the King like compies over a fresh carcass. The

King slumped against his throne, his head lolling to the side, a thin line of drool extending from his mouth across the fine velvet upholstery. His wheeled chair had been placed just out of sight behind a heavy velvet curtain, and Sir Joseph Banks, his loyal Prime Minister, stood behind him, his face impassive as he tried to gently pull His Majesty back to a sitting position.

"Silence!" Banks barked. "His Majesty requires order in this room."

Men scrambled for the available seats. Isambard tried to pull Nicholas toward the front of the room, but he sat down in the back corner, closest to the open door, and shook his head.

"Please do not ask me to sit up there," he said. "In all these important men — there might be one who recognises my face. I will be here if you should need my help, but you do not need my help." He shoved the rolls of drawings into Brunel's arms.

Isambard nodded, and marched toward the front of the room. He straightened his back, squared his shoulders, and stepped forward to greet King George. After some official fanfare, the Council members took their seats, and Brunel spread out the plans and began pointing out the various features of the Wall. On their feet in no time, the Council members crowded around, jostling each other to squint at the complex drawings.

Forgetting his nerves, Brunel was in his element. His hands flew around his head, and his voice rose and fell with each point made. He stabbed the drawing with his fingers, stamped his foot, and stared every man directly in the eye. He wore no religious regalia; only a Stoker pin attached to his freshly pressed collar gave away his standing.

When he called for the crate containing the Boiler to be wheeled in, Nicholas knew it was now or never. Out of the corner of his eye, he noticed a dark shape ducking between the curtains at the edge of the room. He looked again. Maxwell waved at him from behind an arrangement of geraniums. Nicholas ducked away from the gaggle of Council members and approached the gardener.

"This is dangerous. I shouldn't wander off—"

"Tosh," Maxwell flapped his hand. "The King is bonkers and that lot are too interested in your master's preaching to notice your disappearance."

Nicholas looked back. Sure enough, Brunel had the entire room in his thrall. He had the crate open, and while the Boiler steamed up, he moved his hands over it, illustrating functions of various components, while the Council members pressed against each other to get a closer look.

"You're correct. Let's go."

He followed Maxwell down a labyrinth of high, vaulted halls, covered walkways and colonnades, across the North Terrace, and through another wing of residences, 'till they emerged in the oldest part of the castle, in front of the Curfew Tower, an ancient edifice of rough stone and impressive height. Shadowed by the Horseshoe Cloister, anything taking place in the courtyard could not be seen from the nearby St. George's Chapel. Wisteria crept up the stone walls, entwining themselves around the window lintels and arches. He stood on the steps and waited, heart pounding.

Maxwell disappeared and, a moment later, Brigitte

stepped out from behind a holly bush, and his breath caught in his throat. She looked even more lovely than she had before, dressed in a simple blue dress, her unruly brown hair lovingly tamed into a fashionable style, a few stray curls framing her smiling, heart-shaped face.

She walked slowly, her steps controlled. He swallowed, resisting the urge to run to her.

"My lady," he took her hand and kissed it.

"It is good to see you again, Mr. Rose," she replied, her voice husky, quiet.

They remained like this, his lips frozen on her fingers, for several moments, the wind swirling around them. Finally, reluctantly, he dropped her hand.

"I have something for you," he said, pressing the duck into her hands. "To remind you of our last meeting by the pond."

She turned it over and over, bringing it close to her face to admire the exquisite detail, running her finger along the tiny golden beak. "It's beautiful," she whispered, her voice choking. "You shouldn't have."

"Hey. why are you crying?" He wiped a glistening tear from the corner of her eye.

"No one has ever been so kind to me before."

He kissed her hand again. Out of the corner of his eye, he noticed Maxwell gesturing frantically.

"Get down!" he cried.

Grabbing Brigitte's hand, Nicholas yanked her below the planter box, just as Brunel and two of the Council members stormed through the courtyard, followed by Joseph Banks wheeling a screaming King George.

"You!" Brunel bellowed at the gardener. "Have you

seen my companion, Nicholas Rose? He disappeared from our meeting some minutes ago, but he can't have gone far."

"He cannot be allowed to wander the castle alone," Joseph Banks snapped over the King's anguished screams.

Nicholas squeezed Brigitte's hand. She covered her mouth with her hand and stared at him with wide, frightened eyes. *If they catch her here, with me, wearing that beautiful dress, she'll be punished and will lose her job, and it will be my fault.* He wouldn't be responsible for that. He pulled her tighter to him, straining to hear what was going on over the King's cries.

Why do they seem so anxious to find me? And why is the King screaming like that?

He peeked around the edge of the planter. Maxwell lay prostrate on the flagstones, mumbling that he didn't know where Nicholas was. Brunel and Banks towered over him. Banks' hands balled into fists and his face formed a shadow of rage. The Council members bent their heads together, whispering as they glanced from the King to Brunel to Maxwell, unsure of what was transpiring.

"Joseph, take him away," one of the Councillers demanded. Banks ignored him, and kicked Maxwell in the head.

"Tell me where he is, you sniveling blackguard!" he howled.

He kicked Maxwell again. This time, the King screeched, snapping the leather straps holding him into the chair and clawing from the grip of the two Council members. He pounced on Maxwell, who cried out and tried to roll to safety, but the King straddled him, clawing at his back with his long fingernails, shrieking like an animal. As Nicholas watched, horrified, his Majesty King George III bent down and tore a chunk of skin right from Maxwell's outstretched arm.

Maxwell howled. The men grabbed the King under his shoulders and dragged him off Maxwell. Guards rushed in from the castle and carried him — still shrieking and chewing on a chunk of Maxwell's arm — back into the castle.

"Clean this mess up," Banks hissed at Maxwell, stomping away.

Brigitte whimpered. Nicholas, heart pounding, pulled her to his breast, pressing his finger against her lips to stop her crying out.

Brunel did not follow the others back inside. Even though he could no longer see Isambard, Nicholas could feel his gaze searching the flower beds, his boot tapping against the paving stones.

"I know you're there, Nicholas," he said. "I don't understand why you left the meeting and upset His Majesty like this. I'm very disappointed in you."

He turned on his heels and disappeared into the castle.

Brigitte let out a sob and rushed to help Maxwell. He lay on his side, clutching his arm where the King had bitten him, holding the jagged flaps of skin together in an attempt to stop the bleeding. Blood pooled beneath him, seeping between the cracks in the cobbles.

"Miss Julie will fix you right up, Maxwell," Brigitte said, wrapping his arm around her shoulders and hoisting him to his feet. He moaned as blood splattered the front of her dress. Nicholas grabbed his other arm, meaning to steady him, but Brigitte pushed him away.

"I can manage, Nicholas. You must go to Brunel. Tell him you were lost wandering the gardens." She pointed to the southern entrance to the courtyard. "Head toward the round tower, quickly now, and find the gateway into the Upper Ward. You should come out near the South Wing in the Quadrangle. That way, it will look as if you went to look at the Norman gatehouse and got lost."

"Brigitte, I—"

"Go!" Maxwell stared up at him with pleading eyes. She turned away and began hobbling toward the entrance.

What could he do but go?

***

Her heart pounding, Brigitte helped the shaking gardener to his feet. Clutching his wound, he rested his weight against her, and she shuffled him toward the entrance to the servants' chambers.

"I must—" he wheezed, gesturing to the bloodstain on the flagstones.

"Leave it, you silly old fool. I'll send Cassandra to clean it off." She glanced over her shoulder, but Nicholas had gone.

She brought him to Miss Julie in the kitchens, who dropped her rolling pin in surprise. "You're dripping blood in the clotted cream!"

Maxwell responded by slumping hard against Brigitte's shoulder. His eyes rolled back in his head, and he collapsed on the floor with a mighty thud.

Brigitte screamed.

Miss Julie grabbed one of his limp arms and heaved him into a sitting position, propping him up with a flour sack. She fanned his face while glaring at Brigitte. "What on earth happened, child?"

"The King, he *bit* Maxwell." Brigitte clamped down on her lower lip to keep from crying. "It was awful."

Miss Julie frowned as she inspected the wound. When she touched the edge, Maxwell shuddered. Blood pooled under his breeches and spread across the floor.

"Cassandra!" Miss Julie called. The girl came running in from the wash-house next door, skidding to a stop when she saw Maxwell.

"Maxwell will need some whisky. Bring us the whole bottle from the shelf."

"And then go out to the Curfew Tower courtyard and clean up the mess," Brigitte added.

Her face pale, Cassandra rushed off.

Miss Julie got out her sewing kit and threaded up a needle. When Cassandra returned with the whisky, she ordered Brigitte to wet Maxwell's lips with the dark liquid, and hold it under his nose 'till he came round. Miss Julie worked quickly, her deft fingers stitching together the gaping wound. She was wrapping his arm in a bandage when Maxwell opened his eyes.

"What … what happened?"

"The King bit you, in the courtyard, do you remember?" Miss Julie smoothed back his hair. "You'll be right now."

"If only it was that simple, Miss Julie. I fear this is the end for me."

"Nonsense, it's just a bite. I'll have you right in no time."

"You don't understand. The King, he ..."

"What, Maxwell, *what?*" Brigitte grabbed his shoulder and shook him, but his eyes glazed over and he slumped forward, collapsing against the floor.

***

Brunel didn't say a word to Nicholas in the carriage back to the Engine Ward, which made Nicholas apprehensive. He tried to meet the Presbyter's eyes, but Brunel seemed thoroughly engaged scribbling neat rows of sums down one margin of his ledger.

Finally, the carriage passed through the gates of Engine Ward and pulled up outside the Chimney. Brunel set his top hat astride his head and said to Nicholas, "Won't you join me at the pulpit?" It wasn't a question.

Nicholas followed Brunel into the empty church. Brunel ascended the stairs at a leisurely pace, lighting the candles from his Argand lamp on the way. He hummed a tune under his breath, knowing his easy presence was making Nicholas more nervous than ever.

Sweat poured down Nicholas' face. His stomach knotted in on itself. He caught his boot on the steps and stumbled, knocking a candle over and spilling a trail of hot wax down the narrow steps.

Brunel turned around and saw the upset candle. "Tsk," he said. "You are upsetting the order of things tonight."

Nicholas had never been to the pulpit before. They stood on a thin platform, twenty feet above the church, surrounded on four sides by a low shelf containing metalworking tools, worn leather journals and rolls of drawings, all jammed in together in lackadaisical fashion. Brunel paced the length of the pulpit three times. Silence fell, the only sound his footsteps on the grating, and the murmurs of far-off animals.

Finally Brunel spoke, gesturing with his hand to the church below. "Do you see all this?"

"Yes—"

"You're not looking!" Brunel grabbed Nicholas behind the neck, whirled him around, and shoved his head far out of the side of the platform. His arms pinned beneath him, Nicholas had no way of pulling himself back. Brunel pushed him out even further, 'till his feet flailed in the air and he was completely at the mercy of the Presbyter. Two coded plates — notes from the last Supper Club meeting — fell from his pocket and clattered across the grate. His head spun as he watched the floor of the church — the pews, the altar filled with candles and offerings — dance around him. His heart pounded in his throat. *Please, Isambard, don't let go!*

"I can fill this room to bursting with people, Nicholas. *My* people. They love me, *worship* me, and they will do whatever I ask of them. Many of them would gladly kill for the privileges I now show you, Nicholas."

"I—I—"

"No. Don't talk." Brunel dug his nails into Nicholas' arm. "I don't know what you thought you were doing, going off with that gardener, but you were at the castle by *my* grace, and what you did makes me look untrustworthy. A lot of those Councillors don't believe I should have been allowed a church at all, let alone become a Presbyter or be in charge of this Wall. When you strolled away, when they had to break up the meeting to search the castle grounds for you, they think, 'Brunel can't even control those in his employ. He's not cut out to control a church.' They could strip me of my power at any moment, and doom the Stokers to a life of toil. Do you *see?* Do you understand why you can't do this?"

"Y—yes." Nicholas' ears pounded, as the blood rushed through his head, pounding against his skull. His vision swayed and blurred.

"Good." Brunel pulled him back. Dizzy, Nicholas tripped over his own foot and fell to his knees on the grating. Brunel reached down a hand to help him up.

"We've worked so hard for all this," he said. "Not just myself, but you, and Aaron, and all the Stokers. I couldn't bear to see it stripped away now."

"I understand, and I apologise. I don't know what's come over me." He did know, of course, but he couldn't tell Brunel about Brigitte. The engineer would not understand.

Brunel bent down and picked up the two plates, running his fingers over the cold metal. "What are these?"

"It's … a code." Nicholas thought it wise not to lie to Brunel. "Aaron and I worked on it together. We host these monthly dinner parties—"

"The Free-Thinking Men's Blasphemous Brandy and Supper Society?"

"How do you know about that?"

Brunel squinted at the plates. "Buckland is not a man easily given to concealing secrets. It is no matter; I see no reason to report your club to the Royal Society. But why print the code on plates like this?"

"So James can read them with his fingers."

"Genius." Brunel stuffed both plates into his pocket. "You will teach me this code, Nicholas, but not now. You've been distracted this past week. You should rest for a few days. Maybe call a doctor. The Boilers will finish the Wall, but we have much work still to do, and I can't have my favourite architect ill. Go home, and return to me when you feel clear again."

He dismissed Nicholas, swinging open the heavy church door. A biting cold swooped inside, and as Nicholas stepped out, and tipped his hat to Brunel, he felt the hairs on his arms stand up.

Pulling his coat tightly around him, he stepped into the waiting carriage and told the driver to take him home. He pulled down his sleeve and fingered the welts on his arms. *I was selfish,* he realised. *I should never have left the meeting. I would not forgive myself if I destroy everything Brunel and Aaron have worked for.*

Brigitte and I must be more careful.

***

The Times, London, 17 August, 1830

LONDON WALL TO BE COMPLETED IN TIME FOR 1830 SEASON

Isambard Kingdom Brunel, the engineer charged

with the task of ridding London of the dragon menace, should like to inform all interested parties that the London Wall will be completed on Tuesday 24 August, 1830, in seven days' time, several months ahead of schedule.

Construction of the Wall began only three weeks ago, and has moved at an unprecedented pace. Brunel credits the speed of construction to his newest innovation. "The Boiler is a simple machine — a worker who does not eat, sleep or rest. Powered by a fire within the belly, the Boiler can be set upon some specific task, which it then pursues with relentless precision until it is told to cease or runs out of fuel. One hundred of these units have done in three weeks what five hundred men could not complete in a year."

The Great Conductor Presbyter has been beset by requests to purchase Boilers. So far, he has turned away all engineers and manufactures offering money. "I have not yet perfected the Boiler unit," he said. "But when the Wall is complete, I shall have time to improve their workings, and my machines shall be made available on the open market."

Celebrations to mark the completion of the Dragon Wall will begin with a Sermon by Presbyter Brunel in Stephenson's Cathedral, followed by a Grand Supper at the Royal Society and a street parade. Although the internal railroad loop and gatehouses are not yet complete, London residents can expect to be riding across the city in their own luxurious broad gauge carriages by the end of the season.

***

Brigitte crawled under the ornate oak table on hands and knees, pulling her bucket into the awkward space between the footrests. Water sloshed over the sides, soaking the front of her pinafore. She sighed, and went back to scrubbing at the muddy footprints that criss-crossed the marble floors. Even though there hadn't been an official banquet in weeks, the room had evidently been in use recently. Brigitte stared at the neat path of brown splotches running from the door to the table to the corners of the tapestry and back, wondering how someone could have dined in this hall and forgotten to wash their shoes.

The King hadn't left his chambers in several days, and not one of the servants had been allowed past the guarded doors of his private wing. After what he did to Maxwell, Brigitte constantly looked over her shoulder, expecting at any moment to see his wheeled chair looming down on her, his face inches from her own, teeth bared, ready to strike. *And Nicholas ...* Nicholas …

The way he threw me behind that bush, shielded me with his own body so they couldn't see me, lied to his friend Brunel to protect me and—

—that's odd.

She stood up, dropping the sponge back into the bucket, barely noticing the water splashing against her legs. She'd cleaned away the muddy prints from under the table to where they stopped in the corner — just beneath the plinth holding one of the two six-foot high lead candelabras. Here the prints grew confused, as men — at least two — had crossed and circled each other. But that wasn't what had caught Brigitte's attention.

The candelabrum was gone.

A glance to the other corner of the room revealed

the second candelabrum was also missing. Heart pounding, she raced down the stairs to the kitchens, anxious to report the disappearance as soon as possible, lest she be accused of stealing them herself.

"Miss Julie. Miss Julie?"

The portly woman looked up from kneading bread with a sour look, and before she could reprimand her from returning from her duties so prematurely, Brigitte blurted out. "The lead candelabras in the south dining hall have disappeared."

"Nonsense, those weigh a pretty ton. A grown man would struggle to carry one of those from the castle, and to do so without being noticed—"

"There are muddy footprints everywhere, and I swear the candlesticks are no longer there! You must look for yourself. This is awful big trouble, isn't it?"

"Trouble indeed, child, if what you say is true. The last time a piece of silverware disappeared, we all had our wages docked for a month. Turns out Betty Oxtrot had put a dish back in with the terrines by accident."

"We didn't find it 'till the Christmas feast! Miss Julie was fuming," giggled Cassandra. "She didn't half give her an earful."

"Belted that little strumpet right side of the head," said Miss Julie sternly. "Not that it knocked any sense into her. One ought to be less concerned about the contents of the porter's trousers and more concerned about one's duties."

Brigitte thought of Nicholas, and the beautiful china duck hiding beneath her pillow, and felt her ears flush red.

"Fetch Maxwell." Miss Julie turned back to the kneading. "And we'll investigate."

Brigitte found the gnarled gardener tidying the hedges around the pleasure gardens. He worked slowly, his left arm tied in a sling. His recovery from the bite had been swift, thanks to Miss Julie's intervention, but since the incident he'd seemed different — distant, lifeless, a shade of the Maxwell she'd loved.

She tapped him on the shoulder, and he turned. The skin on his face pulled around his eyes, stretched and thin. Strange blisters marked his cheeks. She recoiled in surprise. *Such a change over only a week.*

"How are you feeling?"

"Never better, Miss Brigitte." He gave a forced smile, leaning the shovel against his leg and wiping sweat from his forehead with his free hand. When his fingers passed over his skin, they left red welts behind.

"You seem … out of sorts. Maybe we should—"

"No!" She jumped at the anger in his voice. "I mean, it's nothing to worry about. I'm just feeling a little lifeless. Misbalanced humours from all the blood loss. I'll be right within the week. Now, what did you come running out here to tell me?"

"Miss Julie needs you in the castle," she said. "Someone's stolen the lead candlesticks, and we need your help to investigate."

"No help needed," he bent over his shovel. "I know who did it."

"Who?"

"The King. Or, more precisely, the King's men, on orders of the King. I saw five of them struggling down the hall with one last night."

"Whatever for?"

He shrugged. "Who am I to understand the mind

of a king?" His gaze fell on the sling on his arm, and he sighed.

As he turned back to the garden, his eyes met hers, and she saw a deep fear there. Even though it was a warm day, and she was wearing her cloak, Brigitte shivered.

***

At precisely eleven minutes past midnight, the bell rang in the servants' quarters. Brigitte rubbed sleep from her eyes, and went to Miss Julie's room, to find her still snoring. She shook Miss Julie awake.

"It's the King again, Miss. Do you think he's found out about the candelabras?"

"If you must find out, you can answer him yourself, and let me return to my dreams of saucy French soldiers." Miss Julie folded the pillow over her head.

As Brigitte tiptoed from the room, she could make out Miss Julie mumbling "Oh, Roberto …."

She tiptoed through the maze of corridors, toward the King's chamber in the western wing. Her footsteps echoed through the high arches and cavern-like spaces. The walls seemed to lean inward, closing around her as if they were going to swallow her up. The castle frightened her at night. The beautiful objects cast eerie shadows and every footstep groaned and creaked ominously.

Tonight, the darkness was positively terrifying. Over the shudders of the old castle was the faint, muffled sound of a woman screaming. Brigitte's pulse pounded in her ears.

As she neared the corridor, she passed through the outer doors, guarded by three guards, one snoring loudly, the other two playing whist. They looked up, their faces guilty, as she approached.

"He rang for housekeeping," she declared.

"I'm might sure he did," the younger of the two whist players winced. "Been ringing for all sorts during the dead of night, has His Majesty."

Voices echoed from the hall behind her. A woman screamed, loudly and frightfully close, the piercing sound quickly muffled. Brigitte felt a lump rise in her throat.

"If you want my advice," the younger guard said, "don't enter his chamber, and don't look at anything, lest you wish your eyes be struck from your head."

They waved her through, and she tiptoed down the hall, wishing she could muffle the clap-clap of her shoes against the polished Italian marble. She heard another sound, more like a howl than a scream, so high and piercing. It shook the chandeliers suspended from the ceiling. She took a deep breath, squared her shoulders, and tried to calm her racing heart as she pushed the door to the King's chamber open a crack.

"Excuse me, Your Majesty, you rang for—"

"Lead!" the King screamed. "Bring me lead, now!" She heard scuffling, and the sound of a woman's cries muffled. She dared to peek through the crack, and saw a pair of naked, feminine legs twitching against the red silks of the royal bed. Hands reached and scratched at the flesh, raising thick cuts and gashes which sprayed blood onto the carpet. Brigitte gasped and turned away.

"Lead? Sir, I don't understand—"

"You'll be next!" King George roared. "Soon, you'll all taste the lead! Now, bring me a metallic treat, woman!"

Frightened, Brigitte turned away, slammed the door and dashed back down the hall, her eyes scanning every surface for a lead object. It was then she noticed something strange: every lead object in the opulent hall had been removed — the wall sconces, the candlesticks, even the lion's heads inlaid into the sideboard had been gouged from their settings.

She spied the doorway to the King's dressing room and remembered he kept a lead hat stand in the corner. Trembling, she reached for the door handle, only to discover that, too had been removed.

"You shouldn't go in there, Miss."

Brigitte jumped. "Maxwell! You didn't half give me a fright. What are you doing here?"

The hunched gardener grabbed her by the shoulders. "Did he bite you?"

"What? Maxwell, get your hands off me—"

"*Did he bite you?* Miss, it's very important." The moonlight in the windows above lit his features, gaunt and twisted, his cheeks and lips now pocketed with blisters and his teeth stained black.

"The King? He didn't lay a hand on me, but he was acting frightfully odd. He had a woman with him, and I saw—" she shuddered. "He has sent me to fetch him something made of lead. I remembered the old hat stand."

"He ate that a month ago, Miss Brigitte. Come with me." He hobbled off down the hall.

"He *ate* it? You're not making any sense. Maxwell, what's going on?" He tugged on her sleeve. "Maxwell,

I can't. I have to get back—" He turned again, raised his finger to his lips, and gestured for her to follow.

They crept past the door to the King's chamber, still alive with scufflings and snarlings, and rounded another corner. Maxwell threw open the doors to the private reception hall and hobbled across the pristine marble floor, leaving a trail of grubby boot prints in his wake. Brigitte hurried after him, her eyes scanning every surface for a small scrap of lead.

They passed through a series of ornate receiving rooms, and at last Maxwell pulled back a velvet curtain to reveal a long, narrow corridor. Horrible sounds issued from within — unsavoury creatures demanding to be free.

Before she could protest, he grabbed her arm and yanked her inside. As her eyes adjusted to the gloom, she saw the corridor was boarded on both sides with rows of thick, barred doors. From behind each door, something howled and pounded and screeched.

"What are they?" she breathed.

"Look for yourself."

Handing her his lantern, he cupped his hands and she stood on them, and he lifted her up 'till she was eye level with the thin slit at the top of the door. She stared down into a cell, resting the lantern on the ledge and directing the light downward. She gasped at the full magnitude of what presented itself.

It was a man. At least, it had once been a man. Now it circled and snarled and hissed like a monster, crawling on all fours in an ocean of its own foulness. Filth and blood caked the walls, and as she watched, paralysed in terror, it reared up toward her, screaming as it clawed at the door in its desperation to reach her.

Blood flowed from its cracked fingernails, and it snapped and gashed its burnt, blackened teeth.

It was naked, save the blisters and burns that caked every inch of its body, and the strange metal protrusions which glowed through its cracked skin.

It lunged for her again, clawing at the door just below the slit. She screamed in terror and jerked back, losing her balance and toppling to the ground. Maxwell bent down to pick her up, steadying her with his good hand as she tried to stop shaking.

"What *are* they?"

"I call them the Sunken, but they were like us once. Gardeners, servants, women of the night. That one down here—", he pointed at the door, "was the ambassador of China. Now they are monsters."

"But — *how?"*

"The King, Miss Brigitte. They enter his private chambers as humans, and they emerge … as these — these aberrations! They crave anything made of blood or lead. He feeds them lumps of heated metal that scorch their skin and burn their insides, but they do not care. The more they consume the stronger and less human they become. The King calls them his lead children. And his lust grows stronger. Night after night he calls for more, more blood, more lead." He hung his head. "I have found women in the village for him … I have done horrible things …."

"But tonight you saved me."

"Yes, one life I have saved," Maxwell said, letting out a wretched sigh, "for all those I've helped ruin. For the ruin I've done to myself."

"Maxwell, no—"

He lifted his cast off his shoulder and unwound the

bandages. When Brigitte saw what had become of the bite, her stomach turned.

His arm was completely black. The skin was no longer soft, but burnt and flaking away in crispy chunks. Miss Julie's careful stitches had been ripped out, and the hole stuffed with balls of lead, the leathery, blackened skin growing over the top of them, sealing them inside his body. She covered her mouth, struggling to keep back the bile rising in her throat.

"The King's Physician," he said, giving a wan smile. "He fixed me up good and proper."

"Maxwell, *no.*" Tears steamed down her cheeks. She reached out a shaking hand to touch the protrusion, but he slapped her away.

"Tis fitting, Miss Brigitte. For my crimes."

"You weren't to know, Maxwell." She touched his shoulder. "Can we help them?"

"These … they are beyond help. They will gnaw their own arms off to taste the blood again. They are never full, never sated. The King has more such chambers, and every week the dungeon swells with more of their number. Soon, there will be no one left in Windsor Castle who does not crave the taste of metal or the blood of the living."

"And you, Maxwell?"

He laughed bitterly. "Do not fear for me, Miss Brigitte. You have done me kindness enough."

"I can't just do *nothing*!"

"You must go to your man, Miss Brigitte — your handsome gentleman who writes the notes. You must go away with him, far away from the castle, and never return. If the King lays eyes on you, young and pretty and trembling in fear, I will find you locked away in one of these rooms, and that is more than I can bear."

"But Miss Julie, and Cassandra and … and *you*? What will become of you, Maxwell? I cannot leave the castle without you."

"I will help them. I will try … but your man, he will know what to do." Maxwell said. "I've seen him with the engineer, Brunel. An important man is Brunel. The King trusts him, but Brunel has power over him. Brunel has been in secret to the King's chambers, late at night, many times, but he has not become one of the Sunken. And whenever he leaves the castle, the King is silent. He does not seek the blood. He sleeps. It is the only time he sleeps."

"I can't leave!"

"You must. Immediately. Tonight. Before he calls for you again."

***

She didn't even have time to return to her room to pack her things. Maxwell led her to a staircase she'd never seen before, hidden behind a painting in the Crimson Drawing Room. "This leads down to the cellar," he said. "From there, take the south tunnel toward the gate. It's locked, but you should be able to break through easily enough. Once you're outside, go to the town — there should still be someone at the pub — and find a coach into London."

"My money is back in my room."

"Here." He pressed some coins into the pocket of her nightdress. "It's not much, but should see you safely to London. Be careful, Miss Brigitte."

"I will. Maxwell, don't—" Tears stung her eyes.

He gave her a gruff pat on the shoulder, then pushed her onto the stairway. "None of that now." He slammed the door shut behind her, plunging her into darkness.

She placed a hand on each wall and felt her way with her feet. The stone steps, more crooked and sharp than the other servants' passages in the castle, which had been worn smooth with centuries of constant use, coiled around in a tight spiral. As she descended, threads of a spider's web caught on her face, and something fluttered past her shoulder. She cried out, her foot slipping on the step. She grabbed the wall and regained her balance, her heart pounding against her chest.

Finally, the floor levelled out, and she walked into a heavy wooden door. Feeling around for the latch, she discovered it unlocked, and pushed the bolt through and hurried into the cellar.

And then she heard the howling.

She ran. Past the stacks of beer and wine barrels, past the storerooms of grain, barley, and brandy, past the dark corners concealing nests of compies. Blindly, she criss-crossed through the maze of corridors, surrounded by the shrieks of the Sunken.

She careened around a corner, knowing that she was now completely lost, and found herself in the dungeon. "No!" she screamed, sinking to her knees in horror.

Maxwell had spoken the truth. The Sunken filled every cell, their charred faces snarling from the depths. Blackened limbs flailed through the bars, pawing at the air in their desperate attempt to devour her. They shook the bars with such ferocity she was certain they would tear the castle down.

They can smell me, she realised. *They know I'm not one of them, and they're baying for my blood.*

But the most horrific thing of all was the sound. The high, inhuman wail, the desperate scraping as they gnashed their teeth against the iron bars, the cracking of bones as they crushed one another in their frenzy.

But surely, they can't—

Something clattered against the stone floor. A section of the rotting door to one of the older cells had fallen away. Footsteps pounded down the hall, and two of the Sunken, spittle dribbling from their gaping, blackened mouths, raced down the corridor toward her.

Sobbing, she whirled from the frightful sight, and fled back up the corridor.

I'm dead. I'm going to die and they're going to eat me and turn me into one of them—

She poured on speed. The south tunnel — she would have to reach it before they caught her. *You can lock it behind you.*

Think, Brigitte, think. You know where the south tunnel is.

Back to the cellar. Left, right, left. *Where is it?* She scrambled along another passage, her hands scraping along the bare stone walls. *Not this way.* She doubled back, dove into the right corridor, and there, before her, was the door to the south tunnel. It was blocked with a heavy wooden door.

Yes, yes!

She grabbed the handle and pulled. Nothing. It wouldn't budge. She fumbled around the rotting edges, found the latch, and pulled it across. Still nothing.

Behind her, the Sunken flung themselves around

the corner, scraping their long fingernails against the stone walls. They saw her and sprinted down the tunnel, pulling each other back in a desperate attempt to be the first to devour her.

She screamed, leaned against the door, and fell backward.

Crying in relief, she heaved the door shut and slid the bolt through, just as the Sunken crashed against it.

She ran on, one hand on the ceiling, one on the wall, feeling her way. She couldn't see a thing. These tunnels had been dug many centuries before, as an escape route for the King should the castle walls be breached. Unlike the rest of the cellar, the walls were rough rock, which scraped her hands raw. Still she ran, not knowing how long that door would hold the Sunken back.

Her foot kicked something hard, and it screeched and scuttled away. Something warm fluttered past her face. She squeezed her eyes shut, pushing down the panic.

She slammed into something at full speed, sending her sprawling across the tunnel floor and knocking the wind out of her. Gasping for breath, she reached with both hands to feel out the obstacle. Wood, iron hinges, a heavy lock. It was the door. The door to freedom!

She lifted the padlock and dropped it against the wood, the heavy clatter echoing down the tunnel. *Locked, just as Maxwell said.* He'd also said she'd be able to get through, but how? *I can't go back. Think, Brigitte — there must be a way through this door.*

Feeling with her hands, she searched the hinges for signs of weakness. They had rusted at the edges, but were still solidly attached to the wood and the rock.

Next, she checked the lock. Sure enough, it, too, had rusted, and, although the bolt still remained solid, a deep gash had been gouged in the rock where it bit into the wall. She pressed her weight against the door, and the whole bolt slid back and forth.

She emptied the pockets of her apron. *Please let it be here ... yes!* She held a single brass hairpin, the one she'd worn on her first date with Nicholas.

Bending back the pin, she went to work, scraping the rust from the edge of the lock and widening that gap between it and the rock as much as she could.

She pushed and pulled the door some more, relishing the scrape of rusted metal against the soft rock. She nearly had it. More chipping, more wriggling, and it popped free and swung open, revealing a short stone staircase and a shaft of brilliant moonlight.

She raced up the stairs, and along a path that wound through the forested area to the south of the castle. Lights twinkled on the horizon, just visible between the trees. She headed toward them, hoping the villagers would be well-disposed toward her.

PART II:
THE ENGINE

1820

Boys lined both sides of the dock, some with parents or nannies in tow. Some who'd purchased commissions into the higher ranks wore new uniforms, pressed and neat. Others, like Nicholas, stood alone in their skivvies, folding and unfolding their papers and staring up at the tall ships with worried expressions. The new English flag flew from every mast — that amorphous hodge-podge of symbols representing the ten new sects earning scowls of disapproval from the older veterans.

Overhead, seagulls circled, their thoughts flitting in and out of his head. They'd been summoned by the commotion on the docks — they knew tall ships and crowds of people meant food.

Beside him, James was so excited he could hardly stand still. His mother kept bending down to smooth his shirt. A stout, stern-faced woman, she'd dealt with a lot in recent years. She was a rarity among Stokers, for she'd married outside the sect and made a good life for herself in the city, until tragedy struck. Her husband — James' father — was an officer in the

King's Royal Guard, and had been killed during a raid of an underground Anglican service. His family, who had opposed the marriage to one of the "Dirty Folk", had sent her packing back to the Engine Ward, but not before securing a commission for James as a Naval Volunteer — a fast-track post to an officer's rank. All he'd had to do was survive two years in the Engine Ward, two years under Marc Brunel's tutelage, until he was old enough to go to sea. And now here he was, buttons all shiny, about to be an adventurer for real.

Nicholas — who would have to work his way up from the bottom if he had any hope of becoming an officer — watched her fuss over James, and he longed for his own family. His father had thought him unfit for service, being the scrawnier of the two sons, but he would have bought Nicholas a military commission anyway; not in the Navy, but with the 62nd Wiltshire (his father's own regiment), had he asked for it. But now he would have to make his way without his father's money and influence.

He gazed up, and up, and up at his new home — the flagship *HMS Euryalus*, her imposing hull looming overhead — a solid wall of wood and iron, a veritable floating fortress with four decks of guns. He had to lean right back to catch a glimpse of the tangles of rope and sails jutting at all angles from the masts. Fear gripped his chest. *I know nothing about sailing. What if I fall?*

Isambard stood beside him, hands in the pockets of his green Stoker overalls, his face and sleeves stained with coal. Master Brunel was still being held for questioning regarding Henry's death, and Nicholas wouldn't even get the chance to say *goodbye,* or *thank you.* But Isambard stood on the side of the dock to see them off, his lithe frame jostled in the careless pushing of the more well-to-do children.

"Look at him." He pointed to James, who had pulled his sketchbook out and was scribbling a drawing of the nearest frigate. "I've never seen him so happy."

"All he's ever wanted is to be an adventurer." Nicholas smiled up at the ships that would bear them across the ocean to America. "At least one of us will have a dream come true."

Isambard looked away. "Will you write?" he asked, staring at his shoes.

"As often as I am able." Nicholas wanted to reach out, to embrace Isambard, to cry the tears that threatened to leak from his eyes. But Isambard would not look at him, and Nicholas knew the bond between them stood on a razor's edge. He wanted to offer some kindness, some words of encouragement about Isambard's father, but he could find none that bridged the gap that now widened between them. Instead, he too stared at his boots, the guilt in his heart widening ever further.

"Are you ready?" James reached across and squeezed Nicholas' hand. "They're calling for us to board. I'm over there on the *Cambrian*. She's smaller than yours, but she'll see plenty of action, I'm sure."

Nicholas gathered up his small rucksack, as heavy on his shoulders as a boulder, and, with a last forlorn wave to Isambard and James, he clambered up the gangway to meet his new destiny.

***

"Just a little to the left," Isambard hissed, the tread of his boot shifting uncomfortably into Aaron's shoulder.

Aaron gritted his teeth. Bracing his shaking legs against the brick schoolhouse, he shuffled a few inches left, his shoulders screaming under the full impact of his friend's weight.

"Steady!" Droplets of ink splashed onto Aaron's shirt. He sighed, a strangled sound, his lungs carrying no air. His mother would hang him when she saw the stains.

"I can't hold much longer," Aaron winced. The skin on his right shoulder pinched between his collarbone and Isambard's boot. He leaned his whole body into the wall of the schoolhouse, hoping the lesson wouldn't go overtime.

As Stokers, they were expected to learn their duties from their parents, and weren't permitted into the engineering schools. That was how they had met — Aaron used to sit on the overpass behind the Stoker camp and watch the children of the other sects lining up for classes, their satchels and slates tucked under their skinny arms. One day, he showed up to his usual spot, only to find it occupied by a boy a little older than he, his gaze fixated on the students, tears running unnoticed down his cheeks.

"I'm sorry," said Aaron. "I didn't mean to disturb you." He turned to depart, but the boy spoke.

"Why did you come here? To watch the students?"

Aaron backed away, not wanting to answer. He didn't want to get in trouble. But the boy didn't scold him. Instead, he sighed. "That's why I come here, sometimes. I used to go to school, you know."

Aaron glanced at the boy's green overalls, two sizes too big and identical to his own, wondering how he'd been able to attend a school. Suddenly, he understood. "You were one of Master Brunel's students? My brother Henry went to his school. I wanted to go too, one day, but Henry has gone and got himself killed and they locked Master Brunel away—"

"Marc Brunel is my father." The boy looked away.

"Oh." Aaron didn't know what to say to that. The boy patted the space on the girder beside him, and Aaron sat down. "I'm Isambard," the boy said, offering his hand.

"I'm Aaron. I work in the western furnaces." He didn't mention that he was still only a coal-boy — he was so clumsy around machines he couldn't be trusted with any other task.

"I'm on maintenance team C. Stephenson's church." Isambard spat out the Messiah's name as if it were poison in his mouth. "Sometimes I hide in the broom cupboard and listen to his lectures."

"Why would you do that?"

Isambard stared at him, his gaze fixed and unnerving. "You cannot tell a soul, Aaron."

"I won't."

"I'm going to make a locomotive, just like Stephenson. Only I aim to make mine better."

Afterward, the pair found each other on the overbridge each day, and they would sit and watch and talk and dream. As much as Aaron wished he could cast aside his coal shovel and enter those walls to learn about arithmetic and biology and geography, Isambard wished it more. He cursed his lineage with such ferocity that Aaron at times feared he hated their people.

It was not the Stokers, but the church for which Isambard reserved his ire. After all, it was the conservatism of Great Conductor's priests — appalled at Marc Brunel's radical school — that had demanded his father's arrest. And the church certainly treated the two boys like a pair of pariahs: Aaron with his head in the clouds and his clumsy hands would have made a better farmer than a Stoker; and Isambard, with his surly indifference and unflattering habit of pointing out the mistakes of priests much older and more powerful than himself … well, no one quite knew what to do with Isambard. Even the Stoker children avoided them, when they weren't chasing after them, hurling rocks and cruel words.

And so, they found comfort in each other, though in many ways they didn't understand each other at all. Isambard — like his father — tested the boundaries of Stoker society. His mind connected ideas, toyed with tangents of thought, and although he knew he wasn't supposed to and he was constantly being beaten for it, he couldn't help inventing. He would take a machine apart, figure out how it worked, and put it back together so it worked more efficiently than before. He had a natural way with machines, as if his very mind worked on gears and pistons.

Aaron, on the other hand, spent his youth trying to stay as far from machines as possible. He had only to glance at a mechanism for it to seize and break down. He found the heat and steel stifling, pushing in on him so he couldn't breathe. Sometimes with Isambard, but often alone, he would slip unnoticed through the fences and wander through the city. He often found himself meandering around the many public gardens, ducking between the rose bushes at Kensington or sitting by the duck pond in Hyde Park.

It was here, in these parks, when he first heard — truly *heard* — the voices of the animals. He spent hours following the ducks inside his head, mapping their relationships and thoughts. Far from crowding his head, the voices calmed him. They eased the headaches caused by the constant pounding of pistons and roaring of furnaces.

With the exception of a few chittering compies — tiny feathered dragons who swarmed around food scraps and loved to steal bolts from the workshop floor — the only animals that entered the Engine Ward were already dead — the pigs and cattle put to the flame for dinner. Out here, Aaron felt for the first time as though the world were truly alive.

Despite their differences, the two boys had one thing in common. More than anything, they both desired to escape from Engine Ward forever. And that was why Aaron found himself teetering precariously under the window of a Metic Engineering School with a heavy future Presbyter standing on his shoulders, frantically scribbling down the lessons from the blackboard inside.

"Isambard? My shoulders are separating."

The scribbling intensified. "Got it!" Isambard jumped down, landing on his feet in the damp garden. Aaron slumped against the wall and rubbed his aching shoulders.

"Go on, let's see it, then."

With a smile as wide as a furnace door, Isambard

held up the sketch. A crude drawing of a steam locomotive occupied the entire page; every inch of white paper covered in scribbled calculations and scrawled notations. Aaron squinted, wondering how Isambard planned to make sense of it.

"This is what we're going to make," Isambard said, his smile growing wide. "Except we're going to make it better."

***

Aaron didn't doubt Isambard's determination. If his friend set his mind to something, he would find a way to accomplish it, rules and consequences be dammed. He inherited this trait from his father, who flouted convention at every turn.

Marc Brunel had a reputation. And no Stoker alive wanted one of those. Isambard's father's troubles had begun when he'd lost his foreman job four years earlier after a blasphemous machine had been discovered.

He'd created a tunnelling shield for the Stokers who dug the networks of tunnels under Engine Ward. Though the Stokers now had enormous steam-driven tunnelling and earth-lifting machines, their operation required whole teams of men crowding into tight spaces. The tunnel work was dangerous — rock and debris fell in all directions. One wrong step in the cramped space and a man could find himself sawn clean through by the tunnelling arms.

The shield acted like a giant rain umbrella, protecting the men from falling debris and offering a barrier between the dangerous machinery. Grateful for any concession to their safety, the work crew made no mention of Marc's invention to the clergy, knowing what trouble it would cause.

But a surprise visit to the tunnels by Messiah Stephenson revealed Marc's folly. Appalled that Stokers were creating inventions without the sanction of their church or the Royal Society, he reported the infraction to the Council, and Marc was forbidden to work with machines ever again. Since no other work was open to a Stoker, Marc opened a school.

Marc's punishment outraged the Stokers, who knew that inventions were needed every day to keep the men safe and the works from failing. Surely, they cried, the church can't expect them to seek permission for every single innovation? Stephenson stood his ground — the Stokers were not to innovate without his explicit permission. Discontent between the workers and the clergy escalated: priests found their churches vandalised, indecipherable graffiti scrawled across the walls. Fires soon broke out across the Engine Ward, destroying two churches and severely damaging many more.

"We've as much right to invent as any other Englishman!" was the talk around the Stoker fires.

"Those Stokers have more rights than us, and we're the bloody followers of Stephenson," grumbled the Navvies.

"This Marc Brunel is dangerous, " said the priests, who would never dream of working in the tunnels where they might get their robes filthy. "He blasphemes against Great Conductor and mocks our King's laws."

"But we can't risk making him a martyr for the Stokers," said the Council, who knew the Engine Ward could not function without the Dirty Folk. "How do we make him go away?"

Then, of course, Henry had gone and got himself killed, and the Council and the priests finally had their chance to be rid of Marc Brunel once and for all. So they locked him away while they gathered evidence for his trial.

All of this was known to Aaron, and it made him nervous. But Isambard vowed to succeed where his father had failed, and convinced Aaron to help him construct the design for the locomotive engine in secret.

"When it's finished, the Council will be so amazed, they won't care that it was a Stoker who invented it," he said.

"That doesn't seem the likely reaction of any counsellor I know," said Aaron, once again trying to temper his friend's enthusiasms. "They'd sooner hang us for blasphemy than admit they were wrong."

"So we shall sell it to one of the other sects. Even the Navvies can have it. I don't care, as long as we build it and it is ours."

Once Isambard had perfected the design, they began to scrounge the parts they needed to begin the engine, picking through the detritus left in the scrap yards behind the Engine Ward. They worked in secret, during the few scant hours they could escape from work and chores and their families. Less and less Aaron found himself able to slip away and visit the parks, and Isambard never joined him anymore. His mind was always focused on the engine.

They found an abandoned workshop in the bowels of an old Morpheus church — the abode of a lesser artist whose cult had died with him — and there they dragged their hoard of scrap metal and worked tirelessly for months. Aaron — who barely understood the plans and couldn't fathom the complex nature of the machine — banged and hammered and welded and fitted. Isambard tinkered with the finer mechanisms — the condenser, the valves, the superheater. He stole chalk sticks from the nearby engineering school and drew columns of equations on the dirty walls.

And so they toiled, in the few hours they could escape from the workgangs, with the constant fear of discovery hanging over their heads.

And in the midst of this Isambard's father's trial began. Isambard was forbidden to visit his father in the Tower of London, and his mother — a spiteful, hate-filled woman — increased his sufferings by bringing home a retinue of men, each more despicable than the last. Priests and acolytes spent their nights in her bed, joining her in jeering at her son as he waited outside the door of their shack for her to finish. At her insistence, they would take off their tightly wound horsehair belts and beat him 'till he wept.

Aaron worried for his friend, and for the damning evidence of their own innovations, still lying unfinished in the cellar of the abandoned church. He worried even more when Isambard threw himself into the project with abandon, channelling all his hatred and anger toward finishing the locomotive. He became careless, walking away from his duties as though he didn't care who followed him.

The entire Ward crackled with tension. Every engineer lectured about Marc Brunel from their pulpit — many supported the Council of the Royal Society in punishing Isambard's father for flouting the King's most sacred laws, but others saw the true genius of his invention, and rallied for his immediate release.

But in the end, it was Robert Stephenson, who served as prime witness for the prosecution and spoke with grace and conviction in his Royal Society sermons about the importance of upholding the King's laws, who turned the tide of popular opinion against Marc Brunel. The Council needed to retain control over the unwieldy religious system, and could not back down, especially not for one of the Dirty Folk. But neither could they execute him and risk him becoming a martyr, and so Marc Brunel was sentenced to deportation.

Isambard didn't cry when the priests and their supporters poured out into the streets of Engine Ward in celebration, falling in behind Stephenson's carriage, waving incense in the air and singing songs of praise; nor when he and Aaron snuck out and watched his father being marched on board a convict ship; nor when his mother slapped him about the face for staring and ordered him back to work. When Aaron looked into his friend's eyes, all he saw was hatred, and this worried him even more.

Later, while Isambard and Aaron worked by candlelight in their secret workshop, the priests held a great feast at the church. The scent of roasting meat and the sounds of music and laughter carried across the chilly night, and found their way underground to the boys' workshop. And suddenly, the space seemed very, very small.

Isambard put down his hammer, leaned his face against the cold stone wall, and screamed. Aaron, frightened by the sound of his friend's heart finally breaking, and by the fact that Isambard's screams might at any moment bring the priests running to their hiding place, crawled under the engine and hid there.

A little while later, when Isambard had slumped against the wall and fallen silent, Aaron heard shouts outside. But it wasn't the priests. The shouting grew louder. And now it was joined by screams.

Aaron crawled out from under the engine and grabbed Isambard's hand. "Something's wrong," he said, dragging his silent, shaking friend outside.

Outside, Stephenson's church was alight. Stokers raced through the narrow streets, carrying torches and calling for the blood of the man responsible for condemning Marc Brunel.

As Aaron and Isambard watched in horror, the Stokers surrounded the Navvy workcamp and ordered those inside to bring out Robert Stephenson, to be hanged in revenge for Brunel's banishment. The Navvies, of course, refused, so the Stokers put their camp to the torch.

Aaron and Isambard watched, silent, disbelieving, as the fire spread quickly through the shacks and workshops. Women ran screaming into the streets, their hair and clothes alight. Men trapped inside their homes cried from their windows as the flames engulfed them. Many threw themselves from the burning buildings, dashing their brains out on the streets below. The smoke blew over the whole Engine Ward, bringing with it the smell of burning flesh.

Aaron buried his face in Isambard's shoulder.

As the alarms went up constables and Redcoats poured through the gates of the Engine Ward, and within minutes, they had rounded up most of the troublemakers and shot them, right there in the streets. Aaron dragged Isambard to the pumps, ready to help quench the flames, but a constable shooed them away. "You Stokers have done enough tonight," he growled.

So instead they clambered up the water tower and shared a bottle of whisky Aaron had stashed there. It took several hours to extinguish the flames, and it was only in the light of dawn that Aaron could gaze upon the true devastation to the Ward. The Navvy camp had been completely destroyed, and Stephenson's grand church stood gutted, a blackened skeleton in the early-morning sun. The fire had spread to parts of the Metic and Morpheus districts, but the Stoker camp remained unharmed.

"We will pay for this," Aaron whispered as he stared in horror at the destruction. Isambard nodded, but his expression betrayed his pleasure at the sight.

***

During his first few weeks on board the *Euryalus*, Nicholas hardly thought of Isambard at all. He spent every waking moment clutching the rigging for dear life every time the ship lurched on a wave, and learning the skills of a sailor: splicing and knotting ropes, folding sails, keeping time, and ringing the ship's bell every half-hour.

His small frame made him the perfect size for a sailor, and soon he was swinging from the rigging with the midshipmen. His hands tore and bled as he hauled in the ropes — the boys at night compared their wounds and watched with fascination as their scabs healed into calluses.

And he *listened.* He had hoped being on the ocean might offer him some relief from the voices, but he had been wrong. He could not ignore them, for they were so different from anything he'd ever heard before: schools of fish who thought like compies — one mind with a thousand vessels; molluscs with thoughts like treacle — thick and syrupy as they clung to the rocks for dear life. And far below the surface, in cracks and crevices that stretched right down to the centre of the earth, flickerings of much older creatures, whose thoughts seemed to stretch across eons, alien, and indiscernible.

The *Euryalus,* a 36-gun *Apollo*-class frigate, was one of the few English ships not destroyed in the Battle of Trafalgar, that terrible day in 1805 where Britain suffered such heavy losses to the French and Spanish fleets that her naval power had been crippled ever since. The *Euryalus'* orders were to patrol the Channel in a squadron with four other frigates, and engage the French ships that were disrupting trade between England and her colonies.

It was five months before he had his first taste of battle. He was on the foredeck when the call went up; a strange sail was sighted on the southwest, bearing up the coast toward them. She must've spotted them, because she gave tack, running away toward Ostend. The captain ordered the crew to raise sail, and they gave chase.

Nicholas was with the gunners. His job was to spread the sand on the deck – it would absorb the blood and water that pooled on the deck during an engagement and prevent the men and guns from sliding on the slick surface. He watched the men rolling out the guns – twenty-six eighteen pounders on the upper deck, where he was stationed. The more experienced sailors laughed and joked with each other as they prepared the guns, but the young boys exchanged worried glances. Nicholas knew he should feel scared, but he was excited at the prospect of meeting the French in battle and seeing the guns in action.

With the wind behind, *Euryalus* quickly drew ahead and the Captain gave the order to tack in front of the French vessel, a 31-gun frigate. She fired a broadside. Nicholas ducked as splinters exploded all around him, and the deck beneath him shuddered. He glanced around, but apart from a couple of boys cowering behind the mizzen, no one seemed that concerned. The French ship had tacked away in an attempt to escape, but Nicholas could already see they had made a fatal mistake. The *Euryalus* swung round and, with the favourable wind, was able to cross their line and the Captain gave the order to fire.

All along the decks, the cannons went off. Nicholas' ears rang from the sound, and the acrid smoke clouding the deck quickly extinguished his vision. He coughed, and crawled forward to the bulwark to try to see if they had hit.

When the smoke cleared, he could just make out the deck of the French ship. Her sails had been shredded by their shot, and she was dead in the water. He could see her crew scrambling to ready their guns. The Captain was yelling orders, but Nicholas could barely hear him over the ringing in his ears and the shouts of the men around him as they loaded the guns again.

Another broadside rocked *Euryalus*, splintering the mast above his head and showering the deck in wooden shards. Nicholas leaned against the bulwark and covered his head. The deck shook violently as the guns fired again, spewing powder into the air. Nicholas rolled out of the way as one of his crewmates fell off the arm and crashed onto the deck beside him, blood pouring from his mouth.

A cheer rang out along the deck. The enemy ship had been sighted, and she was in bad shape. *Euryalus* made another pass with the guns, and the French surrendered. The Captain ordered a boarding party over, and Nicholas was chosen to help carry spoil back across to the *Euryalus*. At barely sixteen years of age, he stood for the first time on the deck of a naval prize and felt something like pride for his country, like he might finally have found where he belonged. It was a small victory in an ongoing war that the English were losing, but it filled Nicholas with hope for his future.

Weeks turned into months, and the months faded into a year. Nicholas' voice broke and stubble appeared on his chin and his skin cracked and blistered. He began to feel at home on the sea and with the new voices that inhabited his head. Now that he knew his duties by heart, he spent his days learning about navigation and repairing sails from the midshipmen and officers. While on watch at night he would lean over the edge of the deck and call dolphins to dance alongside the ship. He even tried to summon up one of those monsters of the deep. But as soon as he grabbed a mind, it would push him out again. But he kept trying.

Euryalus travelled down the coast of Europe, chasing down several Spanish privateers along the way, and finally put in at Gibraltar — her first time in port in fourteen months. The crew were let loose on the dockside to stretch their sea-weary legs. While the rest of the men headed to the taverns and bawdy-houses along the docks, Nicholas found the post office to deliver his letters to Isambard. He'd written several while on board, and these he stuffed into an envelope with some sketches he thought would interest his friend.

As he waited in line to buy stamps, he noticed a stand of British newspapers for sale — a few months old, but he hadn't heard news of England in even longer. He picked up a copy of the *Times* and leafed through it while he waited for the line to move.

STOKERS TO BLAME FOR ENGINE WARD FIRE

Following the deportation of Stoker Marc Brunel for causing the death of a child at his school, a gang of Stokers armed with torches attacked the Navvy district in the Engine Ward, killing thirty-seven and razing most of the buildings, including a wing of Stephenson's Cathedral, to the ground ...

Marc Brunel — Isambard's father, his beloved teacher and the only person ever to encourage Nicholas' love of architecture — had been deported. Nicholas checked the date on the paper. *He'll probably in Van Diemen's Land by now.* He skimmed the rest of the article. The Navvies had left London, and anti-

Stoker sentiment seemed at an all-time high.

Isambard. His heart ached for his friend, now truly alone.

***

JAMES HOLMAN'S MEMOIRS — UNPUBLISHED

My ship, the HMS *Cambrian,* was heading to the Americas to join an English force to attempt to win back some of her lost territory. The excitement of finally being on board a vessel and bound for adventure soon wore off when I realised I had months of nothing to look forward to but miles and miles of ocean. I concentrated instead on working hard, taking regular exercise to prevent illness, and earning a good reputation on board, and so it was that by the time we put in at the port of New York, I had earned the esteem of the senior officers and was well on my way to making midshipman on board the *Cambrian,* a fifth-rate frigate in His Majesty's Navy.

Without a huge English naval presence in the Americas, the French and Spanish had been systematically gaining control of the ports, and were exercising monopolies on some of the most sought-after goods; Venezuelan coffee, Cuban sugar, and South American indigo. King George wanted to re-establish a viable trade route, which meant first taking back, and then holding, the strategic port of New York.

After nine months at sea, I was itching to set foot on foreign soil and explore a country completely foreign to me. But it was not to be. The hard work of returning the port to British control had been done before we arrived, so we had entirely missed our chance for glory. Our orders were to patrol the mouth of the port, inspecting the crew and cargo of the vessels entering to ensure they weren't French or Spanish. "Reflagging" of ships (forging their papers) was common practice, so any ship we deemed suspicious was sent to Halifax in Nova Scotia, where its goods could be seized and any American men found on board was impressed into the British Navy.

While the whole operation sounds terribly cloak and dagger, an adventurer couldn't have asked for a worse posting. Since we inspected vessels as they came into harbour, we remained at the harbour entrance and after five further months, we had still not put in on dry land. I saw the ruddy peaks of the new land, of America, jutting up from the horizon, but she was as impossible to reach now as she was from England, and the sight of her taunted me so.

I wish Nicholas were here with me.

***

The Stokers and the Navvies had never trusted one another, but after the fire they were the bitterest of enemies. Stephenson's response to the disaster was quick and devastating. Rather than rebuilding the Navvy camp, he simply moved his entire operation to Manchester, depriving the Engine Ward and the City of London of one of her most profitable businesses. And every time an engineer wondered why there was a lack of skilled workers, or the Royal Society lamented the loss of great minds to lesser cities, they had only to look to that charred patch of the Engine Ward to see where to lay the blame.

And during all this uproar, when the Stokers became overnight the most hated of all men in London, Isambard and Aaron toiled away on their engine, on their own private protest against the loss of Marc Brunel.

Isambard's life took a turn for the worse after the protests. Aaron's own unpleasant home life distracted him from his friend's increasingly manic state, but he couldn't fail to notice Isambard wincing as he worked. No matter how uncomfortable the temperature in the cellar, Isambard pulled his shirtsleeves down, attempting to cover dark bruises and burns on his arms and shoulders.

One day, about a year after they started work on the engine, Aaron entered their secret workshop to find his friend hunched over the bench, his face in his hands.

"Isambard?" Aaron reached out his hand, tentatively brushing his friend's shoulder.

Isambard shrugged his hand away. He lowered his hands from his face, revealing a swollen black eye.

"What happened?" Aaron asked, no longer able to hide his concern.

"Mother has taken up with a new suitor," said Isambard, his voice bitter. "The priest Merrick. He's a brute of a man, more animal than priest. They are to be married next week."

"Do you want to—"

"I *want,*" Isambard growled, "to finish this engine."

***

In a rare moment of maternal kindness, Aaron's mother took him and his older bothers Oswald and Peter to see a menagerie in Regents Park. Perhaps she'd simply wished to escape the tension of the Engine Ward for an afternoon, or perhaps she hoped the fresh air would wash away the stench of alcohol and sadness that pervaded her body.

Since Aaron's father, Henry Williams Senior, had been killed by a falling pylon five years previously, his mother had raised the boys alone, although Aaron often joked with Isambard that whisky had been his real father. After losing her husband and favourite son, she'd found solace in spirits. Her dull eyes barely strayed from the bottle at her side, and her listless voice could scarcely exert any kind of authority over her home. Since Oswald and Peter had both enrolled in the Great Conductor's seminary, Aaron looked after the home, made the meals, brought in a meagre wage from the scrap pits.

Although the Stokers were forbidden from working outside the Engine Ward, and the populace made it clear they wanted nothing to do with the "Dirty Folk", they could not be prevented from otherwise enjoying the pleasures of the city. Being poor, mostly illiterate, and mistrusted by the majority of the populace, the Stokers found that most of London's attractions — the lecture halls, the British Museum, the teahouses and bakeries — were out of reach, but the menagerie cost only a penny, and the proprietor wasn't too fussed about who came in, so long as they paid up.

Aaron had to rise at 4am in order to finish the day's work before lunch. He arrived back at the house to find his brothers, dressed in their black robes, helping their mother outside. She clutched their arms as though they were all that held her upright. They set off, not talking, slipping through the Ward's high double gates and wandering toward the park. Aaron walked ahead, amusing himself by reciting the names of all the animals they would see. For once, their mother didn't seem to mind.

"... llamas and monkeys and ostriches ..."

Aaron heard from another boy that this menagerie included a swamp-dragon, and it was this he most wanted to see. His grandfather had always talked about the dragons — their stealth, their strength, their intelligence. Quartz loved to tell him tales about his grandfather battling with the fearsome creatures. Aaron could barely control his excitement.

As they crossed the city, the familiar thoughts of birds and horses and compies passed through his head. He revelled in their presence, not listening for their individual thoughts but enjoying the sensation of flitting in and out of their consciousness. His mood lifted. *Today will be a special day.*

The menagerie was set up in a corner of the Regents Park. Two wagons stood against an ornate wooden gazebo, and makeshift wooden fences divided off separate open enclosures. Children tugged their parents between the wagons, exclaiming over each exotic beast.

At once, Aaron's head churned with activity, as these large, exotic creatures pushed aside the thoughts of his usual animals. He raced toward the wagons, not heeding Oswald's command to stop. More and more animals pounded against his skull — memories of far-off lands, deserts and jungles and watery swamps. He could see the head of a giraffe above the wagon roof—

And then, he *felt* it. The dragon.

"Look!" Peter cried, running up behind him and pointing at the cage on the back of the wagon.

It loped in circles, its mouth open, its tongue slapping against rows of razor-sharp teeth. Aaron leaned closer, staring into the dragon's eyes. In his mind, the dragon stared back, regarding him with a mixture of revulsion and hunger. It hadn't had a proper meal for several days. A girl threw her sandwich scraps through the bars. The dragon sniffed the corner of bread, its mind torn between hunger and its desire to simply break through the bars and devour the girl. In the end, it nudged the sandwich with its nose, checking it was dead, and gobbled it up. The girl squealed, clapping her hands.

A rough hand grabbed Aaron's shoulder, and his mother pulled him back. "Don't lean over like that, you stupid boy. He'll eat you right up, an' you'll join your brother in the Station of Life."

Aaron shrugged her off, and walked to the next cage, where three monkeys sat on the stump of a tree, huddled together, picking and scratching at reddened sores that covered their rusty fur. He listened to them, felt their sadness, mourned the loss of their homeland.

These animals are so sad.

They lay in their cages, utterly defeated. Many had come from tropical lands, and they were suffocating in the cold. The dragon raised its nostrils and sniffed the air, its mind reaching, longing to race through the trees or sink its teeth into the compies hiding in the flowerbeds.

This isn't fair.

The anger welled up inside Aaron, fuelled by the animals, whose aching desire to break free permeated his every thought. He knew how it felt to be trapped. Raw emotion welled up inside him, a rage building inside his chest, inside his head, pushing against his skull, growing larger and larger, until the emotions flooded from him, escaping from his body like a great cloud of steam from a smoke stack. He bent double, the breath knocked out of him.

And suddenly, they *were* free. Cages overturned. Fences collapsed. Monkeys ran under his legs. The giraffe galloped gracefully across the lawn. Children screamed. Mothers screamed. Men grabbed their families and ran across the lawns, chased by gleeful monkeys. Two ostriches and a small, feathered dinosaur raced for the pond, chased by the red-faced menagerie proprietor waving his whip.

Aaron froze, unable to tear himself away as the dragon, its eyes no longer sad but fierce with anger, strained against its bars. Aaron felt its mind wheeling, straining for its one chance for freedom.

Snap!

The dragon reached through the bars, grabbed the bolts between its arms, clasped them in its claws, and pulled, a motion it must have seen the proprietor perform many times. And now it, too, was free, but it didn't go for the trees, as it perhaps should have, but bounded across the lawn with a grace and power that held Aaron in awe, and with a leap and a slash of its hind leg, tore the tendon in the proprietor's foot.

"No," Aaron whispered. "I didn't mean—"

The proprietor fell, screaming, as the dragon

pounced. It tore at his face, spraying blood over the flower garden. The proprietor, still screaming, raised his hands to defend himself, to grab in vain at the meat of his ruined face, but the dragon bent down and with a quick snap of his powerful jaw, tore the man's left arm clean away.

"Aaron!" His mother grabbed him by the shoulders and tugged him away. His brothers were already halfway across the field, their robes flapping with indignity as they ran toward the gate.

Aaron ran after her, his mind strangely empty. All around him, animals and people fled across the park. Screams followed him, high-pitched and terrified. Behind them, the proprietor's cries cut off. As they raced through the gate, they passed a regiment of Redcoats on their way to contain the mess.

His mother wouldn't stop crying. Oswald tugged her to his breast, stroking her hair and speaking in soft, soothing tones. Aaron leaned against the fence and watched the monkeys clamber up one of the oak trees. His body numb, his mind empty, devoid of thought. Silent.

I did this.

Aaron started to cry. Peter looked like he might slap him. Their mother, all business now, brushed off her skirt and pulled them along behind her, her head down, her face red with fear.

She saw a man selling boiled toffees beside the gate, and she bought a bag and handed it to Aaron. Oswald and Peter eagerly grabbed handfuls of toffees, the incident at the zoo instantly forgotten, but Aaron tucked the rest into his trouser pocket to share with Isambard. He couldn't think about sweets now. He needed his friend.

***

He found his friend on top of the boiler tower, furiously kicking a steel pylon. He didn't stop when Aaron approached, just went on kicking, his hands balled into fists and his face wet with sweat and tears. He winced when Aaron grabbed his arm, and rolled his sleeve up to show him the enormous welts dotted with cigar burns.

"Merrick again," he said. "I wasn't even doing anything, just sitting in the corner, pretending to be invisible. Evidently I didn't try hard enough."

Aaron sat down beside him, and removed the paper bag from his trousers. The toffees had melted a little next to his skin, and stuck together in a big clump. He pulled it into two pieces and proffered one to his friend.

"Oswald and Peter ate most of them already, but I wanted to save some for you."

Isambard looked down at the sugary pile and then looked away. When he spoke, his voice sounded choked. "Please, you eat them, Aaron. You've earned them."

"For what? Leaving you here to suffer while I go away on a nice outing?" He wanted so badly to tell Isambard about the dragon and the proprietor, but he didn't want to give his friend anything else to be upset about. "Hardly deserving at all. I want you to have some."

He pushed the biggest piece into Isambard's hand, and he accepted it without another word. They sat for a while, chewing toffee in silence, each lost in their own dark thoughts.

"I have this idea," Isambard said, biting off a chunk of toffee. "I think we need to change the width of our locomotive track."

"What?"

"I've been working on some calculations, see?" He fumbled in his pocket and produced a faded leaf of paper, printed on one side with an advertisement for cigar leaves. He smoothed it out across his knee and pointed to the rows of scrawled numbers. "The current speed of locomotives is limited by the width of the axle. If I made the track wider, say with an eight-foot gauge, a boarder, heavier engine could operate, effectively able to carry more cargo at greater speed than the current trains."

"I'm not sure you can go around changing rail width and such. Didn't Stephenson standardise it for a reason?"

"I'm not beholden to Stephenson. I can do whatever I want," Isambard insisted. "Whose side are you on, anyway?"

"Mine. Because we've spent nearly *two* years working on that engine, and I'm the one who'll have to re-cut all the pieces of the chassis to fit this new design."

"Don't be such a whiner, Williams." Isambard crunched down on his toffee. "This will revolutionise locomotion. I'm sure you can handle a little remodelling."

***

JAMES HOLMAN'S MEMOIRS — UNPUBLISHED

My eighteenth birthday passed at sea with little incident. I still hadn't set foot on American soil, and the adventurer within me was slowly withering away. But with a new first lieutenant on board anxious to prove himself, we were seizing more and more ships, pressing any men we could find with British ancestry (including deserters and nationalised Americans) and many without into the sadly-depleted British Navy. My fellow midshipman and friend Colebrook used to joke that he shouldn't be in the British Navy, as he had no Yankee blood.

All those seized ships presented a problem — what were we to do with them? We couldn't very well keep them at New York — they'd crowd the port and become a target for pirates. Instead, we had to sail each vessel to Halifax through a bitterly cold stretch of ocean, with only a skeleton crew of men, usually in biting fog.

The duty of captaining these vessels — called being the 'prizemaster' — had hitherto been a great honour, but was being passed out with such regularity mere midshipmen were accepting command of their own vessels.

And this was how, at eighteen years of age, I found myself a prizemaster of a confiscated ship. With a broad smile, I waved goodbye to Colebrook, and climbed aboard my vessel. *My ship.*

This auspicious day in my blossoming naval career was marred by a slight ache in my joints, which I ignored as best as I was able, walking with a stiff foot and setting my boots heavily on deck to minimise the flexing of my ankles. I hoped it would stop bothering me soon.

I hoped in vain.

***

The aches persisted for the entire journey, coming in shooting pangs and settling in for hours — a dull, throbbing pain no amount of exercise could shake off. I endured it as best I could, and we made it to Nova Scotia with the ship still intact.

Once I arrived at Halifax, I sat my officer examination and, with my lieutenancy papers still wet with ink, I switched to a naval flagship — the *Cleopatra*, a British frigate recaptured from the French at Bermuda — with the aim of impressing the Commander with my skills in order to move up in the ranks ... and maybe, *maybe*, land a position that involved some actual adventuring.

It seemed the first lieutenant of the *Cleopatra*, Jacob McFadden, had the same designs, for when I tried to introduce myself, he brushed me aside.

"What are you, fourteen?" he demanded, his cheeks flashing red.

"Eighteen, sir."

"By Isis, but they must be desperate for officers! Listen boy, I don't care who you are. I am not your friend. I am not your mother, and I don't want to hear one word out of your mouth that ain't 'yes, sir,' or 'thank you, sir.' I'm going to be Captain when Old McNeash dies, mark my words, and you'll want to be on my good side, yes?"

I nodded, too surprised to speak.

He kicked me, hard, in the side of the head as I bent to put my things on my bunk. "You're a scrawny little shitter. You won't last long on this ship. As if it wasn't bad enough when O'Reilly took a swim and they brought in that Thorne boy as second lieutenant, all gangly legs and buck teeth and no clue about *real* sailing, and now you're third lieutenant and I'm a bloody *nanny*—"

"James? James Holman? Is that you?"

Ignoring the pain in my legs, I spun around, and there in the doorway, stooping to fit his height through the low door, was Nicholas.

The years at sea had been good to him. He'd gained a foot of height on me, and his shoulders had broadened — his muscles rounding out so they pulled at the seams in his jacket. He'd grown out his hair, and it curled into sandy ringlets at the corners of his face, giving his usual angelic features a slightly roguish look. We embraced, and for the first time since I'd began experiencing the pain, I felt the warmth of joy spread through my whole body. Behind us, Jacob snorted, and made some rude remark neither of us cared to acknowledge.

"But you — how did you?" I cried. "You've been in the Navy only three years, and you started as a mere cabin boy. How do you now outrank me?"

"A combination of hard work and luck," he smiled. "Our fleet came to blows with the French in the waters off Calais, and we managed to board one of their ships. The Captain, foolhardy as he was, got himself into a spot of bother, and I managed to rescue him. The Navy is quite grateful for that sort of thing, so I was hastily promoted. Six months ago I transferred to the

Cleopatra out of Halifax, where I made the acquaintance of our dear friend Jacob here."

From that day onward we were inseparable, as much as two men could be on board a busy vessel. Starved of friendly conversation for the last year, we never stopped talking — first the swapping of news (including the sad story of the fate of Marc Brunel), then the discussion of all our common interests. We spent every mess debating passages of Plato's *Republic*, or recalling what we could remember of our favourite poetry. We bored the other officers quite silly and after a time they refused to converse with us at all.

I had been dabbling with poetry while at sea, in an effort to take my mind from the increasing pain. Nicholas was the first person I invited to read my work, and I did so with trepidation, knowing he would not hesitate to tell me if he thought it terrible.

"Your poetry longs for freedom," he said, setting my notebook down on the quarter galley table with reverence. "You speak not of love for women, as most poets do, but of love for the world and all of her numerous wonders. Yet there is such a great sense of longing."

"I want to see the world," I said. "I have travelled halfway across the globe, and yet my world has shrunk to the size of this ship. I've been away nearly four years, and have spent a total of fifteen days on foreign soil. I feel as though I've seen nothing at all."

"But your advancement has been swift enough, and you have the respect of the Captain and at least one of your fellow officers," he smiled. "You cannot be too impatient, James. A naval career will give you money enough to travel as you wish, if you live simply and contain your enthusiasm for a few more years."

I suspected my legs would not give me a few more years, but I did not wish him to press me, so I merely nodded. I had not told him about the pain — it was mine to bear as best I could manage. "What of you, Nicholas? What is your greatest wish?"

"I too wish for freedom," said he. "But it's freedom of a different sort. It's freedom from myself, from the voices in my head. I had hoped that perhaps the ocean would grant me that much — a quiet space, where I would be free to think. But so far, it's as noisy as ever."

I didn't understand what he spoke of, and he didn't elaborate. Our discussion turned to other matters. That night as I raised myself up from my chair and shuffled toward my cabin, the pains sizzling up and down my legs, he reached across the table and squeezed my hand.

***

I stood the last watch from the helm, correcting the course (southward, through a squall, with no sign of the rest of the squadron), calling sail trim instructions and hailing the lookouts every fifteen minutes.

During calmer nights this was one of the more pleasant duties, offering respite from the crowded confines of ship life. It could be lonely, too, nothing but you and the ocean for miles around, but tonight the thought of my friend Nicholas snoring below decks gave me comfort.

And that comfort was much needed, as the pains shot up my legs and every minute of the watch was agony. The rain assailed the boat in sheets, knocking down men, and tearing the sails. I wore an oilskin over my woollen cloak, which prevented exactly no water whatsoever from soaking through my clothes. I never felt warm, never felt dry, and the aches in my legs grew even more intense.

***

Months passed in agony. The pain now haunted me at rest, so I could no longer lie in peace but thrashed about, tormented by the unending fire.

One night I tired of tossing and turning and listening to Jacob's snores in the cabin next door. I rose and stumbled on deck to see Nicholas, who was on watch, wrapping my collar tightly around my neck to keep out the icy spray. As I made my way gingerly across the pitching deck, I saw his shadow slumped over the railing on the bow, leaning over the edge.

Ignoring the shooting spasms in my legs, I ran to him, thinking he must have collapsed in the cold. He spun around when he felt my hands on his back, and grinned when he recognised me. "Do you want to see a wonder, James?" he asked. "Lean out. I have something to show you."

Gripping the rigging with both hands, I took a deep breath and leaned out over the edge. When I saw what he'd found, I screamed and jumped back.

"That's a—a—a—"

Nicholas nodded. "She won't hurt you."

She was a sea-necker, or *Plesiosaur* in Buckland's taxonomy. Her elongated neck stretched from the water up the side of the boat, and she rested her head on the gun port and stared up at us with narrowed eyes. From the water below, one of her flippers rose from the water below and slapped against the side of the boat, rattling the railing and causing another cry to escape my lips.

To my horror, Nicholas leaned out again, stretching out his hand and rubbing the nose of the creature. She closed her eyes and leaned back into his touch, opening and shutting her mouth so I could see the twin rows of sharp, pointed teeth.

I choked back a scream. "You ... you ..."

He laughed again. "I suppose there's no harm in you knowing the truth," he said. "I called her here to visit me in the solitude of my watch. She will not hurt me, because as far as she knows, she *wanted* to come to me. I *hear* animals, James. Only I hear their minds, and they are inside my head. Their thoughts bounce constantly around in my skull. I feel what they feel — the smells, the tastes, the sounds of nature come to me through their thoughts. And sometimes, like tonight, if I send out thoughts of my own, they will obey me."

I backed away from this remarkable scene, struggling to grasp what he'd told me. "That's impossible. You're not making any sense, Nicholas."

"I hardly understand it myself. As far as I know, I'm the only man in the world who possesses this curse. I've learned to control it, to some degree, otherwise I wouldn't have been able to call on this beauty." He patted the sea-necker's head affectionately, and she gave a snort and flopped back down in the water. I finally let out the breath I'd been holding.

He continued. "I thought, perhaps, if I could take to the sea, I could escape the constant chattering of birds and bugs and beasts. But the ocean teams with life, James, more even than the forests on my father's estate. I must accept that I will never be at peace."

"But how did you—"

He looked down at the great long-necked beast. "Sometimes, I can push with my mind, and I can give an animal thoughts that aren't its own. I can say 'there's a nice man on that ship who will give you a few strips of salted pork if you ease up alongside', and here she is. Usually, I can't influence the thoughts of larger animals at all, but for some reason, ocean-bound creatures are more receptive, their minds more open. Perhaps it is because they haven't yet learned to fear man."

"Nicholas, that's incredible!"

"It's a curse," he said bitterly. "That is why I keep it secret. Men would hate me and women would fear me. In a different time, I would be burnt as a witch."

"I do not hate you."

"There is nothing within you capable of hate." He stared out to sea. "I grew up on my father's estate in Wiltshire, not far from the mysterious chalk horse. My father — a minor Lord — was a shrewd businessman, and although we had family fortunes he more than doubled that amount through local industrial projects. I used to go with him to inspect his properties — huge warehouses that seemed to stretch for miles, mines and wells and a bridge designed to complement the nearby medieval abbey. I adored that bridge, the way the graceful steel beams curved upward into ecclesiastical arches, supporting an intricate lattice of fluted crossbeams. I would sit for hours on my horse and stare in wonder at that magnificent work of engineering art.

"From a very young age, I knew I wanted to be an architect, so I could one day realise such magnificent creations. But I unwittingly destroyed my future the first day I called the animals."

I leaned hard against the railing, ignoring the pain in my ankles as I watched the sea-necker keep stroke alongside the boat. Her neck bent upward, regarding me with those cold, intelligent eyes.

"I loved my father, despite his coldness, and wanted so badly to please him. I was the second of four children — my older brother, Robert, my senior by eight years, and my two younger sisters. Robert would take over the estate one day, so he was of course the favourite. He would torment me relentlessly — pulling my hair, making my horse bolt, putting snakes in my bed — and I could do naught about it, for my father always took his side. My father would take him fox hunting on the estate, and they would always return laughing and joking. He never joked with me.

"I'd always heard the voices. As a child my mother would hit me if I told her what the cat was thinking. My father would whip his horse and I would shake and cry, and he would look at me with such distaste and loathing, it was unbearable. So I quickly learned to keep my secret. But one day, shortly after my thirteenth birthday, I was playing in the courtyard with my sisters. Robert entered with a swagger and announced in a haughty voice that father had given him his first business dealing. He, Robert, now owned the beautiful medieval-inspired bridge that I loved so much.

"I must confess I forgot myself. In my anger, I

threw aside the chess set, and drew up my fists, not sure what I intended to do, only that I hated the unfairness of it. The bridge I loved so much was now in the hands of my loathsome brother. He saw me approach him and laughed, and said he planned on levelling the bridge as soon as possible. He said it was dreadfully ugly, and my sisters laughed, and I felt a great wall of anger push against my skull, and suddenly, the anger was gone. It fell out of me and I collapsed on the ground. My head felt light, as though it might fall off my shoulders and roll away, and my ears rang. I could no longer hear the voices of the animals. I was so scared, I started to scream, and my sisters — not understanding what was happening — screamed too.

"Robert turned away from me in disgust and strolled back across the lawn, when a rumbling from the garden caught his attention. The ground shook and growled beneath me, and I rolled over to see what was going on. And I screamed even louder. But not as loud as Robert. They closed the field in seconds — the horses racing at high gallop, their mouths frothing, followed by the hunting dogs, teeth bared, sweat glistening on their necks, and the loping draft-neckers, and hundreds of foxes and woodland creatures, which must have come from miles around. The sound they made was the most terrifying thing I'd ever heard — a cacophony of growls, squawks, hisses, and barks. But inside my head — nothing. Not a sound.

"Robert barely had time to turn on his heel when they set upon him, and he was pulled down into the stampede. They churned around him, closing in like a whirlpool, and I could no longer see him or hear him scream.

"My sisters and I scurried under the table and crouched low, and I covered my eyes so I wouldn't have to look at the mangled body of my brother, and I prayed they wouldn't turn on us. But they disappeared again, churning the lawn to mud as they charged back toward the forest. The spell had broken. The voices returned, slipping into my head. They had no clue what they had done, or why they had done it.

"My father rushed from his study as soon as he heard the screaming. He came running across the lawn, and he saw the horses bolting away and Robert lying there, his head bent at an impossible angle. He cradled his son in his arms and waited with him while he died."

Nicholas sighed. "He banished me after that. Somehow, he knew I'd caused the horses to bolt. He said I was an abhorrence upon nature and he didn't care if he never saw me again. He said he would throttle me with his own hands if I ever set foot on his lands again. So I came to London. I figured if there were any hope of losing the voices, it would be on the streets of the Engine Ward. So that is where I ended up, and I met Marc Brunel, and he agreed to teach me what he could until I was old enough to join the Navy and try to make a name for myself. But the voices followed, of course."

"Henry?"

"I tried to save him. I sensed Mordred's thoughts, saw he meant to follow his master onto the platform. But I acted too late, and so another person died."

"If the guilt of Henry's death belongs to anyone," I said, my heart clenching upon my own secret, a secret

I'd never voiced until now, "it belongs to me. I let go of Mordred's chain. I was looking at my papers again, and—"

"He would've broken free anyway. I heard the desperation in his thoughts. Henry was down there, in the bowels of that machine, so Mordred would go down there also." He dropped his gaze, and the sea-necker slumped back down into the water. "But I alone had the chance to save him, but I … I did not push, I did not reach for him. I hated Henry, and I wanted to see him hurt." He gulped. "I am so ashamed. My cruelty cost a boy's life, and the life of Master Brunel."

He gave the sea-necker a forlorn wave, and she heaved herself backward and slammed into the water, diving under the churning waves and disappearing from sight. "So you see, James, it is a curse."

"Then, we are both cursed."

He nodded. "I have seen how you walk, and you cry out in your sleep."

I looked up in alarm. He smiled. "It annoys Jacob something terrible," he said. "Don't stop. But James, what is wrong?"

"I don't know. I've never known pain like this before," I said, wheezing as I tried to stretch out my aching legs. "Look at us. Two wretched men blessed by each other's company."

"That we are, James. That we are."

***

It was the drink that took Aaron's mother in the end, of course. She lay in her chair by the doorway with her final bottle, empty, clasped on her lap. She had been dead some hours, and was already stiffening, her skin cold and waxy, tinged with green on her fingers, when he returned from the secret workshop and found her. He pulled a blanket over her and went to find Quartz.

The old man was drinking in his shack, but then, he was always drinking. It never seemed to alter his mood, as it did Aaron's mother. When Aaron told him what happened, he put down his glass, and let Aaron lead him back to his shack. Quartz brought two men along with him, and they lifted Aaron's mother and carried her away.

"It's all right if you want to cry," he told Aaron, straightening her chair and tossing the empty bottle out on the street.

"I know." Aaron didn't want to cry. He felt nothing, no sadness, no anger. He felt numb. He was twenty years old, and an orphan.

Quartz glanced around the room — his eyes taking in the neat pile of blankets in the corner, the candle and worn ledger book propped up against the stove, the pots and pans, clean and stacked on wooden shelves. He walked over to the ledger book and flipped it open, running his fingers over the rows of clumsily printed letters. "You can write?"

Aaron blushed. "Isambard and I taught ourselves. We spied through the windows of the engineer schools. I found that book in one of the scrap heaps. It's what I use to practise."

"You can cook, boy?"

Aaron nodded. "I do most of the work around here. Oswald and Peter are no use."

"Ain't that the truth." Quartz slumped down in

Aaron's mother's chair. "You have everything in hand, boy. Pity, I thought you might have needed an extra pair of hands. But you have no need of an old drunk like me messing things up."

"You want to move in here?"

"If you'll have me." Quartz looked up. "With your brothers in the priesthood, it's your house now, Aaron. No one can tell you what to do anymore. I'm getting on a bit, my home's a tad small and infested with rats, and I could do with a young back to chop the firewood. And you could do with someone to help out with things, someone to keep you out of mischief. And," he smiled, "I can teach you your letters, all proper like. And more things besides."

Quartz sold his own shack to one of his drinking buddies and moved in the next day. Aaron warmed to his presence immediately. They spent hours each evening sitting across from each other at the small table, telling stories, drinking, playing cards, and reading books Quartz had kept hidden in his shack.

Finally, life in Engine Ward seemed less unbearable. But, just as Aaron's life finally took a turn for the better, Isambard decided it was time to mess everything up again.

***

JAMES HOLMAN'S MEMOIRS — UNPUBLISHED

As if my body was doggedly determined to ruin any chance of winning favour on the *Cleopatra*, the pain persisted. First, the dull ache in my legs grew to an agonising drone, a pain that screamed so loud it rung in my ears. I walked stiffly, moving my ankles as little as possible, and praying each hour for the respite of my bed. At night when I kept watch, I paced the deck in agony, silent screams echoing from my lips.

On a naval frigate, an officer does not report to the physician unless he is in rather dire circumstances. If I could not perform my duties, the responsibility would pass to the other lieutenants — Nicholas and Jacob — or worse, to the Captain himself. This was not conducive to the future of my naval career, and I needed that career to facilitate adventuring, and so I pressed on as best I could, my stiff gait the only clue to the searing pains that echoed up my legs.

The day came when my ankles swelled to such proportions I could no longer put on my own boots, and I dragged myself with tears streaming down my cheeks to the office of Dr. Nesbitt, the ship's physician, who confined me to bed at once.

"Rheumatism," he pronounced with an air of confidence after inspecting my swollen legs. "It's common in officers of your age — caused by the sudden temperature changes, hot then cold, cold than hot. Soaking clothes and cramped conditions don't help, either."

"Can we cure it?" I asked, fearing the answer.

"Yes. Many of my colleagues have had much success with fresh fruit, horse-back riding, and plenty of wine-whey."

But, of course, we were at sea, far from fresh produce, horses, and wine-whey. Not surprisingly, as I lay tossing and turning in agony, Nesbitt changed his diagnosis to something he *could* cure — gout. I knew I didn't have gout, which is a disease of the old, the overweight, and the sedentary, none of which I could be accused of. But Nesbitt needed something he could treat (even if unsuccessfully), and the only thing that cures gout is bed rest.

So they let me rest.

***

After two weeks, the pain subsided into a dull, throbbing ache, and after a further twelve days, faded completely. I dared to hope maybe I did have gout, after all. With great delight I thanked the good doctor and resumed my duties.

It was not to be. The pain returned worse than ever. I confided in no one, save Nicholas, who watched my agonised movements with growing concern. After the forth week of torment, when he saw me refuse a meal for the third day in a row, he led me aside and told me to report to sick duty.

"I cannot," I winced, pushing his arm away. "I must endure this, or all my years of work will be for naught."

He insisted on taking the evening watch with me, even though he would perform his own afterward and would get no sleep at all. He sat on the bowsprit and called a pod of dolphins to the ship, and we watched them dive and prance over the waves. A sea-necker joined them, slapping her giant fins against the side of the boat.

"She's the same one," he said. "She follows us. She's the only one of her kind left in all these waters."

"What happened to the others?"

"Fished up and eaten, mostly. Many others died when they choked on debris from the skirmishes on the coast."

The ship hit the crest of a wave, and lurched sideways. I grabbed for the rail, and missed, my hands grasping at air. The sudden tilt of the deck forced my weakened legs to give way, and I toppled forward, pitching over the rail and watching the waves and the churning fins of the sea-necker hurtle towards me. Black spots swarmed in my eyes, before finally enveloping me completely.

***

My eyes fluttered open. Nicholas stared down at me, his face furrowed in concern. My head banged against something hard, and I cried out.

"You're awake," he whispered, he voice wavering, He was carrying me, struggling to fit us both down the narrow steps below deck. "You passed out, James, and nearly fell overboard. The sea-necker saved you. She caught you on her fin. As I dragged you back, you hit your head against the anchor chain, and you've been asleep ever since."

That explained the throbbing, and why my clothes seemed wetter than usual. I slowly registered other objects: the spare rigging and sails stacked against the wall, the barrels of pickled beef and wine on which we subsisted. Nicholas eased open the door of my cabin, and heaved me inside.

We must've woken Jacob, for he lurched into the galley, leaning against the frame of my cabin door and rubbing his eyes. "Is that Holman causing trouble again?" he mumbled. "If he goes back to sick bay one more time, the Captain will have him off the ship."

Nicholas ignored him. As he lay me down on my bunk and wrapped my swollen legs in a blanket, a tear crept from the corner of my eye. Relief washed over me, and fear for my future, and gratitude for Nicholas' kindness.

"Sleep well, my friend." Nicholas lit a fresh lantern and clambered back on deck to finish the watch.

But I did not sleep; the searing pain and my wretched thoughts kept me awake. I thought of my father, who'd scrimped and saved every penny in his life that his only son might have the chance of becoming a gentleman. I thought of the life I longed for — the adventure and freedom that could only come with the prestige and steady salary of an officer. I thought of Jacob, snoring away in his own cabin right next door, hell-bent on making me out to be the worst kind of officer. I knew — pain or no pain — my entire naval career depended on me performing my duties the following morning.

I prayed to the gods for a miracle. Old gods, new gods, forbidden gods — every deity I could think of received a prayer and a pledge of obedience if only they would strike away the pain. But they either could not hear me, or thought my plight a terrible lark, for no relief came.

When his bell rang, Jacob rose, smirking as he lit a candle and dressed himself. "Enjoy your rest," he sneered at me from the galley as he fumbled with his buttons. I had a witty retort all figured out, but the pain rode so great I could not summon the strength to utter it.

When the tenth bell sounded and his watch finished, Nicholas clambered down into the cabin and spooned half his breakfast gruel into a chipped enamel cup. "You'll need to eat if you're to report to watch today," he said. He knew as well as I that I had no choice but to return to my post.

Somehow, I managed to pull my boots on over my swollen ankles and stumble on deck, gripping the railing so tightly my fingers bled and swapping my weight from one leg to the other to give each a brief respite. I bit my tongue and tore shreds of skin from my lips with my teeth, and the food in my belly rumbled and squirmed as the pain caused my stomach muscles to cramp and convulse. I trained my eyes out to sea, and counted back from a hundred, then a thousand. Thankfully, the wind caught my agonised tears and whipped them away before any of the men could see.

***

But it was no use — my valiant effort came to nothing. A week more of this torture and I was in the sick bay again, unable to walk. Nicholas brought me food and water and gave me his single threadbare blanket, and he helped me to my feet to endure my hurried return to service. But after three days I could not bear it — my legs no longer support my weight.

The Captain came to speak to me in my convalescence. Jacob had no doubt told him I was merely being lazy, shirking my duties. As he stood over my bed and stared gape-mouthed at my ankles the size of cannonballs and the tears of shame and agony running down my cheeks, his manner changed to one of pity. He had been a lieutenant once — he knew what my position meant.

"We'll be putting in at Portsmouth in a few weeks," said he. "And I expect you off this ship."

"But sir—"

"You're in no state to serve on board my ship, Lieutenant Holman. You're a good officer; you'll recover from this setback. Go to Bath, get this taken care of, and I'll put in the good word with the Admiralty, see if I can't get you another commission, maybe closer to home this time."

When we finally put in on English soil, I had to be carried off the boat in a stretcher. Nicholas lent me seven shillings for the coach ride to Bath, and a purse of coins to help pay the doctors. I rode on forthwith, my supine body banging and clattering about the carriage, much to the annoyance of the other passengers.

I thought the pain the worst horror of my life, but I was not prepared for what awaited me at Bath.

***

Of all the disciplines to suffer under King George's Gods of Industry, the medical profession has bore the brunt of the damage. Perhaps, if the Church of England's medical colleges had been allowed to continue unhampered, we might have avoided the human atrocity that was the "Heroic Medicines."

A romantic notion popularised by the Morpheus Church, heroic medicine deals with a new methodology for balancing the humors: forcing the malady from the body by subjecting it to various levels of medieval torture.

In the resort town of Bath, where medical men gather in the thousands to hawk their trade amongst the ancient healing springs, I placed myself at the mercy of these barbarians. They rewarded my dwindling savings with the most imaginative torments. They pumped me so full of purgatives I swear at one point I excreted my own viscera. They took so much blood through the lancet and the leech I practically became a vampire. And when this did not ease the pains, they began with the blistering — a most unpleasant treatment where they would strip me naked and flick burning acid upon my skin, so that it would burn and blister and sting so violently it might cast out the gout or rheumatism or whatever they said I had this week. And all of this did not one whit of good. The pain remained.

I quit of them all, and prescribed myself long walks around the city and several hours of daily soaking in the healing waters of the bathhouse, which seemed to slowly loosen the vices upon my legs. I closed my eyes and dreamed I might return to service in a month. With a speedy recovery, there was still a chance my career would not be completely ruined.

And then I discovered a new kind of pain.

I have never before experienced vision problems, and luckily too, because perfect eyesight is essential for naval officers. So on this particular day, as I took up my usual spot in one of the restored Roman baths, I was quite surprised to feel a sharp pressure behind my eyes, as though my skull had shrunk around them.

I rubbed my temples, threw my head back, and lay

in the water to wash them out, but the pressure only intensified. Red welts appeared in my vision, and with reluctance and a good degree of fear, I hoisted myself out of the pool and took myself to a nearby doctor.

"Pain behind the eyes has been known to occur, especially following some kind of trauma to the head," he said. "Have you fallen or bumped your head in recent months?"

I nodded, thinking of my fall on the *Cleopatra*, and how Nicholas knocked my head pulling me back on board.

The doctor — one of the Morpheus Sect — wanted to couch the eye immediately. His theory was that the humors in the lens of my eye were imbalanced, forming an invisible cataract.

"And what does this couching involve?" I asked, preparing myself for another excruciating treatment.

"Well, sir, I take this needle, and I thrust it directly into—"

I didn't stick around to hear the rest. Back at my lodgings, I made myself a cold compress, lay on my bed, and closed my eyes, and tried to will the pain to go away. My heart pounded against my chest as I contemplated the ramifications of this new torture. Sometime later, I drifted into an uneasy sleep.

I awoke again, opened my eyes, and found the world eternally dark.

Fear clung to my chest. I was a lieutenant — a rank that had cost all my mother's money and all my efforts to obtain. It was enough of a disgrace to retire at age twenty as a cripple, but blinded? I would be a beggar. I would never accomplish my greatest dream, to see the world in all her multitudes of splendours.

The days dragged on in unending sadness, and still my vision remained shrouded by darkness. I visited every doctor in the city of healers, trying everything from leeches under the eye, shaving my hair three times weekly, and submerging my bald scalp in icy water, to bleeding via a lancet through my neck and poultices made of diluted brandy and vinegar. Nothing brought back my sight.

And when I could find no more doctors, I turned to those I had scorned — the soothsayers and witch doctors of the engineering sects. The Metics took precise measurements of my face and drew mathematical sigils on my body with hot ash. I subjected myself to brutal psychological experiments by two German Mesmerists. I even saw a phrenologist from the Church of Isis, in the hope he could discern my recovery from the bumps on my head. I met a Dirigire priest in secret in a chamber under the Roman ruins outside the city, who I gave the last of Nicholas' money in exchange for a clockwork device I fitted to my temple, which shot sparks of fire into my cheek every few minutes, causing my face to contort and spasm in pain. But to no avail.

I had to face reality. Not a single doctor, soothsayer, or engineer in Bath can help me. I was doomed to remain a blind man, with no money, no prospects, and no hope.

***

After James' dismissal, life on the *Cleopatra* grew progressively unbearable. After their stop in Portsmouth to discard James, the *Cleopatra* had been reassigned to duties closer to home. King George had lost interest in the Americas, and had his sights set on re-establishing Naval supremacy in Europe, and strengthening the few Industrian strongholds in Europe. Despite his bold plans, however, the French were gaining the upper hand along the coast, and Spanish privateers had been raiding many of the British ports around the Mediterranean. Several British ships had already been destroyed or captured, and morale was low by the time the *Cleopatra* joined the fray. In their first engagement with a French frigate, their prey escaped and they suffered heavy loses, which put the Captain in an ill temper.

Jacob, having got rid of Holman seemingly without any effort, set his sights on Nicholas. Joined by Harold — the new lieutenant brought on board to replace James — Jacob watched Nicholas day and night, reporting even the most minor infractions to the Captain. If his eyes fluttered shut for a moment while on watch, the next day he was summoned to account for his slothful behaviour. His punishments flowed into each other, so his back burned constantly with the bite of the lash and there didn't seem to be a waking moment when he was not engaged in some unpleasant task.

Even accounting for the money he'd given James, if he could survive another year on a lieutenant's wage Nicholas would have saved enough to enter university as an architect, but with hostilities brewing he was likely chained to the Navy 'till death or dismemberment rendered him useless. He thought of the Engine Ward — those high walls of iron and that soot-soaked hovel that had been more of a home than his father's estates. More than anything, he wanted to return there.

The King was sending troops to reinforce the garrisons stationed in the English colonies around the Mediterranean, and the *Cleopatra* was assigned to play escort to a number of vessels landing in Malta and the Ionian Islands with soldiers, supplies and Industrian missionaries off to spread the word of science throughout Europe. This meant ample stops in port, and a chance, one day, if he ever worked up the courage to do it, of jumping ship. He'd have to change his name, of course, and go into hiding. But perhaps he could find an architecture school …

It was a foolish idea, of course, but he was lonely and desperate, and he couldn't help but entertain it. Perhaps his desperation could be read on his face, or Jacob suspected his intentions and had alerted the Captain; for whenever they put in at port, Nicholas was ordered to remain on board as a guard.

So he waited, and he drilled every day on deck with sword and dagger and fist, until his muscles tightened and his senses sharpened. He did not know if he would ever attempt to escape, but he knew if he did, he would need all his strength and wits about him.

The following summer, *Cleopatra* engaged three French frigates off the coast of Italy and suffered a serious defeat. Nicholas was on the quarterdeck when the French guns blew a hole in the hull on the waterline and took out the mast. A wood splinter lodged itself into his shoulder, knocking him off his feet. His men weren't so lucky – eight of them died when another shot went through the deck, and two more died from infected wounds from the splinters flying through the air.

Cleopatra was adrift, and started taking on water at an alarming rate. Clutching his shoulder and gritting his teeth against the pain, Nicholas organised a chain of men to plug the hole. On-deck, Jacob and Harold attempted to raise a Jury mast – if they didn't get back under sail, the French would board and take the ship as a prize.

Luckily, at that moment an English ship of the line, HMS *Friday*, was sighted. The French moved on, and the *Friday* towed *Cleopatra* back to Gibraltar.

As *Cleopatra* limped into port, the Captain called the officers to his cabin and delivered a grim sermon. With forty-six men lost and the vessel in need of significant repairs, the *Cleopatra* was being decommissioned. Hope swelled in Nicholas' chest. *I could go home to England and start my education—*

But the Captain had other ideas. Their orders were to stay with the garrison in Gibraltar until a new commission could be found for them. The English fleet was under heavy fire by the French and there was a constant need for more men. Nicholas thanked the captain and asked to be excused to pack his things; he didn't want to give Jacob the pleasure of reading the disappointment on his face.

The ship needed to be careened for repairs, so everyone, including the Captain and officers, would need to find lodgings for a number of days. The barracks were completely full, but Nicholas easily found a cheap room in town. Thousands of soldiers were stationed at the fortress, and more men came off the ships every day — the town was well stocked with amenities to tickle a sailor's fancy.

After hiding his money and belongings in his room, Nicholas followed the crowds of men as they practically skipped off the docks toward the doss-houses. He pushed his way into a crowded tavern, bought a draught at the bar and slipped toward the back of the room. He didn't want to play dice or cards with the other men, or flirt with one of the doxies making the rounds of the room. He wanted to drink 'till the memories of London faded into a dream.

Leaning against the wall, he tipped his head back and poured his drink down his throat. He closed his eyes, enjoying the warmth washing over his body.

Isambard. James. I wonder what you're doing right now. I wish I could be with you, instead of in the middle of this ridiculous war being shot at by the French every day—

Across the room, something shattered. Nicholas looked up from his drink. Jacob and Harold had entered the bar, and were exchanging some heated words with a group of officers from another ship. One of the officers had smashed a bottle against the table and was pointing it at Jacob. Nicholas could see by the way Harold was leaning against Jacob and Jacob's bloodshot eyes were darting about that they were already very drunk, and ready for a fight.

I have to leave, before they notice me. He couldn't go out the front, as Jacob and Harold stood near the entrance and would certainly see him. Nicholas surveyed the tavern. Stairs behind the bar led up to sleeping quarters above, and men swung in and out of a door into a storage area beyond. Nicholas craned his neck to get a look inside the storeroom, and saw a large space stacked high with barrels and another door beyond, leading into the alley behind the tavern. He set down his drink, inched his way nonchalantly toward the door, and slipped through into the storage room.

"You can't go back there!" someone yelled behind him.

His heart pounding, Nicholas ducked behind the barrels, racing for the second door. Footsteps followed him, and he heard the proprietor yell for some help. *He must think I stole something,* he realised, grabbing the bolt on the door. It was stuck. Panic rose in his belly. He jiggled the bolt, but it wouldn't budge.

"I said, get out of here!" He heard more men shouting behind him. In a moment they'd be on him.

The bolt slid through Nicholas' fingers, and he pushed open the door and slipped out into the alley. He bolted around the corner and down the alley just as he heard the proprietor and his men crash through the door and race after him.

Nicholas ducked around another corner, stumbling into the street and narrowly avoiding being churned under the wheels of a wagon. Heavy footfalls thundered toward him. He dodged through the pedestrians and tore into another alley. He was about to cut through a courtyard when a hand clamped down on his shoulder.

"Oh no you don't, *Stoker,*" said Jacob, stepping out of the shadows. "You're coming with us."

"What's the punishment for desertion, Jacob?" Harold, who held his shoulders in a vice-like grip, asked.

"Why, that would be seventy lashes," said Jacob, a cruel smile plastered across his face. "Followed by death."

"The Captain will hang you right on the dock," Harold cried. "I cannot wait to wield the cat on your treacherous back myself."

"I'm not deserting, you idiots." Nicholas snapped, fumbling for the sword at his belt. Jacob loomed over him, his face twisted into a sadistic smile. Jacob pulled back his fist and punched Nicholas in the jaw, followed by another hit in the temple. The pain blinded him, and he stumbled back across the courtyard, his boots slipping on the cobbles. Rough hands grabbed him, pinning his arms at his side, squeezing the wound in Nicholas' shoulder 'till he let go of his sword. He could smell Harold's rotting breath on his neck. *This is bad. Very, very bad.*

Through his swimming vision, he could just make out the figure of Jacob, his body blocking the entrance to the courtyard and the alley beyond. Nicholas knew he was trapped. *I am going to die right here in an alley, like a criminal. I'll never see London again.*

Desperate, Nicholas did the only thing he could think of — he slammed his elbow back, knocking the wind from Harold and loosening his grip. With a swift kick to the shin, Harold crumpled to the ground and Nicholas dislodged himself. He swung his body around and grabbed his sword from the ground. He whirled around to face the two men.

"I don't want any trouble. Let me go and I won't report this. " Nicholas' voice came out calmer than he felt. Blood ran down his face, obscuring his view. If they rushed him together, he would be done for.

"You struck a superior officer," Harold wheezed. "We don't have to kill you here, you know. When we deliver you to headquarters, they'll hang you on the spot."

Smiling, Jacob drew his own sabre, and took a step forward. Nicholas had seen him duelling on deck and knew he was a skilled swordsman. He regretted his boldness.

Harold was picking himself up, and Nicholas needed to move quickly before the pair overwhelmed him. Jacob advanced a step, and Nicholas backed up, trying to buy himself time to think. He tried to wipe the blood from his eye, but it kept flowing down his face.

Jacob let out a chuckle. He stepped forward again, his blade glinting in the moonlight. Nicholas braced himself for a painful death—

Isambard, I'm sorry. I miss you.

A man barrelled down the alley and, in his haste to enter the courtyard, he slammed into Jacob's shoulder, spinning him off-balance. Yelling something in French, the black-clad man shifted a small package from arm to arm and tore off across the courtyard.

At that exact moment, a soldier passed by on the street. He shouted at the men to lower their swords and rushed toward the confrontation, but not before another man pushed past Harold, knocking him aside.

Seeing his chance, Nicholas leapt forward, easily parrying Jacob's off-balance cut and ducking behind him, sweeping his foot out as he did so and sending Jacob sprawling across the cobbles. Nicholas didn't think twice; he rushed forward and drove the point of his sword into Jacob's belly.

Nicholas yanked his blade free. Jacob made a strangled sound as his blood bubbled from the wound. He stared at the blood on his hands, his face dark with pain and surprise. Then his head flopped back, and he didn't move. Four more officers and a fearsome man wearing the garb of a strange priesthood rushed around the corner and stampeded down the alley toward them. Nicholas tore across the courtyard and dived into the alley, which split off into three directions. He took the left and started running.

He had killed a superior officer. If they caught him, he would be hanged.

"De cette façon!" a voice cried in French. He looked down, and there was the man in the black cloak, only his head visible from the black hole of a sewer. *"Ici-bas!" Down here!*

Nicholas swung himself inside and scrambled down the ladder as the black-robed man pulled the cover closed, plunging them into utter darkness. He heard a match striking, and within seconds the man had lit a candle. *"De cette façon, s'il vous plaît!"* he said, grabbing Nicholas' hand.

The stench rolled over Nicholas, and he gagged. The black-robed man held a putrid hand up to his mouth, ordering him to be silent. Gulping, Nicholas managed to get hold of himself, and he followed the man along the slippery ledge that ran alongside the brown, soupy river. Chittering insects crawled through the slime that coated the walls and crunched under his feet. He tried not to look at the water.

The only sounds were their feet slapping on the wet brick, the drone of the insects, and the splash of discharge as it joined the main flow. His eyes watered, and bile rose in his throat; he swallowed, forcing himself to be silent. After what seemed like an eternity, the man led him off into a smaller tunnel. The river didn't run here, and after a short uphill climb they came to a trapdoor. The man pushed it aside and dragged Nicholas into a small room, stacked high with sacks and barrels – a storeroom of some kind, similar to the one in the bar through which he'd escaped.

Nicholas rolled on the bare floor, couching and retching, his lungs gasping at the fresh air. After a time, he wiped his sweaty face and looked up at his rescuer.

The man was older than Nicholas, perhaps in his late thirties. His face was crisscrossed with fine lines and fading scars, and his eyes blazed with fiery intensity. His black robes were edged with a gold design; Nicholas gasped as he recognised symbols from the Morpheus Church. *What is a French Morpheus priest doing in Gibraltar?*

The man pulled a package from beneath his robes — a parcel of brown paper, about the size of a book, tied up with string — and inspected it. Satisfied it was still in one piece, he replaced the package in the folds of his robe, and turned to Nicholas.

"Qui êtes-vous cachez?" said the stranger. *Who are you hiding from?*

"D'après les soldats. De l'anglais," replied Nicholas. *From the soldiers. From the English.*

The stranger was taken aback. For the first time he seemed to notice Nicholas' uniform. *"Anglais?"* he murmured, staring at Nicholas' feet. Suddenly, he snapped his fingers and grabbed Nicholas' wrist, dragging him toward the door of the storeroom.

"Où m'emmenez-vous?" *Where are you taking me?*

"You won't last two minutes in this town with those clothes," said the stranger, in English. "You killed an officer. They will have the whole garrison looking for you. I will find you some proper attire."

"You mean like yours? No wonder they were chasing us, you dressing as a Morphean in an English port—"

"This is a disguise. I had an errand to run at the local church, when an old priest cruelly interrupted me. You are lucky you found me," he said. "I am Jacques du Blanc. What God do you serve?"

"Great Conductor, but—"

"Then you will come with me. I will get you out of the city; take you to a safe place."

"Thank y—"

Jacques was no longer listening. He rapped three times on the door of the storeroom, and pressed his ear against the wood to listen. Nicholas heard the sound of a bolt being drawn, and a woman's face appeared. Jacques spoke to her in low tones and she left, reappearing a few minutes later with a bowl of brackish water and two bundles of clothes. Jacques handed one to Nicholas. "Put this on."

They were peasant's clothes — breeches and a tunic, and a cloak made of coarse wool. He pulled them on, bundling his uniform under his arm. She stared at him, her pretty brown eyes lingering as she swept her knotted black hair from her cheek. Jacques shooed her away into the room, slamming the door shut behind her. He hid away his robes and dressed himself, too, washing his face in the water and bundling Nicholas' clothes and his parcel into a hollowed-out bale of hay. He opened the door again and led Nicholas through the building — it was a large, derelict warehouse, reeking of old fish and stacked with supplies. The warehouse seemed to be home to several people who crouched in the shadows and hid their faces as they passed. *Where am I?*

Jacques threw open the door and Nicholas followed him into the narrow street. He could see the rear of the port, surrounded by shops and warehouses. Several carriages and wagons loaded with goods rolled past, heading toward the port. One broke away from the line and came to a stop beside them.

"Our ride," said Jacques.

As he settled himself into the carriage, the black-haired girl slipped up behind him and settled herself among the hay bales. She slipped him an apple from inside her dress. He took it gratefully, smiling at her, and she dared a modest smile back.

Jacques took the reins from the driver, who jumped off and slipped away into the crowd. Jacques coaxed the horses into the crowded street, and they were off. Nicholas glanced about nervously, wary of the soldiers posted on every corner. He hid his face in his cloak, but Jacques slapped his arm away.

"You will call attention to us, *Monsieur.* You must be bold. This is how I elude them every time." He winked.

And so, with heart in his chest, Nicholas rode with the strange man with the wild eyes and the silent, black-haired girl out of the town, and across the craggy landscape of Spain, toward the looming shadow of the Pyrenean mountains.

***

They passed into increasingly barren countryside,

the towns becoming poorer, and the faces they passed on the roadside more hardened and rueful. Several times Nicholas asked where they were heading, but Jacques did not answer. Nicholas did not fear the man who had saved him, but kept his scabbard beneath the bench seat, pressed firmly against the heel of his boots, for reassurance.

They stopped often, and each time Jacques ordered Nicholas and the girl — whose name he learned from Jacques was Julianne — to remain in the wagon while he held council with various informants. Nicholas was beginning to understand that he had fallen in with a unique individual. He asked Julianne in his best French where they were going, but she only shook her head.

Once, while Jacques was occupied with his informers, Nicholas opened the corner of the parcel Jacques had taken from the Morpheus church. It contained six thick books on various subjects; chemistry, machinery, medicine, architecture. *Curious.*

On the fifth day of their journey they ascended into the mountains along a crumbling, deserted pass, and camped that night in a cold wood, devoid of warmth, for Jacques would allow no fire. For two days Jacques drove the horses at full speed, 'till at last he stopped on the edge of a ridge and pointed to the other side.

"Bienvenue!" he said. "This will be your home."

Nicholas sucked in his breath, taking in the high walls banked with thick buttresses that seem hewn of the rock itself, the crumbling internal structures, and the precarious stone bridge that marked their path. "What is this place?"

"It was a monastery — a place of learning and worship many hundreds of years ago. But it has been forgotten, except by us." Jacques urged the horses forward, and Nicholas shut his eyes as they bumped over the high stone bridge, barely wider than the wagon.

"You may open your eyes now, *Monsieur* Thorne."

They had parked the wagon in a small, derelict courtyard. The crumbling walls offered some shelter from the biting wind, but most of the verandah roofs and lintels had fallen, strewn in weed-matted lumps across the open space. Doorways lined the crumbling walls, leading into dark spaces beyond. Not a soul stirred. Nervous, Nicholas jumped down from the carriage, his senses on high alert.

A man — dressed in faded black robes bearing the embroidered sigils of the Morphean sect — dashed from a nearby colonnade and began unhitching the horses. He spoke harshly to Jacques in a dialect Nicholas didn't understand, shooting furious glances at Nicholas. Finally, he and Jacques seemed to reach an agreement, and he grabbed the reins and dragged the horses away across the courtyard.

"Auguste keeps the animals in good health. It's hard on them, up here in the mountains. We lose many, but Auguste looks after them. Auguste, this is Nicholas Thorne," announced Jacques.

The man glared at Nicholas, and he saw only hatred in those eyes. His gaze never leaving Nicholas' face, Auguste snarled at Jacques. This time he used English.

"You said there would be no more men. We can barely feed those who we have. And he is an Anglaise — how do we know he won't betray us?"

Jacques didn't reply; instead, he stared down at the man and smiled. That smile carried something —

Nicholas wasn't sure what — but it made Auguste look away, his face flushed. He hurried the horses away. "Do not mind him," said Jacques, placing a hand on Nicholas' shoulder. "He will come around to you. Come. You meet the others."

He followed Jacques and Julianne through one of the monastery doors, pushing aside a tangle of weeds to stoop through the low door. The monastery continued into the bare stone of the mountain, a series of low tunnels leading down into the darkness. Jacques carried no light, but Nicholas saw flickers at the end of the passage. Voices wafted up to greet them. *There are people down here?*

They emerged into a bright, cavernous room, lit by a faded light from two ventilation shafts carved into the vaulted ceiling. But most astonishing of all were the thirty people gathered in this old chapel, divided into groups of threes and fours, each group occupied with a different intellectual pursuit. One man instructed his pairs on the construction of a model bridge, another poured chemicals between glass vials while two men wrote down the results, while many others copied passages from thick, leather-bound books. Dominating the room was a wide stone altar, covered in a stained white cloth and dotted with burning candles, providing the flickering light Nicholas had spied earlier. Where once a Christian crucifix would have stood, there was a golden statue of the God Morpheus.

"This is our sanctuary," said Jacques. "Here we may worship and learn in peace. We have food and shelter, and fresh water from a mountain spring. And we are safe here from discovery and persecution. We are fifty-eight men, and three women — Julianne here, and you will meet Danielle and Marie later. You may stay with us for as long as you wish."

"This is — I don't understand — why have you brought me here?"

"You are a student of Great Conductor, yes? You will find many of your Industrian peers here. We worship together, for we have no other place to go."

"Thank you for your kindness, Jacques, but I cannot remain here. I must return to England as soon as I can buy passage on a ship—"

Jacques laughed. "You will find no such ship leaving from French ports."

"Pardon?"

The Frenchman laughed harder, slapping his hand against his thigh. "You fool! You silly English fool! You picked the worst time to run away. The Emperor Napoleon has blockaded England. He aims to stamp out Industrian influence in Europe completely. His constables travel the countryside, drawing out and destroying the remaining Industrian churches. They hanged two Morpheans in the market square at Marseilles just last week. That is why we live and study here in secret. And now you live here as well." He laughed again. "Even if a ship could get through the blockade, no one would dare take an Industrian on board. No, Mr Thorne, you're a Frenchman now."

The news turned Nicholas cold. He slumped to the floor, his face in his hands. He was a fugitive with no way home. His chances of seeing London and Isambard again shrank to a tiny fleck.

***

Life in the monastery was modest and quiet, but not without its dangers. French troops patrolled the roads leading to the mountain pass, and Jacques said they would sometimes ride up to the ruins to check for refugees. When that happened, the Morpheans would retreat into the lower tunnels, and they had not yet been discovered. They could not have fires at night, nor could they take prolonged exercise on the slopes.

But as days turned into weeks, Nicholas found himself settling into the place. The men — no doubt at Jacques' insistence — accepted him well enough, though they would not resort to speaking English in his presence. His French had much improved, and he was beginning to understand the idioms of the local dialect. It didn't hurt that around every corner he saw Julianne staring back at him through a curtain of tangled black hair. She still did not speak, but for a girl of only nineteen or so her grim expression betrayed her hardship.

His days faded into one another. In the early morning, just as the sunlight appeared between the mountain peaks, Jacques called everyone to the chapel and conducted a church service — daily prayers intoned in his clear, rumbling voice, his conviction apparent as he lovingly removed the statues from their niches and bathed them. The men came from a variety of Industrian religions, and all risked persecution by hiding in the mountains with Jacques.

After church, Julianne and the other women handed around breakfast — a sparse meal of barley gruel seasoned with wild berries that grew in clusters on the slopes of the mountain. Nicholas ate it hungrily, for it might be the only meal he got that day. After breakfast they performed chores — sweeping, cleaning, gathering food and wood for the fires — and finally Jacques called them back into the tunnels to continue their studies.

They had little in the way of tools and provisions, but they had books — some found in the storehouses of the old monastery, the rest smuggled from across Europe by a growing network of Industrian dissenters — and paper and ink. Each man studied according to his own interests, and so it was that Nicholas quickly found books by Étienne-Louis Boullée and François-Joseph Bélanger, great masters of architecture and industrial design. These he devoured again and again, 'till he could quote whole passages by heart.

He shared his studies with three other students. Joseph Ramée — who had been an eminent Parisian architect and outspoken Morphean until the Emperor's reforms had sent him underground — and Auguste, who made no attempt to disguise his hatred of Nicholas. They were joined often by Julianne. She still had not spoken, but read over her notes with a ferocious intensity. Sometimes she would lean over his shoulder as he read, tracing the drawings with delicate fingers. Her hair brushed his face, and all his thoughts and calculations escaped from his head.

***

As his mother and her new lover continued to torment him, Isambard's fervor for his machine only grew. He began to openly flout their rules, returning late, stinking of grease, filling his bunk with minuscule workings of engine parts and crude clockwork mechanisms. He seemed to take the beatings as his personal triumphs, each rasp of his stepfather's whip against his skin only hardening his determination to reveal the machine and prove once and for all that Stokers could be engineers.

"It will avenge my father's banishment." he said. "It will be the locomotive to end all locomotives. Faster than anything Stephenson has ever built. When we are done, I can show the King, and he'll see he was wrong to send my father away."

Every day, Aaron worried about what Isambard would do once he finished tinkering with the locomotive. Did he plan to sell the engine, or use it to incite the workers to rebellion, or to simply buy his way into another sect? They never discussed the subject, and Aaron — knowing the engine was not really theirs, but Isambard's — felt asking was somehow sacrilegious.

Most of all, he worried about being discovered. He worried his love for his friend would soon see his own neck in the hangman's noose.

But as the months and years went by, neither Isambard's mother nor the priests discovered their secret hideout under the church. It was not for want of trying. Merrick paid boys in the village to follow Isambard, but he would weave and duck and lose them in the madness of the underground passages, before emerging and sneaking away to the church. The workers, who still remembered his father and knew Isambard was up to something, covered his shifts and stamped his attendance in the logbook. And though they made a terrible racket, no one noticed the hammerings of two boys amidst the banging and smelting and hissing and whirring of the day-to-day activities of the Ward.

They should have finished the engine a year ago, but at Isambard's insistence, they had pulled the chassis apart and widened her, setting the bearings further apart. Now she was a different kind of beast entirely.

Finally, the day came when they hammered on the last sheet of iron over the boiler, and stood back to admire their work. Their adjustments gave the engine a squat, pygmy appearance — the round boiler casing jutting like a long nose from the high drive wheels. The cab was open to the elements, with barely enough room for two men to pass each other.

"She's beautiful." Aaron breathed, hardly able to believe they had built such an enormous engine themselves.

"Let's fire her up." said Isambard.

They ran down into the tunnels and carried sacks of coal up to their secret workshop. Aaron filled the coal store and spread a thin layer on the floor of the boiler while Isambard knotted rags to the end of a wooden pole, dunked it in oil, lit it, and shoved it in the firebox. They checked the water tank was full, wiped the grime from the pressure dials, and sat against the bare brick walls, waiting for the temperature to climb up.

"The festival of steam will be held in London in the summer," Aaron said. The feast day of Great Conductor and the biggest religious festival on the Stoker calendar would see the Engine Ward filled to bursting with Conductor engineers, their priests, and followers. The streets would throng with food and drink and dancing, and the Great Conductor churches would be packed with worshippers making their pilgrimage during this auspicious time. The Royal Society was holding an exhibition of Stephenson's work that would attract many people to the city, and rumour had it Stephenson himself might even make an appearance.

"The fact has not escaped my attention," Isambard replied.

"Are you planning something foolhardy?"

Isambard laughed. "You know me too well, Aaron. But we're not finished with her yet. She must work perfectly on the day she is discovered; otherwise, all our work will come to naught. Even if everything works perfectly today—"

On the engine, something shot off and clattered on the brick wall above their heads, and the engine belched a cloud of black steam. Isambard grinned.

"—which we knew was too much to hope for, we still haven't run her on a track. That will be our next test."

"But we don't have a track to run her on," said Aaron, a feeling of dread settling in his belly. "The only railway in Engine Ward is built in Stephenson's standard gauge."

"Precisely." The thick, steam-filled air could not mask the gleeful expression on Isambard's face. "So we shall have to build one."

***

Nicholas tossed in his bed, unable to sleep. Above

his head, the carnal pleasures of Auguste and Danielle could clearly be heard, and his mind created images to accompany their cries. He felt his solitude more keenly than ever, and his thoughts cast a dark shadow in his heart. *I am an outlaw, a deserter, hiding in the mountain. I shall never have a wife.*

He could measure his achievements to date by the state of his lodgings. Down in the tunnels, each man had a space of his own, and his was an old storage battery two storeys beneath the chapel, empty save his blankets and a small wooden table on rotting legs. A narrow door led into the passage beyond. The bare rock walls had been carved with crucifixes and other markings by the ancient occupants.

Nothing. I have nothing.

He balled his jacket — on which he rested his head — into a tighter pillow, pulling the blanket around his head to block out the sound. He squeezed his eyes shut, trying to ease his mind into gentle thoughts — thoughts of bridges and factory designs — but they kept being pushed aside by the image of a black-haired face and a life he had lost forever.

The air around him suddenly grew thick. He opened one eye and found that very face staring back at him, her nose only inches from his.

He leapt back in fright. "Julianne, what are you doing here?"

She, of course, did not answer, but lifted up his blankets and slipped underneath. Her skirts brushed against his legs, and a tongue of fire shot up his spine. Instinctively he shuffled away.

"You can't remain here. The men will say—"

"I do not care what they say," she declared

suddenly, pulling the blankets tightly around her.

He sat up in surprise. "You *can* speak?"

"Of course. I—I—I choose not to. I do not want *him* to hear my thoughts."

"Who?"

"Jacques." She spat out his name.

"You speak with such venom, has he done something to hurt you?" Nicholas paused. "I'm sure it was a misunderstanding. He is not a cruel man."

"You do not understand. I did not choose to come here like you and the other men. I am a prisoner. I come from a village near Marseilles. We had one of the finest Morphean churches in the country, and scholars came from miles around to visit our library and hear the great scholars teach. But the Emperor's men rode in on horses, hacking and shooting and setting fire to our buildings. The church burnt down, and they executed many — including my brothers — as heretics. The village had no money, and no one would help us, because they were afraid of the soldiers.

"My father needed money. No one would hire a known Morphean, and my younger broker was sickly, so he sold the only thing he had left — me. I've been with Jacques for four years now, and every year his passions grow more insidious."

"You are his … wife?"

She laughed. "Hardly. He's tried his hand at me, certainly, but I would not let him near me. No, I do the work he deems beneath him — the dangerous work. I deliver messages; I steal from ravaged churches and neglected libraries. Once, I even killed a man." She shuddered at the memory. "You do not know the things he's done. The things he plans to do."

"These men would all be dead if it weren't for him. *I* would be dead if not for his intervention. And here I have access to books, and some of the most learned men in France—"

"Do you think our studies are for the worship of our gods?" she laughed bitterly. "Jacques has a plan in mind for us, Nicholas, and it is diabolical."

She rolled over, pulling his jacket under her head, her black tresses fanning out across the cold floor. Soon, he could hear her breathing heavily, but he did not sleep; the warmth of her body, mere inches away, sending his head spinning with impossible dreams.

***

Julianne came to his chamber most nights, when she felt she could sneak away from her usual bed without attracting notice. She huffed derisively at the sounds of lovemaking from above, 'till Nicholas could only conclude that she had no interest in him in that way, or if she did, she hid it well. Instead, she wanted to learn about architecture.

Huddled around the stub of a candle in a dark corner of his room, they whispered their lessons to each other. She had an astounding aptitude for mathematics; as Nicholas described an engineering concept to her, she could perceive it in time and space without needing it drawn for her. When she struggled with an idea, he would take her hands and form a picture in the darkness.

Snow fell on the mountain, first as a fluffy, flaky sprinkling, and then in a great dumping that iced shut the doors and froze up the monastery's well. Now that the bridge to the monastery was impassable, Jacques sent Nicholas out with the other men to clamber down to the forest and collect wood for their fires.

While he gathered branches to drag back up the cliff, he stuffed his pockets with handfuls of twigs, always choosing the straightest. Back at the camp, he dried them by the fire, and tied them together with twine to form the bridges and factories he saw in his imagination.

As his knowledge grew, he began to fill his room with these creations. It was now more than two years since he'd left the *Cleopatra* in Gibraltar, and the monotony of the monastery had begun to wear on him. He longed again for the freedom and opportunity of a huge, industrial city.

He expressed his desire to Julianne one night, while they huddled together in the light of the candle. To his surprise, she leapt into his arms and planted a kiss on his cheek, sending that familiar fire through his whole body.

"I knew you'd change your mind about this place one day," she exclaimed, forgetting to whisper in her excitement. "We will leave within the month — he'll not follow us down the mountain in winter—"

"No, no, I do not wish—" Her expression froze. "I mean, I have not finished my studies."

"This isn't a university," she snapped. "You have memorised all the books. You have exhausted Jacques' and Monsieur Ramée's knowledge. You cannot live forever in the mountains, drawing cities in your imagination. We must leave soon, before the Spring breaks. We will go north — I've heard the Dirigires will fly people across the border—"

"I'm sure if we ask Jacques, he will drop us near the coast when he next returns there."

Her eyes flashed. "You must not breathe a word to him. How many times must I tell you, Nicholas? He is not to be trusted."

"But—"

"Do you remember I told you I killed a man?" Her voice sounded far away. "He was Louis — the last man who tried to leave here. He snuck out in the dead of night, jumped the fence, and headed east into the mountains. But Auguste was on guard, and saw something moving across the rocks. He chased Louis down and hit him with the flat of his blade. Then he came to find Jacques.

"Jacques has some knowledge of my character, given the arrangement that transpires between us. He wanted to warn me what would happen if I tried to escape. So he roused me from sleep and dragged me up with him. When he found Louis as Auguste had left him, Jacques pressed a pistol into my hand, and ordered me to kill him. He made me straddle the body, wrapping his fingers around mine as he showed me how to pull back the hammer and squeeze the trigger. He said, if I didn't do it, he would, and then he would kill me. And I … forgive me." She looked away, tears sliding down her smooth cheeks.

"He laughed, Nicholas, he *laughed* as that man's brains spread out across the cobbles. I scrubbed and I scrubbed for days afterward, but still the cobbles in the courtyard are stained with his blood. Look for yourself. Look at my skirts." She lifted the hem, bringing it into the light so he could see the dark stains.

"Julianne—" The sight of her tears made him feel helpless. He reached for her, but she recoiled.

"We will escape together," she said. "You and I. And if we make it to London alive, I should like to marry you."

***

Three days after she made this proclamation and Nicholas had promised he would find a way for them to escape, Julianne stopped attending Jacques' morning sermons. At first, Nicholas thought perhaps she was feeling ill, or had been sidetracked with business in the kitchens, but on her fifth absence from the sermons, he excused himself to look for her, and found her in the courtyard. Snowflakes settled on her cloak as she scuffed at the snow with her foot to reveal the discoloured stones.

"I am in private worship," she replied fiercely when Nicholas confronted her. "There's no blasphemy in that. He's not even a real priest. He cannot force me to attend his church."

Surprised by the malice in her voice, he left her alone, and returned to the chapel. Jacques looked up as he came in, nodding as he took his seat alone. Something in Jacques' expression flickered, and Nicholas wondered what had really transpired between him and Julianne.

She returned after the sermon to serve the breakfast with Danielle and Marie. As she shoved Jacques' bowl in front of him, he grabbed her by the wrist and leapt to his feet, sending the gruel across the floor.

"If I may have your attention, please?" he yelled.

The room fell instantly silent. Nicholas lowered his bowl, his stomach knotting. His eyes met Jacques', and he was surprised at the intensity there. Julianne didn't attempt to extract her hand, but her face pleaded with Nicholas to do something. He shook his head, not understanding what was happening.

"I have an announcement to make." Jacques clasped her tiny hand to his breast. "After many years as part of my household, Julianne has finally agreed to be my wife. The wedding will be here, in this very chapel, within the week. It will be conducted in the true Morphean manner."

He left the room, dragging Julianne by the wrist, to raucous applause. A wedding meant a feast, a night to ease the monotony of the long winter. Nicholas remained seated, staring at the departing couple in open-mouthed horror. *This can't be real. Only a few days ago she said she would marry me. She said he had never ... surely Jacques does not mean this?*

As Jacques shoved her toward his quarters, Julianne looked over her shoulder, and the terror in her face told Nicholas all he needed to know.

***

Nicholas retired after the evening meal to be alone with his thoughts. He hadn't seen Julianne or Jacques for the rest of the day, their absence causing all manner of unsettling thoughts to pass through his head. *Surely Julianne has not agreed to this? Jacques is an educated man — surely he would not resort to such barbarity?* The question plagued him long into the evening, 'till he finally drifted into a fitful sleep.

He awoke with a start, his mind awash with images from his nightmares. Something scraped against the stone in the doorway. Someone was in his room.

He could see nothing in the darkness. "Who's there?" he called, reaching for his gun.

"Nicholas?" she whispered, her skirts swishing against the stone. "Are you awake?"

He bolted upright, closed the distance between them in a single stride and embraced her. "I was so worried about you. Are you all right?"

"I shall never be all right again. I could not get away to talk to you," she said. "But now, finally, he is asleep, and I could sneak away. I had to see you."

"What are we to do?" he whispered, pressing her head against his chest.

"We must leave before I am bound to him. It will not be easy. He knows of our … meetings. He is jealous. He will guard me with all his powers."

He pulled her under the blankets with him, and together they formed a plan of escape. She said nothing about what had gone on earlier, her indifference disarming, but he sensed she was fragile, broken somehow. He reached out to touch her face, but she shied away.

What has Jacques done to you?

When the grunting and screaming of Auguste and Danielle interrupted their scheming, Julianne crawled closer to Nicholas and pulled his arms tightly around her. She sobbed; great silent sobs that wrenched her whole body. He ached with need of her, but could not bring himself to do anything more than hold her.

***

The back of the church sloped into a generous garden — now an overgrown mess of weeds and debris, hidden from street view behind one of the tallest scrap heaps. It had once been the burial ground of prominent Christian engineers, but had fallen into disuse with the King's militant stance against the banned religion. Most of the gravestones had been pulled up to decorate the churches of other engineers, but here and there Aaron tripped over the flat corners of a marker. Thinking what might lay only a few feet underground gave him a cold feeling all over.

They didn't have enough space to create a complete loop, so Isambard designed a long test track that extended along the western edge of the graveyard, directly behind the scrap heap, and executed a tight curve, continued in a straight line for fifty feet (just enough time to brake, according to Isambard), and ended abruptly just before the brick wall of a mausoleum. He even built a special machine that moulded and cut the rails to uniform thickness.

But Aaron was the one who had to painstakingly lay each rail according to Isambard's precise instructions. They worked outside in the cover of night — Isambard laid out pegs, while Aaron huffed and sweated as he dragged the heavy rails across the weed-choked cemetery and hammered in the nails to hold them in place. Every night they had to cover their progress with rubbish from the heap, and uncover the previous night's work before they could continue.

Quartz didn't ask Aaron where he went every night, but Aaron could feel the old man's eyes on him as he climbed into bed in the early hours of the morning.

"That Isambard is trouble," he said over breakfast one morning.

"Huh?" Aaron looked up from his bread.

"He's got *ideas,*" said Quartz, "in his *head.* Ideas Stokers ought not to have. And look at you — he's got you out at all hours, burns and bruises all up your arms. I admired Marc Brunel as much as the next man, but I've no desire to join him, and I don't want you shipping out to Van Dieman's Land, either."

"We are careful," said Aaron. "And what Isambard's doing is *important.* I think he could really change things for the Stokers, this time for the better." He kissed Quartz on the forehead as he pulled on his coat. "I'm in Boiler C this morning, and I'll be back late again tonight. Don't wait up."

"If you get deported, I'm keeping the shack!" Quartz yelled after him.

***

They could not risk testing the engine in daylight, for men would sometimes hunt through the scrap heap for salvageable materials. But nor could they test it late at night, where the hiss of the steam and the clanging of the tracks would rouse even Quartz from his grog-soaked dreams. The only time they had available to test the engine was when everyone in the Engine Ward was occupied — during the evening sermons.

So when the bells began to toll the hour, calling people to their prayers, and the churches flung open their doors to accept the waiting hordes of scholars, acolytes, and workmen, Aaron slipped away from the Stoker camp and made his way to the abandoned churchyard.

Isambard waited for him. He'd fired the boiler the night before, so the engine was hot and ready to go, and he'd cleared the debris from the rails, leaving the full length of the track visible. Isambard's smile was almost as wide as his seven-foot gauge track.

"We don't have much time," he said, ushering Aaron inside. They crowded into the cab, which was really a footplate with barely enough room for the two of them to squeeze past each other. Aaron fell to his knees and took up the small coal shovel, while Isambard checked the gauges.

"The pressure is at one-sixty." He released the brake and gave the regulator a squeeze. "Let's go."

And they went. With surprising smoothness they rolled out of the workshop and over the churchyard. Aaron added another shovelful of coal, pushing it right into the corners of the firebox to give an even spread, then looked up at his friend. Isambard leaned against the regulator, whooping as their engine clattered over the track, the heat from the firebox casting dancing shadows over his face.

Down the straight she flew, steam hissing from her pistons, and Isambard pulled in the regulator, slowing her around the corner. Aaron held his breath as they came at it too fast. The wheels slipped on the track, and the whole engine lurched dangerously to the left.

Down they slammed, and the wheels found the rails again, and Isambard closed the regulator and pulled on the brake. Aaron closed the firebox door, and with a screech they lurched to a stop.

Isambard pulled him to his feet. "We've done it!" he cried, embracing Aaron. "We've built a locomotive and she goes! She really goes!"

Aaron couldn't help but beam back at him. They laughed together, hugging each other, patting the engine like she were a housecat, reliving over and over again the joy of that short ride. Suddenly, they were startled from their celebration by the tolling of a bell.

"The sermons are finished," said Isambard, staring in the direction of the churches. "We must get her back inside before anyone sees her."

He pulled on the regulator, taking the corner more slowly this time. The engine, which would have to cool overnight, did not need any more coal, so Aaron leaned against the coal buckets and enjoyed the rush of cool evening wind past his face.

"She's beautiful," he cried as they pulled her back into the workshop, shut her off, and opened the firebox door to cool the engine.

Isambard nodded. "A few minor adjustments and she will be ready for the grand unveiling."

The now-familiar rumble of fear settled in Aaron's stomach. He could not name his fear exactly, but it felt as though he stood at the edge of a swirling black ocean, the waves ready to swallow him at any moment, and Isambard was paddling a boat through the maelstrom, calling for him to pull up an oar.

"What are we going to do, Isambard? We can't simply wheel her out by the cooking fires and expect the priests to hand you a medal."

"You worry too much. I have it all figured out."

"That's precisely what I'm worried about."

***

Isambard had given as much thought to how he would reveal the engine as he had to its design. He knew he had the support of the workers, whose discontent still bubbled just below the surface of the current calm state of affairs. They dwarfed the priesthood in number, but not in influence, and the success of his unveiling depended on his ability to convince at least some of the church authorities — people on the Council of the Royal Society — that he should be allowed to innovate.

The night before the Festival of Steam, Isambard had Aaron drive the engine out onto their makeshift track. They had managed to extend it for quite some distance along the edge of the scrap heap by covering their progress with piles of old, twisted iron. In the early hours of the morning they uncovered the track and cleared away any debris that might impede her journey. They fired up the engine, oiled the mechanisms, and made a few last-minute adjustments to the drive shaft. Isambard hummed while he worked.

In his heart, Aaron had never truly expected the engine to be completed, much less be revealed to the Industrian priests. Now they were on the eve of the reveal, and he was terrified. In the shadow of Marc Brunel's deportation, they'd flouted too many laws and created something too revolutionary to be accepted by the wider religious population. He pictured himself walking on board a vessel bound for Van Diemen's land, his hands in shackles, or worse, standing on the wooden stage of a hangman's porch.

"This isn't going to work," he said aloud, adding fresh coal to the buckets for tomorrow's performance.

"Nonsense. The engine works perfectly."

"You know I don't speak of the engine. Isambard, I know you miss your father, but there's no reason for us to join him—"

"We won't share his fate, I *promise*. If you're so worried about it, I won't let on that you helped with the engine. I will take all of the blame if it goes wrong, but I'll also take all of the credit for whatever transpires."

"Is that a promise?"

Isambard only smiled.

Aaron slept poorly that night, tossing and turning as he thought of what tomorrow might bring. Even if Isambard took the blame, it would be easy for the Council to figure out he had had Aaron's help. Besides, Aaron didn't want to see Isambard hanged or deported as a traitor. When he finally slept, dreams assailed him, fretful nightmares of burning buildings, of an England, years from now, ruled by fiery engines, and of Isambard, wearing the crown of England and smiling from a tall iron tower while the streets below ran red with blood.

Finally, he could take it no more, and pulled himself out of bed. As he dressed, he glanced at the first rays of sunlight pricking the window, dulled by the fog of steam and soot that blanketed the air. He pulled on his coat and, leaving Quartz snoring away on his bunk, went outside to watch the preparations.

As the feast day of one of the Gods of Industry, the Festival of Steam attracted engineers and their followers from all over the empire. Sects who worshipped the Great Conductor travelled hundreds of miles to London to offer up their inventions to his grace. At the centre of the festival, a replica of Richard Trevethick's *Puffing Devil*, the first locomotive ever built, stood on a plinth, its base crowded with offerings.

Worshippers crowded the streets, jostling Aaron out of the way as they hurried to the dawn service at Stephenson's church. The Festival of Steam opened with public honours being given to Trevethick, the church's first Messiah, and to all the church elders and their inventions. Stephenson's cathedral was already filled to bursting, and people crammed into the corrals set up on the street outside. As Messiah, Stephenson should be performing the ceremony, but he'd declined to attend the festival this year, preferring to remain in Manchester. He had, however, sent a contingent of Navvies, who camped on the northern edge of Engine Ward, as far from the Stokers as it was possible to get.

Aaron gazed up to see a regiment of Dirigires, the fanatical followers of Jean-Pierre Blanchard, the first man to fly a balloon across the channel, float across the sunrise. They had arrived the day before, to much fanfare, bobbing over the city in their black-bellied flying balloons, smoke spluttering from their steam engines, before touching down on the great promenade of the Engine Ward.

Aaron skirted around the edge of the promenade, where a parade of all the different sects in Engine Ward was in full swing, the steam rising from their showy inventions shrouding the marketplace in thick mist. Keeping to the early-morning shadows, he scrambled to the top of the scrap heap and looked down. Isambard was there already, running through the final preparations. He looked up, saw Aaron watching, and gave him a casual wave.

Aaron gave a little flap of his hand in reply, not wanting to appear too enthusiastic. He scrambled back down the scrap heap and took a deep breath.

It was now or never.

The parade had just passed by, and the crowd milled about on the street, waiting for the next amusement to begin. Aaron started running, pushing through conversations, using his elbows and heavy boots to dislodge anyone who stood in his way. Men grumbled, women cried out in alarm, and several faces turned from the parade to see what was going on.

"Quick!" Aaron yelled. "There's a fire behind the slag heaps! A church is burning!"

Everyone ran. Isambard was right — each party assumed it was their own church in danger. A great plume of black smoke curled up above the spires, and the crowd panicked. The priests waddled as fast as they could in their constricting robes, quickly overtaken by the tide of people, led by the Stokers and other work groups. They tore over the scrap heap, legs churning, voices raised in surprise, as they discovered just what was going on.

Aaron — who'd been given no explanation of the plan by Isambard — expected to see the spire of the old Morpheus church alight, but when he gazed down he saw it was the church next door, an elaborate shrine to Trevethick — built by the Navvies when they'd resided in the Ward — which was ablaze. Two Navvy priests banged on the glass windows, trapped inside. *What has Isambard done? Those men could die if the engine fails. That isn't part of the plan!*

While men shouted for water to be sent, another plume of smoke approached from the left. With a hiss, Isambard's engine trundled along the final stretch of rail, which stopped alongside the shrine, dragging a wagon containing a small water pump. He pulled on the brakes, and, when he rolled close enough, directed the hoses at the source of the fire. Within a few moments it was over, and he jumped down from the cab, clambered inside the soot-choked building and pulled the Navvies to safety.

Astonishment rippled through the crowd. No one could believe what they'd just witnessed. The men clattered across the tracks and surrounded Isambard's locomotive.

"He saved these two men!"

"That's Isambard Brunel. He's a Stoker. But look at that contraption!"

"Brunel? You mean that chap we had in court a few years back—"

"It may very well have saved them, but what *is* it?"

"And why is a Stoker driving it?"

Oswald pushed through the crowd, and gazed up at Isambard on the footplate with a sneer. "Well, Isambard, you really do take after your father, and you'll soon die like him." He turned back to the crowd. "Rest assured, ladies and gentlemen, this man will be dealt with to the sternest measure of church law."

"There ain't no law against it!" a voice called from the back of the crowd.

"What was that?" Oswald snapped.

Stokers — William Stone and Matthew Harris and, of course, Quartz — pushed through the crowd. Ladies fell over each other to move out of their way, lest the soot on the overalls rub off on their dresses.

"I *said*," Quartz growled, "there ain't no law against Isambard creatin' an engine, if he so wishes." Grumbles of assent rippled through the crowd.

"Stokers are followers of Great Conductor, same as Navvies and Newconens and James Watt's crew. Day in and day out we work under these very streets, keeping the cogs oiled and the furnaces stoked. And if one of our own has the mind of an engineer," he folded his arms as a gasp went through the crowd, "then I say, he knows his craft better than most men."

"How do we know this infernal contraption is safe? How do we know it's not some kind of weapon—"

"It saved the lives of two men."

"You don't even know what *it* is," roared Oswald.

"I think I can explain that."

Every head turned toward Isambard, who disentangled himself from the grasp of a grateful Navvy woman and stalked toward them.

"This is a locomotive engine, built by my hands and my hands alone." His eyes met Aaron's pointedly as he spoke. "She is of a similar design to those run by the Messiah Robert Stephenson, but she runs on a broader gauge track — seven and a quarter inches, to be precise. This gives her a unique advantage. She can ride faster over long distances than any of Stephenson's engines. And she carries a heavier load — like this double-sized water tanker I carry today — and more carriages. When she carries passenger cars, they will be wider and fit more seats in them."

"This is preposterous!" cried a Metic priest. "He dares to argue with the Messiah's own designs!"

"If every Stoker were off inventing locomotives, who would operate the Engine Ward—"

"He should be thrown in the tower!" Oswald cried. "Look at how he flaunts his invention with no regard for his position. He thinks himself among equals here. He should be sent away, like his traitorous father."

"I simply do not see," said Isambard, "why a man's sect should determine his ability to invent something for the good of England, especially when the machine can save the lives of others and improve efficiency and performance."

"You staged this, you rotten—"

"I set a Navvy shrine on fire and then put it out again? Does that sound like the kind of thing a Stoker would do?"

The men looked at each other. Finally, Joseph Locke, the Presbyter of the Great Conductor Sect and a staunch Navvy, stepped forward, shook Isambard's hand, and squinted at the engine.

"Thank you for saving my men." he said.

"You're welcome," said Isambard, smiling broadly.

"As to your engine, I don't believe the validity of your claim this broad gauge will produce superior speed. In order to determine what should be done with you, we must first determine if you speak the truth about your locomotive. We shall have to see what she can do."

***

He floated on a mountaintop, high in the Pyrenees, trapped in the swirling blindness of a snowstorm. Julianne was screaming, her dress covered in blood. He fumbled across the snow, trying to reach her, but with every step, she seemed even further from him. He took another step, but his foot never found solid ground. He toppled over the edge of a chasm and fell, the sheer rocks hurtling past him, Julianne's screams ripping apart the night ...

Nicholas woke with a start, finding himself not hurtling toward his death, but safe in his cold bed in the empty battery beneath the monastery, his blankets soaked with sweat. *It was only a dream. It wasn't real.*

The screaming, however, was real.

The sound pounded against the rocks above, striking him with the force of a physical blow. *Julianne!* Upstairs, somewhere, something was hurting her. He fumbled in the dark for a candle and, lighting it, drew his sword from its sheath and crept silently up the stairs.

It didn't take long to locate the source of the screaming. Julianne's cries faded to a whimper, but they led him directly to the chapel. The door was locked, but he kicked at the bolt with his boot 'till it gave way.

The sight that greeted him froze his blood. Julianne — her hands bound before her and tied to the heavy legs of the altar — was spread naked across their place of worship, her body contorted in pain. Thick red welts crossed her chest where someone had pawed at her, and ribbons of blood cascaded over her breasts and down her face. Jacques loomed over her, naked below the waist, a great grin on his face as he thrust harder and harder into her, while her blood splattered across his thighs.

"Nicholas!" he called cheerfully. "Do you care for

a ride after me? I've warmed her up for you!"

Julianne met his eyes, wide with horror and shame. She tried to speak, but Jacques held his hand tightly over her mouth.

Nicholas' stomach lurched. He coughed violently, and his anger rose along with the bile, welling up from the pit of his belly and coursing through every limb in his body. Remembering the sword in his hand, he held it in front of him and took a step forward.

"I wouldn't." said Jacques cheerfully, reaching behind the altar and grabbing his own sword. He withdrew from Julianne and took at step toward Nicholas. "Do you think the other men don't know what goes on in here? Why, they've many of them had their turns with pretty Julianne while you've slept unawares. If you strike me, Nicholas, you'll have thirty Morpheans upon you in an instant."

"You— you—"

"I am the priest here. I rescued you — *all* of you — from a life of servitude to the false Christian gods. I gave you what you so ardently desired, Monsieur Nicholas — books, and learning, and great scholars who could test your skills. Should I not have something in return?"

"You hide behind the trappings of a learned man, Jacques, but you are a barbarian."

"It is no different to the world left on that boat. Locked up here as we are, with little diversion from our study, a man has urges. And I know you'll agree — Danielle and Marie aren't to everyone's tastes. I have seen the way you look at Julianne — can you say with honesty you have not felt the same compulsion I exercise now? As an honest man, I do not deny my compulsions."

"I am nothing like you." Nicholas spat.

"And yet, you point a sword at me and ask who is the barbarian in this room?"

Nicholas sprang forward, striking at Jacques' chest. But his thrust was wild, driven by anger, and Jacques blocked him easily. He knew as he flung out another thrust that soon he would slip, and Jacques would slit him open.

"I've married her, you know." said Jacques, expertly parrying another swing. "I've performed the Morphean rituals, and we are in every sense man and wife. But this is no Catholic church — I'm a generous man, and I'll share my wife with my brothers. Auguste has his turn this evening, but you may have tomorrow, if you wish—"

Nicholas feigned left and thrust for Jacques' chest, but Jacques stepped back and directed his blow down, throwing Nicholas' shoulder and head forward. Up flicked Jacques' blade, slicing through the skin on his cheek. Blood gushed from the wound, blocking his vision, and pain filled his head. He lost his balance and lurched forward.

Jacques caught him, twisting him upward so Nicholas could see the thin point of Jacques' rapier pointing at his throat. His head swam, the pain stinging like a bee, draining him of strength.

"Very well." Jacques' face twisted into a grin. "Unfortunately, you must understand that I cannot allow you to remain a free scholar here, for if you managed to escape down the mountains, you could easily report our position to the authorities." He snapped his fingers, and Auguste stepped forward and grabbed Nicholas under the arms. "Perhaps you may think about my offer in your confinement, yes?"

***

Auguste dragged him down a flight of narrow, poorly fashioned stairs, much deeper into the mountain than his battery. At the foot of the staircase was a single dark room. Auguste shoved him inside and slammed the door. "Sometimes the monks would go mad up here in the mountains with nothing but their prayers. This is where they kept those men — some dangerous, some simply pathetic." He laughed as he slid the bolts shut. "I know which one you are."

His footsteps disappeared up the stairs, leaving Nicholas alone in the darkness. They'd given him a blanket and a stale loaf, but he had no appetite. He touched the cut on his cheek, sending a wave of pain through his head. It was a clean cut, but he had nothing to cauterize it. He tore the sleeve from his shirt and held this against his face in an effort to stop the bleeding.

The darkness pushed against him, silence embracing him like a wild river, rolling over him and tossing him about, so he didn't know where was up and down. He slept fitfully, waking covered in sweat, his cheek stinging. He tried to pace out the room, but it wasn't even high enough from him to stand without stooping, and if he stretched his arms out wide, his fingers scraped the stone walls.

He passed time in the gloom — it might have been days, or only hours. Twice more, bread was pushed through a slot in the door, the faint glimmer of a torch casting a thin shadow on the rough stone floor. He hammered on the door 'till blood dribbled down his fists, calling for someone to help him, but no one came.

He listened to the voices of the mountain, hoping he might find a mind he could use to help him escape. But all he could hear so deep in the earth were worms and creatures of the dirt and rocks. He hadn't the energy, the power, to form a plan.

He slept and woke again, nightmares clinging to his body. Sweat clung to his clammy skin. There was a noise outside the door.

Footsteps — not slow and careful, but rushed — slipped on the steep steps leading down into the stone passage. A key turned in the lock, and to his surprise, the door swung open and a bright light thrust itself inside his prison.

He closed his eyes against the glare and the imposing shadow that towered over him. *I hope they kill me quickly. I hope Jacques has no use for torture —*

"Nicholas?"

I must truly be ready to die, for I can hear the voices of angels.

"Nicholas!" The angel sounded impatient. He rubbed his eyes, squinting against the bright light as his eyes adjusted. The figure came into focus, hazy at first, a mere shadow. But the light illuminated her height, the curve of her hip, and, finally, her face — scarred and bloody, but utterly beautiful.

"Julianne!" he collapsed at her feet, touching the hem of her dress. "You're alive. Alive! How did you —"

"Ssshh." She knelt down beside him, her delicate fingers wiping his matted hair back from his face. Tracing the wound on his cheek, she pulled his chin up so he could look at her face, and she held her finger to her lips. "I have killed Auguste, so it was nothing to take the dagger from his belt and the key from his pocket. Look at you — you're weak and starving."

He pulled her down, breathing in the scent of her. Her skin felt cold and clammy, as though she were not a woman at all. He ran his fingers over her cheeks, laced with abrasions. When she pulled away, wincing, he saw the bright pink bloodstain splashed across the front of her dress.

"You are hurt?"

"Yes." It came out as a croak. "But this blood is not all mine. We must leave now."

"But how — how long have I been here?"

"Five days, though it feels like centuries," she said darkly, and a shadow passed over her face as she recalled her own horrors. She pressed a bottle against his lips. "For strength. Please, we must hurry, before Jacques discovers what I've done."

He gulped hungrily, the warm alcohol returning some strength to his bones. "But how did you—"

She put her arms under his shoulders and pulled him upright, swinging his arm over her neck and leading him, hobbling, to the stairs. "There was a fight amongst the men for who would be the next to defile me, and Auguste broke the mirror above the altar. Shards of glass rained down on me. I hid one in my hand and later, when the men had retired, I used it to cut the rope. Auguste was charged with guarding me, but the brute was snoring, and I had no trouble at all slitting his throat. I'm going to kill Jacques, too, before this night is done, and I am not ashamed to say I will enjoy it."

The climb seemed to stretch on for days, each lurch of his body sending fresh pains through his aching limbs. Julianne, he knew, was in even worse condition — her dress torn right up the middle, and her legs caked in blood. But she set her face firm and pushed him onward, her determination fueling his own returning strength.

"We will escape." he whispered to her. "We'll go quietly into the night, Julianne. No more blood. No more death. We'll go away somewhere—"

"Where?" She sagged against him as her bloodlust left her body. She shivered against his coat, and pulled him upward, toward the thin shaft of light that marked the hall leading to the chapel.

"We'll go to the Dirigires in the north, and work passage to England, somehow. The north is the stronghold of Catholic France, so he will not follow us there, not wanted as he is."

"But if we leave—" she shuddered. "He will do this again. It will be some other girl. You have seen his charisma — he will soon have more men. He will turn this church into something evil."

"Men always do. Look — I can see the light of the tunnel above. We must be silent now, and move with haste. We don't have much time."

No one stirred as they crept through the tunnels toward the staircase leading to the courtyard above. Julianne sucked in her breath as they passed Jacques' chamber, but the heavy snores emitting from within didn't change as Nicholas pushed Julianne up the stairs.

They took the steps as quickly and quietly as they could, knowing a guard would also be stationed in the courtyard. When they reached the top they stood in the dark chamber for a few moments, catching their breath.

Moonlight streamed in through the gaps in the crumbling walls, and the harsh pinch of winter cold tore at him through his tattered coat. He gripped Julianne's trembling hand and passed into the shadow of the porch that framed the eastern edge of the courtyard.

"Who's there?" a voice called. It was Ramée. Nicholas froze.

He was close, only a few feet away, leaning against one of the upright columns. In the stillness of the night he couldn't have missed their footsteps on the stone.

"Is that you, Auguste?" He turned his head toward them, and Nicholas saw a flutter out of the corner of his eye. Julianne was upon him before he could blink. Nicholas saw the glint of a dagger in the moonlight, and he rushed to her aid.

She stood back, panting. Ramée slumped against the wall. In the darkness Nicholas could not see any blood, but as he reached down to remove the man's sword, a warm, metallic-smelling substance washed over his fingers.

Julianne was already running across the courtyard. Nicholas stood to follow her, and caught a snatch of sound coming up the stairway. *They've discovered we're missing,* he realised. He ran after Julianne and grabbed her hand, pulling her down the path to the bridge.

Winds whipped up from the valley below and circled the bridge, and the ice and snow had piled up on the surface, making their crossing a dangerous affair. But it was the only way. He went first, plunging into the ice on all fours, keeping as low as possible. The winds curled up around him, driving him sideways, trying to suck him below.

"Be careful!" he called back to Julianne, but the wind tossed his words into the maelstrom below.

Inch by inch he crawled across that perilous structure, every muscle taut, fighting against the force of the wind. He wanted to turn around, to see if Julianne was safe, but if he moved his neck he'd be spun off into the abyss below. His muscles screamed as he pulled himself onto the road, collapsing against the side of the mountain to recover his breath. The frigid wind bit into his skin. Julianne fell down beside him.

He glanced back over his shoulder, and caught a glint of light in the darkened courtyard. He rubbed his eyes, straining to see. Yes, there it was again. They had been discovered!

Julianne saw it, too. "Into the forest!" she cried, her words lost in the wind. He pulled her up, and they dashed into the trees. Snow pummelled them from all sides, and Nicholas could hardly see a foot in front of himself. He kept a tight grip on Julianne's hand, fearing that to let her go would be to lose her forever. The wind howled in his ears, the cold stinging the raw wound on his face. He felt certain at any moment they would plunge over a cliff or be shot from behind by one of Jacques' men.

The ground sloped away downhill, and the pitch

beneath their feet became steeper. "Look out," Julianne cried, throwing out her arm just as he nearly sent them hurtling forward down a steep slope.

"Where now?" His whole face felt numb from cold, and his breath came out in ragged gasps. Julianne didn't seem to be faring any better. He knew they were lost, that they wouldn't last long out here without food or shelter.

She yelled something back, but he couldn't hear it. The next thing he knew she had thrown herself down the steep slope, her skirts flapping wildly behind her. He gathered his breath and hurtled down after her.

Immediately, his legs were swept from under him, and he tumbled down the slope, battering his arms against the branches and rolling over the roots 'till the ground drew even and he sailed to a stop, every bone in his body aching as if it had just gone through a grinder.

He opened one eye and saw Julianne a few feet away, dusting off her skirt. She stumbled over and helped him to his feet.

"I know where we are." said Julianne. "If we follow the river, we'll make it down to the pass. That is, if they don't catch us first."

"Even if they ride after us," said Nicholas, "it will take them time to get the horses across the bridge. The wind has erased our footprints, and even if they managed to track us, they couldn't follow us down that slope."

"You mean we are safe?"

"I'm hopeful." Nicholas replied, "but we need to find food and shelter soon. We're not clear of him yet."

"Nor shall you be."

That booming voice sliced through the biting air. Nicholas whirled around and saw Jacques, a silhouette against the moonlight. He stood with two of his men on the edge of the valley, blocking their exit. The men each pointed a pistol at them.

"You forget," he said. "I know every inch of the tunnels under this hill. The old monks created escape routes in case they were overrun, and one emerges not a mile to the west. Your crashing about in the forest made it almost too easy to find you. And now—"

He took a step toward them, drawing his rapier from its scabbard, a broad smile across his face.

Nicholas stepped back, pushing Julianne behind him, and fumbled for Ramée's blade. It slipped through his numb fingers and stuck in the snow.

Jacques laughed, gesturing with his blade for Nicholas to pick it up. "I fancy a bit of sport, *Anglaise.*"

Nicholas stepped forward, losing his balance on the ice, and scrambled for his blade. He gripped it at last, and stood to face Jacques, who took another step toward him, closing the distance.

Snow flew in thick clumps from the trees high above, and great gusts of wind circled around them as they sized each other up, neither daring to make the first move. *He is smiling because he knows he has beaten me. My only chance is my strength. If I can disarm him, I could overpower him, perhaps get a hand on his throat.*

Jacques came at him with a high cut. Nicholas parried, bottling up Jacques' blade. They battled, pressing against each other, 'till Nicholas saw an opening and took it, winding his blade around and opening a long cut over Jacques' right eye. The Frenchman's head snapped back, and blood obscured his vision.

Nicholas feigned left, thrusting for Jacques' belly, but despite his injury, the Frenchman parried him easily, laughing as Nicholas stumbled off balance once again. "Your walk in the snow has weakened you," he said. "You will die soon, *Anglaise*."

Jacques attacked — a lazy cut to the shoulder. Nicholas parried easily, but now he was on the defensive, blocking cut after cut as they came thick and fast. His swung wildly, blocking too high on Jacques' blade, and the mistake compounded with each subsequent parry, 'till Jacques caught him in a bind, bent his sword arm back behind him, and pulled Nicholas' head into his chest. He pressed the thin blade of his rapier against Nicholas' throat.

"You Englishmen, you steal our wealth, you steal our gods, but this is not enough? You must have our women too! I will enjoy very much slitting your throat —"

"Jacques, *arrêtez-vous!*"

Jacques whirled around, wrenching Nicholas' neck around so he too could see Julianne. She stood on the other side of the valley, out of pistol range. She held Auguste's dagger in both hands, the tip pointing inward, aimed at her belly.

"If you hurt Nicholas," she cried, "I shall kill your child."

The winds gusted through the valley, pushing a bitter cold deep inside Nicholas' bones. He felt the shock of this statement descend down Jacques' arm, and he pressed against the jolt, hoping Jacques might loosen his grip enough for him to pivot underneath. But Jacques regained composure quickly, and when he spoke, his voice was cold and firm.

"You can't do that," said Jacques. "I forbid it."

"You are *not* my husband," she said. "You're a charlatan. A liar."

"Please, Julianne," said Nicholas. "Run! Save yourself!"

She stared at him, and her eyes too were cold. "Let him go, Jacques. Let him run into the forest behind me, and do not chase after him, and you shall have me and the baby. This is what you want, isn't it?"

"You are the one who is lying," Jacques spat. "You have said so yourself. You do not want me."

"What I wanted has never mattered to you before. If you allow Monsieur Thorne to go free, I will marry you in front of the men. I will live as your wife, your slave. If you kill him now, I kill the baby, and myself too."

"Julianne, no!"

But Jacques had already made up his mind. He broke the hold on Nicholas' neck and shoved him forward. Nicholas pulled himself to his feet.

"Run," said Jacques. "Run like the cowardly Englishman you are."

He staggered to his feet, his rapier still gripped in his fingers. His eyes met Julianne's as he trudged toward her on the other side of the valley, toward the freedom that had been so bitterly bought. She looked up at him, tears running down her pale skin shimmering in the moonlight, and a cold determination in her eyes. As her gaze locked on his, he realised what she planned to do.

Julianne ... my beautiful Julianne ...

He made to pass her on her left, and as he did so, he leaned in, whispered "*Je t'amie.*" and flicked out his wrist, driving his sword up into her chest, straight into her heart.

She gasped, a horrible, wet, gurgling sound that welled up from inside her. As she went down, her eyes met his, and the hiss of her final breath passed through the air, carrying with it the trace of her words: *Thank you.*

Now he ran.

Up the slope and into the forest, shot falling uselessly in the snow behind him. If they shouted after him, he could not hear them over the roar of the wind and the pounding of his heart in his ears. His chest burning, he reached the crest of the slope and leaned against a tree, resting for a moment. He watched the lamps below — little daubs of light like fireflies dancing as Jacques' men carried Julianne's body back to the monastery.

As they carried her far away from him.

Tears stung in his eyes. He had done what she asked — what her eyes had burnt into him. She would not have allowed herself or the baby — if there even *was* a baby – to suffer in Jacques' hands any longer. She would have killed herself anyway — plunging that knife into her own belly, sacrificing herself in a great ocean of agony, condemning herself according to Morphean law to an eternity of torment.

Now she was free, and so was he, though how he could go on living, knowing the price of his freedom, he didn't yet know.

He ran. Like a coward, he ran on into the darkness.

***

The Council didn't want to take any chances with Isambard, so they locked him in a cell below Stephenson's church while the broad gauge test track was constructed. Of course, they made the Stokers do it, for no extra pay, on top of their regular duties. But the men toiled happily, clearing the ground and laying the wide track alongside Stephenson's line, which ran from one side of the Engine Ward to the other.

"Do you think Brunel's lad will really beat Stephenson?" William Stone asked Aaron as he held the rails in place for William to hammer the nails through.

"His calculations are sound enough," Aaron replied. "But he told me he's never brought it up to speed before. We — that is, *he* — doesn't know how fast it truly runs."

Aaron was allowed to visit Isambard down in his cell, but he had to wait in line while Stoker after Stoker dropped in, each bearing gifts — blankets and food and drink to make Isambard comfortable. He accepted them all gratefully, and stayed chatting and laughing 'till his guards got annoyed and threw in the next visitor. Finally, Aaron was allowed to enter.

"We'll complete the track within the week—"

Isambard sighed. "You're upset."

Aaron gulped. "If Stephenson's locomotive is faster —"

"For the last time, it *won't* be faster. And besides, I've kept my promise," Isambard said. "I've told no one of your involvement. You have nothing to fear."

"You are my friend. I fear for you."

"Your fear is unnecessary. I have done the calculations. There's no way Stephenson will win." Isambard sighed again. "I shall like very much to get out of here. I'm frightfully bored. I've asked that you accompany me on the footplate."

Aaron tried to mask his dismay, but his conversation with Isambard took on a stilted feel, as though they were both going through the motions. Staring at his friend through the bars as he paced his cell in excitement only made Aaron keenly aware of how different they were — of how their very natures divided them.

The Festival of Steam was over, but most of the engineers and their men remained behind, anxious to see what this magnificent engine, built by a boy and seemingly too squat and ugly to be much use, could really do. Stephenson's newest engine — the *Rocket* — was rushed down to the city from Manchester, with the Messiah himself as the conductor. An entire regiment of Navvies marched after him, eager to see their master beat the Stokers once and for all. If Isambard's theory was proven to be false, his punishment would be swift and severe. The promise of a hanging clung to the air, and no one liked to miss a good hanging.

On the day of the trials, a throng of people crowded the streets of Engine Ward. The Council members — draped in all their religious and scholarly robes — gave morning lectures in the great cathedrals, most railing against this upstart engineer, but some showing support for healthy competition. Never had so many come to the Ward to hear the engineers speak or see the result of a public experiment. The city erected a grandstand along one edge of the track near the start/finish line for the engineers, Council members, and other privileged citizens, while the Stokers jostled with the ordinary folk for a view behind a heavy iron fence. Constables patrolled the length of the track, ready with batons in case the crowd got out of hand. Coaches and omnibuses blocked the streets all the way back to the gates — their passengers were forced to exit and walk the rest of the way.

King George III sat on a platform festooned with flowers overlooking the track. He beamed with happiness as he waved at his subjects. As a symbol of his patronage, the workers usually threw bolts and nails at his feet, but the police, worried about injuries and the integrity of the track, were walking up and down with sacks to collect these offerings (which they would no doubt sell later for scrap). Already, four sacks were stacked up against the platform, brimming with loot.

Brunel and Aaron waited together on the edge of the track, while Joseph Banks and two men from the Royal Society checked over both engines for any mechanical tinkerings that might give one locomotive an unfair advantage. Brunel sought out fellow Stokers in the crowd and waved to them, while Aaron hopped nervously from foot to foot.

Only a few feet away, Stephenson waited, surrounded by a crew of Navvies in shiny green overalls. The Messiah had squeezed his wide frame into a frock coat of the latest fashion, the buttons straining under the pressure, and puffed on a cigarette as he exchanged pleasantries with other Council members. He barely even glanced at Isambard's engine, though its broad frame dwarfed his precious *Rocket.*

As the church bells punctuated the day with fearsome gongs, signalling the start of the trials, Isambard helped Aaron up onto the footplate of their squat engine. He waved to the King, and the King nodded in return. Despite the unease settling in his gut, Aaron beamed too, and waved at Quartz. It was a proud day to be a Stoker.

The King gave the signal, and Stephenson stepped on board the *Rocket,* while the Navvies yelled and stamped their feet. The ground vibrated with their adoration, and Aaron felt his gloom sink deeper. *How can Isambard possibly defeat all this?*

Stephenson's fireman stoked the boiler, and soon puffs of steam rose from the engine and floated across the sky like clouds. The timekeeper held up his pocket watch, and at the King's signal, Joseph Banks waved the flag, and the *Rocket* lurched away.

To Aaron's eyes she seemed impossibly fast, much faster than he'd ever seen a locomotive travel when Stephenson used to run them in Engine Ward. She leapt along the track, disappearing from view, save the tip of her smokestack belching black clouds over the cheering populace.

The roar of the crowd grew to such a height he couldn't hear the *Rocket* returning. Instead, he saw her great black face bearing down on them, careening toward the finish line with Stephenson waving his hat in triumph. They screeched to a halt, belched one final cloud of black steam over the wailing crowd, and the time keeper announced their result: "Seventeen minutes and thirty-one seconds!"

A calculating man from the Metic Sect stood by, furiously scribbling sums on his paper. Within a few minutes he announced Stephenson's average speed at 28mph. Aaron gulped.

Stephenson didn't even acknowledge Isambard as he strolled alongside their carriage toward his place of honour on the bleachers. Isambard didn't seem bothered by the snub — he turned to Aaron, grinning from ear to ear.

"Whatever happens," he said, "you have my sincere and greatest thanks."

"As long as I keep my head, you can keep your thanks."

"Just remember, keep the distribution even." he said, handing Aaron the shovel. "Don't forget the corners of the firebox, and don't give her everything 'till she's warmed up a bit. We don't want to drop the fire before we've even begun."

Together, they stoked the boiler — watching the puffs of smoke trotting across the sky — and checked the pressure. Aaron knelt down and took his place in front of the firebox. Easing off the brake and taking hold of the regulator, Isambard tipped his hat to signal he was ready. Banks waved the flag; Isambard pulled the whistle and leaned on the regulator. The train juddered forward, launching itself down the track.

Immediately, they had a problem. Water squirted from one of the hoses, soaking the deck and causing the pressure to drop dramatically. Struggling to find purchase on the slippery deck, Aaron pushed shovel after shovel of coke into the firebox, spreading it out to keep the fire even. His field of vision narrowed, becoming only his shovel and the tiny door of the firebox, and his shoulders heaved with the effort. Sparks flew back at him as he tossed in another shovelful, checked the pressure gauge, and dug for more coke.

Soaked in water and smeared with soot, Isambard threw back his head and laughed gleefully as he let out the regulator even further, and the whole world fell away into a blur of wind and coke and steam. Aaron's fear evaporated, replaced by exhilaration.

Come on, we can do it!

The locomotive thundered across the broader track. His knees wobbled in different directions as they clattered down the straight, accelerating as she dove into the corner. They poured on speed, the rivets and panels rattling with the building pressure. Suddenly, Isambard let off the regulator and slammed on the brakes. They shuddered to a stop, a mere foot before they ran out of track.

"Quick, more coke." Isambard threw her in reverse, released the brake, and let out the regulator, pulling it further and further 'till the whole locomotive shook from the speed.

Now the pressure gauge shot up. Aaron added more water, watching her drop to normal, then quickly shoot up again. The deck shook so violently he had to hold on to the boiler mount with one hand to keep from being thrown. From the corner of his eye he saw the Engine Ward hurtle past, a blur of grey and black. "More!" Isambard yelled over the din. "Faster!"

His teeth chattering, Aaron crouched low, steadying himself against the boiler mount as he flung in another shovel of coke. The pressure gauge shot up again, then down. Two rivets popped from the boiler, sailing across the deck.

"Isambard," Aaron screamed. "We're going to drop the fire!"

In response, Isambard hauled on the regulator as hard as it would go, rocketing the locomotive through the final straight. More rivets popped off as they shot past the bleachers, the boiler belching black smoke from every outlet and the pressure gauge dangerously close to exploding.

Finally, Brunel pulled on the brakes. Aaron dived onto the deck and covered his head just as all three gauges exploded. The engine juddered to a stop, black steam choking the air. The air gushed through the firebox, sucking the fire out through the chimney and depositing it on the side of the track. Firefighters rushed in with buckets to fight the blaze.

Aaron could only just make out Isambard's features through the steam and smoke. He was grinning from ear to ear. His eyes stinging, Aaron fumbled for his friend's hand, grabbed it and squeezed tight.

"Whatever happens now," Isambard said, "I can say I ran my engine through the Ward."

"You won't say nothing if you're dead," Aaron heaved, wiping sweat from his brow.

Suddenly, they were surrounded. Rough hands dragged them from the cab and hoisted them in the air. Stokers, a great crowd of them, singing and yelling and carrying them away on their shoulders. In the madness, Aaron lost sight of Isambard. All around him, people were yelling, and reporters fired a barrage of questions at him, their voices blending together in the din. "What happened?" he yelled between coughs, but no one answered him.

His ears ringing and his eyes full of smoke, Aaron searched the crowd for a familiar face. Someone reached up and tore him from the Stokers' grasp, setting his wobbling legs down on solid ground. "Nine minutes twenty-three!" Quartz jabbed at his watch. "You pulled her through in nine minutes twenty-three seconds!"

"What?"

"We did it!" Brunel cried, throwing his arms around Aaron. "We beat Stephenson's time by nearly half!"

More Stokers broke over the barrier, and they whipped Isambard away again, hoisting him up on their shoulders and carrying him into the steamy haze 'till Aaron lost sight of him. He heard the King speak, but the words were lost in the roar of the crowd. Quartz stood beside him, and William Stone, but even they were swept up in the madness, talking about the great church they would build for the first ever Stoker engineer.

Aaron slumped against the engine, his hands on his temples, trying to make sense of it. His childhood friend was now the head of a religion.

***

JAMES HOLMAN'S MEMOIRS — UNPUBLISHED

The letter I received — from the one and same Nicholas Thorne, whom I'd last seen on board the *Cleopatra* as they pulled me to shore for treatment — contained no apologies for his lack of communication, or platitudes or inquiries after my health. Any other gentleman might think this rude, but Nicholas was too dear a friend for me to bother with formalities.

I had just returned to Travers College following my medical studies, and I was desperate for any distraction from my monotonous lifestyle. I longed still to travel, but my dreams seemed impossible, stifled by the constraints of the very institution that had saved me from poverty. The envelope — bearing no return address and what the maid described as "a most peculiar postmark" — did ignite in me such a terrific hope for adventure that I immediately leapt from my chair, the flaring pains in my legs completely forgotten, and paced the length of the room.

I could smell the road on the letter as soon as I slit open the envelope. That damp, sulphurous scent of rain and dirt and soot clung to the paper, telling me a story more evocative than words. Another smell — familiar, but indiscernible — reached my nostrils, and I knew this to be a letter from someone I knew — one of my friends in a far-flung place. I called in a maid to read to me. If I could not have adventures of my own, I would hear tales of someone else's.

"It's written on fine paper, and there's a watermark along the right side — it looks like some sort of flying machine," said the maid, pulling out the letter. She knew well how to describe every detail to me. "Shall I read it for you, Mr. Holman?"

"If you please, Rose, and I trust you to keep its contents entirely confidential."

The letter I destroyed as soon as I had committed it to memory, for he was right to be cautious of such evidence against him, but as my journals are kept secure in the locked deposit box in my private rooms, I felt it safe enough to record a copy of it here.

Dear James

You may have some idea what has become of me since we parted in Portsmouth. If you had followed the papers you'd know the Cleopatra stayed for a year on patrol in English waters before setting out on duties in the Mediterranean. After being in an engagement, she put in at Gibraltar for repairs and her crew was decommissioned. You may have even read of a young lieutenant who killed his superior officer in a brawl and evaded the authorities by escaping into Spain.

I had intended to buy passage home to England and begin life anew as a student of architecture, but I had not counted on Napoleon making a particularly spectacular decision. Blockading England basically drew a line in the sand — with Industrian England on one side, and Christian Europe on the other. There was not one ship that could take me where I so dearly wanted to go, and French hostility toward Industrians forced me into hiding.

I've been in the mountains for nearly three years, studying architecture with some of the foremost European masters, but circumstances permitted that I return to England with haste, and I hope to find work there under a new name. I will not burden you with the details of my illicit journey, lest this letter fall into the wrong hands. Suffice to say that at the time of writing, I am in the North, and it does my heart well to once more walk on English soil.

I arrive in London on Tuesday, and would greatly desire to meet you for dinner, at 6pm at the Butchers Hall Beef House. You must come alone, and tell no one who you are seeing.

You cannot write to me in return, but I shall wait for

you on the appointed day.

Yours
Nicholas Rose

PART III:
THE METAL MESSIAH

1830

"You want to *what?"*

"Find a coach to take me to London. Tonight, if that's possible."

The barkeeper shook his head. "Ain't no coaches travelling that road for three more days. I will give ye another drink, though."

She took it, the strong taste burning her throat. She swallowed, struggling to hold back tears. "It's of the utmost urgency that I get to London as soon as possible."

"Listen, girlie," the barkeeper said, leaning over the counter, "my job is to serve up the poison, not to organise transport for every pretty stranger who wanders through those doors. I'll tell you what, every week a blind gentleman comes down from the castle, Thursdays at 4pm, has a drink right over there," he said, pointing to a stool at the end of the bar, "and takes a private taxicab into the city. Tomorrow is your lucky day. If you wait around 'till then, you may be able to persuade him to give you a lift."

Mr. Holman? Brigitte knew the blind man, for she sometimes cleaned the Naval Knights' residence at

Travers College. She'd noticed him immediately, as he was younger than the other Naval Knights by some years and moved about with such an affable ease, it was difficult at first to discern his blindness. She'd never spoken to him, and hoped he'd be kindly disposed to her.

For all his gruff talk, the barkeeper took pity on her, and offered her a room for half price. She took it, not knowing what else to do, but she could not sleep. Every time she closed her eyes she saw visions of the Sunken, snarling and snapping, or the woman in the King's chamber, blood running from the gashes in her legs, or Maxwell's sagging, weary face as he showed her his wound.

She awoke to find sunlight streaming in through a tiny window. Not wanting to show her face in the village lest her disappearance had been discovered, she stayed in her room, pacing back and forth and trying to figure out what she should do next. The barkeeper brought her a tray of fresh bread and soup, and, at one o'clock, told her to come and wait downstairs with him.

He put her to work behind the bar, filling glasses and helping in the kitchen. The hours passed quickly, and no one seemed to recognise her. At one point, the barkeeper nudged her with his elbow.

"Your escort has arrived, Missy."

Holman sat on the stool at the end of the bar and ordered a glass of brandy. Brigitte brought it to him and watched while he sipped it, his youthful features serene and untroubled. Finally, she worked up the courage to speak.

"Mr. Holman, sir?"

He turned his head toward her. "You're from the castle, aren't you Miss? One of the maids?"

She nodded, forgetting he couldn't see her. "I am — or rather, I *was*. How did you guess?"

"Tis no guess, Miss. I recognise your voice. When one cannot tell their friends apart by their faces, one must look to other clues. Do you have a name, or shall I simply call you 'she of the gentle tone'?"

She blushed. "I am Brigitte Black. I need to travel to London for an urgent matter, but I'm told no carriage save yours leaves for several days. I wondered if you would do me the honour of allowing me to share your taxi?"

"Anything for the lady who delivers my brandy," he said, flashing her a charming smile. Finishing his drink, he climbed down from his stool and offered her his arm. She took it, marvelling at how he navigated across the crowded bar, out the door, down the steps, and along the road to where his taxi waited. He did not steady himself against her, and he did not sweep the road with his stick the way she'd seen other blind men do. Instead, he moved with a casual grace, occasionally tapping his short walking stick against the cobbles. He explained, when she asked, that he used the echoes produced by the tap to discern obstacles, and by careful listening he built a picture of the world in his mind, and could therefore find his way.

As he helped her up into the carriage, Brigitte looked over her shoulder; certain she'd see the castle guard coming to arrest her. But there was no one, only the dark outline of the imposing castle looming over the town. She stared up at the ramparts, and shivered, tears welling in her eyes again as she thought of

Maxwell and Miss Julie and Cassandra and everyone trapped inside.

Only once they had settled into their seats, and the carriage had pulled away and begun the long and clattering journey to London, did Brigitte let out the breath she was holding. She wiped her eyes with the back of her sleeve.

"Is something the matter, Miss Brigitte?"

Her head snapped up. "What makes you think that?"

"You fidget with your dress, and you are crying. I can smell the saltiness of your tears. Forgive me for embarrassing you so, I had hoped a journey with me would not have left you so distraught."

"No, no," she laughed, taking the handkerchief he offered and blowing her nose. "It has been … a traumatic night. Forgive me, you've been too kind, and I've been a horrid travelling companion."

"I've had much worse. In my studies at Edinburgh, I would sometimes journey into the countryside with a friend from the Navy who had gone completely deaf. Can you imagine what a pair we made, Miss Brigitte? A blind man and a deaf man." He chuckled at the memory.

"Are you off on another adventure today?"

"Only an adventure of the mind. Every second Thursday I meet with a select few individuals — scholars, engineers, doctors, and friends — to discuss matters of the mind in a forthright and unencumbered manner. It's a sort of secret supper society. This week, we're learning about some of William Buckland's biological discoveries, and Nicholas has promised us a wonderful roast pheasant."

She leaned forward. "Who was that again?"

"Nicholas Rose. He's the industrial architect for Brunel's Wall—"

"Mr. Holman," she lowered her voice. "Can you take me to him?"

His face broke into a sudden grin, and he too leaned forward and whispered. "So you are the woman he's smitten with?"

She blushed. "He has spoken of me?"

"Not by name, but he told me of the beautiful maid he met at the castle who has quite stolen his heart. I'd be delighted to take you to him."

The time passed quickly after that. Away from the castle and the frightful events of the night before, her pulse returned to normal. She stretched her muscles — stiff and aching from all the running — across the carriage, wriggling her toes and revelling in her freedom. Holman told her stories of his time in the Navy and at medical school, his yearning for adventure and travel, and of his friendship with Nicholas and how he came to lose his sight. She was so engrossed in his tales she didn't even notice they had passed into London until the familiar tang hit her nostrils. The accumulated filth of thousands of people living atop one another in crowded tenements, the dribbling remnants of rotted meat baked into greasy pork pies and sold cold on the street corners, the ditches overflowing with sewage ... she pulled her collar tightly around her, remembering the horrid conditions at the orphanage.

Holman removed a pocket watch from his pocket and ran his fingers over the raised digits. "We're late," he murmured, "but when Nicholas sees what treasure

I've brought him, he won't worry."

It took Brigitte a couple of moments to realise he was referring to *her.* An even redder blush crept across her cheeks.

Her old orphanage was in Whitechapel, one of the poorest and most notorious areas in London. But she had cleaned houses in Belgravia, Kensington, and Chelsea, and glimpsed the life of easy comfort afforded to the rich. It came as no surprise to her that the carriage stopped in front of the fourth in a row of pleasant terraced boarding houses on the edge of Upper Clapton. She'd cleaned for a doctor and his wife who'd lived just around the corner. Her heart beat against her chest, and she fidgeted with her dress as Holman helped her down and knocked on the door.

"If that's you, James, you are the last to arrive." a voice boomed from behind the door. She heard the latch turn in the lock. "I hope you've brought the brandy—" The door flew open, and Nicholas stood there, a carefree smile on his handsome face. His face sagged when he saw her and he fixed her with an intense stare.

"I'm sorry," she sobbed. "I didn't mean to upset you. I shouldn't have come. I'll leave you alone."

He grabbed her by the arm and pulled her close, and she stared into his narrowed eyes and felt his hand tighten around her arm. After everything she'd seen it was *too much, too much* and she opened her mouth to scream but found he had covered it with his. The ferocity of the kiss tore the air from her lungs. Her chest burst, sending shivers down her arms. Her hands gripped his back, holding her to him.

I'm being kissed, she realised, her pulse dancing. *A*

beautiful man is kissing me.

"Well, I'm mighty pleased my findings interested you so much, Nicholas, that you'd break the rules of our supper club to sneak in a woman."

She leapt back, startled by the unfamiliar voice. A man stood on the staircase, one hand gripping the railing, the other smoothing the pocket of his waistcoat. His comment would have been cruel if not for the grin on his face.

"Of course." Nicholas' mouth twitched into a smile. "Brigitte, this is William Buckland, an eminent professor of geology at Oxford. He was just beginning a lecture on his most recent studies of Ichyosuarus skeletons when you arrived. Buckland, this is my … this is Brigitte."

"Oh, I've interrupted you." Brigitte looked away, hoping the man wouldn't notice how red her face had become. "I'm so terribly sorry! I can leave—"

"Nonsense," Buckland interrupted. "It is no night for a woman to be wandering outside on her own. We have enough bacon sandwiches upstairs to feed an army, and Nicholas might even break open his best brandy now we have a lady present."

"Oh, but I shouldn't intrude—"

"It's no intrusion," Holman said. "A lady adds rather an air of sophistication to our affairs. And besides, I gather your situation is one of great urgency, so you might want to discuss it with Nicholas before he kisses you again."

If possible, Brigitte's ears turned an even darker shade of red.

***

They escorted her upstairs and settled her into the most comfortable chair in the parlour — an over-stuffed wingback upholstered in faded damask. If Nicholas noticed the shabby state of her appearance and the dried mud on her shoes, he did not draw attention to it, but merely wrapped a blanket around her shoulders and handed her a glass of brandy. Holman passed over the platter of sandwiches, accidentally knocking it against the chair arm and spilling a couple on the floor. Without a word, Buckland picked them up and threw them in the fire.

Nicholas introduced the other men in the room, starting with a dark-haired man named Aaron Williams. Dressed in faded trousers and a green tunic, with black soot smeared over his cheeks, he was clearly one of the Dirty Folk, a Stoker. She'd seen them once or twice — soot-caked faces glaring at her from the shadows when she'd gone to church with the other orphans — but never outside the Engine Ward. *I do not want a Stoker to hear my story. Surely Nicholas will ask him to leave,* she thought, but caught herself. *He must be special, for Nicholas and this learned crowd to associate with him.* She smiled at him, but he only stared back at her with brooding, intelligent eyes.

The others were all scholars of one sort or another — a doctor, an artist, a young biologist named Charles something, and a historian. "I can trust these men?" she whispered, her eyes locked on the Stoker. Nicholas nodded.

And so, in a small voice, staring at her muddy boots and clutching her brandy glass as though it were the only thing holding her upright, she explained what had occurred in the castle — from the lead objects disappearing, to the King's inhuman pallor and increasingly erratic behaviour, to the Sunken rattling their cages and tearing at their own skin and all that Maxwell had said. She retold the story of her escape, how they'd chewed through the wooden door in their desperation to devour her, and her chance meeting with Holman. They remained silent while she talked, waiting 'till she had recounted her tale up until she'd arrived at Nicholas' door, and even then they reserved their questions 'till after Nicholas had refilled her glass and she'd had another bite of her sandwich.

"The situation is much worse than we feared," Holman said, tapping his stick against the toe of his boot. Brigitte looked up — she could not understand how these gentlemen, who did not know her and must regard her maid's uniform, soiled and odorous, with disgust, could believe her. But they had already known?

"You knew about this?" Buckland stared from Holman to Nicholas.

"I knew something was not right with the King," said Nicholas, who stood behind her, his gentle hands on her shoulder sending shivers of warmth through her body. "When I'd gone to the castle with Isambard, his manner seemed out of place for a monarch, even one just out of convalescence. He walked about in his nightclothes, so that I could see the fresh scars crisscrossing his chest. He drank a red tea—"

"It was blood," Brigitte said, her eyes wide. "I make it for him with blood from the castle abattoir."

"— and his eyes would not focus — they darted to every corner of the room, coming to rest only on the flesh of his youthful servants. When last I was there I saw him bite a man, tearing a chunk of flesh away like a wild animal. We have all noted his absence from the affairs of the Royal Society — or rather, most of us noted, and described it to James." The blind man gave a low chuckle. "And his dereliction of his duties to his own Gods—"

"He hasn't attended services at St. George's Chapel for nearly three months," Holman said.

"— Holman and I wondered if perhaps he'd gone the way of many kings, falling in with the ladies or gents down on the dockside and contracting syphilis, but this ... this is something else entirely. "

"He is less a man than I," declared Brigitte. "He is a monster."

"A Vampire King," said Aaron.

"The question is," said Holman, "what can we do about it?"

"Without knowing his mind," declared Nicholas, "we can do nothing."

"The castle bursts with the Sunken, his children of lead," Brigitte said. "There are hundreds in the cellar and dungeon, and I know not how many more hidden throughout the castle. Perhaps he means to create an army."

This opened the discussion at great length, and it continued for many hours, each man putting forth a dashing plot which was summarily torn to pieces by his brothers. Brigitte tried to listen, but her eyelids fluttered shut, and she found her head flopping against her chest.

She awoke to the grandfather clock striking three, and felt her body lurch forward as a warm presence carried her up the stairs, bundled her in blankets, and placed her into a warm, soft bed. She slept peacefully, still dressed in her torn pinafore.

***

On this very same night, in a comfortable residence not far from Nicholas' home, Charles Babbage and his wife, Francesca, received two most unlikely visitors.

Annabella Milbanke, heiress and once wife to the gallivanting poet and previous Messiah of the Isis Sect Lord Byron, and a recent convert to the Church of the Great Conductor, was on pilgrimage in London. She'd come from her manor in Kirkby Mallory to see the completion of the Wall, and had brought her fifteen-year-old daughter Ada to see, firsthand, the wonders of Babbage's counting machine.

Babbage had been corresponding with Annabella for some years, and he had advised her upon many texts for Ada's schooling. In contrast to her wild ex-husband, Annabella had pursued a life of order and piety, slavishly devoting herself to exterminating every facet of Byronic psyche from Ada by way of the study of mathematics. It was this very desire to stamp out impulsivity and imagination that had drawn her to Byron, a tumultuous hurricane of a man whom she'd sought to tame with reason and logic. But chaos, of course, had won in the end, and Byron left England forever after an unspeakable sexual scandal involving his half-sister, leaving the Isis Church in the hands of Shelley, his Presbyter, and his daughter in the care of Annabella.

Annabella had spent the years since his departure trying to absolve herself in the eyes of her social circle for any part in their marital breakup. Despite Babbage's fall from grace, she remained a loyal friend, and Babbage secretly hoped her support might one day lead him back into intellectual circles.

Ada, a young woman of exceptional intelligence cursed with Byronic impulses, became Annabella's greatest source of grief. But as Ada and her mother grew apart, Ada and Babbage corresponded with increasing fervour, together extrapolating the intricacies of various mathematical puzzles.

He had not seen Annabella or Ada since his excommunication, and welcomed the sour-faced woman and sprightly beauty into his home with trepidation. He had supported Annabella when her husband's scandals hit the papers, and he hoped she would remember this now, when he asked for her aid in helping him secure some kind of secular, non-engineering livelihood. Without the support of Annabella, he and Francesca would be on the streets within three months, never mind continuing his research on calculating engines.

He knew this visit was vital to their future. Despite their dwindling savings, Francesca decorated the drawing room with fresh flowers and set out a fine feast. Babbage chased away the organ grinders on the street outside with his garden fork and wheeled out his working model of a section of the Difference Engine, the only thing he had to show for his years of work.

While Francesca served tea, Annabella kept up a steady stream of chatter about recent scandals and events, particularly their journey to London with the

Messiah Stephenson and Brunel's sermon. Babbage listened with half an ear, his attention focused on Ada. She sat like a proper lady, nibbling on her teacake. Her eyes betrayed a wit and intelligence far beyond her years. Far from a Byronic terror, this girl seemed mild and well-behaved, if prone to interrupt polite conversation with outbursts of chatter.

"Mother tells me you have been excommunicated," she blurted out. Annabella shot her a filthy look.

"Ada. Mr. Babbage will not want to discuss it—"

He sighed. "On the contrary, ma'am. It is a matter that very urgently needs to be discussed." Annabella's mouth formed a tiny O as he laid out his plans and implored her to reach out to her influential circle of friends and find him something, *anything,* to save them from ruin.

She closed her eyes, and didn't speak for several minutes. Charles studied her prim, drawn face, hoping to glimpse a clue to her thoughts, but he could find none. Instinctively, he reached across the arm of his chair and clasped his wife's hand.

When she opened her eyes again, he could see they were cold. "You must understand, Charles, I cannot do what you ask. I'm already in a precarious position socially, thanks to that rascal of a husband, may he rot forever in Isis' rancid milk. To offer open support for you would be social suicide, and I have Ada's future to think of. What chance have I of finding her a decent husband if it becomes known I'm a supporter of blasphemers? Why, that would be as harmful as declaring myself a Protestant!"

His stomach tightened as desperation sank in. "Annabella, *please,* remember when Byron left and I

—"

She waved her hand in the air. "That was different. In the public eye, I was the victim of Byron's lust. Your support for me opened doors for you. If I support you now, do you think it will open doors for me? Do you think—"

"Is that the Difference Engine?" Ada asked, cutting off her mother mid-sentence.

Annabella frowned, but Babbage was secretly delighted. He was sensing himself dangerously close to falling upon his knees and begging this sour woman for her help. He needed to step away, to collect himself and plan his next move. With a smile, he sat Ada on a stool next to the machine and explained to her how it worked.

"Ada, can you tell me what finite differences are?"

"Adding and subtracting simple equations in sequence to produce new sequences, like square roots or prime numbers. Mathematical tables are computed using finite differences, although sometimes I find mistakes," Ada explained in a breathless rush.

"That's right. You have a keen eye to find those mistakes. They occur because the people who write out the tables, the computers, aren't mathematicians like us. They use the simple method of finite differences because they don't understand anything else, and sometimes they make mistakes. And even if they calculated the numbers perfectly, typesetting errors creep in at the printers. But what if you could use a machine to calculate *and* print the tables?"

"The machine won't make errors. The tables would be perfect."

"Precisely. One of the great advantages which we

may derive from machinery is the check which it affords against the inattention, the idleness or the dishonesty of human agents."

"Can a machine really compute finite differences?"

"It can, and more. Watch." Babbage cranked the handle. The figure wheels wound and dropped and produced the first result.

"Two," Ada read off. Babbage cranked the handle again, producing a four, then a six, then eight, ten, twelve … Ada read off each number with enthusiasm, enthralled with the idea of the machine performing this simple calculation.

When the machine reached fifty, it suddenly jumped up to ninety-two.

"Oh, no!" cried Ada, frowning at the erroneous number. "It's broken." Annabella frowned at him, concerned Babbage had been teaching her daughter on a flawed machine.

Babbage smiled. "It's not broken at all, Ada. You see, I programmed the Difference Engine to add in multiples of two for twenty-five rotations, then to add forty-two before continuing to add in multiples of two."

Ada clapped her hands in delight. Even Annabella, usually severe to the point of indifference, appeared impressed. Babbage, smitten with the child, offered to show her around his workshop.

Having lost his rooms in the Engine Ward, he'd converted the drawing room at the rear of the house into his workshop. Francesca had begged him to give up on the engine after he was thrown out of the Royal Society. "It's over, Charles," she'd said, gently clasping his shaking hands. But he could not let it go.

The few tools he'd salvaged from Clement lay neatly on the bookshelves. His desk remained hidden, buried beneath a mountain of paper — his notes, designs and journals. Academic periodicals — their pages dog-eared and notes and corrections scribbled in the margins — lay stacked in every corner.

Ada went about the workshop in a curious frenzy, her deft fingers tracing the outlines of the counting rods on his plans. She climbed up on his chair and stared at the drawings on his desk.

"What's this? It's not the same as the Difference Engine?"

"That's right. You are really very clever, Ada. This is the Analytical Engine. While the Difference Engine calculates finite difference, the Analytical Engine can calculate many different types of equations."

"How?" Ada picked up the drawing and turned it upside down.

He spread out some plans on the table. "The key is that the machine can remember sequences of numbers and apply them to equations at a later point. Here are the banks of number wheels which function as the machine's memory, and here's the printer that produces the tables. With this technology a machine could perform any number of complex mathematical equations."

"It could do other things, too," said Ada. "It could store information, as a kind of code. You could assign tasks to certain combinations of numbers, and the machine could produce anything you wished."

Babbage, who'd never thought of such a possibility before, couldn't help but be enchanted by the girl, her tiny bonnet bouncing about as she scribbled some notations on a blank leaf, folded it, and tucked it into her dress.

"I shall call on you again next week," she declared, "after Mother has had her fill of Walls and lectures, and you shall explain to me the inner workings of this extraordinary machine."

Babbage smiled in delight, thinking that another week would give him time to come up with a new strategy for winning Annabella's support. Annabella frowned at her daughter's forthrightness and ushered her away, back into the reception room. Francesca kept the conversation flowing, while Babbage mused silently, turning over Ada's observations in his head. *There are so many possibilities ... so many avenues of inquiry I have yet to explore ...*

"Who would have thought," Babbage mused to his wife as she put away the tea settings after Annabella and Ada left. "The only person in all the world to understand the use of my machines would be Lord Byron's fifteen-year-old daughter."

***

Brigitte awoke to find herself in that same soft bed covered in thick blankets. The dim light that marked a London morning peeked through the curtains, and a mug of tea sat beside the bed, steam still rising from the cup.

"Ah," a gentle voice said. "You're awake."

She jumped. Nicholas laughed. He sat in the corner of the room, his tall frame reclining in a faded easy chair, his long legs stretched across the rug. He had dressed himself, and combed his hair, and neither his face nor his demeanour showed signs of the copious consumption of brandy from the night before. "Drink your tea," he said.

She sipped, her mind — fuzzy from tiredness and the effects of the brandy — drifting back to what she could remember of the previous two nights. The King's erratic manner, the Sunken tearing at their cages and chasing her through the cellar, the tavern, her arrival at Nicholas' house, the men, the drink, and someone carrying her to bed. Panic seized her.

"I— I can't remember—"

He reached over and flicked her hair from her face, his touch like fire on her skin. "I slept in the guestroom downstairs, if that is your concern."

She nodded, taking a gulp of tea. She glanced out the window again. Voices called from the street. "What time is it?"

"Nearly midday," he replied. "I wanted to let you sleep. I've had Isabella — that's my maid — prepare lunch for us. James and Aaron will be joining us. You remember Aaron from last night?"

She nodded. *The sullen one.*

He stood, his fingers tracing the outline of her jaw, lingering over her lips before reluctantly receding. "I shall leave you to dress. Come downstairs when you're ready."

She glanced across the bed. Someone had laid out clothes for her — a beautiful dress and woollen coat in dark burgundy, lined with black lace along the sleeves and bustle. She held the fabric to her nose and sniffed. It smelt fresh, clean. *Brand new.* She'd never worn a brand new dress before. She pulled her threadbare maid's dress over her head and stepped into the skirts, fastening the buttons along the front before struggling with the lacings. She finally managed to tie a crooked knot at the back of the bustier, slipped into her shoes, and went downstairs.

She found the men in the kitchen, sipping tea and picking at the selection of bread, meats, and cheeses laid across the table. Nicholas smiled when he saw her, and she blushed.

"I take no credit for that dress," he said. "Holman picked it out." The blind man nodded at her from over his sandwich.

"You have fine taste," she managed, balancing delicately on a stool and surveying the table. Nicholas gestured that she should eat, but she felt awkward, as though she was an intruder on this pleasant world of masculine affairs.

"Look at this." Aaron — the dark-haired man with the penetrating eyes — gestured to an article in the paper. Nicholas leaned across to read over his shoulder, but Holman and Brigitte waited to be told of the contents.

"The King has announced he'll be moving the royal residence to Buckingham Palace," Nicholas declared.

Holman leaned forward. "This is the first I've heard of it."

"That's because you're hardly ever a resident at Travers, James. If you spent half as much time fulfilling your knightly duties as you did studying medicine, gallivanting across the city, and drinking all my brandy, you'd have a better ear towards court affairs."

"Maxwell said this would happen," Brigitte spoke

up. "He said the King would run out of room to house his lead-soaked children. But how will he move them?"

"By locomotive," Aaron burst out abruptly. Brigitte jumped at the harsh tone in his voice. "Brunel has had me working in secret for the last two weeks on an underground London/Windsor line, running from the castle right into the heart of Buckingham Palace."

"And you didn't think to mention this last night?"

"I wasn't sure how it related to the trouble at the castle 'till now," Aaron replied. "Besides, Isambard swore me to secrecy—"

"But why Buckingham?" Nicholas said. "Surely Windsor is a larger castle, and more ideally situated for whatever debaucheries the King wishes to indulge in next?"

Aaron slammed his fist on the table. "I can't believe I didn't see it earlier. The King *wants* the Sunken in the city. He intends to house them inside the Wall."

They fell silent as each pondered the implication of this announcement.

"It would explain why he chose Brunel's competition entry, despite its audacious nature and insurmountable cost. It would explain his insistence in simultaneously constructing the London/Windsor railway and the Wall. He knew Brunel was the only engineer clever enough to build both so quickly and with such secrecy."

"And he knew Isambard would be so grateful for the promotion he would not question the King's motives," Holman added.

"But why the hurry?" asked Nicholas. "Why

constantly push forward the completion date?"

"Perhaps he is losing control of his children," said Holman. "He has made too many of them, and he needs to move them for his own safety. They have no familial feeling remaining — he knows if they were to escape their cages, they would devour him, same as any man. Perhaps his own condition is deteriorating faster than he realised, and he wants to remain in control of himself so he can partake of the carnage."

Brigitte felt sick. The men nodded to each other.

"What can we do?" Nicholas asked.

"Probably nothing," Aaron replied. "I'll return to the Engine Ward and see if I can't get Isambard to divulge something. He's bound to be privy to this decision."

"I have inspections to carry out on the Wall today," said Nicholas. "Perhaps I may find some clue in the structure itself."

"And I'd best return to Windsor," said Holman, "lest my knightly station be wrested from me in my absence. I shall send word as soon as I know more details."

"Tell no one you've seen me!" Brigitte cried. Holman squeezed her hand and smiled in reply.

"Don't go investigating, blind man," Nicholas warned. "I know you. You'll want to see the Sunken with your own unseeing eyes. I'm warning you — don't go inside the castle, or we'll never see you again."

"Nicholas, I'm shocked." Holman clutched his stick to his chest and trembled his lip in mock-hurt. "To suggest that I, a most honourable Naval Knight of Windsor, could be so villainous as to break my sacred vows and enter the palace of my king with the sole intention of proving the existence of flesh-eating lead monsters."

"Just don't do it," Nicholas said. "If what we suspect is true, we've trouble enough ahead without worrying about rescuing you, too."

***

JAMES HOLMAN'S MEMOIRS — UNPUBLISHED

Nicholas was right, of course. I intended to break into the castle and see what I could uncover.

I returned to my lodgings by lunchtime to find the usually quiet boarding rooms a hubbub of activity. The other Naval Knights paced about the common room, wringing their hands and yelling over each other while the maids packed their suitcases and straightened their rooms. No one could tell me anything, save that the whole royal household would move within the week, and until then we would not be allowed out of the castle grounds.

The complaints of disagreeable old men grew tiresome, so I slipped away to my private rooms. Far from fearing the task before me, my mind raced with the pleasure of anticipation. Imagine — a secret army of maniacal lead men created by King George III, the mad Vampire King! And me, the Blind Physician, right in the thick of it!

I began my investigations that very evening by donning my walking shoes, gripping the metal tip of my stick firmly, and beginning the slow, arduous ascent of the Hundred Steps. The chapel stood at the top of the steps, away from the main castle, which we were forbidden to enter. Even I, curious as I was, had always obeyed that rule.

The chapel had — like every other religious building in the King's possession — been remodelled to reflect the new Industrian pantheon. The traditional Christian altarpiece had been torn down and replaced with ten niches, each holding a statue of one of the Gods of Industry. I settled into my stall overlooking the altar, pushing aside the knightly miscellanea — swords, helmets, and wreaths that had accumulated there over the centuries — so I could sit down. The high priest began the usual mass, but I was surprised to hear him joined by the booming voice of the King.

George III had not come to any services for several weeks, and after hearing of his deplorable condition from Nicholas and Brigitte, I could understand why, so to hear him read the prayers in a clear, forceful voice caused the hairs on the back of my neck to stand on end. This was a man in possession of his own mind, in complete control of his body, and far more dangerous than the erratic madman he'd been mistaken for.

Beside me, the other Knights murmured to each other, and I caught snippets of their whispered conversations that filled me with dread. "... his face covered by a red cloth ... hands tremble ... arms strapped to chair ... Banks holding him upright ..."

What do you have in store for us, George? Is this visit to the chapel to convince us of your frailty, or to frighten us?

After mass had finished, Banks bade the Naval Knights march in single file past the altar, so the King could shake our hands and speak to us personally.

When my turn came, and his cold hand slipped into mine, I felt the rough outline of lesions and burn marks across his palm, and I knew Brigitte and Nicholas spoke the truth.

"The Blind Physician," he said, pronouncing each word with care, as though they came to him with difficulty. "Our humble country life must seem quaint compared to your worldly experience."

"It is an honour to serve you, Your Majesty, wherever I may reside."

"You are packed, then, for our little move to Buckingham? I'm tired of living so far from London, tired of travelling so far to attend Council sessions. Now that the shell of my Wall has been completed, the city is safe for kings once again. Buckingham House might not be as grand as this castle, but do not worry, I'll see to it you receive fine accommodations. The finest." He chuckled, and I felt a shiver of fear run down my spine.

"Whatever His Majesty has arranged," I said, trying to keep my voice pleasant and even, "I am but a humble servant."

"Yes, Blind Physician, yes you are." Banks hurried me on, and I hobbled out of the chapel, snuck around the back of the building, and headed toward the castle.

I wanted to see the Sunken for myself.

***

Nicholas hailed a coach to Belgravia, arriving at a quarter past eleven just in time to see the Boilers riveting the last of the steel plate on the double-height Wall. He relieved the night foreman and set about conducting his final structural tests and inspections, while two men cooled the Boilers and loaded them on heavy wagons ready to be returned to the Engine Ward.

A crowd of residents gathered, resplendent in silk pantaloons and fashionable hats, eager to see the completed Wall and the machines that had built it. Nicholas gave them a demonstration of the Boiler's capabilities, showing how it could be used to nail rivets in a pattern.

A well-dressed lady stepped forward. "I am the owner of Lady Vivian's Millenary over on Cross Street, and I'd like to purchase this Boiler to make hats for my store. The two young ladies I employ are lazy and their stitching is crooked—"

"I'd take one for the butchery," said a man in a leather apron at the back of the crowd. "I could use a hand at the chopping block now my shoulder's seizing up."

"These Boilers are even more ingenious than his locomotive design," declared a banker. "I could use one to guard the safe."

"I'll take two!"

"I'll have seven!"

Fists clenched wads of pound notes under his nose. People threw purses down at his feet. Nicholas raised his hands and backed away.

"I'm sorry! The Boilers are not for sale."

"That Presbyter of yours ain't right in the head," said the butcher angrily. "What good's a great invention if ain't no one able to use it?"

Others grumbled their assent.

"The Presbyter says …" Nicholas thought fast. "He

says to spread the word that anyone wanting to know more about the Boilers should come to Engine Ward tonight to hear his sermon."

That seemed to satisfy most of the people, who walked off back toward their homes, clutching their purses and kerchiefs and talking in excited voices ; all save one man, who leaned his impressive bulk against an ornate walking stick as he beckoned Nicholas over. His features — the smooth cheeks, unruly whiskers, and top hat with bright sash — seemed unnervingly familiar. *Where have I seen you before?* Nicholas wondered.

"Excuse me," the man asked, shaking Nicholas' extended hand with a firm grasp. "If I may ask some questions, Mr—"

"Rose," Nicholas replied. "I'm the architect of the Wall. Well, the outer shell, at any rate. And you would be?"

The portly man smiled, ignoring Nicholas' question. "A pleasure, Mr. Rose. And a fine job you have done as far, I see. You must work for this Brunel, then? He's done a fine job, a fine job. And I understand a locomotive will run through the Wall at some later date? Can you tell me what he's done to compensate for the friction in the rails—"

He fired question after question at Nicholas, hardly giving him time to think. Nicholas, who had only a rudimentary understanding of Brunel's engine, could not give any satisfactory answer, and so the interrogation continued. The man clearly possessed a great engineering knowledge, especially about locomotion, but still his identity remained a mystery. *Who are you?* Nicholas racked his brain, but could come up with no answer.

"I am sorry," he said at last. "I am not possessed of much knowledge about locomotion. But if you come to Brunel's sermon this evening, you will learn many of your answers there. Perhaps the Presbyter will even grant a private audience to a learned man such as yourself."

"Oh," the man smiled. "I doubt very much he would do that. But thank you anyway." He gave Nicholas an odd sort of smile. "Our paths shall cross again, Mr. Rose."

Nicholas returned to his coach and rode the entire length of the Wall, staring up in awe at the towering metal edifice that now enclosed the city. The rows of columns, angular and elegant like ancient temples, stretched between the houses, over the streets, as far as the eye could see. *His* design sheltered the city, wrapping London in an iron embrace. *If only Father could see what I have achieved ...*

But he knew he could share his triumph with no one, save Aaron and James and Isambard. And Isambard had a far greater triumph to celebrate. *To think that four weeks ago such a structure did not even exist ... Isambard has singlehandedly transformed industry as we know it.* And he knew, better than anyone, that the Wall was a success. He had heard not a peep from a dragon within the city for the past two weeks, including that dragon Quartz had brought in from the swamps. *Perhaps I was mistaken about the contents of that crate. After all, Aaron never mentioned hearing any dragons inside the Ward.*

He stopped at each of the ten iron gates, checking the guards were on duty, and found the steam-powered lock mechanisms working perfectly. Traffic in and out of the city was already being monitored, and a long line of coaches carrying tourists from the countryside to see the Wall backed up for miles.

Finally, satisfied that everything was in order and the shell of the Wall was finally complete, he returned to the Engine Ward to give Isambard his final report. As they crept toward the black clouds of the Industrian district, traffic slowed, and finally ground to a halt four miles from the gates, where omnibuses, coaches, wagons, and food carts blocked the streets while frustrated drivers yelled insults at each other. It started to rain. Sighing, Nicholas grabbed his coat and umbrella, paid his driver, and made his way down the crowded footpath toward the Ward.

All about him, voices rose over the rain, talking excitedly about the Wall. He rubbed shoulders with priests in coloured robes as they slapped waterlogged tracts into outstretched hands, loudly extolling this and that theorem. Newspapermen in wide-brimmed hats dragged pedestrians from the fray, pens fluttering across cheap paper as they jotted down quotes for the daily editions. The press of people was so intense Nicholas got caught in a crowd outside Stephenson's cathedral and didn't move for several minutes. While he waited, rain pounding against his umbrella and rolling down his trouser legs, he glanced up at the statue of Stephenson adorning the courtyard of the cathedral, and gasped.

You fool, he cursed himself as his eyes sought out every feature of the statue. The rounded figure, the soft hands, the small eyes, and lofty chin were all identical to the man who'd spoken to him earlier about the

Boilers. *How could you not have known?*

Robert Stephenson was in the city. And that could only mean one thing — if he'd come all this way to see the Wall and the Boilers for himself, he considered Isambard's presence a very real threat.

***

JAMES HOLMAN'S MEMOIRS — UNPUBLISHED

Naval Knights are not supposed to enter the castle grounds, but despite the late hour, such a bustle of activity greeted me that it was easy to slip through the hubbub unnoticed. Twice only did a guard stop me and ask my business, and I resorted to pretending I was lost, a trick which evokes only pity when employed by a blind man.

At first, I stuck to the outer courtyards, each step building a map of the grounds in my mind. Growing bolder, I began turning into some of the lofty hallways and drawing rooms, listening for clues to discern the purpose of each room. I cursed myself for not thinking to attempt this before now. The physical exertion and mental challenge it presented gave me a renewed vigor — if I couldn't embark upon adventures outside England, I could at least have one within the confines of the castle.

I passed through a maze of winding corridors, and found myself in an internal courtyard, surrounded on all sides by a covered colonnade leading off into a series of lofty, opulent halls. I stood still and listened. Maids bustled by, pulling down drapes and packing away boxes of fine china. Workmen hauled giant wooden crates onto wagons parked in the centre of the courtyard — these would be taken to the station Aaron had built at the bottom of the gardens.

In the madness, no one paid me any heed as I slipped into an antechamber and pressed on, further and further into the depths of the castle. I laid my feet down carefully, making as little noise as I could on the polished marble floors, listening to the echoes in the cavernous rooms, finding my way to doors and archways by sound. I passed by a doorway, and heard a familiar voice boom from within.

Isambard? What is he doing here?

I flattened myself against the wall and inched my way toward the frame of the door, straining to hear the conversation.

"The first of your children have been loaded onto the carriages, Your Majesty. We will be moving those in the cellars at intervals over the next two days to avoid detection. There will be twenty wagons in all."

The reply came not as words, but as an animalian hiss that stood my hairs on end. Remembering what Miss Brigitte had said about the hundreds of Sunken locked in the cellars, I gulped down my fear and inched closer.

"And we have your guarantee they cannot possibly escape from the wagons? It's vitally important their movement remains secret." That voice belonged to Joseph Banks.

"Of course," Brunel answered. "All the wagons are secured with thick bolts and my own steam-release system. We will move the children only after every last soul has gone from this castle. All the public will see of the train is a brief glimpse of it churning across the countryside, and a few puffs of steam rising from the sewers in London. I've arranged a separate lift shaft to move the children from the underground station to their prepared chambers. My men have laid out a feast of scrap lead for them upon their arrival."

"And your men?"

"When the work is complete, they will be seen to, as per Your Majesty's orders."

"Good." I heard footsteps echo across the room and Banks' voice again, from the furthermost corner. I then heard the sound of liquid falling into a glass. "If the next few days go smoothly, your reward will be handsome."

"I wish only to serve His Majesty and the Industrian Gods. Consideration of wealth and power do not occupy me," Brunel said modestly. "When I have completed the Wall to His Majesty's satisfaction, then and only then is it time to talk of such things."

"The Wall stands, upright and gleaming, after less than a month of construction. It is truly a miracle of engineering. The Royal Society has every confidence in your abilities, Isambard," Banks said, "and in your new thinking machines. If all this goes successfully, you'll be receiving an order for several Boiler units from the Council, and the sum offered will make you very rich indeed."

Their conversation was broken by a snarl, like a hound sniffing out a tasty fox, followed by a shout and something smashing against the marble floor. Banks sighed, and said, "A pity! He was so placid this morning, too. The madness comes more frequently now, and he grows more violent and erratic each time.

I am hoping his children will calm him again. Maybe it is the only thing. Will we see you at the palace?"

"No. I will be busy with arrangements in the Engine Ward."

"As you wish." Wheels creaked across the marble floor, coming towards me. Forgetting my silence, I bolted, the echo of my shoes against the tiles alerting Banks to my presence.

He shouted and gave chase, but he had the King with him, confined to a wheelchair, and he had no hope of catching me. I ducked through room after room, down one corridor, then the next, 'till at last I could smell the fragrance of the flower beds. Not far now. I slowed, panting, searching with my ears for the sound of Banks' footsteps.

Nothing but the songs of nightingales and the gentle rustle of the flowers fluttering in the breeze. I had lost him.

What is Isambard doing at the castle? Although the boy I'd known was a stranger to me now, thanks in large part to my own simmering guilt, I could not imagine Isambard allowing such a blasphemy to continue. But my ears did not deceive me — Isambard not only knew of the Sunken's existence, he was implicated in their relocation to London.

My thoughts turned to Nicholas, who worked with the Presbyter day after day, and had not even entertained the possibility that Isambard might be tied up in this madness. Aaron had suspected something, and I had heard with my own ears the proof that he was right — Isambard had built the Wall and the underground railway in full knowledge of their intended purpose.

Nicholas will not believe me. He quarrels with Aaron over Isambard's motives, and every day he seems to fall deeper under the Presbyter's spell. If I tell him what I've heard, I will only drive him away, force him closer to Isambard, closer to danger.

One thing I could be sure of: they were moving the Sunken into London in two days' time. I had to do something. *I must find Aaron. He will believe me. He will know what to do.*

I hurried through the gardens, vaulting over the low stone wall that marked the edge of the hundred steps, and found myself once again under the porch of Travers College. I stood outside, waiting for my heart to cease pounding and my ragged breath to return to normal before entering the residence. My mind whirred through the possible actions open to me. The castle gates were locked and every exit guarded day and night. I had only one course of action open to me. If I hoped to escape the castle in time to warn the others, I would have to take the same passage Brigitte took — down in the cellars, with the Sunken.

***

"Isambard. Open up!"

Aaron hammered on the internal door. It'd taken him all day to find his way back through the crowds to the Engine Ward from Nicholas' boarding house, and when he'd finally entered the Stoker camp, William Stone informed him the last rivets had been driven in on the Wall, and the Boilers had finished laying the London/Windsor track and building the platforms. All that was left was to test the train in the tunnel and the railway would be operational.

He was running out of time; he *had* to know the truth.

He knocked again, yelling at Brunel to grant him entry. Finally, he heard the bolts sliding free and the heavy door scraping against the floor. Aaron slipped through before Isambard could change his mind, but the Presbyter seemed to have already forgotten him, turning back to his bench and muttering under his breath.

"Is this important, Aaron? The King kept me late at Windsor and I'm behind with these Boiler repairs—"

Aaron stared at his friend's back and yelled his accusation.

"Have I been building a secret railway to transport the King's lead-soaked, vampiric children into London?"

Brunel whirled around. "How do you know all this? You haven't seen—"

"Never mind how I know. Is it true? *Is it true?*"

"Aaron, it's not what you think—"

Red spots flashed in front of Aaron's eyes. He grabbed Brunel by the collar, dragging him up, forcing Isambard to look him in the eye. "How could you do this? How *could you?* Our whole lives I've supported you, helped you bring your dreams to life. How could you let me work on that railway, knowing what it would bring into London?"

"I didn't have a choice—"

"You said so yourself, Isambard. There is always a choice. You must stop that train. If the Sunken are allowed to enter London—"

"Is that what you call them? An apt name — the

Sunken. I think I shall adopt it."

"—if you shut the gates on the Wall, and no one can get out, and no one can get in—"

"Do you think I don't know this? Do you think I'm so blinded by the favour the mad King has shown me that I would endanger the whole city? Do you think I've not put measures in place to prevent such a tragedy?"

"I don't believe you."

"No, clearly you do not. What's happened to you, Aaron? Have all these years of friendship meant nothing to you?"

"What's happened to *me? You* are the one who has changed, Isambard, and not for the better. This power has corrupted you, however much you think otherwise. You've never kept secrets from me before. The Isambard I knew would have given up his church and his power before he agreed to build such a reprehensible device."

"And then done *what,* exactly? King George would have found another engineer willing enough to build him his trap. It is only because of this power I stand any chance of stopping him!"

"Oh, and what a fine job you're doing! Cutting it a little close, aren't we, *Presbyter?*"

Anger flared in Isambard's eyes. "I know what this is about. You're jealous of me."

"What?"

"You heard me. All these years you've been second to me. Aaron the labourer. Aaron the dogsbody. You hated that I got the credit for the broad gauge locomotive *you* helped build. You hate that I am the one who is held up and revered by our people. And most of all, you hate that I am Presbyter and not you."

"Don't be so quick to presume my thoughts. I've never wanted to be you, Isambard. I've never wanted to be an arrogant, self-righteous quack who thinks he is above the gods—"

"You can't stand that I can innovate and you cannot! You hated the Boilers from the moment you saw them."

"You're right about that. I hate the Boilers. They terrify me. Just because you *can* create something, doesn't mean you *should*. You've gone too far, Isambard. You're creating machines to do the tasks that should be left to men. If you have your way, we will soon have no men at all!"

Brunel balled his hands into fists. "Get out," he hissed.

"Excuse me?"

"Get out of my church, Aaron. You're no longer welcome here. You're no longer part of my crew. You have until tomorrow to pack your things and leave Engine Ward."

***

A priest tried to intercept him as he fled the Chimney, but Aaron pushed the man roughly aside. As he flung open the door a torrent of water assailed him — the rain came in sheets, tearing at his clothes and matting his hair across his eyes. He flew down the stairs, forcing back the urge to scream as he came upon a great swell of people waiting to meet the revered Presbyter. His rage bubbling up inside him, he practically knocked the first man down as he pushed his way past. A woman scolded him, and he barked something so offensive at her that she fainted and had to be carried back to her carriage.

Unheeding, Aaron ducked through the gate at the side of the Chimney, picked up a curved iron bar from the pile of tools outside the locomotive shed, and moved toward the Stoker camp. The rain came so thickly everything seemed hazy, coated in a shroud of water. People moved about him, carrying boxes of supplies, moving equipment indoors, out of the weather. He wiped his hair from his eyes and searched for a familiar face.

"Aaron!" It was William Stone. He grabbed Aaron's arm. "Is something the matter?"

"Quartz was right," said Aaron through gritted teeth. "Isambard Brunel is not to be trusted. The Stokers are doomed, William. The whole city is doomed, and we're the ones responsible."

"You're not talking any sense." William grabbed him by the shoulders and shook him roughly. Men walking between the locomotive shed and the camp gathered around them, shouting over the rain that something was amiss.

"That railway we've been building — it's secret because the King is bringing something horrible into London — an army of monsters that lust for human flesh." The men murmured to each other. William looked stricken. "It's the honest truth — Isambard himself confirmed it. It'll take me too long to explain how I know this, but we can't let that locomotive run." He held up the iron bar. "If I can disable the locomotive, then we can buy some time and—"

"You'll do nothing of the sort."

Aaron heard the ominous click of the hammer of a pistol being pulled back. He whirled around and saw his brother, his robes heavy with water and his face impassive behind the barrel of his barker.

"Oswald."

"Little brother." He didn't move the gun away.

"Aren't you supposed to be in the swamps?"

"Brunel called me back. He needs me to hold service for the Grand Opening of the Wall. And I see discipline has grown lax in my absence. Drop the crowbar, Aaron. I'd hate to be forced to shoot my own brother."

Aaron twisted, slowly, to face Oswald, the bar falling from his hands and landing in a puddle. He stared into his brother's eyes, hatred burning inside him. *You've been greedy, Oswald, greedy for power, greedy for the easiest job — I hope the Sunken devour you.*

"Don't be a fool, Oswald," said William. "Put your barker down. We can't have Stokers killin' Stokers, now."

"I don't want any trouble—" Oswald began.

"Well, you're the only one here waving your irons around," Aaron snapped.

"You were given an order. I'm here to ensure it's carried out."

Aaron spat on the ground. "Look at you, a ridiculous man in your sodden robes. Isambard gives you a sup of power and suddenly you forget how much you once bullied him. He's still the same little boy, still tinkering with machines, only now he's put all our lives in danger. And *you* — you don't even bother to ask questions, Oswald. You follow him blindly. You don't even *try* to understand. I'm ashamed to call you my brother."

"And you!" Oswald snarled in return, the arm holding the barker twitching. "You think you know everything, don't you? Aaron bloody Williams — you think you're so bloody clever because you have some kind of magical, special friendship with our Presbyter. Did you ever think that maybe he's been *using* your loyalty all along? You're his lackey, Aaron. Nothing more—"

Oswald's words died as a scream pierced the evening. It came from the maze of Stoker shacks, stacked one atop the other in the blocks behind the Chimney. It startled Oswald, who fumbled with the barker. Aaron saw his chance and broke away, running toward the Stoker camp.

A shot rang out behind him, but he kept on running, William Stone and a growing crowd of Stokers close at his heels. Oswald was a lousy aim, anyway.

He found the source of the screaming soon enough. William's wife, Mary Stone, knelt in the mud in a small courtyard, a pot of stew upset beside her and a body stretched at an impossible angle on the ground before her. A river of reddened water spilled along the narrow alley, sloshing over Aaron's boots as he ran to investigate. She wailed, her screams cutting through the roar of the torrents of water that cascaded from the pitched roofs above.

William gathered Mary into his arms, stroking her hair in an attempt to calm her sobs. Aaron bent down and turned over the body. It was Benjamin Stone, his face bloody and bruised. The bone in his arm stuck out from a jagged cut in his elbow. Aaron felt for a pulse, watched for signs of life, but could find none.

"I— I— I was just takin' this soup over to the fires, when all o' a sudden he comes hurtlin' down like a sack o' potatoes an' lands right there." Mary covered her eyes with her hands.

"He came from where?" Aaron followed Mary's gaze upward, to the precarious pitched roofs that abutted each other along the edges of the courtyard. Water poured from the one of the corners and splashed across his face.

"In this weather? What was he doing up there?"

William shook his head, his face frozen in shock. One of the men piped up. "Maybe he was fixing a leak, an' fell."

"Benjamin wouldn't have fallen," said William, looking over the boy's mangled face. "Even in this weather he was as spry as a compie."

Aaron glanced up at the roof again, but this time he saw a silhouette against the misty London sky — the flash of a dark cloak flapping in the wind. Someone else was up there! He squinted, shielding his eyes from the rain with one hand. The figure — if there even *was* a figure — was gone.

A crowd of Stokers had gathered, blocking all entry points to the square. Many of the women were crying as they recognised the body of Benjamin, and Aaron could hear Oswald toward the back, yelling for reinforcements, trying to get everyone to return to their homes.

"You're all in danger!" Aaron yelled, as heads turned toward him.

"Listen to me! Benjamin Stone didn't fall from this

roof. He was pushed, and by one of Brunel's own priests." A ripple of disbelief coursed through the crowd, while Oswald, hemmed in by the press of people, roared his defiance. "It's true — and more Stokers will die if we allow that locomotive to run!"

William grabbed his wrist. "Aaron, you're scaring them."

"They *should* be scared. William, you have to listen to me. We're in danger —all the Stokers who worked on the railway, the locomotives, and probably the Boiler teams, too. Oswald will return with reinforcements — maybe constables, maybe Redcoats — and if they catch you, you'll end up like Benjamin. We need to gather the men and their families and hide them outside the Ward, or in the deepest, darkest tunnels. Warn everyone they're not to trust the priests, or any of the authorities. Gather what weapons you can."

"What about you? Where are you going?"

"Isambard threw me out of the Ward, and he'll not allow me to live much longer if I remain, but I have friends outside who can help us. I'll be back as soon as I can, and I need you to be ready."

"What will you do?"

Aaron's face was dark. "I need to find out how deep this goes."

***

"Aaron, I don't understand what this is about. Why have we left Engine Ward? What happened to poor Benjamin Stone? And why in Great Conductor's name are we disturbing this man in the middle of his supper?

Aaron, answer me!"

Ignoring Chloe's protests, Aaron dragged his wife up the steps to Nicholas' house and hammered his fists against the door. His blood pounded behind his eyes.

Chloe tugged at his coat. "He's probably already left for the sermon, and besides, he won't hear us over the rain. We could return tomorrow—"

"What is the meaning of this?" Nicholas flung open the door. One sleeve of his pressed white shirt dangled, armless, from the neck of his half-buttoned frock coat. With his free hand he thrust out a candle, his mouth turned up in surprise. "Aaron? What are you doing here? The sermon starts in an hour—"

"That's exactly what I said," Chloe muttered, forgetting her manners. Aaron shot her a filthy look.

"We've been thrown out of Engine Ward."

"We *have?"*

"Quiet, woman! Nicholas, I need to speak with you about Isambard."

Nicholas gestured to his dangling sleeve. "I'll speak to you later. I'm already running late."

"This cannot wait. One of my men has been murdered."

His face grave, Nicholas ushered them inside, took their coats, and hurried them upstairs. Brigitte passed them in the hall, her hands tangled in her hair as she forced it into place with pins. She cried out as Aaron barrelled past, pressing herself up against the wall so he wouldn't upset her dress. Her eyes met Nicholas', and he shrugged.

Nicholas ushered them all into the dressing room. As he held open the door for Chloe, he met her eyes and gave her a sympathetic look.

"I welcome the pleasure of your company once again, Mrs. Williams," he said. "Even if it is under such perplexing circumstances."

"The honour is all mine, Mr. Rose. It is good that we acquainted ourselves on a previous occasion, since Aaron has not been so kind as to introduce us. And this must be Brigitte—"

"No time for that," Aaron snapped, marching back and forth across the dark room. Nicholas used his candle to light the lamps dotting the side-table, throwing an eerie, flickering light over his sparse furnishings.

"I don't understand," Nicholas said, finally managing to pull his arm through his shirtsleeve. He set a bottle of brandy on the table. Aaron grabbed for it before Brigitte had even fetched a glass. "What has made you so upset?'

"Isambard. He's … you won't believe it—" Nicholas fixed him with a murderous stare. Aaron poured a mouthful of liquor down his throat, swallowed, and said, "He knew about the Sunken all along. He told me so himself."

Nicholas paled. "Aaron, this is your oldest and closet friend you're talking about. Are you *certain?"*

"He threw me out of Engine Ward! At best, he's a coward, and at worst, he's … inhuman. He knows the King plans to move the Sunken into the city. He has a plan to stop them, he says, but if it were true he would not have let it get so far. He *knew,* and he built the railway anyway. He let us both become a part of this. He made *me* build the railway with his cursed Boilers, and now Benjamin's blood is on *my* hands—"

"You must slow down. I can barely understand

you. Have another drink. There, now, who is Benjamin?"

"One of my workers. He fell from a roof this evening, and died."

"So not a murder, then?" Nicholas leaned forward, his eyes narrowing. "In this weather, anyone could—"

"He was pushed. I saw a man up there with him." Aaron wiped his mouth, and caught Nicholas and Chloe exchanging a meaningful look.

"You don't *believe* me?" He leapt to his feet, throwing one of the glasses down on the table. Brigitte screamed as the shards rained down on the rug. Aaron balled his hands into fists, anger pulsing through his body as he stared down at his wife and friend. "My oldest friend evicts me from my home, my own brother points a gun at my head, one of my workers dies and you choose this moment to doubt my word." He glared at his wife. "Ask Mary Stone. Ask any of the Stokers. They all saw Benjamin die. There'll be trouble tonight, Nicholas, because word is spreading, and there won't be a Stoker alive who turns up to his post tonight."

"But that would mean—"

"—the entire Engine Ward will be unmanned, and unsafe. Isambard will have to call off his sermon. And maybe, *maybe* we can stop that locomotive leaving the Ward."

"You do realise how crazy you sound. You're talking about going on strike."

"That's exactly what I'm talking about. It's high time all the engineers — Isambard included — realised the importance of the Stokers. Without us, the machines of this city will grind to a halt, and that's exactly what we intend to do. If Isambard won't stop the King from destroying this city, then I will. And you might think I'm as mad as George, but take these words to heart: if that train leaves the Ward tonight, you must flee the city, with or without Isambard."

From the look on Nicholas' face, Aaron knew he hadn't convinced him. "Well," he said, slowly, measuring his words. "I see that you've set your fate in motion. If you'll excuse me, Aaron, Chloe, we have a sermon to attend." He gave Aaron one last, cold stare, and left the room.

***

"Slow down, Aaron. I can't—" Chloe tripped over her skirts again, stumbling across the thin gangway and narrowly missing colliding with one of the overhead pumps.

"We have to act before Nicholas tells Isambard of our plans." Aaron didn't stop, *couldn't* stop. He dropped her hand so he could run faster, but sure enough, as he bolted across the gangway that bridged the next bank of pumps, he heard the clatter of Chloe's footsteps behind him. *That's why I married you*, he thought. *Because you never give up.*

The day shift men were still at their posts, preparing the fires of the evening's work. Voices filtered down through the air shafts — the muffled conversations of the men and women who crowded the streets above, with no idea what was stirring below their feet. Some of the men called out to Aaron as he flew past, but he didn't answer. He had to reach William, had to find the other men, to get them to safety.

Another pair of footsteps clanged behind him, and a rough hand clamped down on his shoulder. "It's too late," said William. "You're too late."

Aaron whirled around. "What do you mean?"

"Five of the lads worked the day shift down in C Deck. I thought it odd when Oswald swapped them all to work together, but I never questioned—" He shook his head.

"They're dead?"

William nodded. "Pipe burst — not half an hour after you left. We've got some lads down there putting the fire out, but the men working there, they can't have survived—" He choked on his words.

"It might have been an accident," said Chloe.

"Aye, it might've been. But I checked those pipes myself but yesterday. And not one of them had a crack. The only thing that could cause one to burst like that was—"

"—if it had been sabotaged," Aaron finished. William nodded again.

"It's just you, me, and the two Nichols boys left from the railroad crew, an' all the men who worked on the locomotive. I've gathered who I could find an' hid 'em in the battery. Word is spreading through all the teams, and ain't no one man who wants to stoke the fires tonight."

"And no man should have to."

"What do you mean? What do you propose we do?" asked William.

"The only thing we *can* do," said Aaron. "The Stokers are going on strike."

***

Nicholas didn't know Aaron's secret passages into the Engine Ward, so he and Brigitte had to navigate through the crowded streets. After an hour of frantic shoving and squeezing, they were barely inside the gates. Nicholas looked up at Stephenson's cathedral to check the time, and at that moment, every street lamp in the Engine Ward flickered and went out.

The crowd erupted into confusion. Women screamed. Brigitte squeezed his hand, and Nicholas pulled her closer to him as the panic swelled around him.

We're too late.

Nicholas knew all the lamps in the Ward worked on a centralised system. A pump fed oil through a series of pipes strung between each lamp. The lamps were lit at the beginning of the evening and would, as long as the oil pump was maintained, burn all night long. The Stokers were in charge of monitoring the oil.

All around him he heard machinery crunching and seizing. The ground below him shook as pumps shuddered to a stop. Two of the chimneys behind the Cathedral belched out great clouds of black smoke, and a fire erupted from a nearby sewer grate, causing the crowd to surge back in alarm.

The panic spread through the crowd in moments, and the situation quickly became dangerous as the people pressed in on all sides, moving back toward the gates. Nicholas wrapped Brigitte in his arms and turned with the crowd — he could do nothing except move with the surge.

On their right, another fire burst from the vents,

engulfing a Metic priest in yellow flames. He screamed and tore into the crowd, the flames leaping from wool coat to wool coat and singeing hair and blistering skin. A gap opened as people struggled to get away from the blazing man. Brigitte screamed, but Nicholas saw his chance.

He made a beeline for the Chimney, pulling Brigitte along behind him. Even in the darkness and confusion he could find it easily, for he had been there many times before, and it was lit with strings of flickering candles that still glowed brightly.

He strode up the steps and charged through the open door, startling the crowd of people huddled inside. He pushed through them 'till he saw Buckland, and he dragged Brigitte over to his friend and flung her into his arms.

"Brigitte, Nicholas? Is something the matter?" the biologist said, resting his hand on Brigitte's hair. She let out a great sob, and Nicholas felt his heart breaking. He wanted so badly to stay with her.

"A man caught on fire right in front of us," he explained. "The scene has left Brigitte quite shaken."

"A fire? I'm told something is amiss outside in the Ward."

"It's Aaron. He's done something stupid. Could you take Brigitte, please, and keep her close to you? Don't go outside — in fact, the safest place to be is probably right inside this church. I have to find Isambard."

"I saw him behind the altar not two minutes ago."

Pushing through the crowds of nobles and Council members, Nicholas ducked behind the altar and slammed his shoulder into the heavy door. Isambard,

Oswald, Peter, and the other priests looked up from where they had been praying.

"Nicholas." Isambard stood. "You're early. We were just—"

"How *dare* you—" Oswald spluttered.

Nicholas crossed the room in two strides, ducked behind the tapestry of Great Conductor, and located the hidden lever there. He pulled it back, and the metal panel obscuring the window slid back, revealing the darkness beyond.

"The lights are out!" cried Oswald.

"And the gate mechanisms, too," said Nicholas. "And every engine and pump room from one end of the Ward to the other."

"By Great Conductor's steam-driven testicles," Isambard swore. "What has happened?"

Nicholas opened his mouth to explain, but the door flew open and an acolyte slumped against the frame, struggling to catch his breath. "The men, sir," he said. "They're all gone."

"What?"

"I've checked the locomotive shed, the Boiler factory, the engine rooms. There's not a Stoker in sight. Old Foxy who looks after the Metic shrine says Aaron told him the Stokers were going on strike. He said they won't work while they mourn those who died last night."

"Aaron? He's not meant to be inside the Ward!"

"Apparently, that message wasn't clear enough," growled Oswald.

"And that burst pipe in C deck hasn't helped matters." Added the acolyte. "The pressure in furnace rooms C and D is already critical. I've shut the fire doors, but that'll only force the fires up the ventilation shafts. There are blockages in most of the western conduits. If we don't get the Stokers down there soon, the whole Ward's going to be an inferno—"

"Stokers? No, Stokers are useless. We don't need *men,*" Brunel growled. "Nicholas, Peter, go to the Boiler sheds and get as many stoked up as you can. Send them down to the furnace rooms. Oswald, I saw Stephenson arrive with a regiment of Navvies. Go and talk to them. Tell them there's a half guinea per man for any they can spare. And keep quiet — the King shall be here tonight, and I don't want a word about this getting out!"

***

In the 1780s, when construction of the network of tunnels beneath Engine Ward began, the design included a series of "safe rooms" — small magazines equipped with stores of food, water, blankets, and lamps, where the workers might go during a cave-in or other disaster to await rescue. As the tunnels expanded, many of these old magazines had been forgotten, save by the Stokers, who made it their business to know every inch of the Ward.

It was in these magazines that Aaron hid the men, women, and children who had dropped their tools and followed him into hiding. As they descended the levels, more and more workers raced from the furnace rooms and joined the exodus. They'd already packed as many as could fit into the magazines under furnace rooms F, G, and K, and Aaron was settling the remaining people into the deepest magazine, under the westernmost corner of the Ward.

The constant vibrating of the walls subsided as men abandoned their posts and streamed into the magazine, coming up from the furthest furnace bays under the Metic churches and the abandoned Navvy camps. The lanterns flickered and went off, but Chloe found a box of Argands and a few matches, and passed those around. Aaron found a crate of salted meat and a few bottles of some foul-smelling concoction, and shared those around, too.

"Are you certain we should hide here?" asked William as he fell in step beside Aaron. "We don't have enough food or water for all of us."

"Each magazine has enough food for thirty men for ten days," said Aaron. "We have many times this number, but we're not trying to last for weeks down here — we're making a point."

"Shouldn't we be marching through Engine Ward instead of hiding under it, and waving signs about and such?" asked Chloe. "When the Metics wanted to be recognised as an official English church they marched around Somerset House for a month, with signs and banners and all sorts—"

"—and the King had his guards open fire on that crowd," said Aaron. "If they want to dispel our protest, they'll have to find us first."

"And what if they simply lock us down here?" William asked. "Shut up all the entrances, block the vents, and suffocate us to death?"

"I know Isambard. He wouldn't allow it." But even as he said that, Aaron felt a chill run down his spine.

***

As Nicholas ran after Peter toward the Boiler sheds, an avalanche of voices seemed to fall inside his head. Each individual voice was faint, as if the animal were reaching out from behind walls of iron, but together the whispers formed a cacophony like none he'd ever heard. *Get out!* He yelled silently back at them. *I've no time to worry about you now.*

Nicholas flung open the door to the Boiler workshops, and was taken aback by the rows of flat metal faces that glared back at him, unmoving, like dolls waiting to be dragged away by children. The deeper into the shed he ran, the louder and more frantic were the voices in his head. The pain of these animals was so intense that he slowed his step, his vision dotted with red as though he himself suffered the same torture.

Why are you calling me from such a distance? Why are you in such great pain? He guessed one of the furnace rooms deep below the workshops had already been compromised, perhaps engulfing a compie nest. Maybe the creatures were running through the pipes, inhaling smoke and losing their way in the flames. He tried to focus on one voice, to see through its eyes, but they were too far away, too faint.

Shaking his head in a vain effort to dislodge the voices, he searched the shed for the tools he needed. "Hurry!" he yelled at Peter. "Grab shovels and wood."

Like any furnace, the Boilers needed a long time to heat up to full capacity. Luckily, Brunel had ordered that several be kept stoked up constantly at a low temperature, in case they were needed for an urgent job. Forty-five units lined the sloping metal belts in front of the coal pit, steam rising from their twin chimneys and snaking along the iron rafters. The shed held a further two hundred Boilers, a number that had never made Nicholas feel uneasy until he was forced to look into the rows of their unseeing faces. Shoving his hands into thick gloves, Nicholas flung open the belly of the first Boiler and began to shovel in more coal.

As the flames climbed higher, licking the edges of the belly, he slammed the door shut, pumped the injector, and set the dials at the back to send the Boiler to furnace room B. With a lurch, the machine set off across the workshop and disappeared down one of the specially constructed Boiler shafts. Peter's unit soon followed it.

He flung open another Boiler and began tossing the coal inside. Bringing them to heat so quickly put intense pressure on their iron bellies — and Nicholas saw a crack appear, radiating out from the hinge of the firebox door. He slammed the door shut, grabbed Peter by the collar, and pushed him to the ground, flattening his body on top of the priest as the Boiler skidded toward the shaft, sparks streaming from the crack along its belly.

After an hour of shovelling his hands were raw and bloody, his face soaked with sweat from staring into the flames, and his eyes screwed shut against the soot and debris. But worst of all, his head throbbed as a different kind of fire consumed it. The sound of so many animals, caught in so much pain, burnt the sides of Nicholas' skull.

They sent all forty-five Boiler units down to the furnace rooms. A team of Navvies, the sleeves of their dress uniforms rolled up past the elbows, arrived and got to work firing up the cold units. Nicholas tossed aside his gloves and walked outside. The lights were back on, and the familiar vibration of the earth under his feet told him the pumps were working again.

Walking back toward the Chimney, he met Isambard, dressed in the robes of his priesthood and surveying the lit-up streets with satisfaction. He waved Nicholas over to him.

"You did it," he said. "The pressure is back down to normal, and the fire in C is being dealt to."

"The Boilers did it," said Nicholas. Isambard laughed.

"Isambard, is it safe to go down?"

Brunel nodded, his attention diverted by Peter, who was dragging him back toward the Chimney. Nicholas heard trumpets, and could see the King's carriage — bedecked in flowers and followed by a regiment of Royal Guards — entering the gates of the Ward. He had only a little time before he had to be at the sermon. He located a nearby entrance to the underground tunnels and clambered down the stairs.

He headed straight for Pump Deck F, located directly below the Boiler workshops. *If the voices came from anywhere, they must have come from there,* he reasoned. As he climbed lower, their intensity increased. He could still not pick out individual animals, but could discern different species — an unceasing cacophony of rodents and compies and even — were those *pigeons* — all in excruciating pain, and all pounding at his skull, calling for help, for freedom.

The fire doors were shut. He rammed them open with his shoulders, and barged into the furnace room, not sure what he expected to see, but anticipating a horror that must accompany the pain of the voices.

But as he slammed open the door to Pump Deck F, he was confronted with something quite different. There was not an animal in sight.

Boilers crowded the tiny space, each one doing the work of five men, stoking and firing and checking the pressure gauges, watching with unseeing eyes as the beam engines creaked and swung through their rotations, adding water to the condensers. Nicholas peered under their feet, watching for the skitterings of compies between their skids. He checked every corner of the room, watching for shadows along the pipes that ran the length of the room, but he could find nothing.

I'm going mad, he thought, pressing his palms against his temples. The voices assailed him, calling through their pain 'till he could take no more, and fled back up the tunnel. He stumbled through the fire door, pushed it shut behind him, and whirled around as another wave of pain shot through his head. More voices, more animals crying out in agony. But where did they come from? *Where?*

His legs gave way and he slumped to the floor, his hands clawing at the iron grating. *What's happening to me? Is the sense somehow broken?* The animals didn't answer, of course. They only sang their sorrows louder, the pain slicing across his temples.

He thrashed about, his hands clamped on his skull, reality and his nightmares becoming one. Sweat poured down his face, and somewhere in his torture he heard himself calling to Aaron, as if by some miraculous occurrence he might be hiding nearby, and would understand his distress and come to him, say that he too heard the voices so deep within the iron, and offer a logical, rational explanation. One that didn't lead to the most obvious conclusion — that Nicholas was going mad.

But Aaron didn't come. Alone in the darkness, Nicholas lost himself. Hours may have passed, or days, but to him they were but one unending spiral of torture.

Hands grabbed him under the arms. Someone lifted him to his feet. He slumped, falling again. More hands steadied him, and voices, real *human* voices, called him back from a dark place.

"Here you are," Buckland said. "Brigitte was worrying herself sick about you."

"I should be preparing for the sermon, not chasing after wayward architects." Brunel pulled Nicholas' arm over his shoulder and began dragging him back toward the entrance. "Nicholas, is something the matter? You look in a dreadful state."

"You were calling for Aaron." Buckland had Nicholas' other arm over his shoulders. "That was how we found you."

He felt tempted to tell them the truth, but he remembered hanging over the edge of the church pulpit with Isambard's hands clasped on his throat. He remembered struggling for breath and seeing the Presbyter's face contorted with — what? Not anger, but a kind of serene indifference. No, he wanted Isambard to remain in the dark about the voices — just in case. Besides, telling Isambard meant revealing Aaron's secret, and that wasn't right by Aaron.

"I'm fine," he managed. "I was looking for Aaron … worried about him, and I must've … tripped and fallen …."

"The church is filling with people, and the King has settled on his balcony. Your woman is waiting for you, and I wanted to see your face as I read my sermon," said Brunel. "You picked a fine time to run off on a fool's errand."

"So you haven't found Aaron?"

Isambard shook his head. "Let him hide. After tonight, I have no use for Aaron, or the Stokers."

***

It was strange being down in the tunnels and not feeling the ache of an evening's work in your shoulders or the blast of hot air across your face. Down this deep there were hardly any animals, save the worms in the ground and an occasional wayward compie. Aaron's mind felt clear.

He hoped the clarity would last, for the lights and machines would've ceased working in Engine Ward, and that familiar hum under the streets had changed to an erratic shudder. Isambard would know by now what he had done, and Aaron wondered nervously what his response would be.

His thoughts were interrupted by a tap on the shoulder. He turned to see a man, about Quartz's age, with thin grey hair and a face scarred by burns. "Excuse me, sir. I don't mean to bother you, but I've just come from the central boilers. The pressure is still unstable in room C." The man paused, as if he were debating something in his mind. After a few moments, he said: "I know we're meant to be on strike, Mr. Williams, but I'd hate for all those people up there to burn, an' it be my fault n' all."

Aaron agreed. He sent William Stone and two other men back up to check on things. "If it's critical, I want you to bring the pressure down to under one-sixty. But you're to touch nothing else. It's Isambard's responsibility now."

William nodded, and raced away. Chloe nestled up against him.

"Some of the women wish to sleep now," she said. "The children are beginning to fuss. I've sent them all to K magazine with orders to send the men back here, but you'll want to have some men keep watch."

He embraced her, pulling her to him, and pressed her warm hands tight against his chest. "Thank you," he said, his voice cracking. "Thank you for everything."

They sat in silence, holding each other, for several minutes. Chloe said, "I'm scared, Aaron. I don't feel safe down here."

"It's the safest place we have. We're Stokers, if we leave the Ward and go out into London, who do you think will hide us? We're much safer in our own tunnels, where we know every secret place and every —"

Above their heads, the lights flickered on. The walls gave a great shudder, and began humming again.

Aaron swore. "I told them to get the pressure back to normal and come straight back. How can we have a strike if they keep *fixing* things."

William sprinted around the corner and collapsed against Aaron's shoulder, his breath coming out in ragged gasps.

"What are you *doing?*" Aaron yelled. "You were only meant to check the pressure, not get all the lights

—"

"Boilers," huffed William. "Boilers … took over. They're manning the Engine Room … and repairing the furnaces …"

"Who's operating them? Who set their controls?"

"No one … I can't see … I don't know." William covered his face with his hands. "There's no one there."

Aaron bolted from his chair. Chloe grabbed at his shirt sleeve, but he wrenched himself away and stomped down the corridor.

The sight that greeted him turned the rage in his veins to ice. Three Boilers blocked the gangways running across the Engine Room, steam curling from their smoke stacks as they opened the firebox doors, shovelling coal inside, and watched the pressure gauges with unseeing eyes.

Everything I feared is coming true.

To keep the Engine Ward running in the absence of the Stokers, to ensure his sermon went ahead without delay, Brunel had done what he promised Aaron he would *never* do — he'd given the Boilers men's jobs. And Aaron could already see that they were better than the Stokers could ever hope to be — three units were doing the work of eight men, and they were *fast* — their hose-like arms stretching and bending in ways no human could ever dream of. They would never need food, never get tired, never make mistakes.

They are the perfect workers, and I've just given Brunel the chance to prove it. Everything we've achieved today has been for naught — the Stokers have been replaced.

***

It was standing room only inside the Chimney, as engineers, Council members, and the high society of London jostled for space. Women decked out in their finest clothing and weighed down by heavy jewels and clockwork parasols huddled together in tight circles, their mouths moving like steam-driven pistons as they shared the latest gossip. The whole room throbbed with anticipation.

The doors had been shut and bolted, for outside thousands of people crowded the streets, corralled behind barriers by the constables but clambering over each other for a good spot. Isambard had rigged two giant gramophones to project the sermon over the whole of Engine Ward, and it seemed every man, woman, and child in the whole of England had turned out to hear the Presbyter speak.

Sandwiched between Buckland and Brigitte, who had not let go of his arm since he'd returned, Nicholas watched Oswald and Peter — the hems of their robes stained with peat from the swamps — make the final preparations on the altar. Isambard had disappeared up into his pulpit, that iron platform suspended fifty feet over the congregation. He wanted to make an entrance.

Nicholas scanned the crowd for Aaron, but could not see him anywhere. He saw Robert Stephenson — the man who'd spoken to him most peculiarly beside the Wall yesterday — as he took his place of honour beside the other Messiahs at the front of the church. His retinue followed behind him, Navvies all dressed in their formal coats, pushing the lesser dignitaries and their wives toward the back of the room. Nicholas watched them filing past, his gaze flicking over all the faces in the room, looking for Aaron.

Wait, it can't be—

His stomach churned, and he jerked his head down so hard his neck cracked. Heart thumping against his ribs, he shuffled closer to Buckland and dared a peek across the room. *Has he seen me?*

The man hadn't turned around. Behind the altar, Peter turned a handle, and the lamps dimmed. The crowd fell silent; the only sound the shuffling of feet and someone coughing. Nicholas leaned over further, watching the man as he faced the altar, his head bent towards Stephenson as though they whispered to each other.

It can't be. It simply cannot be.

There was meant to be a choir of Stoker boys to begin the ceremony, but Nicholas guessed their mothers had dragged them down into the tunnels to join the strike, so instead the crowd watched in silence as Joseph Banks rolled the King behind the altar, the squeaking wheels of his chair echoing through the vaulted room. The King wore a turban of silk scarves, entwined together like coiled snakes, that covered his entire head. More scarves were wrapped around his hands, so none of his skin was visible.

"Let us pray," he said, in his heavy, clear voice. He bowed his head, and so did everyone in the room, and he spoke the prayers to the Gods of Industry, his voice never wavering, his fingers clutching the arms of his chair like talons, twisting and contorting as he recited the ritual. Nicholas watched one of the scarves slip, and he saw the leather straps around the King's wrists.

The room seemed searingly hot to Nicholas, and beads of sweat rolled down his neck. He dared to shift his gaze from the King back to the figure, whose head was still inclined toward Stephenson. The King's voice — rising as his prayer grew more fervent — faded in Nicholas' mind, replaced by the frantic beating of his heart. *Maybe it's not him. Maybe I'm mistaken.*

The man whipped his head around, and Nicholas had no time to look away as their eyes met. He lifted his hat from his head, revealing the long scar running from his ear across his forehead — the scar Nicholas had given him in a cold mountain valley two years ago — and smiled.

Terror clamped down on Nicholas' chest. His head snapped back, as if he'd been slapped, and blood rushed to his head so fast he had to reach out for Buckland's arm to steady himself.

Brigitte looked at him, worry crossing her face. He shook his head at her, unable to explain without bringing further attention to himself. "William," he whispered, tugging on his friend's sleeve.

"Sshhh!" Buckland silenced him with a flick of his wrist. "The sermon is beginning, and I don't want to miss it. He might acknowledge my work."

Nicholas followed Buckland's gaze toward the altar, where the King was being wheeled away, his hand once again covered by the silken scarves. Soft, eerie music flowed from a series of vacuum tubes positioned along the wall. The lamps glowed brighter, and, as the music rose and filled the lofty space, Isambard appeared on the edge of his high metal pulpit and threw his hands in the air. The room fell silent.

"The Wall is complete, and London is safe from

the dragons," he said, his voice amplified by the vacuum tubes sailing out into every corner of the church, so no one would miss his words. "When the King first set me this task, he gave me a timeframe believed to be impossible, but through Great Conductor's wisdom and guidance, I was able to discern a solution and erect the largest man-made structure in England in a mere twenty-nine days. My means of completing this task — the Boiler unit — will be the subject of my sermon."

Nicholas sat numb, Isambard's words falling from the ceiling without sense or meaning. His eyes burnt into the back of Jacques' neck. He didn't realise he was still gripping Buckland's hand 'till the biologist cried out and wrenched it free, wincing as he flexed the fingers.

"Jesus Chr— I mean, by the Gods, man, what is the matter?"

"There's a man, perhaps twenty feet away, standing with Messiah Stephenson. He's—" Nicholas gulped. "He wants to kill me."

"What do you want me to do about it?"

"I cannot allow him to find me, or Brigitte. He's right down near the front of the room, so he can't leave without causing a scene, and he won't want that. I need to leave the Chimney before the sermon ends. I can find a safe place—"

The woman beside Buckland turned around and snarled at them. "Will you be *quiet?*"

Buckland didn't flinch, but he did lower his voice. "I can get you out of here," he said. "And I even know somewhere you can hide. But he will see us leave," he said, gesturing to Isambard, high in the pulpit above, "and with everything that has already gone on tonight, he will be furious."

Nicholas flinched, watching Isambard lean over the edge of the pulpit and remembering how he had dangled over that same edge only a week previously. "If you can bring him to me, in secret, so that he is not followed. I will explain everything. But we must—"

Brigitte let out a yelp as Buckland tossed his glass — full nearly to the brim with dark brandy — at her. It bounced off her shoulder and splashed bright red stains down the front of her dress. Some of the liquid caught.

"Deary me," said Buckland loudly, "that was awfully clumsy of me. Come, let me help you wash up." Grabbing a surprised Brigitte by the hand, he began pushing through the crowd toward one of the side chambers. Nicholas followed, mumbling "excuses me" and "my apologies" as he tried to avoid stepping on the hems of dresses or the heels of boots, while keeping an eye on the back of Jacques' head. *Maybe we can reach the door before he turns around, and he won't notice our absence 'till the end of the sermon.*

Brigitte, still holding on to Buckland's hand, tripped on her skirts and fell into another lady, who stepped back in surprise, knocking the fan from the hand of the lady behind her. The wooden handle clattered against the stone floor, and several heads whipped around to see what was going on.

Although Isambard didn't miss a word, his voice ringing clear and true through the Nave, Nicholas could feel the Presbyter's eyes upon him, his disapproval burning Nicholas' back. *I'm sorry, Isambard. I'm sorry. My past has come back, and I must run again.*

Jacques turned, and his eyes flashed with anger as he saw Nicholas beside the door. He grabbed for his coat and bolted into the crowd. Women cried out in surprise as he pushed them roughly aside. Two of the Royal Guard who stood beside the King rushed forward, swords drawn, yelling for him to stop.

Buckland wrenched a lantern from its socket on the wall and grabbed Nicholas' shoulder, dragging him back into the chamber. "Come on, boy! You don't have much time!"

***

It was no use. By the time Jacques reached the door to the chamber, Nicholas had disappeared, escaping through one of three doors hidden at the back of the darkened room. Jacques tried each of them — locked, of course. He swore and bolted toward the main doors just as two giant hands clamped down on his shoulders and slammed him against the wall.

"What's this all about, then?" A thick English voice, the breath foul with beer, barked in his ear.

"Mrs. Milbanke, is this the one?" another voice called. Jacques was pulled away from the wall and swung around to face a sour-looking woman who was trying to smooth her skirts.

"That's him," she sniffed. "Running through crowd, shoving people aside with no regard for propriety. He travelled in the same carriage from Liverpool as I. That's how I recognised him. French, isn't he? I might've known."

"You a Froggie, then?" The guard shook him. "You a Metic, snuck in here to hurl abuse at the

Presbyter? Or are you an illegal? You know what we do to the likes of them?"

Jacques said nothing.

"I expect you'll take him to gaol immediately," said Mrs. Milbanke. "It would not be wise to have such an unsavoury figure roaming the Ward at night."

"Quite right, M'lady." The officer tightened his grip. Jacques shut his eyes as he felt the rapier blade pressed against his neck. "He's a tight-lipped one, in't he? We might loosen him up—"

"What seems to be the matter here?" a voice boomed. Jacques opened one eye and saw, to his relief, the broad figure of Robert Stephenson looming over the arresting party.

"N-n-n-nothing that need concern you, Messiah," the guard answered. "This man has been causing trouble, running through the crowd, knocking the ladies about. Poor Mrs. Milbanke here was practically knocked over—"

"And as regrettable as that is, I hardly think it worthy of a night in gaol. After all, Mr. du Blanc has apologised, has he not?"

"No," the woman sniffed, "he has not."

"Then allow me to do so, on his behalf." Stephenson reached into his wallet and withdrew a small bag. Handing it to the lady, he said softly, "This will go some way to replacing that fine dress, ma'am, with our sincerest apologies. Jacques truly means no disrespect, he is on a mission of the utmost importance."

Annabella Milbanke grabbed the purse and stormed away into the crowd, Ada following close behind. The guards let Jacques go, and Stephenson gave him his arm while he regained his balance.

"He ran through one of these doors," Jacques said. "I've no hope of catching him now."

"Don't be silly," said Stephenson. "You have every hope of catching him. You are in the house of his new master, yes?"

Jacques nodded, staring up at the wiry figure of Brunel, suspended in the pulpit high above a rapt congregation. On the altar, a live Boiler unit rotated slowly, steam hissing as it bent pipe after pipe to form the crest of His Majesty King George III. Something in Brunel's expression unnerved Jacques— the way he lifted his chin, the way he spoke of the machine as though it were a beloved son. The way he loomed over his audience, his eyes meeting every gaze as he continued with perfect clarity, perfect calm.

"Maybe you need to speak to him, master to master, about your wayward slave."

***

When the sermon was finished and Isambard descended the metal steps from his pulpit, a wave of people surged forward to meet him. The question on everyone's lips was "are the Boilers for sale?" Every one of the rich lords and ladies wanted one, or three, or ten, to run their factory or tidy their home or show up their neighbours. Jacques listened to the praise echoing around him, as Stephenson scowled into his drink.

"I don't like it," Stephenson said, gesturing toward the Boiler with his elbow. "It isn't natural."

Isambard made his rounds of the room, and stopped before Stephenson. He smiled, but his eyes were like coal. "Messiah," he said, giving a shallow bow.

"Presbyter."

"I hope my sermon was to your liking."

Stephenson pointed to the Boiler, which was now demonstrating how it could tie a lady's corset. "That," he said, "is debatable. But at least you're no longer dabbling in locomotives."

Brunel's face was impassive, but his eyes remained hard. "If you remember, sir, it is my engine that will run the first commuter service in London—"

"Yes, yes," Stephenson interrupted. "If you'd be so kind, my friend Jacques has come a long way, and is most desirous to speak with you."

Brunel turned to him. "With all due respect, sir, many people in this room wish to speak to me, and I cannot possibly acquiesce to every reques—-"

"It is about your architect, Mr. Nicholas Thorne."

That got a reaction out of him. He leaned in toward Jacques, so close their noses were practically touching. His eyes were unreadable, his face like stone. In a low voice he said. "He is not here. I saw him leave this building some hours ago, escorted by Mr. Buckland."

"It is you I wish to speak to, *Presbyter*. Might we have a few words alone? It is of a most delicate matter."

Brunel threw a furious glance at Stephenson, who pretended he hadn't seen it. "Very well then," the Presbyter said through gritted teeth. He placed his arm on Jacques' shoulder and pushed him toward another side-chamber. He lifted a lantern from the wall, slipped into a room, and gestured for Jacques to sit. The

Frenchman settled himself into a chair, staring suspiciously at the long table stretching across the centre of the room – three deep grooves cut into its metal surface – and the strange symbols engraved upon the walls. Isambard closed the heavy door and slid the bolt across.

"This is the baptismal," Brunel said. "Worshippers of Great Conductor are brought here to be consecrated in coal and steam. Your Stephenson has a much grander chamber in his cathedral, but I suspect after this evening, it will be emptier than ever. Now," he said, pulling out his own chair, and leaning in closely, "what is it you know about Nicholas? You are the first man in many months to speak his real name."

"He was in my employ, back in France. He owed a debt to me, but he did not finish paying it. I am an important man, Presbyter Brunel, and I have friends in many influential positions. I do not look kindly upon men who cheat me. I have come to take back what is mine."

"Thorne is *mine*. He'll not work for another — he is valuable to me. I shall pay you what you're owed, and that will settle the matter."

"I do not want money. I want Thorne."

"And I say you will not have him." The lamplight flickered across Brunel's cold eyes.

"He ran from your sermon tonight," said Jacques. "He is a coward — always running from his duty, from his punishment. Death follows him wherever he goes. He murdered my wife, did he tell you that? The French authorities look unkindly upon men who brutalise women and then escape across the border to England. Even your English courts will not spare such a man.

And think what such a scandal would do to your newfound reputation—"

"Why are you *here?*" Brunel's eyes narrowed. "If you're as important and influential as you say, why not simply send French soldiers, or your own private ships, to exact the justice you seek?"

Jacques laughed. "I am a philosopher, not a madman. My sect is unpopular in France. If I were to send a ship to Industrian England, I would be assumed a traitor and dealt with in the usual way. But I am one man, Presbyter Brunel, and one man can go where an army cannot. I must again command you to deliver to me Nicholas Thorne."

"And I again state that you will not have him. We are done here." Brunel pushed his chair back, but Jacques reached over and clasped his wrist.

"You still protect him, after he has left you in your greatest hour? He has not even told you the nature of his crime, for if he had, you would not hesitate to hand him over."

"I trust him," said Brunel. "If Nicholas committed any crime, he would have reason, and I would not betray him, even if I knew where to find him, which I do not."

"Then you are unwise, Presbyter. Nicholas Thorne is not to be trusted."

"You dare to come in here, a follower of Stephenson, and make demands of me?"

"I follow no man," Jacques said. "And certainly not an Englishman. I am here, at great personal peril, to look after my own interests, and to avenge the death of my wife, whom Nicholas Thorne stabbed right through the heart as she stood before me. I have not yet gone to the authorities on this matter, Mr. Brunel, but I could. And when I do, the brutal nature of Mr. Thorne's crime will be made public. The press — not to mention your fellow priests and Councillors — will use the story to crucify you." He gazed up at the low ceiling of the chamber, sweeping his arm in a circle to encapsulate the whole of the Chimney. "You have to ask yourself if you're willing to risk everything you've created here for the sake of a man who has walked from your church without apology, for a man who has kept secrets from you and fed you lies and falsehoods, for a cold-blooded *murderer?*"

He watched Brunel's face for a sign, the twitch of a muscle, the flicker of emotion that might tell him if he'd achieved his goal. The Presbyter stared into the flames of the lamp, and his face never changed. He remained silent so long Jacques became uneasy, wondering if he'd drifted into some sort of trance.

Finally, in a low voice, so quiet Jacques had to lean forward to hear him, Brunel said, "What do you want me to do?"

***

Buckland ran ahead, the faint light of his lamp bobbing down the winding staircase. Brigitte followed, her arm sore from where he pinched it between his enormous hands, her slippered feet sliding across the slick stone as she tried desperately to keep her balance.

"Nicholas! What on earth is the matter? Why are we running? Is it Isambard? Is it—"

"Ah hah," cried Buckland in delight. "Here it is! I was worried I wouldn't find it — I've never come this way before."

They crowded onto a landing, facing the stone wall. Buckland held his light up and examined the stones. Nicholas squeezed Brigitte's hand. She opened her mouth to ask again what was going on, but Buckland gave a cry of triumph and leaned his weight against a particular stone. With a groan, he pressed his whole body into the wall, and to Brigitte's great surprise a whole section of it slid inward, revealing a low, dark passage.

"After you." Buckland gestured to Nicholas.

"Thank you, friend." Nicholas clasped the man's shoulders. "Please take Brigitte and find her a room in the city. He won't come after her — it's me he wants, but she should not go back to my lodgings—"

"Excuse *me,"* she cut in, her patience finally run dry. "But I have been dragged from a sermon I was quite enjoying, sent running after you two all night, stained my dress and ruined these slippers, and now you're sending me from your presence with not a word of explanation. I *demand* to know what's going on, "

"Brigitte, *please—"*

She folded her arms and leaned back against the stone wall. "I'll not move from this spot 'till you tell me why we've left the Chimney to crawl around in dark tunnels in the middle of the night—"

"Someone's trying to kill me," Nicholas said, his face slick with sweat. "And I'll be damned to the Great Conductor's fiery furnace before I let him get you, too."

"Nicholas—" she reached out, wanting to comfort him.

"Keep away from me!" He slunk back, hiding in

the shadows. "You must go with Buckland. Please, Brigitte."

Tears brimmed in her eyes. She shot out her elbow and knocked Buckland's arm aside, ducking into the dark passage next to him. "I'm not leaving you," she said.

"Don't be absurd, Brigitte. You are safer if you return to the city, pretend you don't know me—"

She shook her head. "I'll pretend nothing of the sort. I gave up my livelihood for you. Don't think for one moment I'm leaving."

"You don't understand. If he catches you with me—"

"Then we had better make sure this man, whoever he is, doesn't catch you," she said firmly, taking another step into the dark passage. "I've decided, Nicholas, and I'll not hear another word to the contrary. We don't have time to argue about it anyway, by all accounts. Now, where does this tunnel lead?"

"Into the Wall," Buckland answered, stepping in beside them and pulling the stone door back into place. "The structure isn't solid inside, but contains many rooms and chambers for Brunel's use. I've been working here on a project for Brunel, and I've had a chance to explore some of the tunnels and rooms around my workshop. I know a place you can hide."

"What project?" asked Nicholas. Brigitte detected a note of suspicion in his voice.

"I cannot say. Ah, here we are. Watch your head, Miss Brigitte." She had to get on her hands and knees to crawl under the banks of lead piping that crisscrossed over their heads. The air here felt warmer, and everything around her hummed and vibrated beneath her hands as though it were alive. Warm air moved under the pipes, caressing her bare arms, and in the distance she could hear a strange, regular *whoosh.*

Buckland stood, and helped her to her feet. She dusted off her dress and saw by the dim light of a lantern they were at one end of a long metal walkway, suspended over a floor of beam engines, all turning in unison, the rise and fall of their arms creating the *whooshing* sound.

Buckland stepped out on the gangway, and Brigitte followed, her eyes falling to the machines below, each one rising and dipping with the grace of a dancer. She saw the faint glow of fires moving between the machines — Boilers, keeping the engines running. *But what do all these engines power?*

On the other side of the gangway, Buckland pulled down a steel ladder and motioned for Brigitte for ascend. "When you reach the top, lean down and I'll hand you the light," he said. "When Nicholas is up there with you, I will push up the ladder and close the gate on the other side. Only Brunel and I have the key, so it should be impossible for anyone to find you."

Brigitte gathered her skirts in one hand and clambered up the ladder, pulling herself onto a cold metal floor. She reached down, and Buckland placed the heavy old lamp in her hands. She hauled it up and set it in the centre of what was a low, square room, barely ten foot from end to end. It was devoid of furniture and decoration, save the square grating of a ventilation shaft in the corner.

Nicholas heaved himself up the ladder, and knelt beside her. He looked back at Buckland. "Please," said Nicholas. "Explain to Isambard what has happened. He saw me leave, and he will not be pleased. And do inform the other Blasphemous Men, if you should cross paths with them."

With a cheerful wave, Buckland hurried back across the gangway. Brigitte heard a steady creak as he drew shut a metal gate on the other side. The clang of his boots against the metal faded into the darkness, and she was left alone with Nicholas and his secrets.

***

Brigitte set in with persistent questions, but Nicholas, so weary from the day's activities and their flight he could no longer stand, begged for time to rest before he told his story.

"I deserve to know."

"Yes," he sighed. "You do, but, please … not now. We are out of immediate danger, and it is a long tale, cruel in the telling, and I have not the strength to tell it." He slumped against the wall, and lifted up his arm.

Brigitte snuggled under it, and fell asleep quickly, her warm cheek pressed hard against his chest. But every time Nicholas' eyes seemed to be closing, he would hear a noise or sense an animal or see an image of Julianne dancing under his eyelids, and he would be jolted awake again.

The Wall was not nearly as secure as the tunnels under Engine Ward, and Nicholas' mind jumped from compie to compie as they raced along the pipes. Through their eyes he could see where they'd already gnawed through the metal structure in places, creating for themselves a network of secret tunnels. If he lived through this night, he'd need to have Brunel dispatch a crew to tidy up the gaps.

The compies spoke a complex language of scents, sounds, and signals, which he was only just beginning to decipher, but he'd learned enough to know that they had sensed the presence of the humans in this room. Used to the company of Boilers, these compies were wary of humans, and their scent signal leapt from body to body. *Be alert.*

But they were wary of something else, too. Some great and terrible shadow lurked in the corner of their minds. They could not see it in the dark, but they had heard it, smelt it. It worried them.

Nicholas could feel this shadow also, a looming presence on the periphery of his sense. He was too weak to hold onto it, and it was too great and dark for him to sense properly, but he knew whatever it was, it was nearby, and it was hungry, and very, very angry. But he had enough to worry about now without succumbing to a nameless fear in the darkness. He tried to ignore the presence and follow the compies in his mind, skipping from one to the other as they made their rounds of the tunnels. He knew if they sensed more humans in the tunnels, so would he.

Hours drifted by, and their lamp — the oil already low — gave a final flicker and went out, plunging them into total darkness. Sometime later — when, he could not tell, for no light penetrated their cell, and he had lost his pocket watch somewhere in the tunnels — the compies did indeed sense a human presence. This man came by a different route, down from the official entrances above. The compies knew his smell instantly, and so did Nicholas. It was Isambard.

He heard the gate swing open, and the Presbyter's

footsteps across the gangway, and he prayed to the Gods that Isambard had not come to give him over to Jacques.

"Nicholas!"

The voice rang out like a battle cry in the silent darkness. Brigitte shuddered away and gripped Nicholas' hand as they listened to Isambard climbing the ladder into their hiding place. There was nowhere to go, nowhere to hide. Nicholas opened and closed his mouth, his throat dry and his words dying on his lips.

"Nicholas?" The voice was softer, but so close Brigitte screamed and leapt back. A second later, a match struck, and a shaft of light penetrated the room. Isambard's face appeared at the top of the stairs. He held up a lantern and a parcel.

"Buckland said you had no food, so I have brought some. And some oil for your lamp." He crawled in beside them and set the package down on the floor. "Nicholas ... why didn't you *tell* me?"

"You are not angry with me?" Nicholas leaned away from him, remembering Isambard's face when he'd threatened him on the pulpit.

"If I am to understand correctly, a threat has been made on your life. I am concerned for you, and determined to keep you safe, at least as long as I am able." Isambard opened the parcel and spread out a bounty of bread and butter, jam, and a draught of beer. Nicholas could not bring himself to eat, but Brigitte ate hungrily, stuffing bread into her mouth faster than she could chew. "I am saddened you did not come to me earlier. I have power now, and what good is such power if I can't use it to help my friends?"

"There is a good reason for my silence. The man

that follows me does not simply intend to kill me — he will hurt anyone in my life if he knew their deaths would wound me. I intended to keep a low profile, to claim friendship with no one, to extract myself with little disruption from London if he did find me here. But you two—" he said, glancing from Isambard to Brigitte, and sighing.,"you have destroyed my hope of this, for I care about you too deeply. Now that he has found me I must once again go underground, for I cannot have him catch me and destroy your lives in the process. Brigitte has, against my protestations, decided to go with me, but I'll not have you forsake your own life for my mistakes."

"This man hates you so much?" Tears streamed down Brigitte's face.

"If you knew my crime, you would not be so quick to side against him."

"Nicholas." Brigitte's voice seemed firm, large in the darkness. "I am hiding in a tiny box in the deepest reaches of an iron wall. I am cold and I am frightened. Your friend Isambard has come down here to tend to you when he should be celebrating. It's time you told us what is going on."

"We cannot help you until we understand the nature of the man we're up against," Brunel added.

Nicholas sighed. "Very well, but when you hear what I have done, you will change your mind and cast me forever from your life, and you will be all the happier for it."

So he told them the tale of his escape from the Navy, of his meeting with Jacques and the beguiling black-haired woman named Julianne, of his days spent studying, of his nights holding her while she cried, of how the atmosphere at the monastery had slowly turned poisonous, of his discovery of Jacques' brutality, and of their desperate flight that ended in him driving his sword into the heart of the woman he loved.

When he finished, he was weeping, the tears hot against his cheeks. Isambard pressed the beer into his hands, and he drank, long and heavy, 'till the rawness of the memories floated away.

All three were silent for a long time, the only sound in the room the steady dripping of water somewhere in the distance and Nicholas' wretched sobs.

Brigitte spoke, her soft voice cutting the air like a dagger. "I could not ask you to do this."

"Brigitte—"

"She was selfish, this Julianne. She wanted you to do this for her, knowing you loved her so, knowing what it would do to you thereafter."

"It wasn't like that—" He caught himself. "Perhaps she didn't expect me to live much longer."

"But live you did. And now you're in a world of mess, and it's *her* fault."

Nicholas felt a strong sense that he should be defending Julianne, but he said instead, "You do not hate me?"

"Why should I? You fulfilled the last wish of a dying woman, a woman who was already numb and dead inside, and you've carried the guilt of that memory like a shroud ever since. Do you think me so fickle that my love for you could be extinguished by some past crime? Do you think you alone own all the sorrow of the world?"

Love ... she had spoken that word. He'd not thought

about it, not dared to utter it, since that night in the valley. And here she was before him, this maid who knew nothing about him save his one greatest secret, and yet she professed her love for him.

"I do not think you fickle," he choked, trying to keep his voice steady. "But you should not profess such things, for they cannot be taken back, and you may yet meet the same fate as the last person to utter those words to me."

"She will not," said Isambard. "Buckland has done right to hide you here, for du Blanc cannot possibly find you. As soon as Buckland told me of your flight, I sent a guard to your home. He saw Jacques arrive there but three hours ago, with two Navvies in tow. They broke the front window and stirred your papers into frightful disarray, but they left soon after. He tracked them back to Stephenson's London residence, but they have not emerged since."

"He aims to make my death look like a simple Stoker/Navvy rivalry," Nicholas said.

"That is my guess, too. It was probably Stephenson's idea. It will take all my cunning to design a solution to this dilemma. I do not know when next I can return to you, but when I do, it will be with your salvation."

"Could you send someone else? What about Aaron?"

"He's still playing hero with the Stokers. I'll not trust him again," Isambard said. "Apart from Buckland, I'm the only one who knows about these tunnels and this room, and I intend to keep it that way. But just in case, I have brought you this." He drew from the darkness a long, thin object: Nicholas' sword.

He took it gratefully. "Thank you, Isambard. For everything."

With a nod of his head, Isambard retraced his steps back down the ladder, and Nicholas listened to his footsteps fading into the gloom. He reached across and clasped Brigitte's hand.

"Brigitte?"

"Mmhmmm?"

"If we make it out of this alive, would you object to marrying me?"

"Nothing would make me happier."

***

JAMES HOLMAN'S MEMOIRS — UNPUBLISHED

A night and a day had passed since Brunel's sermon, and I was no closer to London. I had been ready to sneak off toward the castle after the night mass, when another Knight took it upon himself to be unusually talkative, and I was unable to slip away. I had already heard one carriage clatter away into the darkness — no doubt laden with a cargo of Sunken — and I knew I could not remain here much longer with the King's disturbing secret weighing heavy upon me.

I made sure to leave Travers College at the earliest possible hour, and upon reaching St. George's Chapel, some thirty-five minutes before service was due to begin, I took up a stall closest to the exit. I needn't have bothered, for as the minutes drew out and the priests at last began their incantations, not a single other Knight appeared. They'd all decided to absent themselves from duty. Maybe luck would be with me tonight.

After the service had finished, I slipped around the side of the church, hid in a flower bed, and listened as the priests locked the chapel for the night. When I was certain the courtyard was empty, I slipped from my hiding place and crept toward the servants' quarters.

Brigitte had said there was an entrance to the cellars in the castle kitchen, and although I'd never been there before, I'd have no trouble locating it. A short walk through the northern wing of the castle revealed a sharp scent of fresh herbs on the breeze. I'd found the kitchen gardens. From here it was a simple task to feel my way along the wall 'till I found the door to the kitchen. It was unlocked. I pushed it open and crept inside.

The door to the cellar could probably be found in the larder. I stood in the doorway of this unfamiliar room and rapped my knuckles against the wooden bench, once, twice … I listened, the echoes creating an image in my mind. The shapes and positions of objects — though not their form or function — became clear to me. I took a cautious step forward, careful to avoid knocking any pans from the overhanging rack.

A blind man builds his image of a room in a very different way from a man with eyes. While the sighted man can take in the basics of a room in a single glance, I build my perception in layers — first, the position, density, and relationships of objects, then the intricacies of the space that surrounds them, and finally a complex map of textures, scents, and sounds. Normally, I would build this "image" over weeks, visiting a room many times to familiarise myself with every detail, but this night I didn't have the luxury. I stepped to the right to avoid the wooden table, my hands at my sides, fingers running across the surface of the object. Slowly. Methodically. Every sense on high alert.

I took another step.

On the other side of the room, a door creaked.

I froze, listening hard. There was a window beside the door, just behind where I stood. If the moon was high in the sky tonight, my silhouette would be illuminated to anyone looking in on the room.

I held my breath.

After several moments, I could detect no further movement, no other human presence. Satisfied it was just a draught, I took another step into the room.

A woman cried out, and a heavy object slammed into the side of my head. Pain arced across my eyes, and I felt my knees wobble and give way. I pitched forward and hit the side of the table with a *thud,* and everything around me passed into silence.

***

I came to and found myself propped up awkwardly in a hard wooden chair. A harsh female voice barked orders at another girl, and some smelling salts passed under my nose. I pushed the hand away.

"My head hurts," I said.

"An' that's no one's fault but your own," snapped the rough voice. "Fancy sneaking in here in the middle of the night, frightening two helpless young women and all."

The voice sounded neither helpless nor young, so I

concluded there were at least three women regarding me from around the table. The matron cleared her throat. Clearly, I was required to furnish an explanation for my intrusion.

"Forgive me, ladies. I had hoped to navigate the kitchens without rousing you from your beds. I am Lieutenant Holman, one of the Naval Knights of Windsor, and I am trying to escape the castle before we're forced onto those trains."

"What do you know of it?" The woman sounded suspicious.

"I know that unholy creatures haunt this castle, and I know that tomorrow we're being moved to a new residence in London, but the creatures are moving with us, secretly, so no one in London can glimpse them. I know our residence is behind a high iron Wall that promised to keep the dragons out, but will instead lock the citizens in."

The matron and her companions — their voices belonging to young girls — gasped.

"And I know that tonight is my last and only chance to escape that fate, so I might find my way to London and send up some warning, perhaps stop Presbyter Brunel from closing every exit through his Wall—"

"Travers College is all the way down the other end of the garden. How do you know of the Sunken?" the woman cut in.

"Brigitte Black told me of them. She used to be a maid in the castle, but—"

"—she left," a girl's voice, high and musical, interrupted. "She had a gentlemanly sweetheart, and so she left. And not a moment too soon, for the very next day the King was calling her to his chambers."

The matron's voice remained hard. "You know of Brigitte? She is safe?"

"Safer than any of us. Her sweetheart, Nicholas Rose, is my very dear friend, and he is architect to Presbyter Brunel. He is, at this very moment, working to avert this crisis."

"Maxwell the gardener's gone, too," the first girl piped up.

"Cassandra."

"Well, he *has,*" she sniffed. "Last we saw him was the night Brigitte disappeared. He'd been so ill—"

"He helped Brigitte escape through the cellars," I said. "This is where I am going. She told me about a door—"

"There's no escaping that way," the woman said. "Them creatures have overrun every inch of the cellars. If you put your ear to the door you can hear 'em, chomping and snarling. You won't get ten feet before they tear you apart."

"What are we to do, then?"

"We?" the second girl asked, her voice trembling.

"I can hardly leave you ladies here alone now, can I? Not when you've shown me such hospitality." I smiled, rubbing the lump on my head.

"Me an' Cassandra an' Rebecca have our escape all figured out. There is perhaps room for one more, but you must listen carefully to all we say and follow us without question. It will not be easy for a blind man."

"Nothing ever is. When?"

"Tomorrow. You will remain here with us, and we make our escape early in the morning. You will sleep here, in the scullery, and you'll *not,*" she said sternly, "move or make so much as a sound, or that frying pan will be the least of your worries."

***

"I'm worried about Holman. And Isambard." Nicholas hunched forward, folding his arms across his chest, then letting them fall at his sides, then clasping them together. If the room were tall enough to stand up in, he would be pacing, but it wasn't, so he folded his arms again.

Brigitte leaned against the other wall, spreading her skirts over her knees. "Why? Is someone trying to kill them, too?"

"The Sunken—"

"—are not our biggest concern of the minute, Nicholas—" She stopped mid-sentence. He started to speak, but she hushed him. Then he heard it, too. A clank, like someone trying to open the gate on the other side of the gangway.

"It could be a compie," he said, straining his ears and his sense to listen. He heard it again — more scrapes and clangs in the gangway below. They were definitely footsteps — someone was coming.

"It must be Isambard. I hope he's brought some more food and oil." Nicholas stood up, picking up the lantern — which was running low again — from beside her. "I'll help him—"

"Please?" she tugged on his trousers, her eyes large in the glimmer of the lamplight. "I don't want to be left in the darkness."

Sighing, he stroked her hair and placed the lantern back on the floor beside her. Lowering his feet over the edge of the ladder, he climbed down onto the platform at the end of the gangway. He could see the faint glow of a lantern bobbing toward him, the figure shrouded in the shadow of a heavy cloak.

"Isambard?"

"You are mistaken," a voice rasped close to his ear. Nicholas leapt back, just as Jacques brought up his lantern and slammed the metal bracket across his face. Reeling, Nicholas cracked his spine against the metal ladder. He kicked out with his boot, but he was disoriented and the blow glanced off Jacques' shoulder.

"You'll have to do better than that," said Jacques, and Nicholas heard the slice of a rapier being drawn.

He had no time to fetch his own sword, still sitting on the floor next to Brigitte, so Nicholas let go of the ladder and flung himself at Jacques. The Frenchman fell backward, hitting the grating with a crack, Nicholas' full weight bearing down on top of him. Jacques' lantern clattered across the grating.

Nicholas pinned Jacques' sword arm with his knee and slammed his fist into the Frenchman's face. He felt no fear at all, no anger, only an odd sense of calm, as if he were merely a spectator to the fight instead of a participant. Jacques tried to rock his body over to free his arm, but Nicholas landed another blow to the side of his head and he slumped back down.

Something moved behind Nicholas on the grating. "I'll grab the sword!" Brigitte cried, rushing to his side and grabbing Jacques' arm.

"No! Go back!"

He turned and saw her prying Jacques' fingers from the hilt, but as he turned, his weight shifted, allowing Jacques to free his left arm and land a blow on

Nicholas' cheek.

Brigitte stomped on Jacques' wrist with the heel of her boot, and he howled. Nicholas felt his arm slacken and knew without turning that Brigitte had freed the sword. He pinned both Jacques' arms again, and landed another blow across his face before he heard more footsteps clanging across the grating.

How foolish I've been. Of course Jacques wouldn't come here alone.

Hands grabbed him, pulled him up, away from Jacques, whose cries of pain turned into peals of laughter. He shouted a warning to Brigitte. She stood her ground, sword raised, eyes defiant, but though she swung and thrust and opened a deep cut across a man's cheek, other men closed in around her and overpowered her with ease.

Nicholas struggled against his captors, but it was no use. They wrenched his arms tightly around him, and he watched, helpless, as Jacques — blood gushing from his nose — yanked the sword from Brigitte's grasp and held it to her throat. She whimpered as the blade pressed against her skin.

"Leave her be," Nicholas cried. "She has no part in this. It's me you want."

"Ah," said Jacques, smiling, and Nicholas' blood turned cold. "And by your very admission, Monsieur *Thorne*, I conclude she is exactly the person I want. Does not our situation here seem familiar to you? It does to me. Two years ago you murdered my wife — the woman who was carrying my child. I held her in my arms and felt the life drain out of her, while you ran into the forest like the coward you are. And so, tonight, I will murder the woman *you* love, and you too will know the pain I've lived with ever since."

He spoke to his men in French, and they grabbed Brigitte's limbs and pinned her to the grating, her arms and legs spread wide. With a slash of his blade Jacques split open her dress. Brigitte screamed, but he silenced her with a slap so hard it jerked her head right back. Nicholas' eyes met hers, and he saw his own fear reflected there.

Nicholas gathered his strength, kicking and thrashing against the men who held him, but they did not loosen their grip. Memories flashed before him — another woman he loved, another life he had not been able to save. Jacques raised the sword high above his head, the blade glinting in the dim lamplight.

"No!" Rage burnt in Nicholas' limbs, and his vision darkened with spots of red. His anger welled in his stomach, growing larger until it took over every limb, every pore, until it pushed out all other thoughts.

And, when his mind was clear, the mind of something else entered his body.

The thoughts slammed into his with such force his whole body jerked forward. The rage disappeared, replaced by a burning hunger that seemed to squeeze his muscles, wringing every shred of strength from him. His vision swirled and changed, the colours disappearing, replaced by a flowing, bubbling mass of wafting scents and energy. As he looked again at Jacques, he no longer saw the man who had hunted him for two years, a man who at this moment raised a sword to his beloved Brigitte.

He saw dinner.

Nicholas could only stare through the eyes that weren't his, a stranger in his own body, as the mind inside him *pushed*, pressed against some invisible force. Jacques drew the sword higher. Brigitte screamed.

The gangway lurched to the right, and Jacques — arm in the air, mouth open in silent surprise — fell back against the railing. Two giant rows of teeth clamped around his body, as a dragon rose up from the depths of the Wall to meet him. His leg exploded in a geyser of blood, and his sword clattered over the edge.

Jacques' scream echoed from every metal surface. The men holding Nicholas cried out, slackening their grip as they took in the horrid scene.

As quickly as it had come upon him, the dragon's mind left Nicholas, expelling with it the gleeful rapture to hunt. He fell to his knees, his head devoid of thought, his body without sensation.

The dragon swung his head up again, bones cracked, and the scream was cut off abruptly. The men seemed frozen, unsure of what to do. With a final heave, Nicholas freed himself and took a step across the swinging platform toward Brigitte.

Brigitte got on her knees and crawled across the grating — now slick with Jacques' blood — to collect Nicholas in her arms. The scent of her — warm with sweat, and very much alive — slowly brought him back from the blur of his thoughtlessness. He clasped her to him and pulled her down, shielding her body with his in case the dragon should return for another meal.

Jacques' men, their confusion giving way to terror, fled back the way they'd come, only to find the corridor blocked with Isambard and two of his Boilers, short hoses attached to their blow-off valves. Isambard reached behind and pulled a lever, and a shower of scalding water met the men, sending two of them sailing over the crumpled railings to meet their deaths twenty feet below. The dragon growled, snapped its teeth, and the men no longer screamed.

One man remained twitching on the grating, his chest, arms, and the right side of his face turning as the scalding water worked its way through his skin. His screams resonated around the chamber, like some horrifying spectacle of industrial worship. Isambard stepped over his writhing body, and the Boilers simply rolled over him, mangling his corpse into a bloody pulp.

The Presbyter's face appeared before Nicholas, his mouth drawn in concern. Isambard's hand — always impossibly cold, despite the heat in the room — cupped Nicholas' forearm. "Go back up the ladder to the room," he said. "The Boilers will take care of our friends here."

After helping a shaking Brigitte up the ladder, Nicholas clambered back up himself, his thoughts slowly returning, and the full horror of what he'd just seen finally reaching him. The way that dragon had risen up from deep in the Wall, filling his mind and body with its malice. The sensation of feeling what it felt as it closed in on its meal. The sound it made as its teeth closed around Jacques.

"Great Conductor be praised you both are safe," said Isambard, swinging himself up the ladder after them. "I'm only sorry I didn't arrive sooner."

"You arrived perfectly on time," Brigitte said, gathering her torn skirts around herself and burying her head in Nicholas' chest.

"I brought you that blade for a reason," Isambard said, pointing to the rapier still lying in its scabbard against the wall of the room. "You should've guessed he'd come down here after you."

"But how could he know we were here?"

The Presbyter's eyes darkened. "Stephenson has been helping him, which means Jacques had access to the extensive network of Navvy spies operating throughout London. One of them would've seen Buckland bring you here, or me coming to find you."

"And the dragon? Why are you keeping a dragon inside the Wall?"

"He was a present from Quartz and the Stokers in the swamps. The King wishes only to keep the dragons out of the city. But I wanted to *understand* why they desired to come here in the first place. If the Council caught wind of my experiments, it would be the end of me, so I hired Buckland and set up workshops inside the Wall, so he might conduct his experiments without interruption—"

"*What* experiments? Why the sudden interest in biology?"

Isambard smiled. "Your friend Buckland once said something that stuck with me — that if man ever wanted to create the perfect machine, he had only to look toward a living body. The intricate workings of vessels and veins, the heart like a great bellows, pumping blood around the body, the reactions and behaviours of the four humors ... these are machines created by the Gods. If I can understand them, think of what I too can create."

Nicholas crossed the room and shone the lamp into the corner. "There's a vent here," he said. "And this goes out across the gangway and down to the floors below. Your dragon must have caught the scent of men from his pen." He pressed his hand against his temple, remembering the sensation of the dragon inside him, but one look at Brigitte's tearful face and Isambard's glazed, faraway look told him it was not yet time to reveal his secret.

A bang and crash outside revealed the dragon was still wandering around under the gangway. Isambard picked up the sword and made to return down the ladder. "I must see to my dragon," he said. "The cages will need reinforcing."

"I mean no disrespect, Presbyter," sniffed Brigitte. "But we've had quite a fright, between our fight with Jacques and that dragon … all that blood …. But now there's no question Jacques is gone. I wonder if you think it safe for Nicholas to return to his home?"

"Of course," he offered his hand to her. "I forget, sometimes, that there are more pressing matters than my engineering projects. With Jacques dead, Stephenson has no argument against you — at least, not one that will hold up in court. He certainly won't risk the lives of any of his Navvies. I will have two Boilers watch your lodgings — did I tell you they can now be set to perform basic guard duties? — and you should be safe in the city."

***

JAMES HOLMAN'S MEMOIRS — UNPUBLISHED

I crouched in one of the sculpted flower beds that

lined the road leading to the King Henry VIII gate. The sun hadn't yet risen, and a crisp breeze rustled through the leaves. Fresh dew dripped onto my trousers, much rumpled from my night's sleep on the scullery floor. Beside me, little Cassandra held my hand tightly, her breath coming out in nervous gasps. Rebecca clutched my other hand, her warm fingers stroking my palm.

"I see him," Miss Julie said, from the branches on the other side of me. "Quiet now, we mustn't alert him to our presence."

A night sleeping next to the cellar door and listening to the snarling below had convinced me I could not have escaped that way, but Miss Julie's plan was no less foolhardy. "A farmer from the village comes every morning at 5am," she explained as she roused me from my fitful sleep. "He brings a delivery of fresh blood from the abattoir, stored in barrels to prevent suspicion. The blood feeds the Sunken, though they are never sated. That is why they snap and snarl so, all day and night. The farmer unloads the barrels and loads the empties, then leaves by the same entrance. But tomorrow when he passes through the gates, we shall all be hiding inside the barrels."

"But why would they feed the Sunken on this, of all mornings?"

"You don't know the strength of them! If they're not fed before they're moved to the train, they'll tear apart the carriages before they're even out of the station," Miss Julie said. "I heard the Prime Minister place this morning's order with my own ears. Hurry, we don't want to be late!"

Her original plan had relied on her either bribing or threatening the man into allowing them to hide amongst the barrels. Having met Miss Julie, I could immediately see that she had great skill in both these areas. But with me joining their party, we now had another option.

"Here he comes," Cassandra whispered, squeezing my hand.

The wheels rolled past, slowing as they rounded the corner toward the castle. Miss Julie sprang up, and raced after him.

Seconds later, I heard the thud of a familiar rolling pin, and something warm and heavy was pushed down beside me. Miss Julie and her girls worked quickly, tossing the unfortunate man's garments into my arms. "Quickly now." Hands yanked at my sleeves and grabbed at my buttons.

I pulled on the man's coarse clothing, bundling my lieutenant's jacket into his satchel and covering it with his paper-wrapped lunch. I left my other clothing items in the garden, and climbed up on the footplate. My three passengers had already concealed themselves inside the barrels. It was up to me to drive them from the grounds without attracting suspicion.

And therein lay the plan's greatest flaw. I'd never driven a carriage in my life, nor indeed even ridden a horse, and to begin now, a blind man charged with rescuing not just himself but three plucky ladies who'd placed their lives in his charge, had me paralysed in fear. I sat for some minutes, the reins slack in my hands, the horses snorting in impatience, wondering how I could possibly manoeuvre the carriage through the garden complex without attracting suspicion.

"Mr. Holman, you really must get a move on." The muffled voice of Miss Julie from the barrel behind me jolted me out of my stupor.

"Of course, of course." I clenched my fists over the reins and pulled them toward me. The horses sprang to life, jerking the carriage forward so hard I nearly slipped from the bench. Steadying myself, I held the reins loose in my fingers, focusing on the tugging as the horses trotted away.

"Steady now," said Miss Julie from inside her barrel. "If we dash away the guards will think something's amiss."

I found the clop of the horses' hooves against the wide path served the same purpose as the tap of my walking stick, and I managed to navigate down the path toward the gate without running over the flowerbeds. I was just beginning to enjoy myself when Miss Julie hissed at me to stop the carriage.

"We've reached the gate," she said. "A guard is approaching on your right."

Panic rose in my throat as I pulled the reins up, bringing the horses to an abrupt halt. Heavy footsteps approached the carriage, and I felt the weight shift on the axles as a man leaned against the footplate.

"What do you think you're doing, aye, chappy?" barked a Royal Guard. Stray droplets of spittle splattered against my cheek. I fought to keep my voice calm as I spoke my answer. "I'm returning these barrels to the abattoir—"

"Not today you ain't. No one leaves the castle grounds. That's a direct order."

"But—"

"I'll draw this sword on ye if I have to."

"Lieutenant Robbins, what seems to be the trouble?"

All the swagger left his voice as he replied, "Nothing, sir. This man, sir, he wants to leave the castle grounds."

"Well, is he a servant of the King or isn't he?"

"I'm a farmer," I cut in. "I deliver barrels from the abattoir every morning, and I'm returning—"

"Let him through," the officer barked. I let out the breath I was holding.

As I bent down to pick up the reins, the officer's voice rasped close to my ear. "When you're outside, give those horses hell, do y'hear? Don't stop no matter who comes after ye. I aim to save one life at least today."

"Thank you, sir." I picked up the reins and drove the horses forward, listening to the clop of their hooves against the cobbles. I sensed the great arch of the gate and we drove under it, then the turn in the road as we passed over the threshold of the castle and continued down the hill.

"Are we outside?" came a muffled voice from behind me.

"Ssssh!" I strained my ears to listen. The gate hadn't been locked. I could hear the soldiers arguing. I drove the horses into a trot.

"We need to turn right at the—"

The thunder of hooves erupted from the gate behind me, followed by the clap of a cannon that landed on the road beside the carriage, cracking the cobbles and starting the horses into a run. I grabbed the reins and gripped them tightly, and behind me Cassandra screamed as the carriage tore around the corner at speed. Two of the empty barrels tumbled out and crashed against the ground.

Hooves beat toward us, single riders, probably cavalrymen with rifles and sabers. They would overtake us easily. Another cannonball buckled the ground beside us, and my own horses squealed in protest and careened off the path. We bounced over green lawn, and I gripped the reins as tightly as I could. I had lost all control — we were completely at the mercy of the horses.

Miss Julie threw off the lid of her barrel. "They're gaining on us!" she cried. "Quick, toward the village. If we dump the carriage we may lose them in the crowds. Cassandra, Rebecca, get out of those barrels."

My teeth clattered together as we rumbled over the rough ground. We rattled over a steep drop and landed hard on a cobbled road, the wagon groaning in protest. Men yelled obscenities at us as they swerved their vehicles to avoid a collision. Miss Julie clambered in next to me and tore the reins from my hands.

Hooves pounded on either side of the carriage. I heard a *swoosh* as a blade hissed through the air, missing my head by inches. I pulled myself down, pressing my head against the dasher, hoping Miss Julie could keep us on the road.

Our carriage swerved hard right, and a horse cried out in pain as our wheels collided with its flanks. I heard the crunch as the rider was thrown to the ground. "Sterling work, Miss Julie!" I cried. That only left one more soldier, the man who swung his sword wildly, and who now drew up beside us for another swing.

"Use this!" Cassandra passed something flat and heavy to me — a barrel lid. I flung it at the man, and heard him yelp, but he didn't give up his pursuit. "Hand me another." I cried. She dumped another in my hands and I lobbed it in the direction of the man, hoping to knock him off his horse.

I heard a crunch, followed by the sound of splintering wood, and our entire carriage pitched violently to the left, toppling me bottom over bootstraps onto the hard ground. I landed on top of Miss Julie, and the wooden ash of our flipped carriage landed on top of me, pinning us to the earth.

"What do we have here?" It was the voice of the young lieutenant. "I recognise both your faces. You're the kitchen maid, and you're one of them Windsor Knights. Well, your escape attempt didn't fool me. It's back to the castle for all of you."

I cried out in protest, begged them to take me and spare the girls, but they heard none of it. Rough hands grabbed me, bound my arms, threw me into the back of a carriage and sent us all back up the hill. Miss Julie lay beside me, warm blood from a wound in her face trickling onto my sleeves. Neither she nor Rebecca uttered a word. Cassandra wailed, clutching her hand, which they had broken.

They took us in through King Henry's Gate, but instead of returning us to the castle proper, they took a meandering path through the garden, down toward the southern corner, 'till I had no doubt in my mind where we were headed.

The carriage stopped. I knew at once we were in grave danger.

The smell hung thick in the air — blood and piss and excrement, and the unmistakable tang of rotting flesh. But it was the sound that turned my blood cold — a chorus of animals, snarling, hissing, barking, fingers clawing at each other in their frantic attempt to crawl closer to us.

"What have you brought me, Lewis?" a familiar voice asked. Joseph Banks, the Prime Minister, leaned against the carriage and rapped his stick across my back.

"We found these four trying to escape, sir. I figured you'd best know what to do with 'em."

"Right you are, Lewis. Bring them down to the pit."

Hands grabbed us again, and pulled us out, threw us on the ground. I tried to stand, but the butt of a rifle slapped me across the face, and I fell to my knees, whimpering. I could hear them, *smell* them. The Sunken — hundreds of them, in a pit only a few feet from me. Each one had once been a person, but the sounds the emanated from that hellish pit were not the sounds of men. Miss Julie landed beside me, and she reached out and felt for my hand.

"The girls first," said Banks, as his men wrenched Cassandra and Rebecca high in the air and tossed them, screaming, into the pit.

I tried to stopper my ears, to take my mind far away, but I could not turn away from the screams of those girls as they were thrown down to the beasts. The Sunken pounced, and their howls enveloped the screams as they supped their full. Cassandra's scream rang out. Every tear of her flesh, every squelch of her innards pierced by their bony fingers, every snarl as they fought over the morsels of her body reverberated off the sides of my skull. I forgot myself in my panic, giving my body over to my terror. Something warm ran down the side of my leg, and from my mouth spewed forth an incoherent stream of delirium.

Someone kicked me in the head, and I toppled over,

unable to bear up my own feeble weight. Miss Julie's hand was torn from mine, and she yelled at me to be brave as they heaved her over the side. The Sunken took much longer on her, as if the delights of her ample body should be savoured.

One of the soldiers leaned over beside me. "They're not clawing the sides anymore," he said, puzzled.

"That's what the flesh does to them," Banks said. "They get lethargic once they've had their full. I remember the day I came down with the body of the Crown Prince and two of His Majesty's other children. They could hardly move at all after that feast!"

"That won't do," said Lewis. "We're meant to keep 'em somewhat stimulated before they go on the train. I don't want my own self to be thrown in there amongst them for disobeying orders."

"Very true, very true," said Banks, thinking. Behind us, up at the castle, a horn sounded.

"Time to move out, lads," Banks said.

"What about this one? Shouldn't we—"

"Toss him in the train with the others," said Banks. "He'll be in the hands of the Sunken soon enough."

***

Chloe watched Aaron pacing the length of the magazine, his face twisted into a ferocious scowl. She sat at the table beside William Stone, her shoulders knitted with tension, watching her husband as he made that silent trek from one end of the narrow room to the other. Above their heads, the engines purred, the familiar vibrations punctuated with a new sound — the low rumble of more Boilers entering the tunnels, making their way to the workstations abandoned by the Stokers.

She was prepared to admit to herself that she was afraid of Aaron. Ever since Brunel had been made Presbyter, her husband drank more than ever. He came home with wild eyes and strange ideas. His advances, which had once been tender, were now fuelled by a kind of inner fury that made her dread their nights together.

After only a night of self-imposed imprisonment, he seemed ready to snap at any moment. She feared he had become utterly lost to her — his mind consumed by hatred for Brunel. William met her eyes across the table and she knew he shared her fears.

"Aaron." William addressed him, quietly, questioningly. "We can't remain down here forever."

Aaron spoke nothing in reply.

"We will run out of food in two days," said William. "And every hour we remain away from our posts, and those Boilers stoke our fires and tend our furnaces, is an hour closer to the end of the Stokers. We are proving nothing, except that those machines can do our jobs better than we ever could.

"Today they have taken over our jobs, but who is to say they aren't capable of expelling us from this place by force." Chloe shivered at the thought. "Isn't it time we returned to the Ward and tried to salvage what we can of our livelihood?"

"We *are* in the Ward." Aaron hissed his reply through clenched teeth. "We are in the heart of the Ward — the very soul of this cursed place."

"Our homes are up there—"

"I said no!" Aaron spun around and kicked the

table across the room. Chloe shrieked and buried her face in William's shoulder.

"By Great Conductor's steam-driven testicles, Aaron, you're scaring your wife," William snapped. "You're scaring everyone. What do you expect? That we will stay down here forever?"

"We don't even know what's happened up there," said Chloe. "What about the Sunken? What about Nicholas and James and—"

"They threw their lot in with Isambard. What happens to them is not my concern. As for the Sunken — if they even *do* exist, let them feast upon this ungrateful city 'till her streets are piled high with bones. Why should we care for them—"

"This isn't you. This isn't my husband talking … the man who has such empathy for every living being. What's *happened* to you?" Chloe angrily wiped fresh tears from her cheeks.

"Isambard happened to me. He turned his back on the Stokers, and on me, the minute he fired the first Boiler. He—"

"But he was your *friend,* your oldest and dearest friend, and you abandoned him when you could have been his one voice of sanity. You could've saved the Stokers, Aaron. You could have stopped Isambard, but instead of showing him a better way, you let your anger overcome you, and you hid down here and sulked—"

"I'll *not* be talked to like that—"

"Enough." William pushed his chair back. "I will go to Isambard myself, and I will see if I can make him understand the Stokers' position."

"No. I will go," Aaron said. He pulled his

shoulders back, and took a deep breath. Chloe caught his expression; saw him battling the anger, pressing down his temper so it did not impair his decision. She stepped back, wiping her tear-stained face. Aaron would not let his anger override his concern for the Stokers. He would do what was needed. He was still the man she loved. "It was my idea to strike, to hide down here, and it was our leaving that has caused Isambard to issue forth the Boilers. No Stoker will be put in danger because of me."

"You will talk to Isambard?" Chloe asked. "You will find a way to end this?"

"I will," he pulled his coat close around his face. "But first I shall find Nicholas." Chloe glared at him. "No, you don't understand. I have treated him poorly, but I must show him what we're up against. I must help him understand what I've done here, why I did it. And together we might be able to stop Isambard before he destroys the Stokers, and London, and everything we hold dear."

***

JAMES HOLMAN'S MEMOIRS — UNPUBLISHED

The carriages were closed on all sides, without windows to let in air or light. Anyone who might see the train as she made her clandestine journey would not know the contents of her cargo — would not see the fear that spread like a fire through every inch of the claustrophobic space.

It was standing-room only — maids and Knights

and footmen and cooks pressed up against each other in the darkness. I had secured myself a spot in the furthest corner, my back against the wall, hemmed in on both sides by the stooped shoulders of my fellow Knights. The other carriage — longer still, but no less cramped — contained the courtiers, priests, handmaidens and the King's private staff. No one knew what was happening or why they were being moved to the new court like cattle on the way to market.

No one except me.

My mind raced with the memory of those horrid creatures, trying to discern a way out of this mess. Nicholas and Aaron must learn what I'd heard — they needed to know that Brunel could not be trusted. I knew if I reached Buckingham Palace, I would not be able to leave again, but the door to the carriage had been padlocked behind us. Besides which, I didn't fancy leaping from a moving train at this speed.

The train rocketed over a rough stretch of track, and everyone lurched backward, slamming me against the wooden wall of the carriage. I heard a crunch and felt a cold breeze blow past my elbow.

A breeze ...

I felt along the wooden struts, hardly daring to hope ... but my fingers slipped through a gap in the wood. When building the wagons the Boilers must've malfunctioned — or a programming error had caused them to miss adding the rivets on three planks in this corner. Now, the clattering of the train at high speed had forced the planks apart.

Twisting around in my crevice, I grabbed the planks and began wriggling them free. The first flew off in my hands, sending me stumbling backward into a fresh round of grumbles from my fellow Knights.

With a swift punch of my walking stick, the second plank clattered onto the tracks below. Another couple of whacks dislodged the final plank, and a cold gust of wind hit my bruised face. I felt the edges of the gap I'd created, ensuring it would be large enough for me to escape through.

Aaron had told me that the locomotive would slow when it reached the city, for too much speed in the underground tunnels could cause a cave-in. Judging from the smell of soot and excrement on the breeze, we were passing through the outer boroughs of London. Sure enough, the train began to slow, the clattering of the rails spreading out, and the whisper of buildings whooshing by less discernable.

Paying no heed to the protests behind me, I dropped to my knees, creeping forward and ducking my head under the limber so I crouched, like a frog, on the edge of the wagon. I manoeuvred my stick through the hole and clutched it tightly in my hand, and listened to the pace of the train, trying to gauge a speed that would ensure my survival.

The wind on my face grew suddenly colder, and the sound of the train changed, becoming hollow and amplified, as if it bounced back from a surface close by. We must have entered the tunnel. Now was my chance.

I took a deep breath and launched myself from the carriage, landing hard on the track and rolling clear as the train clattered away into the darkness. The shock jolted up my legs and back, and I lay in a crumpled heap between the rails for many minutes, trying to calm my racing heart. Slowly, I pulled myself up to a sitting position, my fingers tracing every inch of my body, looking for cuts or broken bones, but I could find none.

Standing on shaking legs, I realised I could only just hear the low rumble of the train as it disappeared deeper into the tunnel. I had to hurry. Thrusting my stick in front of me and tapping it against the rails to hear my way, I set off toward the entrance at a brisk pace.

After a few hundred yards I found it, emerging into a damp ditch between two rows of tenements on the edges of metropolitan London. I slipped into the street and found my way to a coach house, where I dug out two shillings and paid for a cab to Nicholas' residence.

When I arrived Brigitte answered the door, her voice registering her surprise. "James? By the Gods, what's happened to you? I thought you—"

"I need to speak to Nicholas. Immediately."

"I — of course. Come in. Aaron is here also. He just arrived." She held open the door, and I stomped upstairs to Nicholas' study while she fetched Nicholas. He entered the room soon afterward, followed by Aaron. He told Brigitte to wait in the kitchen, and shut and bolted the door behind her.

"James Holman, just look at your face, all battered and bleeding! I'm not even going to ask if you went snooping in the castle, because I already know the answer. The question is, what did you find?"

"More than I ever wished for, and I barely escaped with my life. Brunel was there," I said. "And Banks." Quickly I recounted the conversation as I remembered it. I told them of my foiled escape, the pit of Sunken, and my subsequent ride on the train. As I described the deaths of Miss Julie and Rebecca and Cassandra, I thought I heard a sob come from the hallway, but no one else acknowledged it.

"See?" Aaron said. "We've been blind, Nicholas. We both believed Isambard had no part in this."

"He could merely be referring to the safe transport of some other royal children," Nicholas replied. "I don't see how this proves any of your crazy notions—"

"There are no other children," I said. "Banks had them thrown to the Sunken. I heard that, too."

"And what about my men?" I heard a crash as Aaron leapt from his chair. "Benjamin Stone thrown from a building, and five others burnt to death—"

"This is ludicrous," Nicholas shouted. "We have no proof. Perhaps Brunel had no choice."

"I know what I heard, Nicholas. For whatever reason, Brunel is helping Banks smuggle the Sunken into London," I said. "And if we're all agreed the King bringing his lead children into the city would be a bad thing, perhaps we should stop debating the motives behind Brunel's involvement in it, and come up with a way to stop them."

"Have any of us even *seen* the Sunken?" Nicholas yelled. "Perhaps they're not what we assume them to be. We have the testimony of James and Brigitte, but James is blind, and his observations cannot be given full weighting in this matter—"

His words hit me with the force of a blow.

"—and Brigitte is young and vulnerable and afraid. She could have mistaken what she saw."

"You're mistaken, Nicholas, if you insist on blindly believing Isambard means well for England! The only

person he's looking out for is Isambard!" Snarling, Aaron yanked open the door, and Brigitte, who had been standing behind it, eavesdropping, shrieked as he stomped past. Nicholas called after him, but the front door slammed. Aaron had already gone.

"You doubt my word?" Brigitte addressed Nicholas, her voice rising with every syllable. "You claim to love me and then call me weak?"

"Brigitte, I—"

"Don't bother." She stomped down the stairs. Another door slammed.

"Nicholas, perhaps you should sit down."

"I've had just about enough of this!" Nicholas thundered. "Isambard is a brilliant man who's brought this country naught but greatness. Why must you and Aaron be determined to drag his name into the sewers?"

"I'm not denying his contributions to engineering, Nicholas, merely reporting what I know. And what I *know* is that Brunel's transporting the Sunken — dangerous, blood-starved creatures — into this city, a city now surrounded by a high iron wall. What I heard was Brunel making a deal with Banks, the very scoundrel responsible for popularising all this religious fervour and making himself filthy stinking rich into the bargain!"

"And I say Brunel is a good man, without malice or corruption. If he has done such a thing, it could only be without the full knowledge of its consequences, or because he had no other choice. But we could sit here all night and argue, or we could settle this once and for all."

"How?"

"I'm going to speak to Isambard." He rose from his chair and collected his things.

"What, right now?"

"No time like the present. Do you wish to join me?"

"Someone should remain here to watch over Brigitte. It's a dangerous city out there tonight, and she's rather distraught."

Nicholas sighed in exasperation. "If you must." And without a further word, he too was gone.

I went downstairs and knocked on each door 'till I found one that answered, "Go away!" in angry, strangled sobs.

"This is James. You can let me in. Nicholas has left."

"Of course he has," she sobbed, opening the door and collapsing into my arms. "He's left me, because I am weak and vulnerable, and apparently, a liar."

"I do not believe he truly thinks those things."

She snorted. "He said them, didn't he? And after all we've been through. Oh, James, this man came to kill him, and he had a sword and Isambard rescued us and Nicholas said … he *said*—"

"You must understand how difficult this is for Nicholas. Tonight he has heard proof that his oldest friend and most admired colleague, the man who gave him work, sheltered him from harm, who saved his life, is involved somehow in the most heinous of crimes. He wishes so badly not to believe it that he seeks any way possible to invalidate the evidence before him, even if it means hurting those he loves the most."

"Including me?"

"*Especially* you. But he'll come around." I tried to suppress the tight fear gripping my chest.

"Where has he gone?"

"To confront Brunel. He needs to know, tonight, of his master's part in this plot."

She bolted upright. "If what you say about the Sunken is true, he'll be killed. We must go after him, James. You must talk him out of such madness."

"I have sworn to stay here and protect you, and protect you I shall. Besides, what chance would a blind man and a weak woman have that an armed man would not?"

"He took his barker?"

"I heard him slip it from its holster and stuff it into the pocket of his coat as he left. Evidently, even Nicholas Thorne, Brunel's most ardent follower, believes I might be right, and his master is up to no good."

***

"Isambard?"

Brunel looked up from his workbench, and he recoiled in surprise to see Nicholas leaning against the pylon, his features drawn into a worried frown. One of the Boilers had been moving crates from Brunel's workshop to the upper floors, and Nicholas had snuck down on the elevator as it returned for another load.

"I understand you're busy, but if I could have a moment of your time."

Brunel nodded, gesturing for Nicholas to have a seat.

"I'd rather stand, if it's all the same. I must ask you

something, and I beg you not to take offence."

"Speak freely, Nicholas, but make it quick. I have urgent business."

"I have … friends, who have informed me about the situation at Windsor, of the King's lead-soaked children. I trust you know of them?"

Brunel nodded.

"My friends, they say these creatures — *dangerous* creatures — are being moved into Buckingham Palace in secret. They say that you are responsible for this, that you built the Wall not to keep the dragons out, but the people in. They say … you have a deal with Banks, that you will be named Messiah if you deliver these creatures safely into London, and ensure no one escapes. Is that true?"

Brunel stared at him, unblinking.

Nicholas slammed his fist down on the workbench. *"Is that true?"*

Brunel held up his hands. "Yes, Nicholas, it is true, and yet also not true, for there is much you do not know."

"I would really prefer to know now."

"Yes, the lead children, the Sunken, they are real, and they are terrible. Ask Dr. Joseph Banks, and he will tell you how several years ago, back when he was a regular doctor and not the Royal Physician or the Prime Minister or the head of the Council or any of his other titles, he was called to treat the King for acute syphilis — you know of his indulgences down at the dockside. He prescribed a tincture of lead, twice a day, 'till the pain subsided. But the King had an unusual reaction to the lead, and became as the opium addict, feral and crazed, desperate for greater doses of the metal. And it came to pass that he no longer craved food, or wine, but only the acrid taste of lead. You saw his condition with your own eyes — the sunken skin, the boiling welts upon his flesh, the snarled teeth and the bulging, monstrous eyes. And this fetish led to another, even more unthinkable, abomination: the taste for human flesh."

Nicholas recoiled, his mouth agape.

"The King took unfortunates into his chamber — at first, he sought street walkers and homeless men, cripples and condemned prisoners, starved and weak. But then, he began to take those of his own household — footmen, soldiers, maids. Some he tore limb from limb, their screams muffled in his darkest chambers, and the bodies buried by his guards. Others he took as his own, feeding them on lead and flesh and locking them away 'till they became as mad as he. The Sunken is an apt name for these unfortunates — the children of the Vampire King."

Nicholas thought of Brigitte, all alone in that castle, her pretty features marked for that fate. Anger bubbled within him. "And how did you become embroiled in this madness?"

"Because of the Wall. I was so pleased to win the contract; I ignored the signs of his approaching madness until it was too late. And with Banks' power to make or break my career, I admit I made several ill-advised decisions. By the time I had grasped the situation and had seen the King's lead children with my own eyes, I had made a contract from which I could not extract myself.

"Yes, I constructed the underground railway for a nefarious purpose. Yes, today we have moved the

Sunken into Buckingham Palace. But if you were in my position, you would have done exactly the same thing. By earning the King's trust, I've been able to remain in favour, and thus, I have access to Buckingham Palace via my own underground passages. I have the means — *should I wish it* — to commit the ultimate treasonable act."

"You mean—"

"*If I wished it.* We are, of course, speaking hypothetically." He moved down his workbench, inserted a fresh plate into his press, and arranged the symbols of the code Nicholas and Aaron had invented. He pulled down the handle and handed the newly inscribed plate to Nicholas.

Nicholas stared at the message, his heart pounding. Brunel outlined his plan in the coded message. What they were about to do was treason, and Brunel wasn't taking a chance that one of the King's men might be listening to their conversation.

"When will this—"

"Tonight. It must be tonight. Go out to the streets and find us a cab. I'll meet you outside the Chimney in a few minutes."

Nicholas tucked the plate in his pocket, shook Brunel's outstretched hand, and left the chamber.

As he walked back through the Engine Ward, he sensed a change in the air. Fires flared from the sewer grilles, and the crisp evening breeze carried the sound of women crying.

"Nicholas!"

He turned, recognising Aaron's voice, who ran towards him, a stricken look on his face. "What are *you* doing here?" he asked.

"I came to talk to Brunel," said Nicholas. "Where's Chloe?"

"Safe with the other Stokers in the tunnels. I'll be joining them after I wring Brunel's neck with my own hands."

The dark tone in Aaron's voice frightened Nicholas. "You intend to kill him?"

"Five of my men *died*," said Aaron, his voice choking. "Killed when a pressure valve burst in one of the Boiler rooms — a valve that was in perfect working order only the previous day. Someone has to stop him—"

"Look." Nicholas handed Aaron the plate.

"Did Brunel write this? How does he know about the code—"

"Just read it."

As Aaron's fingers danced over the letters, his expression changed.

"You shouldn't be so quick to think ill of your friend. He has been manipulated into this, and he admits he hasn't navigated it in quite the best way. But he plans to fix it, tonight. And I shall go with him."

"You're going to the Palace? After what Brigitte said?"

"If nothing else, I *must* know the truth."

"I should come with you."

"No, Aaron. Think of how that would look. Go to your wife. Go to your people, and keep them safe. They need you."

"You're a foolish man, Nicholas. You're walking into your doom."

"Maybe so, but if returning to this city has taught me anything, it's that you have a duty to *do* something with the knowledge you've obtained. If I can save London from the Sunken," he shrugged, "perhaps I'll finally be at peace with my crimes."

***

JAMES HOLMAN'S MEMOIRS — UNPUBLISHED

"What do you mean, I can't leave the city?"

"My apologies, Mr. Holman, sir." The constable adjusted his nightstick from one hand to the other, his voice betraying just how sorry he felt. Behind him, a row of surly-looking guards protected the heavy iron gate, which had been drawn shut and barred. "Boss' orders, sir. No one is to leave the city tonight. Best you go home and have a mug of cocoa, sir."

We'd already had our cocoa, and our brandy, and an entire plate of cream biscuits. Hours had passed and Nicholas had not yet returned, and we feared the worst, and Brigitte declared she could no longer remain inside the house. So we'd taken to the streets, securing the last ride at the coach house and proceeding at a snail's pace toward the gate, where we'd met this cheery fellow.

"And just who exactly is your boss?"

"My, Joseph Banks, sir. Thousand apologies, sir."

"And did he say why we are to endure this forced imprisonment?"

"No, sir. Said I had permission to shoot anyone who disobeyed. Present company excepting, of course, sir."

I sighed. In the carriage behind mine, a man yelled

obscenities at another constable, obviously anxious to escape the city. A crowd of foot traffic swarmed around us, shouting in indignant surprise. Our coachman grumbled and reined in the horses, which were becoming agitated with the thickening press of people. The air crackled with tension, and it wouldn't be long before anger gave way to violence. I clasped my hand over Brigitte's, in case the horses should bolt and surprise her.

"There's nothing else for it," I said. "We shall have to find another way."

I jumped as a shot rang out in front of us, and the crowd screamed and swarmed back. I clenched Brigitte's hand as the horses squirmed. The driver yanked back the reins, turned the horses around, and asked me what I wished to do next. I told him to try the next gate.

When we arrived at the Stamford Hill gatehouse, we found the story much the same. A great horde of people were trying to escape the city and had found the road blocked. Farmers from the neighbouring villages returning from the market with empty wagons growled in gruff voices about this imprisonment. Lords and ladies attempting to flee to their country residences huffed and spluttered their indignation. The unfortunates, used to the whims of the rich affecting every aspect of their lives, said nothing at all, sloping away again into the night.

Smoke billowed from the blow-off valves positioned at intervals along the Wall, and the London air — which had never been exactly aromatic — now stank with burning coal, stinging my eyes, nose, and throat.

We got caught in a traffic jam along Holloway Road and sat next to a carriage of country ladies who had been shopping in the city while their men attended a Council meeting. They seemed unperturbed by the delays, gossiping together about the latest court scandal. I spoke to them through the window and learned that the Oxford gate entrance had been closed, too. "I don't understand what's the trouble," sniffed one of the ladies. "No one in the accursed city seems to know what's going on."

Someone knew all right, but I had a feeling he was tucked up in his Chimney, safe behind an impenetrable wall of iron.

We tried the next gate, and the next, each teaming with disgruntled commuters and backed-up coaches. The news passed from carriage to carriage. Every gate in the city had been shut on the King's orders, and we were advised to return to our residences at once. When my spirits and my pockets could take no more, I bid the driver return to Nicholas' residence, where he could collect his not insubstantial fee.

We had barely made it past Birdcage Walk in the crawling traffic when we noticed something else wasn't right. Traffic ground to a halt as every passenger, driver, and coachman turned his or her eyes toward Buckingham Palace, which Brigitte informed me had been lit by thousands of glimmering lanterns. "It shimmers like a star," she said. "And all the gardens have been strung with streamers and bright red flags. People stream from the palace doors. It looks as though the King is hosting a grand ball."

The street was now dangerously crowded. Onlookers packed the narrow footpath, pressing against each other in a desperate attempt to see inside the palace grounds.

"It seems odd word of such an occasion hasn't appeared in the papers," I said. I couldn't read the papers, of course, but the other Knights discussed them constantly.

Brigitte gripped my arm. "I'm certain there is an explanation for all this. We should find—"

She was interrupted by the ripple of panic that darted along the crowd, passed from soul to soul by some invisible force. It swept the people into a frenzy, and as one they bolted toward Westminster. Several horses reared up, and our driver expertly swung us into a side street as soon as a gap opened up. Brigitte caught a glimpse of the palace grounds as we hurtled along the fence, and cried out. "That's no party! Something is terribly wrong!"

And then the screaming began.

***

Aaron watched Nicholas and Isambard climb into a cab together and speed off toward Stephenson's church. Nicholas' final words to him echoed in his mind. *If I can save London from the Sunken, perhaps I'll finally be at peace with my crimes.* Peace. Aaron longed for peace, longed to be free of the anger that gripped his chest.

When he was certain the Ward was again deserted, he dashed across the empty Stoker workcamp to the lifts. Down he went, down past the Boilers toiling on levels C and D, down to the darkest places, where the Stokers waited for him.

He heard them as soon as the elevator clanged to a stop, drinking and talking in low, solemn voices. He stood awhile on the darkened gangway, listening, hoping to catch a smatter of conversation, to understand the sentiment of the men he would call upon tonight. *Have I done right by them? Would they still follow me?*

But he could hear nothing over the hum of the engines above. He stepped into the first magazine, unnoticed by the men huddled in groups on the floor, heads pressed together as they whispered to each other. Aaron touched one on the shoulder.

"Willy?"

William Stone whirled around, splashing his drink across his overalls. "Aaron? Is that you? I can hardly see in this gloom."

Aaron stepped into the light of the lantern.

"Did you find him? Is everything going to be all right?" William asked.

Aaron paused. "I don't know. William, I'm so sorry. I'm sorry you lost your son. I'm sorry I didn't figure this out sooner. I hated it from the start, but I didn't have a—" He stopped. *There's always a choice.* "I did the cowardly thing, and it cost us all dearly. I didn't know what to do. That makes a man angry, do you see?"

William nodded.

"Do you still trust me?"

William nodded again.

"Something terrible will strike in London tonight, and I'm damned if I'm going to stand by and watch it destroy this city. I need you to round up every able-bodied man willing to return to the surface with me, and any weapon you can find, and meet me outside the South Gate in thirty minutes."

"What are we—" But Aaron had already left him.

He found Chloe in the second battery, with the other women, fast asleep with her back leaning up against the wall and her hands clasped tightly around his battered barker. Aaron ran his hand over her soft hair and eased the weapon from her grip. "Sleep well, my wife," he said. "I am sorry. For everything."

He met William on the gangway, with forty men in tow, each man carrying weapons of varying levels of effectiveness. The sight of them made Aaron's chest swell with pride.

"I know you've never been taught to equate the word 'Stoker' with bravery," he said, "but in the last three days you've all proved your worth a thousand times over. When Isambard was accepted into the engineering elite, we all held him up as a model Stoker, the man we could all aspire to be. But Isambard isn't one of us, not really, not anymore. And he makes mistakes, just like any of us — the trouble is, when a great man makes mistakes, the consequences are hundredfold, spreading out into the world and infecting those around him. When that happens, when the great men of this world fall into darkness, it's up to ordinary men like us to bring them back to the light.

"If we don't do something, this city will burn tonight, and vile creatures the likes of which you cannot even fathom will be set loose upon her streets. London has never been kind to us, and I, like many of you, would rather hide down here and let them suffer, but these creatures … they will find us. And it will be your women and your children who will be defiled and devoured. The army will not stand against them … the Metropolitan Police are useless, but we Dirty Folk, we Stokers, we will be the ones to save this city."

The men yelled their approval, and crowded into the stairwell and lift shafts in their haste to get to the surface. William looked at Aaron, tears in his eyes. Aaron smiled back.

If Nicholas wants to throw in his lot with Brunel, that's his business, but we have a city to save.

***

Deep below Stephenson's church, Nicholas followed Brunel down a long tunnel; his back bent double to prevent scraping himself on the roof. The barrel of his pistol jammed in his hip, and once again, he bent down to adjust the belt.

Brunel kept up a vigorous pace, despite the heavy rucksack of equipment on his back. He would not look back or wait for Nicholas, who at times had to sprint to catch up.

Suddenly, Brunel stopped. Nicholas stumbled over him, fumbling wildly to keep the lamp from smashing against the stone floor. "What did you—"

Brunel held up his hand, and Nicholas fell silent. "Can you hear that?"

He could. If he closed his eyes, he could hear faint sounds from the city above: carriage wheels bouncing over the cobbles, the clank and grind of London's great machines. And over this, faint but unmistakable, he heard screaming. Women and men screaming, and heavy footfalls as hordes of Londoners rushed back and forth, shrieking all the while.

"We're late," whispered Brunel. "It's already begun."

Nicholas thought of Brigitte, and Holman, shut up at his home. *Please, Great Conductor, let them be safe there.*

"We're nearly there," Brunel said. "The station is right underneath the Palace."

After a time, the tunnel narrowed, pressing against Nicholas' shoulder, so he had to squeeze through sideways. He tried not to think of Aaron's men, holed up in tunnels such as these, mourning the deaths of five of their number. He followed Brunel up a narrow staircase and found himself on the platform at an underground station.

The whole structure glowed with eerie yellow light, illuminated by wall sconces and moonlight shining through grates in the ceiling. An opulent, tiled platform stretched on into the distance, much longer and wider than Nicholas expected. *Surely Aaron was wrong ... surely machines didn't create all this?*

A huge, black locomotive waited at the platform, steam still curling around her. She had not long been used. Several carriages waited behind her, and as Nicholas walked past them, he could see dark smudges across the walls. Blood.

"It's not perfect," whispered Brunel, stretching out his fingers to touch the locomotive. "I designed it myself, but Banks insisted on letting Stephenson look it over. He installed the vents to carry the steam and smoke out of the tunnel, but they don't work as efficiently as I'd hoped. Actually, they don't seem to work at all. When you exit the train, it feels as though you are walking into the smoky pits of hell."

Nicholas nodded, too stunned to speak.

A grand staircase wound up into the palace proper, but Brunel led him through a nondescript wooden door down a stairwell and up into a steep vertical shaft. A ladder made of iron pins mounted into the stone served as the means of ascent.

"I had this built secretly, while we constructed the platform," said Brunel, heaving his broad figure up onto the first rung. "When I first laid eyes on those deplorable creatures and was given the job of constructing this railway, I knew the time would come when I would need it."

"How far must we go?" Nicholas asked, slipping his hand through the metal handle of the lantern and grabbing the first rung.

"Not too far," answered Brunel, in a tone that implied he climbed precarious ladders up thin ventilation shafts every other day.

Up and up they climbed, Nicholas holding his breath and trying to ignore the heat from the lantern as it banged against his arm. Brunel stopped, pushed open a tiny trapdoor, and wriggled his way through. Nicholas followed, squeezing his shoulders together and thrusting himself through on a jaunty angle. He slammed his shoulders on cold stone and slid a few feet down a winding staircase.

"Servants' access," Brunel whispered. "We must hurry."

A strange noise penetrated Nicholas' ears, a kind of buzzing, almost like a swarm of insects trapped behind the walls. From somewhere within the palace, more screams echoed, and the fear tightened in his chest. As quietly and quickly as they could, they descended the steps into a long, low hall, with thin wooden doors on either side, probably leading to more halls — a maze of passages extending throughout the palace grounds, to allow servants ease of access to every room without being a nuisance to the royal family and their guests.

Brunel led the way, strangely confident of his path for someone who should never have spent much time wandering through servants' passages. The sound was even louder here, and Nicholas thought perhaps he heard individual voices, hissing and crying, producing the hideous cacophony. He remembered what Aaron had said, and wondered if Aaron had been correct in no longer trusting Brunel.

Maybe I'm being led into a trap ... he remembered how frightened he'd been when Brunel held him aloft over the pulpit. *No.* He shook his head, trying to shake off the thoughts. *No. Brunel was angry with me, and rightly so. He is placing himself at great risk to save the city. I trust him.*

They rounded a corner, and thumped down a flight of small steps. At the bottom, Brunel stopped abruptly, and Nicholas crashed into him, sending the pair of them into the stone wall.

"Argh!" Nicholas cried as his head scraped against bare stone. His vision blurred, and pain shot through his skull. From somewhere outside the pain he became aware that Brunel had picked himself up, and was facing away from him, his back rigid.

And then he heard the animalian snarl from somewhere in the darkness, and his chest tightened in fear.

"Nicholas," Brunel said, his voice strained. "You

need to get up and run back down the passage. You need to go *now!"*

Seizing every ounce of courage, Nicholas heaved himself to his feet. His vision swam and he toppled forward, grabbing the edge of the stone staircase, and scrambled away, barely able to tell if he were going up or down. He heard Brunel cry out behind him, but he couldn't look back. He ran, his feet sliding out from under him on the slippery stone.

Down the corridor he stumbled, around one corner and the next, not sure where he was going. Footsteps thundered behind him. "Nicholas!" Brunel called out. "Not that way!"

He reeled around, the hallway spinning in a whirlpool of shadows. He stumbled into the wall, banging his temple against a protruding candle sconce. Black dots appeared in his vision. The creature hissed, so close now, he could hear it breathing, panting, and salivating for his flesh. *I'm going to die,* he thought. *I'm going to die here in the palace and I'll never see Brigitte again.*

Brunel grabbed his shoulder and shoved him forward. Nicholas stumbled over his feet, falling forward, spinning out of control. Rough hands yanked him back, and Brunel groped for the pistol on his belt. The creature hissed again, and pounced. Nicholas caught a blurry glimpse of that horrid, disfigured face and bulging eyes as it tore at his shirt with emaciated fingers. He shut his eyes and waited for the pain.

The gun went off, and the creature screamed. Its hands tore from Nicholas' chest as it bounced against the wall. It crashed in a heap, squirming and screaming as it clutched at the wound. Brunel leaned over it, and stomped on its neck. Once, twice … Nicholas heard the bones crunch … and it was dead.

"Are you all right? Did it bite you?" It was Brunel's voice in his ear, softer now. He pulled Nicholas to the ground and inspected his chest.

"No … I don't think so."

Brunel untied the powder horn from Nicholas' belt and refilled the barrel, using the ramrod to pat it down. He wrapped a ball in wadding and dropped that in on top, then handed the pistol back to Nicholas.

His vision stopped swimming, and the dim world came into focus once more. His head throbbed, but he thought he might be over the worst of it. In front of him, on the stone ground, the creature twitched, groaning as it sank into death. Nicholas leaned over, straining his eyes for a look.

It had once been a man, and wore a tattered tunic and trousers much like Nicholas' own, but the resemblance ended there. The skin on its face and arms hung from the bones like wet sailcloth, slick with sweat and mucus that oozed from the hundreds of weeping boils that covered its skin. The eyes bulged from the skull like a reptile, and Nicholas recoiled as these blinked once before rolling back in the creature's head. Where the mouth had once been was now a gaping hole, surrounded by charred flesh. The jawbone protruded, stained green by a diet of lead, and a metal protrusion extended from the cheeks and chest, like unholy surgeries gone wrong, surrounded by more patches of charred, broken skin.

"This is madness."

Brunel tugged his jacket. "More will be coming for us soon, if we don't get to the King's private chamber.

Are you able to walk?"

"I think so. My head hurts, but the dizziness has subsided."

"Good."

Something skittered along the corridor. They both whipped their heads around, but couldn't see anything. Brunel tightened his fingers around Nicholas' arm.

"We need to leave these tunnels, *immediately,*" said Brunel. "Follow me, and for Great Conductor's sake, don't fall again."

***

JAMES HOLMAN'S MEMOIRS — UNPUBLISHED

It was not party guests who swarmed from the palace gates, but hundreds of hissing, snapping creatures. They fanned out across the street and ducked and weaved around the carriages. I heard the unmistakable sound of teeth tearing flesh, of bones being crushed as the creatures tore down their first victims. Two vehicles careened down the street beside us, a pair of snarling creatures in hot pursuit.

The Sunken were not locked away inside the palace, but had been let loose here, on the streets, to tear the population of London limb from limb.

"Nicholas!" Brigitte grabbed my hand. "He wanted to stop them. James, what if he went into the palace? We must go to him!"

Before I could dissuade her, she ordered the coachman to turn the carriage around and drive with all speed toward the palace. "Bugger that, you're a madwoman!" he cried, slowing the coach, leaping off and sprinting away into the night. A sensible lad, if ever I saw one.

Brigitte pulled herself onto the coachman's bench and gathered up the reins. "Holman, I need help!"

"Hand me the reins," I said, clambering onto the bench beside her, "but you'll need to direct us."

And for the second time that day I found myself, a blind man, on the footplate of a carriage, navigating a horse and cart through London's narrow streets when they swarmed with terrified citizens and lead-soaked vampires. We turned off the main road and careened through the smaller, narrower streets at a pace I wasn't entirely comfortable with, Brigitte calling out directions and me trying frantically to learn the right signals for left, right, stop, about turn. All around us, bedlam reigned. Terrified people ran in all directions, throwing themselves to the road to be crushed by the carriage wheels rather than succumb to the tortures that awaited them.

Phantom hands groped at my legs, crying out to be let on the carriage, but I knew if I stopped we'd share the same fate as Miss Julie and Rebecca and poor, sweet Cassandra. Men shouted at me, women sobbed, bodies pressed against the wheels before being dragged under. I felt their bones breaking as we wheeled over the top, but we could not stop. And over it all, that inhuman sound of the Sunken hissing, snarling, and tearing apart their victims in their frenzy.

***

Through the gates of Engine Ward they rolled, two

abreast, like an army spilling forth from a fortress of steel. Some carried weapons – hoses and blades and crude bludgeoning devices. But all carried a fire in their belly. All carried a message from their master.

The Boilers fanned out across the city, placing themselves at strategic points around the palace, spreading out across the boulevards, weaving around the traffic, smashing their way through roadblocks and buildings, relentless in their haste to carry out their mission.

Their instructions were explicit; destroy the lead creatures. Destroy them all.

***

Charles and Francesca Babbage had just seen the last of their dinner guests to the door. Francesca pulled the downstairs curtains while Charles lovingly carried his miniature Difference Engine back to the study and locked it in the cabinet under his desk.

He was just replacing the key in the spring-loaded secret drawer behind his typewriter, when Francesca called him from the hallway. He went to see what was the matter and found his wife with her head pressed against the front window.

"Something's happening out on the street," she said. "I heard a woman screaming. I'm worried about the Faradays. We only just sent them on their way — what if they're being mugged right at this very moment!"

Charles stared into the dark street, but could see nothing amiss, save the outline of a lone organ grinder pacing the curb in front of the house. He gritted his teeth in irritation, and was just about to tell his wife it must have been the wind when a piercing shriek cut through his thoughts.

"See?" said Francesca. "What if that's Mrs. Faraday?"

The song of the organ grinder — a tuneless version of "The Stoker and the Navvy's Wife" — suddenly ceased.

Babbage threw open the door. "Hand me that lantern," he ordered his wife.

He stood on the stoop, still in his evening finery, and shone the lantern into the darkness. It was no good. The city hadn't got around to installing street lamps in their neighbourhood yet, and the houses on either side of him had their lights off, so he could barely see across the street. He descended the steps, straining in the darkness to see if the Faradays' carriage was anywhere in sight.

He heard a scream again, from the eastern end of the street, probably the organ grinder trying to lure him out into the street. But no, the organ lay on its side at the bottom of the steps, the grinder nowhere in sight. He squinted at the cobbles. *Is that blood?* He stepped onto the road, thinking to walk as far as the corner to investigate.

Something hissed as it brushed past him and leapt up the steps.

He whirled around in time to see a blur of movement as the intruder disappeared through the open door. He heaved himself up the steps, and pushed the door open just as Francesca let out a wail.

He shone the light into the dim hall and froze. The sight that greeted him cooled his blood. His wife, backed up against the bookshelf, faced a creature so loathsome it must have come from the very pits of hell. It walked like a man, but hissed and snarled like a predator, gnashing its teeth against its puckered, blackened jaws.

"Hey, demon, over here!" The creature whirled around, its bulging eyes narrowing on Babbage. He inched along the wall toward the hat stand, where his walking cane rested in the basket. Inside was concealed a thin, retractable blade.

The creature took a tentative step towards him, a dry hiss emitting from its puckered, burnt mouth. Not daring to take his eyes off the creature, Babbage fumbled with his fingers and grasped the handle of his cane. He gestured to his wife to move toward the staircase.

He pulled the cane to his chest and pressed the spring-loaded catch. Francesca bolted for the staircase. The creature's eyes darted between the two of them, then sprang onto the balustrade and lunged for Francesca.

Her scream tore Babbage's heart. The creature caught her by the throat and bit her, tearing the flesh from her cheek. Babbage raced across the hall, knife poised for the kill, but by the time he reached her, it was too late. With a twist of its head, the creature tore out her throat, and his beautiful wife fell silent and sagged against the staircase, her blood cascading over the creature like a waterfall.

Babbage howled as he bore down on the beast, slashing with the knife and tearing at it with his bare hands. He dug his fingers into those bulging eyes and felt the hatred surge. The creature squirmed and screamed for escape. With a final bellow of triumph, he thrust the knife deep into the creature's chest, driving it through the ribcage and into the heart, if it even had a heart. He twisted the blade, and the creature sagged.

He threw the beast to the floor, his rage unquenched. With tears clouding his eyes, he kicked the body, stomped on the head. He screamed as he pummeled the fiend with his best leather boots, trampling its oozing viscera into the hallway carpet.

In defeat and disgust, he turned away.

"Francesca," he knelt beside her. The creature had torn open her bodice, ripping the buttons from her favourite dress. It had also torn off most of her face, leaving her beautiful visage a pooling mess of veins and muscle. Her eyes, still intact, stared at the ceiling. He cradled her in his arms, pressing his face to her chest and hoping to hear the faint beat of her heart.

Outside, in the street, the organ grinder started up again, tuneless and ugly. His shoulders shuddered with sobs, and he threw himself down next to her and howled with pain.

***

Brunel pushed open a wooden door leading into one of the opulent connecting halls of the southern wing of the palace. Although they could hear screaming from the palace staff while the Sunken feasted on what they fancied, the sounds were muted, confined to the Georgian wing.

Nicholas followed Brunel through a series of halls and drawing rooms, each more opulent than the last.

The sounds of the madness faded, 'till he could almost pretend the horror was all in his imagination.

Outside the entrance to the King's private wing, Brunel dragged him behind a door and gestured to the pistol on his belt. Nicholas drew the barker, and Isambard silently slid his sword from its sheath. Isambard gestured for Nicholas to go ahead.

Nicholas sucked in his breath, held the pistol against his shoulder, and crept up to the heavy doors. He wondered, briefly, why the door was bolted on the outside. As silently as he could, he slid the bolts across, leaned his shoulder against the carved wood, and pushed inward. The door opened, revealing a dark, empty reception hall.

I am going to kill the King of England.

The thought stopped Nicholas cold. He'd been so worried about the Sunken, so concerned for the welfare of the city and for Brigitte's safety, that he hadn't contemplated the deed 'till now. If he killed the King, he would be a traitor. He would be a murderer. He could be put on trial and hanged, and he'd deserve it, too, for betraying his King and country.

"Isambard?" he whispered, hearing his mentor step behind him. "We can't kill the King."

"Shhhh!"

"It's treason. We will hang for this."

"It needs to be done, Nicholas. He cannot be allowed to live. Trust me. I will look after you."

Nicholas made to protest some more, but Brunel held his finger to his lips.

Around the corner, Brunel pushed open a wide double door, and the horrible stench of raw, rotting meat invaded Nicholas' nostrils. He gagged, covering his mouth with his hand to try and keep out the smell.

More doors, more empty rooms. They passed into the inner sanctum — the private chambers of His Majesty King George III. As Nicholas' eyes adjusted to the gloom, he could see what made the horrid smell.

Scattered about the room, piled on the bed, hunched by the curtains, lay the torn, twisted bodies of several young girls. Naked and sprawled in vulgar positions, their limbs scattered about them, their bellies torn open and organs strewn across the floor, tangled about the satin pillows and Turkish rugs.

Hunched over the broken corpses, more women — their naked backs puckered with pustules and scars — chewed on discarded limbs, digging their long, thin fingers into the bellies and stuffing whatever delicacies they could find into their gaping mouths.

Nicholas pressed his hand to his mouth, forcing himself to follow Brunel, ignoring the bile rising in his throat. The smell made his head spin — the putrid stench of a slaughterhouse and a public urinal washed over him.

Look at your boots. Just don't look at them. He followed at Brunel's heels, his hand pressed tightly against his mouth, as they moved, unnoticed, through this monstrous feast, out through the doors onto the King's private balcony.

And there he stood — George III, the maker of this madness, the Vampire King. He hunched over the railing, sickly, but strong enough to stand. His thin fingers gripped the wrought iron lattice, and he stared out into the night, drinking in the chaos he had wrought. His wheeled-chair lay in pieces, strewn across the balcony, the axles bent at unnatural angles and great chunks of flesh hanging limply from the torn ribbons of its upholstery.

The screams from the city rolled over them, wave after wave of terror that rocked Nicholas on his feet. In the courtyard below, soldiers fought against the Sunken, wrestling the loathsome creatures to the ground and slitting their throats with their curved rapiers. But they were few, and they would soon be overpowered. The battle had long been won.

"Your Majesty." Brunel spoke.

The King whirled around, and Nicholas cried out and staggered back. Where his face should have been was nothing but a raw, blistering, bloody pulp, the eyes grey and bulging, the lips burnt away to reveal jagged, rotting teeth. The skin was pulled from the bones and hung in bulbous clumps under his cheeks, and through the mess ran ribbons of cold lead, solid bars nailed right through his bones, as if those protrusions were all that kept his body strung together.

The thing that had once been the King of England opened its jaw, and Nicholas thought it would snarl like the Sunken, but instead, it spoke, in the rough, commanding tone of a ruler whose time had only just begun.

"Have you seen my city, Presbyter? She has never been as beautiful as she is tonight, with her streets bedecked in red ribbons and the song of her people arching across the skies."

Isambard said nothing. He took a tentative step forward, and unsheathed his sword.

The King threw back his head, and laughed.

"Don't point that needle at me," he said. "I have drunk the blood of hundreds of men. I am immortal.

You will not kill me."

Before Nicholas could cry out or turn away, Brunel flicked the blade up, and sliced clean through the King's neck.

The head balanced in mid-air for a moment, as though suspended on strings like a balloon. And then it fell, bouncing on the balustrade and toppling into the courtyard below, landing with a splat upon the tiles and strewing across the pavement. The King's body crumpled against the railing.

Brunel lowered the sword, his eyes downcast, expressionless. "It's over," he said.

"No." Nicholas whirled around, raising his pistol. "It's not."

Noticing at last the two intruders and the crumpled body of their master, the Sunken had discarded their morsels and rushed towards the balcony door, clawing the air with their sharpened nails, eager to be the first to devour the murderers.

Isambard sized up the horde in one glance, and flung himself over the balcony.

Nicholas leaned out over the balustrade, horrified he might see his friend sprawled across the courtyard in a pool of his own blood. Instead, Brunel swung from a window cornice, his right coat arm pulled back to reveal a remarkable device strapped to his skin — a metallic claw which had extended and gripped the edge of the cornice, supporting the engineer's full weight while he fumbled, one-handed, with a rope.

"Isambard!"

"Only a few moments more," Brunel called up, securing the rope with a knot. He swung the end up, and Nicholas reached out. Missed. Something grazed his back. He swung up his shoulder and knocked the creature across the face, the force of his blow sending it flying over the balustrade.

He fired his pistol into the approaching horde, knocking another to the ground. The others, wary now, stepped back. He reached out, Brunel swung the rope again, and this time he caught it.

Without stopping to look down Nicholas leapt off the balcony and swung out toward Brunel. The rope sliced through his fingers and he slipped down, crying out as the palace wall careened into view. Suddenly, the rope pulled taut, and the shock released his hands, and he fell backward.

"Oh no, you don't." Something cold grabbed the top of his arm. He dared to look up. Brunel gripped his shoulder with his strange metal claw, the mechanism somehow supporting his entire weight.

"The rope, on your left — grab it!"

Nicholas reached for it, gripped it with both hands, and swung across. Brunel unlocked the claw from his shoulder and retracted it into his sleeve. He hung from the windowsill, his weight on the rope allowing Nicholas to plant his feet against the wall and guide himself down. When his feet landed in the soft earth of the flower beds, he tied the rope around his waist and sat back, allowing Brunel to climb down.

Isambard landed beside Nicholas in the flower bed, stopping to untangle the rope from his waist, and wiped the sweat from his brow. As Nicholas struggled to calm his frenzied stomach, he noticed his friend didn't even seem out of breath.

"What *was* that?"

"What was what?" Brunel jumped down from the

flower bed, unsheathed his sword, and held out a hand to help Nicholas, who still felt shaky on his feet.

"That ... *thing* that came out of your shoulder. That machine that saved my life."

"Oh," Brunel replied, flashing him a wicked smile. "You'll learn all about that soon, Nicholas. I promise. At this moment," he pointed across the courtyard to where a horde of Sunken had gathered, swarming over the bodies of the guards on duty, "we have more pressing issues at hand."

Nicholas gripped Brunel's arm, his nails digging into his friend's flesh. Guards screamed as the creatures pounced on them, tearing the flesh from their faces with their teeth. One wrenched a guard's arm so hard Nicholas heard the *snap* as the bone broke in two. The man howled as the Sunken gnawed at his wound.

Run. Get out. He tried to force his body to move, but he was frozen in place, unable to tear his eyes away from the horror before him. His heart thundered in his chest, and blood rushed to his head.

"They should be here." Brunel whispered beside him. "Why aren't they here?"

Nicholas wanted to ask what he was talking about, but his tongue had frozen to the roof of his mouth.

One of the Sunken raised his head, sniffing the air. He turned, and his cold, hungry eyes found Nicholas. The creature snarled, and leapt forward, racing across the courtyard toward them.

Paralysed by his fear, Nicholas could only stare at the animal eyes of the creature as it closed the distance between them. At any moment it would pounce, and his life would be over. *I'm sorry, Brigitte. I hope you are safe—*

At the corner of the courtyard, Nicholas saw something flash; a glint of metal under the lamps. Suddenly, a jet of water shot across his vision, catching the creature on the head and knocking it down. The Sunken screamed, pawing at its face with clawed fingers, crying in agony as its skin fell away under the stream of boiling water.

"Let's go." Brunel tugged on Nicholas' arm, but he still couldn't move. He watched, horrified, as more Boilers poured into the courtyard and set upon the Sunken. The creatures dropped their victims and raced to deal with this new threat, leaping and crawling over the machines as they swung with pipes and blades.

One Sunken tried to sink his teeth into a Boiler's belly, but the Boiler swatted it away. The creature sailed through the air, landing in a marble fountain. It slumped in the water, not moving, a pool of red spreading out from its body and a stream of blood pouring from the broken teeth in its mouth.

Another Boiler picked a creature off his shoulder and flung it into the palace wall. Its skull cracked open, leaving a red stain across the stone as it fell to the ground.

The Sunken began to hang back, confused. They didn't understand why they couldn't eat the Boilers. Their hungry eyes darted anxiously between the units, searching for escape. But the Boilers soon had them surrounded, and began to roll forward as one unit, weapons raised, faceless soldiers moving in for the kill.

They used to be men. I am watching the Boilers ruthlessly, mechanically, killing men.

"How did the Boilers know to come here?" Nicholas

asked.

"Because, I told them to," Brunel met his eyes. "I figured we would need their help. We must go, Nicholas. There is nothing left to do here."

With a last look over his shoulder at the carnage, Nicholas allowed Brunel to lead him away to the edge of the courtyard.

***

"William, there's another one!"

Lead pipe raised above his head, William let out a roar and swung it down hard on the creature's head. Its skull split in two with a sickening crack, spewing blood and gore across William's already filthy face. He swung again, flinging the limp body into the window of a ladies' hat shop, where it slid down the glass and rolled into the gutter.

"That's for my son, you filthy leadbag," William growled.

They charged along Oxford Street, dodging crowds of scattering citizens. Out of the corner of his eye, Aaron saw two of his boys bring down another of the Sunken, hacking it with their axes 'till it was reduced to a bloody puddle.

They'd barely run a block when they heard more screams, and turned off Oxford, following the sounds of shrieking women 'till they stood outside the British Museum. Two Sunken circled a crowd of tourists, pouncing whenever someone tried to dash away. They huddled in a protective circle in the corner of the courtyard — women and children in the middle, men facing the beasts, their stricken faces betraying their terror.

Panicked scholars poured from the ramshackle Montagu House, only to be met by this monstrous pair. Men ran across the courtyard, letters flying everywhere, pursued by the Sunken, who had the instincts of true predators — pick off and corner the weak and the slow. They pounced on two men hobbling along on walking canes, slashing and gnashing with their terrible teeth, 'till the men went down in a fury of blood.

While they were feasting, Aaron and William charged them with their axes, hacking their heads off from behind the neck. His blood boiling, Aaron cried as he swung, like a medieval warrior clamouring for blood. Again and again he hacked, the creature's blood splattering across his face and overalls,' till well after the creature was dead. William had to pull him away.

"Plenty more where that came from, boyo!"

Aaron turned away, wiped the blood from his eyes, and followed William down to Fleet Street. They chased the screams along the Strand, toward Somerset House, the imposing residence of the Royal Society. Several Sunken crowded around the grand entrance, crawling over each other in a great pile, snarling and snipping at their comrades as they lunged at their prey.

"Holy Conductor's Turds," breathed William.

A shout from behind Aaron tore his gaze away. A group of men approached him, their fine coats stained with blood. Londoners from the nearby well-to-do neighbourhoods, these men carried fine swords and loaded pistols. Their leader signalled that they wished to help, and Aaron called his men back. They stood, gasping for breath, allowing these fresh-faced chaps the honour of hacking down the monsters.

They attacked with gusto, flinging each corpse aside and pulling out the next one, bellowing praises to their various gods as they swung and slashed and stabbed. The swords, thin and flimsy, sang as they sliced through the air, removing limbs and heads as though they were slicing fruit fresh from a tree.

At the centre of the horde, they saw what the Sunken had been scrabbling for: Joseph Banks, or what was left of him. One of his hands still clutched the ornate door handle of Somerset House, but his hand was no longer attached to any other part of his body. *He must've been trying to escape when they set upon him.* His body slumped forward, and his face twisted around his neck so he faced the sky, his mouth open in a silent, terrible scream. His flesh, muscles, and organs had been torn away, leaving only crackcd bones dripping with gore.

Aaron turned away, his stomach heaving. He bent over, trying to calm himself. William grabbed him by the shoulders and turned him away.

"You can stop this now. They're saying the King is dead!" he cried. "They are shouting it from rooftop to rooftop. Listen!"

Aaron gazed up. Sure enough, a cry had been taken up, passed from citizen to citizen. "The King is dead! The King is dead!" The sound of those four words was as sweet as a symphony to Aaron's ears.

"We did it, William," Aaron huffed, as two Stokers pulled down another creature and stabbed it through the chest. "The Stokers saved London."

William shook his head. "Not the Stokers. Look."

He pointed up the street. Aaron squinted, and

could just make out a horde of Sunken running into an alley, screaming as they fell over each other in an attempt to flee their pursuers. He heard the sound of steam rushing through chimneys, of gears turning and wheels clanking. He knew before he saw them what pursued the Sunken so relentlessly. *Boilers.* Boilers chased the Sunken into the alley, surrounded them, and hacked them down with blades already slick with blood. One creature leapt over the wall of iron soldiers, only to be hit with a stream of boiling water from one of the Boiler's hoses. It fell to the ground, screaming as its skin was scorched away. A great cheer rose up from the people crowding the streets. "Long live Brunel!" They cried. "Long live the Metal Messiah!"

Aaron slumped to the ground. *Of course.* Brunel had set everything up so neatly. He had laid the trap, he had set the Sunken loose within the Walls, and then he sent his mechanical army into battle to reclaim the city. Now the king was dead and all of London was praising his name.

Brunel and his machines had saved the city. And Aaron had made the Stokers into Brunel's enemies.

I've doomed us all.

***

JAMES HOLMAN'S MEMOIRS — UNPUBLISHED

With no regard for propriety or London's traffic laws, Brigitte ordered me to swing the carriage through the palace gates. We careened up the drive, the horse snorting in protest as I drove them onward at a frantic pace. The Sunken, aroused by the scent of fresh meat, raced from every corner of the lawn to circle our carriage. I heard them snarling around us, and felt the carriage judder as one flung itself at the canopy, its hands swiping at our heads. Brigitte screamed, and I ducked, yanking the reins. The horses swerved, flinging the Sunken off the carriage into the screaming horde.

"Over there!" she cried, tugging my arm. "Oh, James, it's Nicholas. He's alive!"

I turned hard left, dashing several sculpted flowerbeds under the horse's hooves, and pushed the horses at full speed across the lawn. The heavy stone palace raced alongside, and the Sunken still circled, teeth snapping in anticipation of a fresh meal.

"James!"

It is Nicholas. I slowed, wondering how I would make it to him without having the carriage overrun by Sunken. A heavy object thudded on the roof of the canopy, followed by another. "Go, man, go!" Nicholas screamed, and I took off, flying those horses for all they were worth.

"They're everywhere!" Brigitte cried.

"I'm aware of that," I snapped, trying to focus on getting the carriage safely outside the palace gates.

"No, not the Sunken. Boilers! They are chasing down the creatures."

I focused my hearing. She was right. The sounds around me had changed. Before, we had been surrounded by the snarling, snapping creatures. Now, the hiss of steam and the clang of metal hitting metal punctuated the air, broken only by the screams of the Sunken as the Boilers took them down.

We hurtled through the gate at top speed, and tore out into the street, leaving those horrible anamilian screams behind us. Only when we were back on the street and Brigitte reported no Sunken in sight did I slow the horses and allow Nicholas and his companion to climb down into the carriage.

"James Holman, you bloody scoundrel. You were meant to remain in my home to protect Brigitte, not take her on a midnight carriage ride through a blood-soaked city! And why are *you,* of all people, driving this carriage?"

"Needs must be met, when a woman is distraught and the city is overrun with lead-soaked vampires," I answered. "Where to, gentlemen?"

"To Engine Ward, please," said a familiar voice — grating and controlled. Isambard. I nodded, and pulled back out into the empty streets.

"For once, James had nothing to do with this," said Brigitte. "It was all my idea. I couldn't bear the thought of you out here trying to save the city singlehandedly."

"Woman, you are incorrigible. I may as well marry Holman here for all the grief you cause me."

"What happened, Nicholas? What have you done?" Brigitte demanded.

Isambard answered. "Nicholas and I have … solved the problem. My Boilers will take care of the rest." He leaned forward, clasping his hand over my shoulder. "A real pleasure to see you again, James. I see you have not lost your bold spirit."

"Even *my* lust for adventure has been tested tonight," I said, shuddering under the touch of his cold hand. "People have been shouting that Somerset House is overrun with the Sunken — you are very lucky to be alive. I would pay you the correct observances, Presbyter, but under the circumstances I think we can both agree that would be unwise."

"Indeed. Drive on, Mr. Holman. And call me Isambard."

The news of the King's death had spread through the streets. All around us we heard people shouting from window to window, their voices rising with joy as they passed on the happy news. The Sunken had all but disappeared from the main streets, butchered or chased away by the Boilers. Only scattered screams in the distance reminded us the fight still continued.

Inside the carriage, however, all remained quiet. Beside me, Brigitte still gripped my hand, speaking only to give me directions in a small, frightened voice. Finally, she broke the silence.

"Forgive me for what I am about to say, but … won't you be … is the … will you be punished for what you have done?" she directed the question at everyone, but it was clear she worried for Nicholas. I worried also, knowing full well the penalty for such an act as they had committed.

"That remains to be seen," Brunel answered. "Is it treason to kill someone who was already dead? Most of the King's supporters on the Council died alongside him tonight, and he has no immediate heirs. We have done England a great service, Miss Brigitte, and she will look after us."

"But—"

"Don't fear, my love." Nicholas leaned over, placing his hand on top of Brigitte's and mine. "The worst is behind us. From now on, every day will be filled with promise. Nothing approaching this scale of horror could ever be repeated."

How wrong he turned out to be.

***

They poured down the street like a river, their furnace bellies glowing in the moonlight, their blades slicing the air like a siren's song, calling the Sunken to their doom. They fell into formation with languid ease, as if they had fought off hordes of once-human-lead-vampires hundreds of times before. Descending upon the city with immaculate precision, they finished what the Stokers had begun — sweeping the streets clean of the Sunken.

Aaron could only pull the Stokers back, well clear of the carnage, and watch the Boilers with a mixture of reverence and disgust. Wiping the blood from his face, the full horror of what he'd fought against came crashing down on him. Watching the Boilers at work — the ease with which they mowed down their enemy, the ruthlessness of their mechanical blows — forced him to see them as something other than a mechanical workforce; they were a true killing machine, answering only to one master. The notion struck his heart with a deeper feeling of fear and unease than he'd felt all night.

William patted his shoulder. "Time to go home," he said.

Home. Aaron shuddered. *We have no home anymore.*

They trudged back toward Engine Ward, the only place they could go, their spirits broken, their bodies shaking off the thrill of the killing and taking up the burden of their belated terror. All around them, the night's horror forced itself upon them. The dead littered the streets, piled up in the doorways, draped across the gutters and sprawled in mangled heaps under the wheels of wrecked carriages. Blood mixed with raindrops and flooded through the cobbles, collecting in the drains and forming scarlet ponds that glimmered in the moonlight.

So many dead, and for what? What could drive a king to this madness, and what made Isambard allow him to do so? He could have stopped this. He should have stopped this. So many have died so he could be the saviour of London.

They marched through the gates of Engine Ward, wishing only to sink back down into their tunnels and sleep off the horrors of the night. But the madness on the streets outside had penetrated the high walls of the Ward, for men and women ran through the streets, torches blazing, drums beating, voices screaming and cackling as they rushed in and out of narrow streets and ramshackle buildings.

Aaron pulled his men into an alley. "It seems we're not out of danger yet. If the Sunken have penetrated Engine Ward—"

"But why is the Chimney ablaze with light?"

"And why is everyone singing?"

"Singing?"

William peeked around the corner. "I don't believe it."

Aaron leaned out, and he couldn't believe it, either.

It wasn't a massacre, but a celebration, and it was attracting a great crowd of people, who poured in through the main entrance. Priests from the Metic and

Isis churches rolled barrels of wine from their cellars into the streets and pried them open, while eager hands dived in, bottles and tankards at the ready. Men dragged instruments from their homes — strange devices made from steel pipes, broken steam valves, and empty drums. A great cacophony rose up — grating at first, but as the musicians found their places, it became melodious, a dance to lift the heart of the Engine Ward. Multi-coloured robes of every sect intermingled, twirling and weaving through the streets, dancing together, the wearers laughing *with* each other.

As they walked, awestruck, toward the Chimney, hands reached out to embrace them, voices calling blessings and thanks. Their praises brought smiles to Aaron's men, and as they neared the Chimney, he saw the lanterns had been flicked on, and a group of revellers congregated on the steps, dressed in dirty overalls, but welcomed by all and wrapped up in the frenzy of the dance. They were led by a familiar figure, draped in grey and handing out candies to laughing children. He bolted into the street before William could grab him.

"Chloe, what are you *doing* up here?"

"You left me all alone in that hovel," she snapped. "We could hear the screaming through the vents. What was I *supposed* to do, Aaron? Wait for them to break into the Engine Ward and devour us? I heard them, everywhere I heard their horrible snarls, and you were gone, so I came here — we *all* came up here — to see what could be done."

"What has happened here?" Aaron grabbed his wife by the shoulders. "Why is everyone celebrating? The Sunken are not yet defeated. We've lost two men, and the city is drowning under the weight of the dead. What could there possibly be to celebrate?"

"Haven't you heard? The King is dead," she answered, her face breaking into a smile. "Brunel has killed him. The Council has seized control of England. The Boilers are rounding up the rest of the Lead Children as we speak."

"I heard, but—" *But what about the Stokers? What about all we did?*

"Long live Brunel!" The shout rang out from the horde of Stokers.

"Long live Brunel!" The cry was taken up by the other men congregating in the streets — Metics, Morpheans, Dirigires, all chanting praise to Brunel. Aaron stepped back, his stomach tight with horror.

"Long live Brunel, the Metal Messiah!"

Everyone — his people, his enemies, even his wife — was under Brunel's spell.

EPILOGUE

Nicholas watched from his place of honour behind the altar in the Chimney as Robert Stephenson, who could barely disguise his disgust, placed a new sceptre, forged of steel, into Isambard's hands. Isambard repeated an oath, spoke in Latin, containing his promise to watch over all the peoples of England and her Empire, to uphold the laws of her Council and the will of her Gods. He raised the sceptre high in the air, and the whole Nave erupted with applause. Nicholas stood and clapped loudest of all, a genuine smile on his face.

After the Boilers had cleaned the streets of the Sunken, and the remains of the dead were piled up in the market square in Engine Ward, a public funeral was held and hundreds reported to collect what body parts they could recognise as belonging to loved ones. All that remained were buried under a memorial stone in Kensington Gardens. The bodies of the Sunken were deposited on the lawn of Buckingham Palace, and set alight.

The Council of the Royal Society convened an emergency meeting and confirmed what the populace of London knew already — in the absence of any immediate heirs to the throne, there was only one man fit to rule the Kingdom, and that man was Isambard Kingdom Brunel.

He took the title of Lord Protector, and would not wear a crown. He was given other honours — he would take over from Stephenson as Messiah of the Sect of the Great Conductor, and would replace Joseph Banks as President of the Royal Society. There were only two men in all of England who opposed the changes: Robert Stephenson, now demoted to the mere rank of priest, and Aaron Williams, who had disappeared into the tunnels and hadn't been seen for days.

Brigitte squeezed Nicholas' hand. "You were right," she said, leaning into his shoulder. "Isambard is a brilliant engineer, and a truly great man. What better leader for this country than he?"

Nicholas smiled back, but in the back of his mind, questions swarmed. *An engineer instead of a king — what does this mean for England? More importantly, what does it mean for Isambard?* He'd not been near Isambard since the night they entered the palace. Isambard had been swept up in the affairs of state, but Nicholas wondered if the new responsibilities sat well with his friend — if the adoration of the populace, the responsibility of running a country, the title "Metal Messiah" being hailed from every corner affected him. Nicholas wondered too if Aaron knew of Isambard's appointment, and how he would be taking the news.

"And now," said Buckland, the new Prime Minister, "the Lord Protector Sir Isambard Kingdom Brunel will give his first sermon: On the Adoption of Boilers and the Nationwide Adoption of Broad Gauge Rail."

A great cheer rose up. Brunel stepped up to the podium, the grand sceptre out of proportion with his wiry frame. As he waited for the applause to die down, he turned around, searching the crowd. Brunel met Nicholas' gaze, his eyes shining with delight and humility, and he smiled.

Nicholas smiled back. He had nothing to worry about, after all. Isambard was perfectly fine.

***

Within the Engine Ward, every bell chimed, every whistle blew. Breathless messengers rushed from street corner to street corner, passing the word through the huddled crowds.

The Metal Messiah, the Metal Messiah is about to speak ...

The Stokers had gathered around the rear of the Chimney, confined to stalls — a corral of high fences set up especially to keep the Stokers away from the populace of London, as though they carried some kind of disease. Aaron frowned as Chloe tapped her fingers impatiently against the high bars. "This is a *fine* way for heroes to be treated. After all this, we're *still* the 'Dirty Folk'."

"Hush, husband," Chloe laid a gentle hand on his shoulder. "No one saw what you did. They only saw the Boilers. Give Isambard a chance to work his magic on them. He knows he would be nothing if not for the Stokers. He will lift us up as he has been lifted."

All around them, Stokers chattered about Brunel's sermon, certain it would honour their efforts in the battle. "Do you think he'll announce a new engineering project, now that the Wall is finished?"

"Maybe he's had a message from Great Conductor?"

"I hope he's giving us a pay-rise."

Aaron remained silent, not wishing to destroy the mood with his suspicions. Below his feet, the engines whirred away, safe under the watchful eye of their Boiler furnace masters.

A loud buzzing emitted from the row of horns protruding from above the grand entrance, startling the crowd and causing Aaron to jump. This was followed by a sound like an elephant's trumpet, and then Brunel's voice grated across Aaron's temples.

"Despite the tragedies of recent weeks, progress must continue unhindered if London is to thrive and move on from this tragedy. The success of my most recent Boiler prototypes has inspired me to create a new model, which will begin production immediately. The Boiler Version 3 ... an iron machine that can be programmed to perform any mundane task. Thanks to a generous gift from the Royal Society, we will begin immediately constructing the new Boiler workshops. These new buildings — designed by the brilliant Nicholas Thorne — will occupy the western quarter of the Engine Ward, behind my Chimney—"

"That's where our homes are!" cried Chloe.

"—and from right here in the Engine Ward, I can produce Boilers to order for all your engineering needs. With my machines stoking the fires of Engine Ward, we'll work with an efficiency never before experienced, and this city's legacy of innovation will be unparalleled. London will be known across the globe as the city that engineered the world."

A cheer rose up from all around — the people clapped and screamed their applause for Brunel's vision for the city, but the Stokers remained silent, too shocked to utter a word.

Finally, someone spoke.

"Drop my balls in sulphur and call me a Navvy!" William swore. "I bloody knew that pox-ridden scallywag was up to no good. He's gonna flatten our homes to build more of them rotten machines. Oi, Williams, get your lead-puckered arse back here!"

Aaron vaulted the railing of the stalls, pushed past the Stoker guard who, used to seeing him walk where he pleased, didn't attempt to hold him back. He shoved his shoulder into the riveted door and swung it inwards, stalking through the Nave, where the gentry seated inside clamoured with the exciting news. The gentlemen talked with ardent gesticulations as they ran their hands over the shining Boilers that rolled up and down the aisle. Aaron saw Holman and Nicholas and Brigitte standing in the far corner, and they called to him, but he ignored them, stormed past the ranks of priests, and ascended the stairs to the pulpit.

"You can't go up there—" A young Stoker priest grabbed for his arm, but Aaron jerked it away.

"Someone has to stop him, Johnny Ringley," Aaron hissed. "Someone has to tell him that with our homes flattened and these metal beasts at the fires, the Stokers will be ruined. Someone has to tell him he's ruined his own people. How will your daddy pay for that fancy priest school now, Johnny?" The kid let go of his arm.

Aaron grabbed the chain and pulled, and the collapsible metal staircase — a trademark of Nicholas' industrial designs — slid down from the ceiling and uncoiled into an ecclesiastical spiral. Aaron raced up the stairs, three at a time, and fell, panting, onto the platform in front of Brunel's pulpit. He banged on the door of the hatch.

"How dare you disturb me—" Brunel flung the hatch open. "Aaron?"

"How dare *I?* How dare *you!*" Aaron's rage flew

from his mouth. He grabbed Brunel's collar and pulled him onto the platform. "Have you no concept of what you have done? You've made us redundant. You're turning our homes into workshops for those abominable machines."

Brunel smiled, and in that instant, Aaron knew what he'd suspected for many months; Isambard was forever lost to him.

"You misunderstand me," Brunel said, his voice calm. "I know exactly what I'm doing. I'm sending the Stokers back to the swamps, to hunt once again."

"You're sending ... us ... *away?*"

"Yes, as you have pointed out, the Stokers are useless here in London," Brunel said. "I have no need of them anymore. But I do have a job for them, one my Boilers cannot do. I need them to hunt in the swamps, to send as many live specimens back to London as possible. The larger the animal, the better."

"Why?"

"My experiments are of no concern to you. You will be the foreman, of course, and you will lead the hunters, just like your grandfather. Isn't that just what you wanted, to live with the mud and the animals?"

"You ... you ...." Aaron had no words. He balled his hands into fists.

"You can thank me for this boon later." Brunel shoved him back toward the staircase. "But right now, I have a congregation to address. You'll receive your new instructions tomorrow." He clambered back into the hatch, pulled the door shut, and locked it from the inside.

Aaron beat his fists against the grating, barely noticing the rough steel cutting his hands. He buried his face in his hands, slivers of blood mixing with his tears as he wept for the friend he had lost and the doom of his people.

***

"Nicholas! Open this door!"

The window on the upper story flew open. "Aaron? What are you doing? It's three in the morning, *again*—"

"Now you see what your beloved Messiah has done?" Aaron roared, beating his fists against Nicholas' door. "He's no friend of mine!"

"You'll wake the whole neighbourhood!"

"He's sending the Stokers away! We finally have the opportunity to make a good life for ourselves here in the city and he's sending us away!"

"Stop yelling. I'll be right down." Nicholas' head disappeared from the window. Aaron paced across the stoop, his rage boiling, until he heard the bolt slide across the lock and saw Nicholas open the door.

"He's a rotten scoundrel and I hate him!" Aaron yelled in his friend's face, painfully aware he was being uncouth and vile, but too drunk and angry to stop himself.

"You need to calm down." Nicholas grabbed his shoulders and shook him roughly. "You're drunk, aren't you? By Great Conductor's steam-powered faeces, man, we'd best get you inside before you wake the whole neighbourhood."

He pulled Aaron into the downstairs drawing room and settled him into a chair. "I saw you in Mass today, climbing up to the pulpit like a drunken fool," he said sternly. "I can see you've further inebriated yourself."

Brigitte appeared at the doorway, clutching a candle, her nightcap askew. "Aaron? Nicholas, what's the matter?"

"He's just a little upset. Could you fetch us some water, love? And perhaps a bread roll for Aaron." She disappeared across the hall.

"Do you *want* to stay in the city, Aaron?" asked Nicholas, holding his friend's face upright. "Is that what you want? Because I can talk to Brunel for you and see if he'll let you stay—"

"No!" Aaron bolted upright, his eyes flashing. "My people need me, and I will be stronger in the swamps. Every day I live inside that Ward, surrounded by iron and without the comfort of the voices, I feel the press of my own madness, Nicholas. Even if there are no tricorns anymore, I want to walk where my grandfather walked, hunt with the dogs, feel the breath of the dragons on the back of my neck."

"If this is what you wanted, why are you so upset?"

"Brunel has sent the Stokers to a death trap. Those swamps are swarming with dragons, and no one knows how to hunt anymore. When Stephenson hears Brunel intends to connect London and Bristol, he'll descend with force. Even though he's not a Messiah anymore, the Navvies still outnumber us five to one, and they'll fight us to the death to keep the southwest free of broad gauge. I won't allow my son or my wife to die in the mud, not while I still have breath in my veins."

"Blood in your veins, Aaron. Breath in your lungs, blood in your veins, although I think yours might be well supped with alcohol."

Nicholas remembered Quartz' warning, not to allow Aaron to return to the swamps. He brushed the thought aside. That was the last thing Aaron needed to hear right now.

Brigitte returned with a roll and a pitcher of water. She set them down on the table in front of Aaron. He stared at her with reproach, then leaned over and snatched up the roll.

"I think you misunderstand Brunel's intentions—"

"I think *you* misunderstand," Aaron cried, globs of sticky bread dribbling down his shirt. "Did you know these new Boiler workshops would be built over our homes?"

"No, of course not—"

"I know how his mind works, and he's consumed by those machines. His entire being is focused on their creation, on their *perfection.* He doesn't care about the Stokers — he never has. He doesn't care about you, Nicholas. I'm his oldest friend, and look what he's made of me." He gestured to his bedraggled frame.

"You did this to yourself," Nicholas said. "He cares for you very much. He thought this was what you wanted."

"Is that what he told you? No, Nicholas, he stopped caring about me when that first Boiler rolled out of the factory. He—" Aaron fell back into the chair, his eyes glazing over and his head flopping onto his shoulder. He started to snore.

Nicholas patted Aaron's hand, and together, he and Brigitte stretched him out across the couch, placed the pitcher of water beside him, and left him be.

***

Nicholas stood outside the door of Isambard's workshop, peering through the gap, just wide enough for a thin man to squeeze through, into the gloom beyond. Brunel sat in his wingback chair by the roaring furnace, the spidery apparatus that had sprung from his sleeve on the night they'd killed the King now holding a teacup to his lips. "May I come in? I want to talk to you about Aaron—"

"I don't want to talk about Aaron," Brunel snapped.

"He thinks you hate him. He thinks you're sending him away."

"Don't I? Aren't I?" Brunel smiled. "Pull up a seat, Nicholas. Let me tell you about Aaron Williams."

Nicholas squeezed through the door, found an empty crate under the workbench, tipped it over, and sat facing Brunel. The mechanical arm held out a teacup for him, but he waved it away.

"Don't you like it? Without this arm, I couldn't have saved your life, remember?"

"I remember, but why do you wear it?"

"I like it. A man can never have too many arms." He extended the limb to its full length. "Besides, it has more strength, more flexibility, and more *functionality* than both my real arms put together."

"Is it painful?" Nicholas saw parts of the machine — gears and rods — extended under Brunel's shirt, into his skin.

"Not at all. It is partly my own design, partly made with Dirigire technology. Those Frogs understand fine clockwork better than I understand steam. Now, I was going to tell you why I sent Aaron away."

Nicholas leaned forward.

"He's not taking this very well." Brunel gestured around himself, at the Chimney, the Boilers, and his mechanical hand. "When we made the engine all those years ago, he told me he didn't want any credit. He didn't want to hang if anything went wrong, and so he left me, alone, to live or die by the whim of the priests. Things could have gone very differently for me, and Aaron knows it. He knows if I had died, it would have been on his hands. He feels guilty, because he deserted me when I needed him most. And over the years, that guilt has turned to resentment, that resentment, to jealousy, and that jealousy to his current rage. He hates me, Nicholas, and has hated me for a long time. Here in the city, hemmed in by my success, he's falling apart. He's drinking more than ever, haven't you noticed? And Chloe ...." He frowned, leaning forward and lowering his voice, even though there was no one else to hear. "I've seen her, Nicholas, walking through the Ward with bruises on her face and arms. The men fear his temper. He's cracking up. He needs to leave the city as soon as possible. I had to send him away. Do you understand?"

Nicholas felt ill.

Aaron loved his wife, he would never ... but Nicholas remembered how rough he'd been with her when they'd shown up at his home, how he'd dismissed her, how his eyes shone with hatred, how he saw fault in everything Brunel did.

"Yes," he nodded. "Perhaps you're right."

***

Holman and Nicholas saw Aaron off at the train

station. They were two of only a handful of non-Stokers present, for the Stokers' work and insular society afforded them few friends in the city. Brunel, the Metal Messiah himself, was not in attendance.

The train they piled into was barely functional. The carriages had no walls, only wiry metal frames secured with chains. The locomotive itself spluttered, spewing sickly gases through a cracking blowpipe. Aaron knew his men could have done a better job, but men hadn't made this locomotive — Boilers had. He'd seen them churning away in their new workshops for the past two weeks, putting together this prototype to send the Stokers away.

Aaron settled Chloe into one of the forward carriages, then rushed up and down the length of the platform, checking the supplies and machinery had been correctly loaded and secured. He was the last to board the train when the whistle blew.

His friends waited for him, and he faced them both, shrugging off his exile with his usual bravado. It was Holman who broke the silence first, extending his hand a little from his body in the habit of a blind person, and Aaron reached over and shook it.

"Goodbye, friend." Holman's voice was kind. "I trust you to be safe and look after this sorry lot."

Aaron smiled. "As well as I'm able, James. And you stay out of trouble."

"You know that's too much to ask." Holman let go of his hand, and Aaron turned to Nicholas, the only other man who understood the voices, the man whose peace he'd shattered and whose drawing room he'd thrown up in.

"Goodbye, Nicholas, and good luck with

everything."

"Thank you, Aaron, and ... I'm sorry."

"I know."

Nicholas leaned forward and embraced him, patting his shoulders. Aaron returned the embrace, savouring the texture of his friend's wool coat and that familiar smell of fresh aftershave.

"How will we contact you?" asked Holman.

From the hidden pocket inside his greatcoat, Aaron pulled a thin metal plate, which he pressed into Holman's hand. "There's a woman in this village. You can trust her, but to be on the safe side, you should use the code."

He shook each of them by the hand again, his eyes imparting more than his lips could say. He collected his bag and climbed the steps onto the train. Setting down his rucksack, he leaned out against the railing and gave one final wave just as the whistle blew and the train lurched forward. For the last time, he stared at the soot-stained London cityscape, her regal buildings and lush pleasure gardens whizzing by in a blur, the great Engine Ward far in the distance — a black smudge on the skyline. He knew he would never set foot inside the city again.

He was going home.

ᴀ NOTE ON THE TEXT

Fiction is a reworking of established truth. All things subtly shift under the author's pen, and even the most infallible facts become relative. As the *Engine Ward* series is set in an alternate history, I have taken certain liberties with the historical evidence. For your interest, I've detailed some of the more blatant fallacies below.

Brunel, Banks, Babbage and Holman are all historical figures, although whether any of them met in life is not recorded. Joseph Banks died in 1820, ten years before his appearance in this book, but I figure if he could keep the King alive well past his time, he was probably cheating his own death a little, too.

James Holman was blinded at age twenty-five in a manner similar to that described in this book. He returned to London, took a degree in medicine (secretly), and, after securing a post as one of the Poor Knights of Windsor, he set out on a journey across the world. The most thorough account of Holman's unique experiences can be found in Jason Robert's riveting biography, *A Sense of the World,* which I highly recommend.

George III's mania was believed to be caused by prolonged exposure to arsenic, resulting in the malady *porphyria*. Victims of porphyria suffer from abdominal pain, vomiting, seizures and mental disturbances. Porphyria affects *heme* (a vital molecule for the body's organs), causing the skin to blister when exposed to sun and the gums to retract around the teeth and the canines to become pronounced. Many scientists have speculated that porphyria accounts for some historically documented cases of vampirism. Canadian biochemist Dr. David Dolphin has popularised this theory with research suggesting ingesting human blood relieves the symptoms of porphyria. Scientists tested follicles of George III's hair and found large amounts of arsenic, known to be a cause of the disorder. He was not, to the knowledge of any historian, actually a vampire.

Isambard Brunel was appointed chief engineer of the Great Western Railway (affectionately known as the *Goes When Ready,* due to its rather loose interpretation of a "schedule") in 1833, and the first train ran in 1838. He built several notable English bridges, including the Clifton suspension bridge and the Royal Albert Bridge – and two of the largest and most innovative ships of his time – the *Great Western* and the *Great Britain*. He had no delusions of godhood. Probably.

Lastly, the widespread occurrence of dirigible flight has been altered dramatically. All these decisions were not made lightly. Nicholas' world called for these divergences and each was necessary to create the story and anchor the setting. I did not lead you down a false path. I am a spinner of tales. I hope you have enjoyed this one.

S C GREEN

Want more trains, dinosaurs and mad scientists?

Enjoy the first chapter of *Engine Ward 2: The Gauge War*

COMING SOON

Want to be the first to know when the new *Engine Ward* novel gets released? Want access to exclusive previews and fan-only stories? Sign up to the mailing list at: http://www.steffmetal.com/subscribe.

JAMES HOLMAN'S MEMOIRS — UNPUBLISHED

Aaron said he would write in his first week in the swamps, but warned us we may not receive the letter for some time. After two weeks, Nicholas commented he'd been checking with the post office twice a day. After four weeks, he was concerned, and after eight weeks with no word, we both wrote worried letters inquiring after him and mailed them off to his contact, but still we received no reply.

So, I felt a great deal of relief when the housekeeper delivered to me a letter. I had hoped it would be from Aaron, but as I turned it over and felt the crossed gauge nails that formed Brunel's official seal, my heart leapt in excitement.

The letter had been written using the raised, punched code Nicholas and Aaron had developed. They must have shown it to Brunel. The letter stated His Holiness the Lord Protector and Messiah of Great Conductor Sect was most looking forward to meeting with me on my next trip to London.

I turned the letter over, and read it again, just to be certain I had not mistaken the message. What could the Metal Messiah possibly want with me?

With my walking stick tap-tap-tapping on the ground I wound my way through the narrow streets toward the Chimney. Since I'd last visited, the Ward had become even more crowded, as engineers flocked from all over the country, all over the world, to acquire one of Brunel's Boilers and seek their fortunes amongst London's industrial elite. On every street corner, scientists and natural philosophers extolled this or that theorem. "Banish your boils!" yelled one, trying to herd me inside his church. "Heal your blindness!" cried another, waving a foul-smelling concoction under my nose.

And everywhere, priests of the various sects bustled past, their strides confident, full of self-importance, their thick robes trailing along the cobbles. Metics, Morpheus, priestesses of Isis, even some Dirigires in their leather flying costumes ... I could hardly tell them apart, for all their clattering.

Despite the cacophony of the crowds around me, I found the Chimney with ease. The great steel face loomed overhead, dominating the Ward and casting a great shadow over the streets below. As I neared its giant iron entrance, sounds around me changed, the echoes morphed by the huge presence of the Chimney. I ascended the wide stone steps and braced my shoulder against the heavy door, which swung inward on an internal spring, barely requiring any effort at all.

Not being a time of service, the Nave sounded deserted, save for a few mumblings of the priests tending the altar. I found myself a seat on the left of the aisle, fumbling for the hands of my pocket watch. I was a few minutes early, so I leaned back and waited for the Metal Messiah to arrive.

"Welcome, James. "

I jumped. He'd either been waiting behind me with the specific purpose of startling me, or had entered the room so silently I hadn't heard him. Either option made me uneasy.

"I'm sorry to startle you so. I was so deeply engrossed in these mathematical designs sent down from Charles Babbage's office, I'm afraid I didn't even hear you enter. You must think me frightfully rude."

"Oh, not at all. It's my pleasure to meet with you again, Isambard."

"It's always a pleasure in the company of old friends." He laughed. "I knew when I saw you driving that getaway carriage you'd be the right man for this job."

I rose and extended my hand, and he clasped it in his, tracing my knuckles with his cold fingers.

"You've created a beautiful retreat for the mind within these walls," I said, nervously, wishing to fill the awkward silence.

"I often enjoy sitting in this lofty room when a sermon isn't in session. The sense of space around me and the rhythmic cadence of these priests soothes the aches and pains of the workshop."

"Forgive my ignorance, Your Holiness, but you spoke of a job. Is this why you called me here today?"

He leaned forward, his hand brushing against the back of my hair. "You always did yearn to travel," he said, by way of introduction. "I remember well how you devoured the journals of great adventurers, memorising their escapades and planning how you might cope in similar situations. Tell me, has the loss of your eyes quieted your dreams of adventure?"

"I must confess that it has not," I said. "But they must remain just that — dreams. As a Naval Knight of Windsor, I'm expected at the castle for the twice-daily ordeal of climbing one-hundred-and-thirty-eight steps to attend mass. My last application for leave on medical grounds was declined."

"Why do you not simply quit the Naval Knights and travel as you please?"

"I am still a blind man, Your Holiness, subsisting on an officer's half-pay and a small stipend from the Naval Knights. Without the salary afforded to me I could not fund travel, or indeed even feed or house myself, and I refuse to resort to begging."

"Ah." I heard the smile in his voice. "Then I think you and I can help each other. I need a job done, and I think you're just the man for it. I had ordered the Stokers to send me living specimens of various species from the swamps, but, apart from a splendid dragon they sent some months ago, all they've managed to send so far are a few piddling reptiles and two mangy birds, which proved useless for my needs. I am unsure if Aaron's presence will bring forth greater results, but I wish to search further afield. I need someone to travel across Russia and through Siberia, alone, and bring me back a selection of specimens. I have made arrangements and prepared detailed descriptions of the specimens, but finding a man willing and able to undertake this mission has proven a hard task indeed. When I saw you at the reins of that carriage, I realised you'd be the perfect man for the job."

"Siberia?" I could hardly contain my excitement.

"I realise the danger involved in attempting to cross the untamed continent. To follow some of the migratory paths you will need to gain access to Siberia via the Russian Tsar, and you will need to negotiate with many locals. I know you have the temperament and skill with languages to make this mission a success. Of course, you will be paid handsomely, enough to fund many years of travel and to set you up with your own residence in London."

I leaned forward, heart racing. The offer seemed

too good to refuse. I could complete Brunel's job while making my way across the Russian continent. Then, once the last specimen was safely on board a vessel back to England, I could continue my circumnavigation of the world across the land bridge and into the Americas. With my own London residence bought and paid for, I would not need to seek permission from the Naval Knights. *I could quit the order of cantankerous men forever.*

But it all hinged on my ability to complete the mission Brunel had set. "What kinds of specimens are we talking about? Will I be able to catch and transport them on my own?" I imagined myself swatting blindly at rare species of butterfly with a net attached to the end of my walking stick.

"No. You will need to hire teams of men in the villages. I will give you all the currency you require. I wouldn't ask you to hunt yourself, of course, only to manage the teams of men who will trap the animals. I need them to reach England alive — this is paramount. The animals will travel by ship, so you'll arrange for them to be sent under escort to the coast, where my ships will be waiting. With Buckland's assistance, I've had the artist J.M.W. Turner make you some engravings of the species I require."

He dropped a stack of metal plates on the table. I counted them gingerly — ten in all. Ten different species: a monstrous task. I picked up the first and ran my hands over the drawing.

I gasped. It was a creature the likes of which I'd never encountered before. Low to the ground, it appeared almost as a tortoise with a great shell upon its back, only the long, clubbed tail and spiked face gave away its true nature.

I held up the next engraving: a seven-foot necker with thick legs and a thin, whipping tail. Another showed an incongruous herbivorous dragon with a great crest atop its head. I studied them in turn, each more monstrous than the last. Turner had listed the measurements on each drawing: four feet tall, nine feet tall, twelve feet tall. Stunned, I set the stack back down.

"As you can see," said Brunel. "It is not a delicate task I ask of you. What say you, old friend?"

My heart beat with a furious urgency, and my fingers tingled at the possibility of finally setting off on an adventure. I thought of those great monsters I would be charged with trapping and transporting to the shore, but my stomach sank a little. But I knew, despite the danger, what my answer would be.

"I am at your service, Messiah."

=

Want to be the first to know when the new *Engine Ward* novel gets released? Want access to exclusive previews and fan-only stories? Sign up to the mailing list at: http://www.steffmetal.com/subscribe

Visit the author's website at www.steffmetal.com

Follow S. C. Green on facebook.com/steffmetal

Made in the USA
Lexington, KY
15 May 2015